LOR MANDELA

Four Hundred Days

L. CARROLL

TO MILDRED AND HER SECRETARY (EVEN
THOUGH HIS EFFICIENCY IS OFT TIMES CALLED
INTO QUESTION). PARENTS DON'T GET ANY
BETTER THAN THIS.

TABLE OF CONTENTS

	PROLOGUE	7
I-	A VICTIM OF TEMPTATION	11
II-	NO MORE CRICKETS	17
III-	GLARON'S CELL PHONE	31
IV-	JONATHAN'S PLANS	37
V-	MIKIL TU SHADOW	47
VI-	THE SOLOM CLAN	58
VII-	ANOTHER RIDDLE	65
VIII-	THE SCHEMER	75
IX-	THE NEW CLEST ANARIA	82
X-	DE NOBLE LORTU'S BEST OFFER	93
XI-	TEEDEE VENILWORTH	106
XII-	MIKIL'S SURRENDER	116
XIII-	THE HOUSE THAT TEEDEE'S…	123
XIV-	A SQUANKI	134
XV-	THROUGH THE PORTAL	143
XVI-	SÍORAÍ CASTLE	150
XVII-	HODGSON CAN HELP	160
XVIII-	ACCUSATIONS AND REVELATIONS	168
XIX-	RYANNON RETURNS	177
XX-	GUARDS OF THE DEAD	188
XXI-	THE GHOSTS AT THE ROCK	194
XXII-	DALLIN'S TURN	212

TABLE OF CONTENTS

XXIII-	BARGAIN FULFILLED	216
XXIV-	TABBIT'S TRINKLE TRANCE	223
XXV-	A PERFECTLY ORCHESTRATED PLAN	232
XXVI-	LOVE INDUCED SUICIDE	242
XXVII-	THE UNINVITED ENTRUSTING GUEST	250
XXVIII-	DALLIN IS OUR FRIEND	258
XXIX-	THE PRESIDENT'S ARMY	264
XXX-	THE CALL OF THE BIG PIG	270
XXXI-	A NEW PLAN	275
XXXII-	DECLINE OF A VRITESSE	284
XXXIII-	THE CLEST ANARIA'S BOOK…	295
XXXIV-	A STRANGE, BUT LUCKY COINCIDENCE	301
XXXV-	HERE WE GO AGAIN	313
XXXVI-	FORCED INTO IT	320
XXXVII-	SURPRISE RESCUE	334
XXXVIII-	KABLAZAM!	339
XXXIX-	ANY OF THESE ELEMENTS MISSED	348
XL-	LORTU DECIDES	357
XLI-	FOUND	363
XLII-	A FRIEND TO RELY ON	372
XLIII-	FROM ONE NIGHTMARE TO THE NEXT	379

Prologue

The only visible thing outside of the cement, one-windowed room was a hazy blanket of black — a thick, inky gloom so dense that neither moon nor stars penetrated it. Inside, the small room was similarly shrouded in stale blackness, except for a tiny sliver of one wall weakly illuminated by three shining, green buttons. In their faint glow, the sharp edge of a metal door glinted on the otherwise barren slab of concrete. A musty odor — similar to that of a dust field stirred by the wind prior to a thunderstorm — hung heavily between the cold, damp walls and seemed a fitting aroma for a mill which was left dead and decaying by its former owners.

On a simple, grey, utilitarian bench — sterile and hard, and haphazardly jutting out from a corner — sat a tiny creature, curled in a dismal, rocking ball, quietly sobbing and shivering. The faint chirping of crickets in the distance no longer appealed to her. In fact, the sound that would have normally held an irresistible fascination now created a sickening knot in the pit of Tabbit's bulgy, brown tummy.

"Squankis don't tells," she blubbered, "lady comes backs . . . lady comes backs . . . return the powers . . . four hundred days . . . four hundred days."

LOR MANDELA

Four Hundred Days

L. CARROLL

CHAPTER I

A VICTIM OF TEMPTATION

Tabbit was hungry — not an unusual state for a Shadow Squanki — but tonight, the gracious spread of succulent meats, exquisite cakes and pastries, and exotic fruits at Lor Mandela's Celebration of Light was doing little to squelch her appetite. She craved one thing and one thing only — crickets from Drolana — and her hunger, which had been nagging all evening, was finally getting the better of her.

She tried to resist. After all, Atoc Jonathan, the highest ruler on Lor Mandela, had forbid her people from opening any more portals to other worlds. But crickets didn't live on Lor Mandela, and none of the bugs here tasted quite the same.

"I cans be careful," she breathed in a squeaky whisper to herself, rationalizing the scheme she was concocting in her head. "I could finds a secret place . . . a hiding secrets place. Ryannons of Brashnell would never finds."

She glanced around the glistening, alabaster room at the chattering hordes of ladies in their many colored gowns and gentlemen in their dress uniforms. Her wispy, white hair floated dreamily about her head and demure, bare brown shoulders as she took note of the location of each of the Nobles, all of whom seemed quite occupied with the festivities and their guests — a further reassurance to Tabbit that she would not be missed.

Gathering up the lower edge of her flowing, peach ball gown, the famished little Squanki tiptoed backwards out of the Terrace Ballroom, snuck across the stained glass entrance foyer, and bounded out of the palace toward East Mystad Field, dodging in and out of the thin shadows cast by the scraggly trees that bordered it. She stopped about half way across to scan the area for a private spot to set her plan in motion.

Near the edge of the grassy field, a massive, twisted, angular tree jutted up into the evening sky. Its broad canopy of bluish-black leaves rustled in the warm evening air. The tree, known as the Ator's Anaria —the special place of retreat for the female leader, or ator, of the Mandelan's — seemed to perk slightly in response to Tabbit's approach.

"Hello Anarias! You is perfects," Tabbit giggled, bouncing along in a lively zigzag toward it. Her initial intention, to slip behind the tree and create her portal, changed suddenly when she rounded its imposing trunk and, much to her delight, found the entrance to a large tunnel carved into its rough gray surface. She squinted and peered into the dark chasm and squeaked, "Even mores perfects!"

After a quick, cautious glance around, she slipped sideways into the tree. "Ator's Anaria," she whispered, "no ones comes *heres* anymore. Ator Lady Kahlie nots has had its cleaned up yets! Nots since big light come crashings down in earthquakes!" She fidgeted with the stiff taffeta skirt of her gown, and then started in a cheerful skip down the long, dim corridor.

The floor was littered with glass which crunched softly under her bare feet. She ran her hands across the smooth, damp walls, singing as she flitted along, "Squanki feets are tough. Nots hurt by glass and stuff. Glassies feels like fluff. Doobee doot, uh . . . puff, puff." Moving through the tunnel, she repeated the bouncy tune until finally she reached the Anaria's big main room.

She bounded into the room and gazed around in awe. Little shards of sparkling crystal covered everything, and looked rather lovely glistening over the big, amber sap blobs hanging from the walls, and dotting the rich, jewel-toned velvet upholstery that was strewn indiscriminately throughout the room.

One

"*Doobee doot puff puff,*" she breathed quietly, and spun around in a circle to make sure she was alone. Once content with her solitude, she raised her petite hand skyward, and rolled her fingers into a tight little ball. She opened and closed her fist and was just beginning to repeat the motion when she noticed something sparkling in the dim light of an olive glass wall sconce at the back of the room. There, sticking out of a particularly large blob of sap was a glinting spiral of silver metal.

"Ooooo! Pretties!" she giggled, momentarily abandoning her plans and hopping over to it. Upon close investigation, she discovered that it was a part of the chandelier that had twisted into an odd swirl when the massive fixture had fallen and had embedded itself in the sap-covered wall. It was whimsical with its curly shape, shiny, and very appealing to the playful little Squanki. She reached up with one hand, and then the other, and grabbed a hold, tugging and jerking with all of her strength in an attempt to free the swirl from the sticky sap. She shifted her stance and grip several times in order to get a better hold, but the swirl wouldn't budge. She stood back and tilted her head side to side, staring determinedly at the defiant object. Her alabaster hair floated back and forth a second behind her head, as if it had to decide for itself whether it should move or not.

"Hmmm, stucks good!" she huffed, spitting into each of her hands and rubbing them together. Taking a deep breath, she gripped the swirl again, and began yanking. She struggled and strained, lifting her feet into the air, and planting them against the wall. Just as her tiny toes touched the sappy, bark-like surface, the wall shuddered and then melted away to reveal a maze of sprawling tunnels. "Oooooo," she breathed excitedly, her already huge, blue eyes as big as saucers, "a mysteries!"

All but forgetting the glittery trinket she was trying to extricate, she dropped to the ground and sauntered into the maze. It was dark and shadowy, with thick, tangled root walls and a warm dirt floor.

"Wheee!" she squealed as she lifted her arms to the side, leaned backwards against the roots, and slowly dissolved into them. Her small body melted into the deep brown wall behind her until only her bulgy round eyes remained visible, merrily blinking on the twisted surface. She stayed hidden in the roots for a few seconds, enjoying the damp coolness against her back, before sliding out of the shadows and continuing further into the maze.

As she ambled along she investigated every inch, tracing her tiny finger over the surface of the roots, whispering a quiet, "smooths," or "bumpies," or "scratchies," after a careful examination of each twisted tuber. She had just begun to study a peculiar stubby root when a loud bang from deep within the labyrinth startled her. "Oooo, Ator's comings!" she whispered, and quickly scurried back toward the main room.

As she rounded the corner into the glass-covered chamber, she crashed right into something with a *smack*, and fell hard on to her backside. Without so much as a second to react, she was grabbed by the hair and hoisted high into the air.

"Well, what have we here?" a smooth, deep voice asked.

Tabbit raised her eyes and found herself face to face with a tall, dark-haired man with red flecks dancing in his dark eyes — absolutely the last person she wanted to see.

"What have we here?" Tabbit repeated in a whisper. "Ryannons of Brashnell," she gasped.

"Ah, if it isn't my good friend, Tabbit," he sneered, "or should I say Atoh Audril's good friend, which would make you . . . let's see, my enemy!" He lifted her a bit higher and studied her little shape.

"Let's see, my enemy," Tabbit echoed with a growl. "Lets me goes!" She swung ferociously at Ryannon's face with her tiny, clenched fists and kicked at him with her scrawny legs. "Puts me down!"

Ryannon was not fazed by her assault in the slightest. "I don't think I will," he replied, "you see, I really should kill you now . . . while I have the chance, but I think it might be more advantageous for me to keep you around." He chuckled and added, "I can have you stuffed and mounted later."

Tabbit snarled and took another swing at him, this time with an open hand. Her sharp, claw-like fingernails sliced across his neck and square jaw, gouging deep into his skin and catching him so off guard that he dropped her to the ground.

She quickly scooted backward, sprung to her feet and zipped into the maze as fast as her petite legs would carry her.

Ryannon raced after her. "Stop!" he commanded, lifting a gloved hand equipped with nearly two dozen long, thin, golden spikes. He took aim and clenched his fist. With a loud metallic swish, the spike dart shot from his glove and hummed through the maze, whizzing past Tabbit dangerously close to her left ear.

He missed her intentionally, and Tabbit knew it. Ryannon was renowned for his deadly accuracy. He had been trained in combat from the time he could speak. If he wanted to hit her, he certainly would have. She kept running, fully aware that he had the ability to take her at any second. Her only hope was to keep moving, and pray that he was having an off day.

Another crisp, loud *shink* rang out from the spike dart glove. A moment later, a searing pain exploded through Tabbit's right leg. She dropped to the dirt floor and tumbled across it. "Owwws!" she cried, as she rolled, end over end, to an abrupt stop. She struggled to get to her feet, but her leg collapsed the moment she put weight on it, and she fell with a smack to her knees.

Even in the darkness of the maze, she could see the long spike dart glinting in her upper calf where it had lodged after slicing a long, deep gash. It throbbed and pounded as warm, crimson blood oozed from the wound and soaked into her pretty party dress.

Ryannon strutted over to where she landed, his boots making soft thuds as they hit against the dirt ground. Tabbit was helpless to do anything. Poison from the dart had begun seeping into her veins and had rendered her unable to move.

Ryannon stopped and looked down at her weak, shaking form, and then scooped her up like she weighed no more than one of the leaves on the

15

Anaria's floor. "Now then," he began, "I need a portal, Squanki, and *you* are going to open one for me. Right here should be just fine."

Without warning, he reached down and yanked the dart from Tabbit's leg; she let out a scratchy, mournful yelp as it ripped through her already burning flesh.

Ryannon grabbed her hand and forced her fingers into a fist, prying them open and shut, open and shut; her small knuckles crunched and cracked under his strong grip. As he pulled her fingers open a third time, a tiny sliver of azure light appeared in the air next to his left shoulder.

Tabbit struggled to get away and as she did, the blue portal slid from its levitating position, easily five feet in the air, and dropped to the tunnel's dirt floor.

"How convenient," Ryannon smiled. With Tabbit in hand, he stepped forward onto the blue light.

The portal expanded with a loud sizzle and, in an instant, the oddly contrasting pair became enveloped in its blinding glow and then disappeared with a pop.

CHAPTER II

NO MORE CRICKETS

Ryannon and Tabbit exited the portal into an abandoned shopping mall in the small Midwestern town of Glenhill, Iowa. It was late afternoon on Saturday, but rather than the usual cliques of gossiping teens, exhausted, stroller-pushing parents, and over-dressed, under-paid employees that usually spent their weekends at Glenhill's one and only hot spot, the mall was completely empty. The gates and doors of the darkened shops were plastered with rodeo fliers and hand written signs indicating the reason for the stillness; today was Glenhill's fiftieth annual Founder's Festival Rodeo.

Just shy of ecstatic over the perfectly ideal circumstances, Ryannon flung Tabbit over his shoulder, turned to the glass doors of the store next to where they had emerged — Pet Land — and peered inside. From behind the doors, the gentle chirping of crickets danced through the quiet air.

"So, this is what you were doing in the Anaria, isn't it? You were hungry," Ryannon smirked.

Tabbit, who was weak and dizzy from blood loss and the poisoned tip of the spike dart, listened to the chirps. Her desire for yummy crickets was no longer a craving — sustenance was necessary for her to regain her strength. As she lay limp across Ryannon's broad shoulder, her round belly gurgled and growled.

"Ohhhh my," Ryannon tsked, "poor little thing. Let's get you some of those lovely bugs, shall we?"

He reached into his coat pocket, produced a small black ball and pointed it at the set of glass doors, which began to vibrate and buzz wildly. Within a second or two, the lock at the bottom made a strange grinding noise and started to smoke. Its tarnished gold patina darkened to nearly pure black and then turned a glowing hot orange as it slid out, and landed with a clunk on the floor. Ryannon pulled the door open and kicked the lock, which screeched and sizzled as it skated across the smooth, white tile.

Toward the back of the store, a low green cabinet droned with the twitter of hundreds of crickets. He carried Tabbit to it, and lowered her onto the clear sliding doors on the top of the case.

Her head slumped to her chest, giving her a clear view of her injured leg, which was still bleeding profusely. The blood-soaked fabric of that section of dress was hiked up and clinging to her thigh above the wound. Just the sight of it made her queasy. She teetered side to side on the cabinet as she breathed deeply, fighting to stay conscious.

"Tabbit," Ryannon began as he casually glanced at the back of his gloved hand. "I've done a bit of reading about Drolana crickets, fascinating creatures they are. You see, these crickets are sold as food which is exactly what *you* want them for." He slid one of the doors open just wide enough to reach his hand through, scooped out a few crickets and held his fist out to her.

With all of the energy she could muster, Tabbit reached out a shaky little hand, took the bugs and pressed them into her mouth.

"There, that's better," he oozed with an odd hint of amusement. "Would you like some more?"

Tabbit weakly bobbed her head up and down, which was almost more than she could manage; her eyes rolled around in the sockets as she did.

"First, let's fix this," Ryannon smirked as he grabbed a hold of the bottom of her beautiful gown with both hands, ripped a large swath of fabric from the hem, and tied it tightly around her leg.

Two

He reached back into the cricket cabinet, swooped up a few more of the jumpy critters, and offered them to Tabbit. He watched her eat as he continued, "As I was saying, these crickets are live food for lizards and other animals. But did you know that crickets, when hungry, will become the hunters and snack on the very animal that was supposed to eat them?" He lifted her from the cabinet and slid the top all of the way open. Two or three of the little chirpers hopped out at the chance of freedom. "Tabbit," he whispered in her ear, "when do you suppose these crickets were fed last?" He picked up one of the escapees and studied it for a moment before tossing it back into the cabinet. "Let's find out if they're hungry." Without hesitation, he stuffed Tabbit into the cabinet and slammed the doors shut above her.

She reached up and pushed against the Plexiglas doors — panic glaring in her eyes — but Ryannon just smiled and shook his head.

Hundreds of crickets jumped onto her; the combination of their creepy legs and antennae twitching against her skin, and the agonizing throbbing in her thigh, created a sensory overload. Horrific, panic-induced thoughts of being devoured slowly over the next several hours raced through her mind as the bugs squirmed over her, chirping wildly. Their frenzied buzz amplified as more and more of them hopped onto her.

Suddenly, a strange stabbing sensation prickled in her fingers and toes. At first, Tabbit didn't know what it was, but then the terrifying realization struck. The crickets were starting to eat her! They were all over her — on her hands, arms, legs, back and face — chirping, crawling, looking at her with their emotionless glazed eyes, and gnawing on her skin!

She frantically batted at the bugs, struggling to knock them off, but there were too many of them. Terrified, she tried rolling her hand into a fist, but several of the insects crawled over her palm, preventing her from shutting it all the way. In a desperate effort, she lifted her arms out to the sides as far as they would stretch inside the enclosure, and leaned backwards against the cabinet wall. Several of the creepy bugs crunched and squished under her weight, as more and more of them jumped onto her. She pushed harder against the side of the cabinet; the sound of squishing, slurping and chirping filling her ears, along with the painful nipping of the crickets' mouths was almost more than she could stand. A sickening nausea rose in her throat as insects crushed against her back. At last, she felt the wall begin to give way behind her and she faded into it; her bulging, frightened eyes — each with three or four crickets crawling across them — were the last to disappear. She slipped through the other side and landed on the hard tile floor with a *thwack*.

"Oh, well done! Good thinking," Ryannon taunted. "I'm glad to see that you are clear headed . . . just how I need you to be. Now come on, Tabbit. Let's figure out exactly where on Drolana we are." He grabbed the exhausted, mortified Squanki by her messy white hair and started for the front of the store. Once outside the glass doors, he flopped her back over his shoulder and strode down the length of the mall, looking into shops for further clues to their whereabouts.

In the center of the mall's main corridor was a three-sided lighted sign, with the word "INFORMATION" glowing in scrolling yellow letters across the top. On one side was a mall directory, on another, a vintage-looking poster about the Founder's Festival Rodeo — but on the third side, the presence of a detailed map of the town of Glenhill proved the ultimate find. Ryannon studied the map thoroughly for several minutes and seemed to be memorizing every detail. Finally, he turned his attention away from the map, and moved to the side with the Rodeo poster on it. "Sponsored by the Glenhill High School Drama Club," he read the credit at the bottom of the poster aloud, "Gabrielle Pearson, President . . . Maggie Baker, Vice President." The red, sparkling flecks in his eyes intensified and the same delighted smile he'd had when they arrived in the ghost-town of a mall returned. "Well, how perfect, Tabbit," he sneered, giving her a demeaning swat on the backside and turning toward the exit doors. "It's time to make our presence known."

Just beyond the mall parking lot — and in a glaring contrast to the interior of the mall — the town of Glenhill was quite active. People, horses and long, gleaming horse trailers crowded Main Street.

Across the street from the mall were two large buildings. One was Palmer Equestrian Arena, where most of the throngs of people were gathering, and the other was Glenhill High School. Ryannon headed directly for the school, weaving his way through the masses. A few people eyed the nearly six and a half foot tall man carrying a limp, white-haired rag doll over his shoulder, but no one thought much of it. It wasn't uncommon for the rodeo and other Founder's Festival activities to turn out colorful characters each year.

Tabbit couldn't even lift her head now. The ten or so crickets she'd eaten had done little to rejuvenate her.

In front of the high school, a big, cement marquee sign which read "Glenhill High Panthers" rose from a small section of lawn. Ryannon moved toward the covered and locked structure and lowered Tabbit's inanimate body onto the top of it. He reached into his pocket, and this time pulled out a glowing, purple crystal shaped like two entwined hands. On one side of the oddly shaped crystal, were a square black button and a display window. He pushed the button a few times almost in rhythm, and strange green symbols flickered and scrolled across the display. "There we go," he smirked as he depressed the button once more. The entire crystal blinked twice and then evaporated into thin air.

Ryannon stared at the marquee for a minute, and then smiled as though he'd hatched a brilliant idea. He retrieved the black ball he had used on the door at Pet Land and aimed it at the lock on the sign, which rattled a bit, heated to glowing amber, and then popped out and dropped to the grass, crackling, steaming and sputtering as it lay on the damp ground. He then quickly went to work, using the spare letters that sprawled across the bottom of the sign to change the "Welcome Rodeo Guests" message into something more suited to his requirements.

Once finished, he tossed Tabbit back over his shoulder, and nearly sprinted back to the mall. He returned to Pet Land, marched quickly to the cricket cabinet, pulled a clear plastic cup from a stack next to it, slid open the top and scooped out a generous cup full of the chirpy little creatures.

He plopped Tabbit back onto the cabinet, held the cup to her mouth, forced it open and started dumping crickets in. Tabbit gagged and sputtered as Ryannon pushed her jaw up and down. She swallowed hard, struggling not to choke as crickets dropped down her throat wriggling and squirming the whole way. For the first time in her life, crickets were revolting. She didn't want any more, but Ryannon pried her mouth open again and shook in another large helping. Then, reaching back into the cabinet, he refilled the cup, picked up a vented lid from another stack, and popped it on top.

"Time to go," he sneered. "It's time to find our lovely friend, Audril."

He lifted the tattered lower edge of Tabbit's dress, ripped another piece from it, and tied it around her mouth. "You make so much as a peep when we get back to Lor Mandela, and I will lock you in a whole room full of hungry crickets and let them enjoy *you* piece by piece. Your magic will do little to save you then! Do I make myself clear?" He shook the cricket cup tauntingly in front of her.

Tabbit nodded, her eyes even wider than normal.

"Excellent," he snarled, as he tossed her back into the usual position, dangling over his shoulder.

He rushed to the portal that shone on the woodwork outside the Pet Land doors and started through. A loud hissing permeated the mall air, and out of the corner of her eye, Tabbit caught a glimpse of a huge fiery burst. A second later, they were sucked into the flash of the portal, emerging into the labyrinth of tunnels at the back of the Ator's Anaria.

Ryannon wasted no time. He pulled some of the thinner roots from the walls and used them as cords to bind Tabbit's small hands, arms and feet, taking extra precautions to make sure she couldn't roll her fingers into a fist, or lift her arms out to the side. He then tethered her waist to one of the thickest roots.

Two

"Now, Tabbit," he began, "I'm off to find our beloved friend, Audril. You stay put!" he insisted, patting her forcefully on the cheek. "I'm counting on *you* for later."

Ryannon knew where he would find Audril tonight. Everyone who was anyone in Mandela City would be at the premiere event of the year, the Celebration of Light. He left Tabbit and made directly for the gardens outside of Mandela Palace's Terrace Ballroom — a room so named because of the spacious, beautiful outdoor terraces, lush plantings in every imaginable color, and lacy, gazebo-like structures that bordered it.

It was not uncommon for the festivities to begin in the ballroom, and then trickle out into the luxuriant surrounding stair-stepped gardens as the evening progressed — as Ryannon was well aware. He had himself romanced his fair share of young ladies over the years at the Celebration, and now used this familiar area to gain a different sort of advantage.

After seeking out a secluded spot behind a long, meandering hedge near the bottom-most terrace, he waited, earnestly scouting the area for any sign of Atoh Audril. Several minutes passed, and he was forced to watch snuggling couples wander through the gardens as he searched. Finally, he spotted her inside one of the smaller, more intimate gazebos dancing cheek to cheek with a neatly groomed young man with a strong build and brown curly hair.

"There you are," he sneered in a whisper, as a searing flood of jealousy burned through his core, "and with that freak of a loner, Dallin Doone. I thought you had taste." Ryannon's blood boiled. Dallin was too close — touching and holding *his* Audril. He was breathing in her perfume and feeling the motion of her body against his. Dallin's hand, which was on the small of her back, was sliding slowly up into her silky black curls.

"How dare you," Ryannon hissed, raising his gloved hand into the air and taking aim. Dallin was an easy target, and one that Ryannon would be only too delighted to watch fall. He held his arm steady, locked on Dallin's neck, preparing to fire, but then stopped himself. "No!" he seethed, coming to the realization that a murder at such a public event would draw far too much attention. Furthermore, he needed Audril for his plans to succeed, and unless she came to him willingly, things would become more complicated than necessary; killing her little boyfriend, as gratifying as it may be, would have to wait for now. Ryannon hesitantly lowered his arm and growled, "Later, farm boy, *later.*" He glared angrily at Dallin for a few more seconds and then skirted around the shrubberies, moving in closer to listen and observe.

Ryannon located a spot behind a row of large-leafed weeping trees with hanging sickles of deep purple blossoms, close to where Dallin and Audril danced. He ducked behind them unnoticed and could now hear their conversation perfectly.

"You wanna take a walk?" Dallin asked, looking as desperate and pathetic as any man Ryannon had ever seen.

"As a matter of fact, I do," Audril answered. "There's somewhere I've been *dying* to go see."

Ryannon stared at her lips as they moved; those lips that had twice been against his. They were full and silky coral, with the slightest hint of a pout. "Soon, Audril," he breathed, "even if I have to take it by force again." His breath caught in his chest as his gaze licentiously wandered over her. Her vivid blue eyes glittering under the flickering lights in the trees above; her raven curls cascading in soft ringlets down to the middle of her back; her long, dusky lavender gown hugging each subtle curve; everything about her was fueling his insatiable carnal lust. "Yes, soon, Audril," he practically panted.

Another violent surge of anger washed over Ryannon as Audril locked arms with Dallin, who playfully leaned his head onto her shoulder. "Where have you been *dying* to go?" he asked.

Her response soothed Ryannon's rage a bit. "The Ator's Anaria," she answered.

"Well, how very fortuitous," he whispered. A devious smile played across his lips as he watched Dallin lead her back into the ballroom. He waited until they were out of view, and then turned on his heels and raced away from the terraces and back across the field.

Two

Once he reached the big tree, he ducked quickly into the cave inside the massive trunk and went down the hall. He crossed the main room into the maze of tunnels to wait for Dallin and Audril to arrive.

He had barely set foot inside the largest tunnel, when he realized that something was not right. Tabbit was no longer where he'd left her. He scoured the shadows for any sign of the little Squanki, but she was nowhere to be seen. "Ghandentel," he barked, "the portal!" He kicked violently at the root wall, leaving a deep white gash in one of the twisted masses. "Ghandentel!" he repeated.

He hurried back to where the sliver of blue glowed on the tunnel floor, and was just about to step into it, when suddenly there was a flash and a pop, and two figures materialized before him — one, a bulky, muscular, dark-haired man roughly the size of a brick wall, and the other, the still-bound and struggling Tabbit, who was being held firmly around her mid-section by the brawny man.

"Milord," the imposing man muttered as he lowered to one knee and held out the squirming Squanki. "I thought you might like this back."

"Grayden?" Ryannon gasped, clearly shocked to see the man kneeling before him. "What a charming surprise. I didn't realize you were still alive. You're the last person I expected to run into. How ever did you find the portal?"

Grayden rose to his feet and patted Ryannon on the shoulder, and together they strolled back into the Anaria's main room. "Well, let me see. I heard reports of a town that had been completely destroyed in a single explosion, right up to, but not exceeding its borders. No one on Earth has that technology; not many on Lor Mandela, either. It had your name written all over it. Naturally, I came looking, though I must say, I was rather hoping to find you there and not this thing," he scowled as he pointed at Tabbit, who Ryannon had flopped over his shoulder yet again. "But at least she was somewhat helpful in leading me to the portal."

25

Tabbit lifted her head to snarl, but the exertions of the evening finally overcame her, and she slipped into a dark unconsciousness.

Ryannon rolled his eyes, and lowered her to the ground. "Shadow Squanki," he groaned, "aside from their periodically useful skills, they really are such pests." He flicked Tabbit hard on the side of the head, but she did not stir.

Grayden nodded in agreement.

"So, General," Ryannon began, "You've been trapped on Drolana all this time? How did you find it?"

"Pitiful," answered Grayden, "most of the people there are so wrapped up in their own petty problems, they've lost all potential. I did find one interesting woman, though. She's intelligent, yet easily persuaded. She's been helping me these last few months . . . helping me work on a plan to get back here."

"Last few months?" asked Ryannon with a confused grimace. "Excuse my ignorance, General, but exactly how long were you on Drolana?"

"Nearly ten months, sir . . . why?"

Ryannon's surprise was evident, but then a knowing sneer reminiscent of the evil smirk that used to grace the face of his father suddenly spread across his rugged, handsome face. "Ten months . . . of course! Ten months. Why, General, this is quite excellent, isn't it?"

"Excellent?" quizzed the general. "What is so excellent about it?"

"Oh, trust me, Grayden. This is going to be something you won't want to miss." The crimson glints in Ryannon's eyes flickered as he continued. "This woman friend of yours, can she locate shelter for us on Drolana? The more remote the location, the better."

"Her family owns an old wood mill building in an abandoned town. I don't think you could find a more remote location. I've spent a few *memorable* weekends there myself. Trust me, sir, there's no one around to hear you scream."

"Perfect," Ryannon smirked, "follow me and bring the Squanki!"

26

Two

As Grayden lifted Tabbit's limp body, he unknowingly grabbed her by the wound on her leg, and Tabbit awoke with a scratchy, squeaky, blood-curdling scream. "Ahhhh! *Noooo!*" she shrieked loudly.

Her sudden outburst startled Ryannon, who stumbled backward and bumped against a bookshelf that was already teetering awkwardly atop a pile of rubble. The shelf tipped and crashed to the floor with a loud bang which echoed through the tunnels.

Ryannon raised his arm and angrily back-handed Tabbit across her face with enough force to render her unconscious once again.

"Tabbit! Tabbit! Where are you?" Audril's concerned voice rang out from the maze.

"Come on!" Ryannon commanded, pointing at Tabbit. "Bring her!"

They raced to the portal, stepping on it just as the shadows of Audril and Dallin appeared at the end of the corridor. The glint of blue light expanded beneath their feet, followed by a loud, whooshing roar. With a pop, they emerged in what were now the charred remains of Glenhill, Iowa.

"Over here," instructed Grayden. He led Ryannon to what was left of a cinder block wall a few feet away, and they dove behind it.

A few seconds later, a flash of blue blasted through the air, and Audril and Dallin appeared from out of the portal.

"A portal?" Dallin yelped. "I thought the Squanki were s'posed to destroy 'em all!" He looked at Audril who was staring out in horror. All of the color had drained from her face, and she was barely breathing.

He followed her gaze to see what had caused such a reaction, and was met with a scene unlike anything he'd ever witnessed. Piles of what appeared to have recently been buildings lay smoldering across the landscape. Trees and shrubs were blackened and smoking. There was no movement at all — no activity and no life whatsoever — for as far as the eye could see.

"Oh, no." Audril's nearly inaudible voice shook. "Dallin, we're in Glenhill."

The expression on Dallin's face dropped as he surveyed the annihilation before him, but then, as his eyes fell upon one particular sight, it changed from a look of shock and dismay to one of sheer terror. He grabbed at Audril, catching the skirt of her dress with his hand. He yanked frantically, pointing with the other hand, while keeping his gaze locked on a single structure — the only one that remained intact. Audril looked in the direction of his finger to where the high school that she had attended once stood. There, surrounded by a brownish haze, was the school marquee sign, and across it in black plastic letters were the words, "**WELCOME BACK, ATOH AUDRIL BORLOC.**"

Dallin quickly grabbed Audril around the waist and pulled her back toward the portal. "What are you doing?" she screamed, struggling to get away.

"No, Audril!" insisted Dallin, "I'm getting you out of here! Now!"

"But this was my home! I've got to. . . ." she shrieked as he lifted her from the ground.

"NO! We need to get . . . ." his voice vanished abruptly as he yanked her backwards and they disappeared back through the portal.

Ryannon stood and calmly brushed some stray dust from the legs of his pants. "Well," he began, "that couldn't have gone much better."

"What do you mean?" Grayden asked, rising from his crouched position behind the jagged wall, leaving Tabbit lying unconscious on the charred and dusty ground. "What are you plotting?"

Ryannon's reply was vague at best. "That, General . . . that was almost too easy. I didn't expect to get her here so soon. This should speed things up tremendously," he muttered, pacing back and forth.

"Speed what up?" Grayden tried again.

Suddenly, Tabbit bolted upright with such abruptness that it made both of the men jump. The wisps of her white hair which were bound under the gag started to weave and thrash wildly. They pushed, twisted, writhed and snaked until at last, the gag slipped from her mouth and dropped down around her

Two

neck. Her bulgy blue eyes were even larger than normal and devoid of all expression.

She turned her head toward Ryannon and locked him in an eerie, catatonic gaze. "What we do know, Atoha, is dat de answers you seek . . . de answers only you can find . . . day are steel hidden from you. Day are steel hidden in de Advantiere." Her accent — deep, flowing, and hypnotic — perfectly mimicked that of a Shadow Dweller.

Ryannon and Grayden listened in astonishment as she continued but this time in her own squeaky tonality, "Squankis don't tells . . . lady comes backs . . . lady comes backs . . . return the powers . . . four hundred days . . . four hundred days."

Ryannon leaned down and gave her a robust jab in the shoulder with his index finger. "What are you rambling about?" he demanded.

"Squankis don't tells . . . lady comes backs . . . lady comes backs . . . return the powers . . . four hundred days . . . four hundred days," she chanted again.

Grayden sighed in disgust. "Well, there you have it. She's lost her mind. Why don't we just shoot her and get it over with?" From a worn leather pouch at his hip he pulled out a black and silver hand-gun and aimed it at the mumbling Squanki.

"Put that away!" Ryannon barked. "Didn't you hear what she said? She said that the answers are still hidden in that wretched Advantiere! What does that mean?" He turned a disapproving eye on Grayden who was reluctantly stuffing the gun back into the pouch. "Really, General . . . ? Primitive," he scolded, shaking his head.

"It's nonsense. It doesn't mean anything, sir," Grayden replied, ignoring Ryannon's rebuke. "She's off her truglunt, that's all!"

"Listen, General," Ryannon hissed, the flecks in his eyes surging brighter. "You would be wise not to dismiss things so easily, especially where Shadow Dwellers and Squanki are concerned." He turned his attention back to Tabbit who was still droning on.

29

"Squankis don't tells . . . lady comes backs . . . lady comes backs . . . return the powers . . . four hundred days . . . four hundred days."

Ryannon lifted her from the ground, a bit more gingerly than he'd done previously, and wiped some of the soot and dust from her tattered dress. Tabbit didn't as much as blink; she simply continued repeating her cryptic message over, and over, and over again.

After listening with intrigue for a few seconds, Ryannon turned to Grayden; his confident sneer had returned. "General, I need you to introduce me to this intelligent, yet easily persuaded woman, with the old wood mill in an abandoned town." His eyes were almost a solid, glistening red as he added, "My little plan just gets better and better by the minute."

Three

CHAPTER III

GLARON'S CELL PHONE

T he sun was just beginning to peek over the northern mountains as a taller-than-average, athletic guard — General Glaron of the Trystas — made his final early morning sweep of the areas surrounding Mandela Palace. Following the alarming events reported by Audril and Dallin after the Celebration, Atoc Jonathan had placed his generals on high security alert.

Glaron's green eyes diligently scanned terrace gardens for any sign of trouble, but the only mischief taking place was the odd straggling, romantically involved teenaged couple who hadn't been able to part at the end of the night — nothing that a playful threat of parental notification didn't cure.

Glaron whistled happily as he moved around the front of the palace, toward the magnificent courtyard. He was hurrying another youthful pair on their way as a tiny form bounced into view near the edge of East Mystad Field.

The visitor, who was no larger than a child, had a shock of thick, messy white curls atop his head, which flopped unnaturally as he bounded closer. "Oh, Master Glarons!" he squeaked, his bulbous grey eyes widening to the point of creepiness when he realized he'd found exactly who he was looking for. "I haves a message . . . er, um . . . a *somethings* for you." The small messenger hopped over and stopped very close to Glaron. His basketball-sized stomach protruded out above dusty brown pedal pushers, and from underneath an ill-fitting, floral print shirt. It sloshed and bounced up and down like a water

31

balloon as he moved. He looked up nervously at Glaron, rolled up onto his tiptoes, and snapped his hand to his forehead in a salute.

"Good morning, Guddlebee," Glaron greeted, taking a small, retreating step for fear that the chubby little Squanki's belly might throw him off balance and send him tumbling backward. "What is it?"

Guddlebee, whose demeanor usually bordered on obnoxious enthusiasm, glanced around uncomfortably and breathed, "Strange newsies, Master. Very strange newsies! I don'ts knows what it is." He reached into a black satchel bag at his side and pulled out a shiny, rectangular device. He seemed terrified to touch the thing as he lifted his shaky hand toward Glaron.

Glaron's emerald eyes widened. "*What?*" he gasped, "Guddlebee, where'd you get this?"

Guddlebee whimpered and shook his head frantically back and forth. Unspilled tears shimmered in his large eyes. "It was ats the courier's offices when I arrived. I swears! I don't knows where it came froms! Please, Master Glarons! I'm just doings my jobs!"

"Guddlebee. It's all right, calm down," Glaron soothed, handing the distraught Squanki a pouch full of bugs and stones. "You're not in any trouble. It's just that . . . well . . . this device isn't from Lor Mandela."

Guddlebee gulped and stuffed the pouch in his satchel; again his big eyes bulged eerily in their sockets. "Bewares, Master Glarons! Bewares of the evil things! The stars speaks to Guddlebee. Things on Lor Mandela aren't rights." He stroked one of Glaron's forearms in a tender gesture of warning, before turning on his toes and abruptly bounding off in the direction from which he had come.

Glaron turned the device over in his hand. There was a small note taped to it that read, "Under videos. File name-Glenhill."

"Great big son of a slarp," he breathed. "How in the world did this thing get *here*?" His long, sandy hair dropped forward, and though the wavy locks nearly hid his emerald eyes, they did little to shield the look of worry on his tanned face.

Three

He pressed a couple of buttons on the thin gadget, and a dignified, middle-aged female appeared near the top on a small screen. Glaron recognized her from his time on Earth, Shawna Spence, a tenured and popular reporter from KRLN — a television network out of Omaha, Nebraska. Behind her, the air was a thick cloak of brown dust punctuated by weak swaths of heavily filtered sunlight. It was hard to tell through the haze, but it looked as though nightfall was nearing. A sense of helplessness and awe was apparent in Shawna's expression as well as the uneasy shakiness of her voice as she spoke. Glaron noticed immediately that her words flowed far slower than usual.

"Authorities have no explanation for the strange and tragic explosion that leveled the entire town of Glenhill, Iowa this afternoon. The blast, which took place at approximately four o'clock p.m., Central Standard Time, ripped through Glenhill just as many of the residents were gathering for the annual Founder's Festival Rodeo. Officials are on high alert, and are only allowing a few news teams into the area at this time. We are seeing first-hand, Mike, the total annihilation of this once quaint, peaceful Midwestern town."

Images of rubble piles, charred trees and plants, and a blackened landscape flashed across the screen as the report continued.

"We've confirmed accounts that the explosion was oddly confined to the borders of Glenhill. As you can see, there is absolutely no damage whatsoever where I am standing . . . just five feet away from Glenhill's eastern border . . . in the neighboring town of Palmerton. In fact, this strange blast, powerful enough to nearly disintegrate an area eight miles wide and six and a half miles long, did not harm any of the surrounding towns in the slightest. Crews continue to search for survivors in the rubble, but rescuers fear that the chance of finding any of the missing twenty-five hundred plus residents, and as many as one thousand Festival visitors, alive is very slim. Michael . . . back to you."

Glaron didn't wait to hear more. He stuffed the device into his pocket, and rushed across the neatly manicured courtyard toward the palace. He rounded the end of a rich green hedge, and sprinted up a sprawling, curved marble staircase which led to two towering, etched glass doors. A stocky guard in a meticulous pale grey and black uniform bowed respectfully and pulled one of the doors open for him. "Where is the atoc?" Glaron asked, barely slowing.

The guard cleared his throat and replied, "In court six, sir."

Glaron ran through the stained glass enclosed foyer, and down a shimmering hallway toward the courts. After a nearly three hundred yard dash, he erupted through the large wooden door of court six, surprisingly full of breath, and exclaimed, "Jonathan, Kahlie, you need to see this. Guddlebee just delivered it."

Atoc Jonathan's face twisted into a perplexed grimace as Glaron pulled out the device. "Is that an MP3 player? Glaron how did *that* get *here*?" he asked.

"No, it's not an MP3 player," Glaron corrected. "It's a cell phone . . . my old cell phone, to be exact. But that's not what I have to show you. It's about Glenhill." He fumbled with a couple of the miniscule buttons and held the phone up at eye level in front of Atoc Jonathan and Vritesse Kahlie. Again, the devastating report played, and as it ended, the screen darkened, and a voice — deep, slightly distorted and equally as disturbing to encounter — sounded from the phone's miniscule speaker.

"Hello, Atoc . . . Vritesse . . . Ryannon of Brashnell, here. I do hope you enjoyed my little video. I wanted you to see what I've been up to since we last met."

Kahlie gasped and looked at Jonathan, whose cobalt eyes blazed with loathing as he listened to the voice of the man who had murdered his first Entrusted, and then tried to kill his daughter.

"Atoc? Are you familiar with Catorian explosives? Perhaps my father mentioned them to you. They are amazingly accurate and far-reaching . . . as you saw from my little test detonation documentary. It worked so well in your old hometown that I've decided to expand my efforts. I've placed about seven hundred of them in some of Drolana's most intriguing locations. I'm sure that once one or two more of these beauties go off, the governments of this planet

34

will be quite anxious for answers. So, when I come forward and convince them that the Highest Ruler of the distant planet, Lor Mandela, ordered such a violent and senseless attack on the billions of Earth's inhabitants, I'd just bet that they'll be more than willing to retaliate. You and your insignificant army will be grossly outnumbered, and won't stand a chance."

There was a brief pause, and then the recording resumed.

"Of course, all I need from you, Atoc, is one thing . . . your enchanting daughter. Have her come through the portal in the Anaria . . . the same one she and her boyfriend came through earlier; only tell her that HE isn't welcome this time. I can guarantee you that no harm will come to Audril if you cooperate; she'll just be a little less powerful when she gets back . . . that's all.

"And Jonathan, don't you dare try to trick me. I'm counting on you to see this through according to my instructions. You have two weeks. By then, I will probably become impatient. I think Los Angeles might be a nice place for my next test. You are familiar with L.A. of course . . . three million people or so . . . ."

There was a click, and the recording ended. Jonathan stared at his shoes for a few seconds, and then turned his gaze to Glaron. A passionate anger was evident in his squinting eyes and clenched jaw. "Find Statlen and the two of you meet us back in our chambers," he seethed. "I thought I ordered all of the portals, except the one in the Bogs, closed!" The volume of his tone escalated as he spoke. "Send Guddlebee to the Anaria and have him close that portal, immediately!" He took a couple of deep breaths to calm himself, but they didn't appear to have the desired effect. In a tone every bit as scathing as the one he had just used he sneered, "I'm going to go have a talk with my daughter."

Glaron nodded and slipped out of the room.

"Jonathan," Kahlie tried, "let her sleep. She was pretty upset about Glenhill. I think she was up most of the night. We can get to the bottom of this in a while."

"She lied to me, Kahlie! She said that the portal was down by the lake! What was she doing in the Anaria?" Jonathan fired back.

"She's next in line to be the ator, dear. She has every right to go to the Anaria whenever she wants," Kahlie argued but in a tone far more composed than that of her Entrusted.

"Yes, she does! Which brings me back to my point," he snipped. "Why did she lie?" He didn't wait for a response. "I'll tell you why! She knew that I'd have the portal closed! She was going to use it to go back there! After I absolutely forbade her! No wonder we couldn't find one at the lake!" He paced around the room, flailing his arms in a full fledged tirade. "No! She's done sleeping! She has some explaining to do!"

Kahlie tried to calm him by placing her hand warmly on his arm, but to no avail. He shook his head and stormed from the room, leaving his Entrusted without saying another word.

CHAPTER IV

JONATHAN'S PLANS

"**W**hy should we even worry about it?" boomed General Statlen. "It doesn't concern us! What happens on Drolana is their problem!" The tangle of battle scars about the older general's worn face did little to hide the deep lines of concern in his forehead.

"We can't just leave them to die!" Glaron argued. "They're in this mess because of us!"

"They're in this mess because of Ryannon, not because of us!" Statlen fired back.

Ator Kahlie observed the argument from her maroon velvet chair, remaining silent as the generals bickered between themselves. At the moment, she was more worried about the likely unpleasant scene happening across the hall in Audril's chambers, and wondered why she hadn't heard Jonathan's shouts echoing from behind the quarreling generals.

In an uncharacteristically aggressive manner, Glaron moved his face close to Statlen's and barked, "Atoc Jonathan and I spent thirteen years on Drolana, and he is not about to let a world he called home for that long be obliterated by some lunatic!"

"Glaron, relax," Kahlie warned, in a tone befitting the highest ranking Trysta on Lor Mandela. "I'm sure we'll think of something. Why can't we send travelers to retrieve him?"

Glaron glanced at her apologetically, but then sneered back at Statlen. "He said that if anyone tries to stop him, he'll destroy Earth. You saw what he did to Glenhill, Vritesse. It's beyond anything I've ever seen. We'd be risking the lives of everyone on that world."

"And again, I say we should just stay out of . . . ."

All at once, the large wooden door at the back of the room flung open and Jonathan burst in. Kahlie rose to her feet, and the generals lowered to their knees. "We have less than twenty-four hours . . ." he blurted as he strode authoritatively across the room, barely acknowledging the reverence being shown him. "Less than twenty-four hours to formulate some sort of plan."

"What? Why?" quizzed Kahlie, tucking a lock of her wavy raven hair behind her ear.

Glaron and Statlen stood and exchanged heated glances.

"Audril and I were there for thirteen years," Jonathan explained, "yet only one year passed on Lor Mandela. If time on Earth passes thirteen times faster than it does here, two weeks will pass there in about twenty-four hours."

"I should have realized that," Glaron whispered, disgusted with himself for not having made the connection.

Jonathan paced from where Kahlie and the generals stood to the stately pedestal desk at the opposite side of the room. He leaned over it, placing both hands on the desk's burled top, as he struggled to organize the ideas racing through his mind. "This is insane," he whispered, "less than a day." He remained hunched over the desk for several moments, lost in deep thought. Kahlie lowered back into her chair and General Glaron and General Statlen took seats on opposite sides of the room.

Suddenly, Jonathan bolted upright. "Glaron," he gasped, spinning around so quickly that it startled the unsuspecting general. A surprising smile graced his lips. "You're familiar with altering, right?"

"Y . . . yes, sire," Glaron spluttered. "I've witnessed one, and as you know, I've had a tendency to alter myself on occasion." His eyes sparkled mischievously.

Four

Jonathan chuckled as he recalled his best friend on Earth. For thirteen years he'd known him as Dr. Paul Brockman, a gifted surgeon and calming force to his own often high-strung personality, but in actuality, Dr. Brockman — for all of those years — had really been the altered Glaron. "How long does the altering process generally take?" Jonathan asked.

"About six hours," Glaron replied.

Kahlie's sapphire eyes lit up. "Are you thinking what I think you are?" she asked. "That's perfect!"

General Statlen rose from the brown leather chaise, and nodded in understanding. "An altering . . . of course."

"If he wants Audril, we'll give him Audril," Jonathan answered, winking at Kahlie. "Vritesse, your permission to recruit a Trysta Warrior with altering powers?"

"Absolutely," she beamed, "Branlor and I were just discussing his niece, Mikil, the other day. She would be perfect! She's a commander in the Seventh Order, and she's altered many times in the line of duty." She touched Glaron on the shoulder and asked, "Will you see to it, General? Have her alter right away and then bring her back here."

"Of course, Vritesse," he replied as he bowed and promptly headed for the door.

Jonathan turned his attention to General Statlen. "Mikil will need assistance. What do you suggest?"

"I can ready a division of our soldiers to accompany her, sire. But won't that be rather conspicuous? Perhaps . . ." he seemed to weigh his thoughts carefully before proceeding. "Perhaps we should send Dwellers, Atoc," he suggested. "As long as they stay hidden in shadow, Ryannon won't be able to see them."

"Hmmm, Dwellers?" Jonathan replied, stroking his chin. "Yes, that's an excellent idea. Dwellers are exactly what we need. See if you can find Lortu and have him join us right away."

Statlen nodded and he too hurried from the room.

Kahlie floated over to Jonathan, kissed him on the cheek, and gave him a tight squeeze. "This is a wonderful plan, my love. Now, we just have one more little problem to deal with."

A scowl played across Jonathan's handsome face. "A problem?" he asked. "And what problem is that?"

"We have to tell Audril."

Jonathan's deep cobalt eyes dimmed.

Kahlie studied his expression earnestly and then explained, "Jonathan, we can't very well send Mikil without allowing her to learn Audril's mannerisms and speech. She'll be discovered the second she opens her mouth. Audril will have to brief her, especially on encounters she's had with Ryannon. She has to be in on this if it's going to work." She placed a hand warmly on Jonathan's cheek and asked, "She is still speaking to you, isn't she?"

Jonathan listened, but did not respond. He walked to the desk and plopped down into the burgundy and gold tapestry chair behind it. He drew in a deep breath, blowing it out slowly as he placed both elbows on the desk and buried his head in his hands. "I didn't wake her. I was too upset," he mumbled. Thick locks of his straight, black hair slid around his fingers as he added, "This is going to be one intense conversation."

Kahlie lowered back into her chair; she appeared suddenly exhausted for a woman of just nineteen. "I wish there was another choice, Jonathan. I suppose we could tell her that we're sending Mikil and the Dwellers to capture Ryannon and bring him back, but she'll want to know why a Trysta Warrior would have to alter into *her* to do that."

"I know," he moaned, "but if she finds out that he is holding the entire Earth ransom for her, she'll do whatever she can to get there." He repressed a shudder. "Who knows what he's planning on using her for? He's even more of a monster than his father was . . . and that's saying something!"

Four

Just then, the door squeaked open, and Audril's black curls appeared around it, followed by the rest of her. "Good morning," she began hesitantly, almost as if it were a question.

"Good morning," Jonathan replied, "come over here."

Sensing that she was in trouble, she glanced nervously at Kahlie as she crossed the room, and then lowered onto the arm of her father's chair and kissed him on the forehead. "You know, Dad, I should go to Earth. If I were to go, with say . . . ."

"Out of the question," he snapped.

"But, Dad, you're not even listening!" she whined, jumping to her feet.

"There's nothing to listen to, Smaggs! You're in hot water so deep you'll be lucky if you get as far as Delovic anytime in the next six months! You told me . . . ." Before he could finish his sentence the door flew open, and Dallin stood wide-eyed and out of breath in the doorway.

"Audril! It's Bridgette! She found out about Glenhill!" he gasped.

"What? Oh no! Dad, I gotta go! How? I mean . . . she was supposed to be sleeping!"

"I don't know," Dallin blurted, "but she's hysterical!"

Audril didn't wait for further explanation. She raced from the room, grabbing Dallin by the shirt and yanking him along behind her. Her best friend, Bridgette, had accidentally been transported to Lor Mandela three weeks earlier. She had been having such a magical, romantic evening with Glaron at the Celebration the night before that Audril didn't want to ruin it. She had decided not to tell Bridgette until morning that their home town had been destroyed.

"You weren't supposed to say anything!" she shouted over her shoulder to Dallin as she sprinted up a flight of marble stairs and down a pearly corridor toward the hall that housed the guest chambers. "We were going to wait until she woke up!"

"I didn't!" he insisted, "I wasn't even with her! I ran into a guard who was lookin' for you or your dad. He's the one who told me about her!"

41

Audril stopped outside of Bridgette's room, pausing to catch her breath. "Then who was it?" she panted.

"I don't know," answered Dallin.

Audril acted like she hadn't heard him. "Who would do this, Dallin? Who would tell her? Who would want to destroy her like this?" All at once Audril's mood plummeted as if an emotional dam that had been waiting to burst for the last several hours had suddenly ruptured. She could no longer conceal her own shaky emotions — let alone deal with Bridgette's. She looked pleadingly at Dallin, as a big, glistening droplet jumped from her eye and rolled down her freckled cheek. The full weight of the tragic events washed over her in a choking wave. She gasped sharply and burst into tears as the picture of the smoldering scene in Glenhill jumped to the forefront of her mind. An agonizing, wrenching pain twisted in her stomach, followed by the horrifying realization that the home that both she and her best friend had shared for most of their lives no longer existed. Apart from Bridgette and her dad — all of her friends — all of the people she'd grown up with were gone. "I can't do this," she breathed and fell, sobbing, into Dallin's arms.

As he tried to soothe her, Jonathan and Kahlie turned the corner into the corridor. Neither of them said a word, but Jonathan's face bore a peculiar expression of concern and disappointment — both of which seemed to be directed at Dallin.

Kahlie took notice. "Here," she said, calmly coaxing Audril from Dallin's embrace and into her own. "You two go ahead and help Bridgette and we'll be along momentarily."

Dallin rushed to open the door for Jonathan who didn't look at all pleased with the effort. He whisked past without making eye contact, and entered the room.

"She's dead!" Bridgette wailed, "My mom! My mom! Everyone! Lorri, Gabby, Ms. Devereaux, Principal Stockman, Brian, Charlotte! They're all gone!" A female Shadow Dweller stood by the bed, tenderly stroking Bridgette's long, blonde hair as she sobbed.

42

Four

Jonathan sat down next to her, and placed his hand on her arm. "Oh, plea-heeease! My mom! My mom!" She fell against him and buried her head in his chest. Her muffled cries were the only sound filling the uneasy air in the room.

Jonathan gently folded his arms around her and kissed her softly on the top of her head. "Okay, sweetie," he soothed, "I know."

The sad truth was that he did know. Ryannon's father, Darian, had murdered both of Jonathan's parents, and now a portion of the pain, anger, and fear he had felt when he found them strangled and mutilated on the dining hall floor stabbed into his chest beneath Bridgette's tears.

After a few minutes, Kahlie entered the room alone and calmly approached the bed. She placed a hand on Bridgette's heaving shoulders, and turned her around so that she was facing her. Her blue eyes emitted a soft, hazy glow which seemed to instantly calm Bridgette.

Jonathan stood and watched in awe as she guided the now subdued young woman down onto the fluffy mound of pillows and smoothed the white rumpled blankets over her. "Get some rest, sweetheart," she whispered so quietly that only Bridgette heard. Within seconds, Bridgette's reddened eyes drooped shut as she sank into a deep sleep.

Without another word, Kahlie locked arms with Jonathan and they walked from the room, followed by Dallin and the mysterious Shadow Dweller, who continued past them and faded away into a darkened spot in the corridor. Audril was sitting against the wall with her head lowered onto her knees.

"Come on, Buzz," Kahlie whispered as she offered a hand to help Audril from the floor. "Bridgette will be all right. She's sleeping now. I'll walk you back to your room. Your dad and Dallin have some things to discuss." She glanced sideways at Jonathan who knew he shouldn't be surprised by her Trysta powers, including her ability to read his thoughts, but he was, nonetheless. He hadn't yet fully grasped the concept of the woman who had once been the companion servant to his former Entrusted — and who he remembered very well as an awkward, gawky teenager — now being the most powerful woman on Lor Mandela.

Audril lifted her bloodshot, teary eyes, sniffled and took Kahlie's outstretched hand. Kahlie placed an affectionate arm around her waist and led her out of the hall, glancing back and smiling reassuringly at Jonathan and a visibly nervous Dallin.

"How may I help you, Atoc?" Dallin asked as he shifted his weight from foot to foot and refused to look Jonathan in the eyes. The air was tense as he waited for the reply he feared — the reply that came quickly and painfully.

"I want you to keep your distance from Audril," Jonathan muttered with an unmistakable seriousness. "Do I make myself clear?"

Dallin stared at him in a stunned daze. The response was even blunter than he had anticipated. It felt like a dull blade had been plunged into his chest. How could Jonathan do this to him? They had been friends since before Audril was born. Why was it so terrible that he was spending time with her now? Didn't his happiness matter? Didn't hers? Dallin gathered all of the strength he could muster, took a deep breath, and answered, "Yes, sir. You make yourself very clear." Again he inhaled deeply and then blurted, "It's just . . . I think I deserve an explanation."

Jonathan studied Dallin's rugged face. All he could see were the dark eyes of a man who had never come to terms with the blows that life had dealt him — a man who, after his parents had died, had retreated so far within himself that Jonathan questioned his ability to ever feel happiness again.

"Don't you understand, Dallin? I have to protect my daughter," Jonathan replied.

"Protect her? Protect her from what?" Dallin blurted, his tone far from respectful. "What do you think I'm gonna do to her?"

"She doesn't need any distractions right now," Jonathan snapped back. "She's young and naïve and it could be very dangerous for her to. . . ."

Four

"Dangerous? Dangerous for what? For her to get close to someone? Is that what you're sayin'?" Dallin interrupted. "You know I would protect her with my own life, just as I would you, or Kahlie! Besides, she's not really in any danger! You heard Lortu . . . she's immortal!"

"There are worse ways to hurt someone than by taking their life," Jonathan retorted quietly.

Dallin choked back a rising lump in his throat. Could this be happening again? Was he being denied yet another chance to be happy — and by someone he trusted and admired?

"I would never let *anything* happen to her," he breathed, fighting the emotions that were threatening to overtake him.

Jonathan's eyes seemed to soften, but then changed in a second as he delivered his next blow. "I need you to go to Drolana, Dallin. Bridgette's mother may still be alive, and I want you to find out one way or another."

"Drolana?" Dallin questioned, fully aware that Jonathan's intention was to initiate a plan that would keep him as far away from Audril as possible. "But sire, no one would have survived that. Anyone who was there would be dead."

"Precisely. Anyone who was there," he repeated, "but Bridgette's mother may not have been there. We've been so caught up in our own lives here that none of us remembered that time goes by much faster on Drolana. Bridgette has been gone for months now . . . I can only imagine what her poor mother has been through." He stared at the door to Bridgette's room for a second or two before continuing. "At any rate, she was often away on business and may not have been in Glenhill at the time of the explosion. You will find out if she is alive, and if she is, let her know that Bridgette is safe. You can bring her back here if she wishes."

45

"Surely Glaron would be better suited. . . ." Dallin's rebuttal was stopped short by Jonathan's raised eyebrow, which adequately expressed that the subject was closed to debate.

"That will be all, Dallin," he insisted.

"Yes, sire," Dallin groaned reluctantly as he bowed and sulked away to prepare for a mission that seemed rather ridiculous, and that would keep him worlds apart from the one person that he longed to be near.

CHAPTER V

MIKIL TU SHADOW

Standing outside of a scrolling metal gate — the only break in the imposing amber stone wall surrounding Trysta Palace — Glaron stopped briefly to marvel at the beautiful edifice before him. The way that Trysta Palace played seamlessly into the bordering foothills had always astonished him. Seven domes — one large and six smaller — carved into the rock formed the Hall of Warriors, which literally glowed as the sunlight shimmered across the glass roofs and danced through the tall, spiny trees growing from the domes' sides. Down the center of the grassy main courtyard, seven stone pillars — hewn from the same marbled rock as the wall — reached skyward, each one a symbolic representation of the seven Trysta disciplines: Courage, Strength, Wisdom, Honor, Self-Control, Unity in Nature, and Dignity in Death. Glaron recited the disciplines aloud as his emerald eyes trailed from one pillar to the next. After quoting the final discipline, he stated loudly, "Glaron, son of Maylinda, chief advisor to Vritesse Kahlie." With his words the heavy metal gates slowly swung open.

He hurried across the courtyard, and up to a majestic evergreen that stood off to one side of the Hall of Warriors. He pushed against the rocks that ran alongside the tree, and its needled branches rustled and shuddered before swooping downward to reveal the main entrance into the Hall.

The room he stepped into was even more impressive inside than it was out. Six beautiful, weeping evergreens surrounded the main dome — each

47

concealing doorways to one of the other smaller domes. The soft grey walls were covered with a dewy mist that glistened in the criss-crossing beams of filtered sunlight pouring through the cut glass ceiling above. Pockets of deep green mosses covered in clumps of tiny colorful blossoms grew up from the cracked rock and rich soil floor, clinging to the lower third of the wall, weaving artistic scrollwork around the entire room.

Unfortunately for Glaron, there was no time to linger and take in the beauty of the stunning room today. He needed to find Commander Branlor immediately.

Branlor — who had been chief advisor to the previous vritesse, Ultara, and had earned his rightful place in the Hall as a dignified and skilled soldier — resided in the Dome of Self-Control. However, since Ultara's death, the discipline of self-control had grossly eluded the broken-hearted commander. His life had become quite meaningless and dissolute, and although he had managed to hide his destructive tendencies from Vritesse Kahlie, Glaron knew all too well of Branlor's wanton binges and debauchery.

"Branlor?" Glaron called out when he reached the tree guarding the Dome of Self-Control. "It's me, Glaron."

The commander's gruff and raspy voice called back, "Glaron, my boy. Come on in."

A female gasp followed, as the branches of the tree descended and a young woman, at least half the commander's age, fumbled for a red blanket to hide her nakedness. Glaron frowned at her as she wrapped the blanket around herself and jumped from the bed to retrieve her clothing.

"Get out," he demanded, pointing at the door. She let out a frightened whimper as she ran past him and exited the room.

The interruption didn't seem to upset Commander Branlor in the slightest. "Welcome, my friend. To what do I owe this honor?" he smiled, grabbing a black robe from the post of his bed and slipping it on. He staggered across the room to a table that was littered with bottles, odd wrappers, and half-eaten fruit. "Can I get you a drink?" he offered, draining one of the bottles into a tall wooden cup. "I've got Meronica. Tastes like seeva nectar in these wood things." He tapped a gnarled finger on the side of the cup, causing some of the contents to slosh over the side and splash onto the leaf-covered floor.

"I don't think *you* need any Meronica, Branlor," Glaron scolded as he pulled the cup from the commander's hand. "You can hardly stand as it is."

The commander plopped down into a large green chair and stared blankly at Glaron for several seconds. "Hardly stand?" he repeated. After a long, awkward pause, he dropped his head into his hands and rolled it back and forth. His disheveled brown and silver-tinged hair flopped from side to side as he mumbled, "Oh, I'm sorry, Glaron. I just get so thirsty. So very thirsty. You know, Ultara used to call . . . ." It sounded as though he was crying as his voice trailed away, but then, as suddenly as his mood had changed before, he sat upright and grinned widely at Glaron as he said, "How can I help you today, sir?"

Glaron shook his head in awe of the fallen man in front of him. "I need to know where I can find Mikil," he answered. "The vritesse has an assignment for her."

Branlor struggled to lift himself from the deeply cushioned chair, and wobbled over to Glaron. He wrapped his arm around Glaron's shoulder, winked and jabbed his elbow into Glaron's side. "The vritesse has an assignment for her, eh? I think *you* have an assignment for her." He winked and nudged Glaron again.

"Will you stop?" Glaron insisted, shoving Branlor away. "I don't have time for your games right now, Branlor. Just tell me where she lives."

"Of course, of course!" Branlor wheezed. The stench of his liquor-scented breath nearly knocked Glaron over. "She lives in Koria South. Eighty-fourth parcel, I believe. Big place with lots of Verulcae trees around." He sank back into the chair and mumbled, ". . . bushes with red and purple flowers. The Greelan bugs will eat those things if you're not careful. Such pests . . . such pests." His head sunk to his chest and he let out a long, rumbling snore.

Glaron breathed a disappointed sigh as he touched the rock that opened the tree door and headed back into the hall's main dome.

After leaving the palace, it didn't take long for him to reach the Koria South region, where he soon discovered that there was no such parcel as eighty-four. However, after nearly an hour-long search, he came across a large home with mature evergreen Verulcae trees surrounding it, and since its parcel number was forty-eight, he deduced that this was the place he was looking for. He started for the door, and was almost to it when a loud, wailing cry emanated from somewhere behind the house.

Glaron dropped the satchel bag he was carrying, and quickly yet cautiously snuck around the side of the house. Three tall, twisting Verulcae trees grew perpendicular to the back wall, providing a convenient place for him to hide.

He jumped behind the tangled trunk of one of the trees, and was just poking his head around it when, "HEEYAAHHAAAOOO!" another shriek howled through the warm afternoon air. He pulled back instinctively, but then inched his head between two large clumps of glossy green needles and peered out. There, wielding a pair of enormous sword-like weapons was Mikil Tu Shadow — a tall, young woman with peachy brown skin and long, pure white hair. She flipped and spun the swords around as she ran from one side of the clearing to the other, whooping and wailing as she went.

"She's part Dweller," Glaron breathed as he observed her disappearing and reappearing whenever she would run through the shadows cast by the trees.

"Keeeeyaaahhhhaaa!" she screamed again as she planted one of the swords into the ground and used the hilt to launch herself skyward. She rolled in the air two or three times, landed, yanked the sword from the ground, and then faded into a twining shadow. When she reappeared she was panting heavily and glistening with perspiration. Glaron watched as she set the swords reverently onto the ground and then wiped a stray bead of sweat from alongside one of her pale, yellow eyes.

He couldn't help but gawk a little. After all, here was this beautiful, physically perfect, scantily clad, mysterious warrior who'd just performed one of the most amazing battle sequences he'd ever witnessed. He leaned out a little further to get a better look, shifting his weight onto one foot, and causing a tiny twig beneath his boot to snap.

In one fluid motion, Mikil picked up the swords and vanished. Before Glaron could even react, she was behind him holding a sharp, jagged blade to his throat. "Awwww," she moaned as she realized that she was about to slit the throat of the vritesse's chief advisor. "What are you doeeng heah?" Mikil's voice, which was deep, sultry and melodious, fit her perfectly.

Glaron turned to face her and bowed low. "Commander, I bring an order from the vritesse. She requires the honor of your service."

Mikil seemed pleased with Glaron's show of humility. "At least the vritesse has taught you how to act in de presence of a female Trysta Commandair. What is it dat she requires of me?" She plunged the blades of both swords deep into the soft ground and looked at Glaron smugly. "I assume it is eemportant." As she spoke, her hair floated outward and twisted itself into a long, white braid before coming to rest on her nearly bare back.

"She requires you for a mission on Drolana," Glaron explained. "There is not much time to go into details right now, but she would like you to alter into Atoh Audril."

"Peh!" Mikil spat with a look of disgust on her face. "She wants me to alter into a selvish brat and go to de stupidest planet in exeestence. It is a good ting that you represent de vritesse. I would keel you right now if you brought dis assignment from anybody else!"

"I tink . . . um, *think* you would have killed me before I even opened my mouth if you hadn't recognized me as the chief advisor," Glaron snapped authoritatively. He had shown Mikil all the courtesy he was going to. He was second in command to Kahlie and Mikil's blatantly disrespectful retort would not be tolerated.

Mikil realized that perhaps she had lingered in her defensive warrior persona for a little longer than was necessary. "Dat's what you get for sneaking up on me," she whispered sheepishly. "Forgive me, Glaron. I will, of course, serve de vritesse."

"Thank you, Commander. Now, what do you need for the altering? Time is running short. You'll have to alter immediately and come back to Mandela Palace with me."

"Altering takes perhaps seex or seven hours. De palace is a five hour journey. I weel begin de process heah, and den we can leave for Mandela City. I have all I need," Mikil answered as she strode quickly toward the house.

"You're going to alter while we travel?" Glaron gulped. "Will you be all right?"

Mikil spun around and glared at him.

"Oh, okay, I guess you will be," Glaron apologized as he watched Mikil evaporate into the shadows.

About twenty minutes later, a very different version of Mikil emerged from the house. Dressed in an orange and red ankle length skirt and a flowing white blouse, she looked feminine and refined. Her hair was pulled to the side and hanging over the front of her shoulder in pearly, cascading waves, and was complemented by a big, frilly, red flower tucked behind one ear. She didn't say a word as she approached, but she didn't have to. Her clenched-jaw, furrowed-brow expression spoke volumes of the pain that was twisting through her entire body. "Let's go, Chief," she muttered as she marched past Glaron.

Glaron followed her around to the front of the house, where he paused only to pick up his satchel bag, and then sprinted up behind Mikil. They walked swiftly and in relative quiet for nearly a mile. Every once in a while, Mikil would gasp or cringe or close her eyes and bite down on her lower lip.

Five

Following a particularly anguished gasp, Glaron decided enough was enough. "Mikil, would you like a Greelan chew?" he offered, hoping that the small amount of Greelan bark contained in the candy would help ease her discomfort.

He was fumbling through his bag trying to find one when Mikil stopped in her tracks. All at once, her breath caught in her chest and her eyes became wide. "Mikil?" Glaron tried, racing to her side. "Oh . . . you shouldn't be doing this! Come on! Let's go back," he pleaded.

Mikil placed her hand on his shoulder and forced a smile, "I . . . I weel be all right, Master Glaron," she sputtered as the roots of her hair began to darken, and dozens of thick, black, curly strands popped randomly from her scalp, sending the red flower floating to the ground. The black hair twisted and twined itself around her alabaster waves. Within mere seconds, every strand of her bright white hair was surrounded and replaced by curly locks of rich, raven black. She lifted a few of the curls and studied them before muttering an approving, "Mm hmm," and starting off again as though everything was as right as rain.

Glaron ran to catch up to her. "You know, I appreciate your willingness to suffer like this, but it really isn't necessary. I calculated altering time into my plans. It'll be all right if. . . ."

Before he could finish, Mikil whipped around and glowered angrily at him. "And I appreciate your concern, sir," she seethed, "but seence you have no idea how this works, let me assure you, I am fine. I do not want to have to say eet again." As she spoke, her eyes pulsated eerily and transformed from light yellow to vibrant blue. Again, she gasped sharply as an excruciating, stabbing pain pulsated in her forehead.

"It so happens that I *do* know how this works," Glaron retorted loudly. "I've altered three times myself! And I can assure you that you are not fine! We are stopping when we get to Koria!"

Mikil opened her mouth to retaliate, but as she did, an agonizing pang sliced through her stomach. She folded nearly in half and let out a long, mournful groan. Glaron put his hand on her shoulder and she reached up and struggled to grab a hold. After a few failed attempts, she finally found his hand and squeezed it so hard that his knuckles cracked and popped under the strain. She whimpered miserably, and seemed to be straining for breath, when all of a sudden her upper body rolled to the side, and she crumpled, unconscious, to the ground.

Glaron dropped to his knees beside her. "Mikil?" he tried, shaking her gently on the arm, but she did not respond. He rolled his eyes and dropped his bag from his shoulder onto the leaves and twigs that all but covered the path they'd been following. "Well, I guess we're stopping here," he muttered.

He was just getting comfortable when a strange noise emanated from somewhere beyond the nearby trees, filling the late afternoon air with a jumble of odd clicks. "Oh, slarp drool!" he gasped, "Rynolts." He patted Mikil frantically on the cheek, "Mikil? Commander? We've gotta go. Rynolts . . . Oh, come on! Mikil? Wake up!"

A screeching roar blasted from behind the trees, followed by the thudding of approaching hooves.

"Aw, man," Glaron whined, quickly grabbing his bag, and pulling Mikil's limp body into a position which would enable him to lift her. After one or two tries, he finally managed to maneuver her over his shoulders. With a grunt, he rose to standing and started running as fast as his legs would carry him. Unfortunately, it wasn't fast enough.

With the crack of snapping branches and the rustling of leaves, a huge, scaly rynolt burst through onto the path not more than fifty feet behind him. Its two cobra-like heads weaved in the air, sniffing wildly and searching for prey with their silver, glowing eyes.

Glaron dove behind a nearby rock that was not nearly large enough to hide him and Mikil, but was the only cover in sight. As he dove, Mikil slipped down his back and her head smacked against the rock. "Aaa! Sorry," he mouthed as he frantically struggled to fold her legs in.

Five

The rynolt's horse-like body pranced excitedly as its eyes locked on Glaron and Mikil. It let out another series of clicks, reared up on its massive back legs, roared loudly again and started its charge.

Glaron picked up a jagged rock from the ground and hurled it at the approaching beast. It whacked into the side of one of its snaking necks, but did very little to slow it.

Now the rynolt was just a few feet away, bearing its long, razor-sharp fangs. One of the mouths opened widely and raced down toward Glaron, snapping shut on the hem of his pant leg. The beast pulled back and Glaron's feet went out from under him. As the rynolt dragged him across the ground, his shirt rolled up his spine; rocks and sticks scraped into his back, slicing painful gashes in his skin.

He felt himself being jerked violently into the air when all of a sudden, a strange surge of heat rippled through his skull. All he could think was that his head had been bitten and that the sensation he was feeling was death creeping into his body.

What happened next was quite unexpected. The rynolt let out an ear-splitting screech, and dropped Glaron to the ground; he landed with a thud on his back that knocked the breath out of him.

The searing heat in his head caused him to instinctively lift his hands to his forehead. As he did, he noticed something strange; his hands were glowing bright blue. In fact, everything around him was glowing bright blue.

The rynolt thrashed and twisted as though it were in agony. Glaron hurried to his feet as the creature raced shrieking back into the distant trees.

Glaron breathed a heavy sigh and patted himself to assess his injuries. All at once, the fire in his skull and the blue glow faded away into nothingness.

"Wh . . . how?" Mikil's weak voice gasped behind him. He turned to see her standing behind the rock with a look of utter shock on her face. "I deedn't know you are . . . ." Before she could finish, her body convulsed wildly and Glaron literally saw her shrink a couple of inches. She grappled to steady herself on the rock as her eyes rolled back in her head and she again collapsed unconscious onto the ground.

Glaron rushed to where she lay and dropped down beside her. Her face was twisting and contorting in a most bizarre manner. A big red goose egg, evidently inflicted when her head hit the rock, protruded almost an inch off her forehead. "Ewww," he muttered, gently touching his index finger to the swollen knot.

The sun set beyond the eastern hills, and the sky faded from brilliant orange to pale grey blue. Glaron paused for just long enough to regain his energy. He worried that if they didn't hurry along, more rynolts and other equally ferocious nocturnal creatures might show up and present more deadly deterrents. Leaving his satchel lying on the ground, he gently lifted Mikil in his arms. "Off we go," he breathed and started toward Koria.

It was several minutes later when Mikil finally regained consciousness, and not a moment too soon. The muscles in Glaron's arms — particularly in the right arm which held the bulk of her weight — started to burn and felt as though they would soon give way. He lowered Mikil to the ground and smiled as he observed progress of her transformation. She looked more like Audril than she did herself now, and the bump had magically vanished. "You're almost done altering," he announced as he massaged his right bicep.

Mikil lifted a hand to her cheek and felt around. "I tink so," she whispered, eyeing Glaron like he'd sprouted another head.

"What?" he asked, "Oh, the hitting your head thing? Yeah, I'm sorry. I didn't mean to . . . I mean, are you all right?"

Mikil gaped at him for a second or two and then spun around and walked away.

"Hey! I said I was sorry! It was an accident," he called after her. "Thank you for saving me though."

Mikil froze in place and then slowly turned to face him. "You tink *I* saved *you*? Dat is so teepical!" she huffed, spinning around and stomping off again.

56

"Wait! What?" Glaron questioned as he rushed to catch up. "What's typical? I was about to be ripped apart by that stupid rynolt until you used your eyes, so yes, Commander, I do *tink* you saved me!"

"Why can you alter, Chief?" she snipped. "Don't you tink eet is odd?"

"I was on Drolana when I did it. I can't do it here. Ultara had to alter me when I came back," he explained, "I guess it's just different on Drolana."

"Was Ultara with you when you tried to alter yourzelf?" Glaron finally managed to get a little ahead and was keeping up with her rapid stride. "No, why?"

"Noting," she fired back, "just forget about eet."

"Forget about *what*?" he tried, "You're not making any sense, Mikil!"

"Just keep walking," she barked, "I don't have the strength to eexplain dis to you now."

Glaron shook his head and let out an exasperated sigh.

They traveled the rest of the way to the palace in a strained silence. Mikil didn't stop except for briefly, just outside of the Sybran forest, when her legs were transforming in such a way that walking in a straight line was nearly impossible.

They finally reached East Mystad Field, and were starting across it when they noticed two people walking together in the shallow water at the edge of Mystad Lake. As they came nearer, the duo — Atoh Audril and Bridgette — stopped what they were doing and stared at them in surprise.

"What in the . . . ?" Audril breathed as she observed the exact replica of herself standing a few feet away. "Glaron, what's going on here?"

"Now don't go getting all freaked out, Boo," he cautioned. "I'm sure your dad will explain everything."

"My dad?" she retorted, "Ugh! He's sending her to Earth, isn't he? What is he, nuts?" Without another word to her friend, she took off in a full run for the palace.

"Audril! Stop!" Glaron yelled after her, but she didn't slow. He glanced at Bridgette who was gaping in utter shock at Mikil. "It's okay, Bridge. I'll explain later." He grabbed both girls by the arms and pulled them quickly toward the palace.

57

CHAPTER VI

THE SOLOM CLAN

Audril burst through the main palace doors just as Kahlie and Jonathan rounded the end of a hallway and stepped into the foyer. "You . . . her . . . why?" she shrieked, rushing up to Jonathan and pointing an accusing finger in his face; the deep red color of her countenance perfectly expressed her outrage. "She's not . . . how could . . . this is the most . . . !"

"Now, just relax, Smaggs. I have my reasons," Jonathan replied in a tone more scolding than soothing, as he put his hand on top of hers and guided it down to her side.

"So you're willing to risk *her* life? Good grief, Dad! He can't hurt me! You know that! Why are you sending someone he can? What's wrong with this picture?"

Jonathan took a couple of calming breaths and then quietly, yet in a manner still charged with authority, replied, "I said I have my reasons."

Audril opened her mouth to retaliate, but before she could speak, Glaron, Mikil, and Bridgette rushed in through the huge glass entry doors. Jonathan waved a dismissive hand at his furious daughter and approached the out of breath group, followed by Kahlie who shrugged her shoulders and smiled at Audril in a feeble attempt to smooth things over. Audril responded with a scoff and an indignant flip of her head.

"Commander Mikil, thank you for coming," Jonathan began, wiping a small bead of sweat from his forehead.

Mikil lowered to her knee and bowed her head respectfully. A proliferation of jet black ringlets cascaded forward, blocking her face. "Tank you, Atoc . . . Vritesse. It is an honor to serve."

She raised her eyes and looked with adoration at Kahlie, who signaled for her to stand. Kahlie's hand twitched awkwardly, clearly expressing her discomfort in her newly discovered Noble status.

"This is ridiculous," Audril huffed.

"This is ridiculous," Mikil repeated in a perfect impersonation of the disgruntled atoh.

Audril glowered at her in disgust. "Okay, that's *so* not funny! Do you even know what you're getting yourself into?"

Mikil thrust her hands into her sides, mimicking Audril's body language with exactness. "Okay, that's *so* not funny! Do you even know what you're getting yourself into?" she repeated.

"Stop it!" Audril snapped.

"Stop it!" Mikil echoed.

Glaron let out a pathetic whimper in an attempt to hold back the laughter that was welling at the back of his throat.

"Ugh! That's it!" Audril yelped, throwing her hands in the air. "I'm old enough to decide for myself, you know! I'm going to Earth whether you all like it or not!" Without hesitation, she turned and started in a sprint across the foyer.

"Young lady!" Jonathan called out.

"No," Kahlie cried, "Jonathan! She's going to transport!"

Jonathan raced after her, but she was too far ahead for him to catch up. She looked skyward and loudly shouted, "The Anuh . . . ." but before she could finish, a hand slapped over her mouth from behind and a strong arm wrapped around her midsection, stopping her dead in her tracks.

"Are you nuts?" Dallin's whisper sounded through clenched teeth. "They don't know that the portal's in the Anaria, remember? Are you trying to get us into even more trouble?"

"Let go of me," she sneered, struggling to free herself. "Dallin, I swear, I'll . . . ." As she twisted her body she suddenly found herself nearly shoulder to shoulder with her fuming father with his stabbing eyes and embittered scowl.

"Let me spell it out for the pair of you," he hissed, locking them both in an uncomfortable stare-down. "I know all about the portal in the Anaria; it's being destroyed as we speak." Audril's eyes lowered and Dallin blushed to an unbecoming shade of purple. "Ryannon wants you brought to him, Smaggs. I don't know why; I have no idea what he's planning, but I am not about to take him for granted and let him have you for whatever evil he has in mind. He knows you're immortal, and yet he still wants you for something. Do you understand that I have a responsibility as your father and the atoc to protect you? And do you understand that as atoh, and the Child of Balance, *you* have a responsibility to the people of Lor Mandela to protect yourself?"

Audril continued staring at her feet as Jonathan scolded, "Don't make me lock you in one of the dungeons in order to fulfill my responsibility, young lady."

"Dad, you wouldn't!"

Jonathan's expression indicated that he was anything but joking. "With a full contingent of guards, if I have to," he replied. "Mr. Doone. . . I believe you have an assignment."

Dallin felt very much like a small child who had just been caught with his fist in a forbidden cookie jar. "Um . . . y . . . yes, Atoc," he stuttered, "I was just coming to let you know that I will be ready to leave first thing in the morning."

Audril shot him a bewildered stare. "Leave? Where?" she asked.

It was her father who answered almost before the words finished escaping her lips. "That is a private matter, which I will discuss with you later."

She gaped at Jonathan, and then back at Dallin. Both her face and Dallin's bore nearly the same wounded expression. "When will you be back?" she tried, but was interrupted by her dad clearing his throat loudly.

At that moment, a strange orange light began surging throughout the entire hall; it seemed to be coming right out of the walls.

"Solom," Mikil gasped, both excitement and fear evident in her voice.

Everyone else was so occupied in trying to pinpoint the source of the strange illuminations that no one noticed her drop to her knees in a humble bow.

"Glaron! Get everyone dat is not Noble DOWN," she shouted. "Dey'll keel you if you are steel standing!"

Bridgette didn't hesitate. The warning was enough for her and she quickly dropped into the same position as Mikil. As she did, the glow intensified, and then gathered and formed what looked like hundreds of tiny orange flames flickering on the walls of the room. Within seconds, the flames condensed even more and then transformed into sets of haunting, pupil-less amber eyes.

"Get down!" Mikil shrieked again, and this time Glaron and Dallin listened and lowered to their knees.

The walls of the foyer began to ripple and distort, darkening as they waved unnaturally. Dozens of large, black, bare feet started to materialize at the floor, followed by long, thin black legs. Suddenly, and with a strange swishing pop, creature after creature slinked out of the shadowy mass and moved further into the hall, eyeing the Nobles and weaving their heads side to side as they did. These beings were unlike anything Audril had ever seen before, and seemed to her rather like what one would witness in a demonic nightmare. They all stood at least seven feet tall — even the women — and had pure black skin. In fact, the only things on them that weren't as dark as night were their eerie orange eyes, the long, golden loin cloths worn by the men, the short, golden toga-type dresses worn by the women, and the jagged pewter daggers they held out in front of themselves. Perhaps the most startling feature however, was the thick, black, scrolling ram's horns on either side of their heads, which made their heads oddly disproportionate to the rest of their bodies.

As more of the creatures snaked out of the shadows, a shock of white hair appeared in the center of the group, followed by a familiar face. The form of Lortu emerged right out of the bodies of two of the black giants and — with knuckles dragging on the floor — he approached Atoc Jonathan. He looked oddly tiny and pale in the midst of his companions, but still carried himself as though he were the leader of the group.

"Atoc, you zent for us?" he began in his thick, deep voice as he rose up in front of Jonathan. "De Solom Clan is 'ere to zerve."

The atoc placed his arm around Lortu's grey shoulders and whispered, "Solom, Lortu? How in the world did you arrange this?"

Lortu smiled and replied loudly enough for everyone in the room to hear, "Ahhh, dat is a question for Mikil, sire."

Mikil, who was smiling and staring at one of the tallest Solom warriors, glanced at the atoc and sheepishly answered, "Lonoren . . . my Entrusted." The warrior walked over to her and gently helped her to her feet before bowing to Jonathan. Three other Solom held their hands out to Dallin, Glaron and Bridgette.

"We will accompany Commander Mikil to Drolana, Sire," Lonoren offered. Although the heavy accent possessed by Lortu and the other Northern Shadow Dwellers was absent from his voice, Lonoren's tone was still deep and intoxicating. "We . . . the Solom are cousins to the Dark Watchers of Drolana, and can call upon them for assistance, if needed."

Bridgette, who was standing close to Kahlie, leaned over and asked in a whisper, "How did he know she wasn't Audril?"

"Oh," Kahlie quietly chuckled, "all Dwellers can see through an altering. He just sees Mikil."

Bridgette nodded slowly and went back to eyeing the group of tall, freaky creatures.

"Can I please say something?" Audril decided that she had held her tongue for long enough, and pushed herself between her dad and Lortu. "This whole thing is really stupid . . . I mean, no offense to you guys," she nervously added, nodding toward Lonoren. "I just don't understand why we're going through all of this when I could just . . . ."

"Not now," Jonathan insisted loudly.

"Then when, Dad?" Audril replied in a manner oblivious to the fact that she and her father were not alone. "You haven't listened to a word I've said since last night! It's just your way or no way at all! I can't even have an opinion! I'm the Clest Anaria for Heaven's sake . . . the Child of Balance . . . I freakin' saved this whole planet! But apparently that doesn't mean anything to anyone!"

"ATOH!" Jonathan barked back, as he grabbed his daughter by the arm and forcefully led her across the foyer and out of earshot of the rest of the assembly. "You are WAY out of line, young lady! I've already told you that I have my reasons for not letting you go back to Earth! And how dare you question me in front of everyone? What are you thinking?"

"I'm thinking that this is the only way you'll listen to me!" she retorted. "Can't we at least discuss this?"

"Discuss what?" he fired back. "You want me to just let you go to Earth and do . . . do what? Have you even thought about what you're gonna do once you're face to face with Ryannon? Are you planning on tackling him to the ground and hog-tying him? Honestly! It's obvious that you underestimate what he's capable of, and that in and of itself is one very good reason why I *will not* let you go." Before Audril could counter, he added, "Ugh, I don't have time for this right now. . . Lortu?"

Lortu, who was talking with Dallin, rushed to the atoc's side.

"General, would you please have a few of your friends escort my daughter to her room?"

"What?" Audril gasped.

"Bridgette can go with you," he replied nonchalantly, and then spoke again to Lortu. "She is not to leave her chambers until I say so; is that clear?"

"You're placing me on house arrest, Dad?" Audril sneered. "What . . . like I'm five years old or something?"

Jonathan ignored her.

Kahlie, who'd watched the scene unfold from across the hall, started toward them. "Jonathan, dear, don't you think that's a bit drastic?"

But Jonathan would not be persuaded. "General?" he raised his eyebrows at Lortu. "I meant now."

"Yez, sire," Lortu answered softly and pointed his bony, grayish finger at one of the Solom. "You der . . . take tree more and ezcort de atoha and hair friend to hair chambers."

Audril gaped at her father in shock. "Dad," she pleaded, "don't do this."

"I'm sorry, Angel, but you leave me no choice," he replied. "Commander Mikil will be in to see you momentarily. I expect you to help her wholeheartedly." He looked into her eyes and earnestly added, "You must understand that she will be in *grave danger* if you don't give her what she needs."

As the Solom escorts approached and surrounded her, with Bridgette in tow, Audril fought the impulse to kick and scream and run. While it was not in her nature to give up easily, fighting seemed pointless at the moment. After all, four large, intimidating warriors stood next to her, towering over her and her best friend. Furthermore, they had plenty of back up standing in the foyer behind them. With an indignant stomp and an evil glare in the direction of her father, she allowed one of the giants to place a massive black hand on her shoulder and guide her from the room. As they walked away, Bridgette complained aloud, "Why am I in trouble? I didn't do anything wrong."

Seven

CHAPTER VII

ANOTHER RIDDLE?

It was just after two a.m. when a faint rapping sounded at Audril's door. She and Bridgette were not sleeping, but the pair was far from their energetic selves. The few words they shared in their hours of confinement were shallow at best. Neither wanted to talk about the loss of Bridgette's mom or how Audril's dad had cruelly sentenced them to a humiliating "time-out."

"Who in the world . . . ?" Bridgette breathed.

Audril shrugged her shoulders and crossed from her bed to the beautifully carved door at the other side of the room. She opened it to find Glaron beaming with an expression of wonder and awe across his face. "That was so cool!" he bubbled. "I could see the light coming under your door . . . through his feet!" He chuckled, pointing his thumb toward one of the Solom guards who looked far from amused.

"What are you doing here?" Audril asked, shaking her head at the ease in which Glaron was entertained. "Let me guess, Dad heard us talking and sent you to put a stop to it?"

"Harsh, Boo," Glaron replied as he walked right past her and over to Bridgette. "Hey, Pretty Dude. How ya doin'?"

Bridgette rose to her feet and wrapped her arms around Glaron's shoulders. "Better now that you're here," she smiled and the two of them commenced in what Audril thought was a disgusting display of passionate kissing.

She waited almost patiently for about ten seconds before clearing her throat loudly and slamming the door shut. "You didn't answer my question, lover boy. Why are you here? Or did you just come to make out with my best friend?"

"You're in such a sun-shiny mood, Blue Eyes," Glaron retorted, prying himself almost painfully away from Bridgette. "As it so happens, I was going to the kitchens to make sure Kahlie's criwa cake didn't go to waste, when I saw your light . . . shining through that guy's foot, I might add . . . and I thought I'd stop in and check to see how *both* of you are doing."

Audril flopped back down onto her bed. "We're sensational! There's been so much to do in here; we've hardly had a moment to think!" The sarcasm in her voice was not difficult to detect.

"Well, at least you didn't let your sweetness interfere with what you had to teach Mikil. Ya know, it's spooky how much she sounds and acts like you now, right down to the 'tude." He walked over and poked her gently in the side. "But then, she had a bit of her own attitude to begin with, so I guess that was the easy part."

Audril glowered at him.

Bridgette observed her bitter expression and blurted, "Ugh, she's been like this all night!"

In a split second Audril was on her feet. "Well, I'm sorry to inconvenience you both with my 'sun-shininess'!" she shrieked. "My dad just arrested me . . . had me locked up, for Heaven's sake! Am I supposed to be all happy about it? Oh, sure, Dad! Why don't I just sit here and do nothing while your precious little changeling, Mikily-poo, gets herself killed? Sheesh! I don't even know who he is anymore. Ever since we left Glenhill, he's all serious. I swear! If I even blink he freaks out!"

"Listen, Boo," Glaron tried, "I've known your dad for a long time. He gets like this when he's stressed out, and you know as well as I do that the things he's stressing out about now are a lot bigger than what he was used to back in his accountant days in Iowa. Eventually he learns how to cope and goes back to being his normal, fun-loving self, though. Just give it some time."

His attempt at soothing her was unexpectedly interrupted by the quiet sobs of Bridgette. They both turned to face her as she whimpered, "At least you still have a parent."

Glaron rushed to her side, and Audril sighed and joined him. "Come on, Bridgey, hey, come on," she comforted. "I'm sorry. I haven't been there for you today, have I?"

"It's okay, sweetie," Glaron interjected, "Don't cry. I'm sure Dallin will find your mom."

The room fell silent. Both Audril and Bridgette turned their heads slowly toward Glaron, gaping. He looked like someone who had just been tricked into confessing to murder.

"What . . . are you talking about?" Audril began. "*Dallin* is going to Earth?"

"My mom is still alive?" Bridgette asked, her brown eyes wide.

Glaron dropped his face into his hands. "Oh man, I am so dead," he mumbled through his fingers.

"Oh . . . you will be if you don't spill," Audril demanded.

With a heavy sigh, Glaron lowered into a small chair the color of robin's egg blue — one of four surrounding a shiny, chocolate-colored table — and groaned, "You have to understand, Boo . . . your dad will hang me from the tallest tree in the Sybran if I tell you."

Bridgette and Audril joined him at the table. "But Glaron, my mom . . . ." Bridgette whined, beseeching him with her big mahogany eyes. "Please tell me what you know . . . is she alive?"

He glanced at Audril, hoping to see an understanding face, but was met instead by batting eyelashes and a pathetic pout. "You promised you'd never keep secrets from me, Doc, and this seems like a pretty big one. Besides, we're not gonna tell Dad. It won't leave this room . . . we promise."

Bridgette nodded emphatically.

Glaron took a deep breath. He was never very good at resisting the pleadings of his beloved Goddaughter. "All right . . . fine . . . I'll tell you," he relented, "but if you breathe a word of this to anyone, I'll make sure that both of you are swingin' from that tree with me."

Audril winked at Bridgette in triumph as Glaron explained how Jonathan was sending Dallin to Earth to find out if Bridgette's mom was actually in Glenhill at the time of the explosion. "She traveled so often that it's quite possible she was gone. He didn't want you to know, love, because he didn't want to raise your hopes . . . ya know, just in case."

Bridgette's lovely face was solemn. She'd hoped for better news.

"Oh . . . um, I guess I understand," she whispered.

"Well, at least there's a chance," he tried, to which she responded with a barely detectable nod.

Audril leaned her head against Bridgette's shoulder. "Come on, Bubbles. Glaron's right, you've got to hold on to what you can."

The atoh's sincere show of compassion impressed Glaron. For the first time that day, she chose to focus on someone else's feelings rather than her own. He rose to his feet and kissed her on the top of the head before holding his hands out to Bridgette to help her up. "I think I'll leave you two ladies to get some sleep now. It's probably pushing three." He embraced Bridgette, who responded by pressing her lips to his.

This time Audril didn't interrupt. She sat in quiet reflection and waited until they were done. When at last they moved apart, she asked, "Hey, Glaron? Did my dad give any reason why he would send Dallin and not you? Dallin's never even been to Earth . . . I'm just curious."

"Nope, it didn't really make much sense to me either, but I'm sure he has his reasons." He gave Bridgette another quick peck, tousled Audril's raven curls, bade them both goodnight, and then ducked out of the room.

"You okay?" Audril asked, hugging her best friend warmly.

"Yeah, I'm . . . ."

Seven

A sudden loud rustling — like someone folding stiff paper — bristled from a shadowy corner, stopping Bridgette mid-sentence. Both girls glanced in the direction of the sound but could only see vague sections of black silhouettes cast by an antique doll house and an old child's chair.

"What was that?" Audril mouthed as she cautiously started across the room. Bridgette rushed up behind her and followed, clutching her by the arm. They took only a few steps when, once again, the strange noise permeated the darkness — this time followed by faint whispering.

"Hello?" Audril tried, while Bridgette nervously whimpered behind her.

The rustling became more frantic, as though whatever or whoever it was didn't relish the idea that it had been discovered.

As the girls took another wary step, a single sheet of slightly crumpled paper blasted out of the corner, with an unnatural force considering its size and weight. The breath in Audril's chest seized sharply, and Bridgette jumped and let out a tiny, high-pitched "eep." As the stiff, wrinkled page zipped through the air toward them, they stood frozen in place, watching it propel itself closer and closer, but then quite suddenly — and in a manner more characteristic of paper — it caught the air, and floated dreamily to the floor a few feet in front of them.

Audril reached for the lamp that was arms-length away on a small glass-topped table and switched it on. The light flooded the corner from which the paper had come. To both her surprise and overwhelming relief, no one was there. She started toward the strange paper but before she could take a second step, she was grabbed forcefully by the arm.

"Don't touch it!" Bridgette warned in a terrified whine. "It might be cursed."

"Cursed, Bridgette . . ? Really?" Audril questioned with a roll of her eyes. "I think you've seen way too many movies."

"Noooo, like that grasping thing your dad told us about! It killed your grandparents! Don't you remember?" Bridgette was practically trembling.

"This is not a grasping curse, Bridge," Audril smirked. "A grasping curse has to be on a sealed note, and do you see any creepy black hands?" She leaned down and picked up the paper. "This is just a harmless . . . ."

She stopped short and scanned the mysterious words which were scribbled haphazardly across the page.

Who did tell of the Advantiere?
To make it so in merely one year.
Share with the schemer; the Channeler stays,
to keep what was lost for four hundred days.

The answers are still hidden in the Advantiere, Atoh. But you must try to find them TONIGHT! Time is ticking.

"Ugh, what is it with this place and these ridiculous riddles," Audril sighed, handing the note to Bridgette, who studied it for a moment before handing it back. "I mean, would it be so difficult to just say, 'do this, and something cool or, ya know, something outrageously life-threatening will happen'?" Audril pointed to the words *the Advantiere* on the note before continuing. "First, the Advantiere . . . a mysterious glowing message that shows up on a wall . . . and now some elusive note? Yikes!"

"So, what do you think it means?" Bridgette asked.

"No idea."

Audril walked over to her bed and dropped down onto it, reading the cryptic scribblings once more. "Who did tell of the Advantiere? Who did tell . . . Oh, come on!" She took a deep breath and rubbed her forehead. "Okay . . . so I guess that would be my grandma, Lantalia."

"Well, that's helpful," Bridgette chimed in, joining her friend on the bed. "Won't it be a little difficult to ask her anything? Didn't she die, like, years ago?"

Audril grimaced. "I'm just trying to figure this out, Bridge. It says, 'who did tell of the Advantiere?' I don't really know of another Advantiere, do you? And Lantalia was the one who told it to my mom."

"Okay. Well, where I come from spirits of planets don't deliver messages through some random person, so honestly, I don't know what. . . ."

"Bridgey! That's it!" Audril blurted, "That's why *who did tell* and *the Advantiere* are underlined! Look . . . ." She shoved the paper toward Bridgette.

"So what?"

"The spirit of the planet!" Audril explained, "That's who told the Advantiere! Lantalia was just the messenger. I've got to . . . Oh my gosh, I wonder if it'll even talk to me?" Suddenly she sprung up from the bed and started frantically sliding furniture toward the center of the room. "Help me!" she yelled to Bridgette as she attempted to move a large chest of drawers.

"Help you what?" Bridgette exclaimed, rushing to her side and leaning against the dresser. "What are we doing?"

"I need to clear a path!"

"A path for what?"

Audril didn't answer. She continued pushing everything away from the walls into a large pile in the middle of the floor. Bridgette shrugged and joined in moving two tables, six chairs, a stack of tapestry covered boxes, a dozen or so stuffed animals, a mountain of books and a myriad of other things. After a few minutes, there was a clear race track-type path circling most of the room, and a mass conglomeration of textures, colors and shapes heaped in the center of it. Audril rushed to a closet and pulled out a ragged grey sweatshirt. "Thanks, Bridge," she smiled as she tied it around her waist. "I'll be back in a while."

"Back from where? You can't leave, remember? You're supposed to stay in your room!"

"That's never stopped me before," she winked, "besides, I have to do this. I promise I won't be gone long. Well, here goes . . . ." With a deep breath,

71

she started running around the circle. Bridgette had to jump backwards onto the bed to avoid being knocked over as Audril sprinted past.

After two complete laps, Audril lifted her head skyward and shouted, "The caverns!"

Nothing happened.

Again she ran, this time doing three laps, trying to build up more speed, but the short distance between turns made it difficult to go fast enough. "The caverns!" she yelled, even louder than before.

"This is ridiculous," Bridgette observed. "It's not working."

Audril didn't give up though; after circling the room five times in a frantic dash, she raised her eyes to the ceiling and bellowed, "THE CAVERNS!" But to no avail. This time as she rounded a sharp turn and tried to stop, she lost her balance and tumbled with a shriek into the pile in the middle of the room.

Bridgette sprang to her feet. "Are you all right?" she gasped.

"I'm fine," a shaky voice replied. "Just get over here and help me up."

As Bridgette approached, she found Audril with her legs tangled in a couple of bras and a t-shirt, her rear end stuffed into a crushed tapestry box, and a lamp balancing precariously against her head.

"Oh, how regal," Bridgette giggled, as she lifted the lamp and set it back on the table from which it had fallen.

Audril freed her legs from the attacking laundry, and held her hand up to Bridgette who planted her feet squarely and pulled. As Audril lifted from the floor, the smashed box which had formed itself to her backside dropped and smacked her behind the knees, causing them to buckle. As she started to fall back, she grabbed wildly at Bridgette's free arm, which was only effective at pulling Bridgette down with her. The girls toppled — Bridgette landing right on top of Audril — and crashed with a bang into the side of a small nightstand.

Audril moaned and pushed Bridgette to the side. "Awesome," she groaned as she examined the long, red welt burning on her upper arm.

Bridgette started to giggle. "That was beautiful," she snorted, her giggle erupting into full fledged laughter. "Can you tell me one thing? Why, exactly, do they call you the Child of Balance?"

"Oh, tee hee! Very funny, Bubs," Audril responded with a small slap on the back of her best friend's head, "but now how am I going to get to the Caverns?"

Bridgette, who was still sniggering, slid out of the pile and got to her feet. She grabbed a hold of a big wooden wardrobe in a teasing attempt to better anchor herself, and thrust her hand enthusiastically toward Audril. "What are the Caverns, and why do you need to get there so bad?" she asked.

Audril pulled herself up, with success this time, and brushed herself off. "They're where the soul of Lor Mandela lives. You said it yourself. The spirit of the planet delivered the message through Lantalia. If the answers are hidden in the Advantiere, then I need to go straight to the source."

"But wait. Didn't you tell me that only the vritesse can call upon the planet's soul?" Bridgette asked, wiping a stray tear from her laughter.

"I have to try, Bridge. Everything's outta whack and that stupid riddle thing says that I have to find out what's going on *tonight*."

"But how do you know the riddle's for real?" Bridgette tried. "We don't know who wrote it, or anything."

"It was obviously a Dweller. They're the only ones that can appear and disappear like that. Dallin once told me that Dwellers seem to know things long before anyone else does. I don't think I'm gonna take any chances."

"Okay." Bridgette leaned back against the wardrobe. "So then how *are* you going to get there? You have four huge, black, goat people hanging out outside your door, remember?"

"I know . . . even if I get past them, I won't be able to transport. They'll know right where I'm going." She paced back and forth in front of Bridgette. "And they're Dwellers. They can get there almost as fast as I can." She continued pacing for a few more seconds, and then all of a sudden stopped; a smug, knowing smile spread across her peachy lips. "Hey, Bridge, I have an idea. We both got A's in drama."

Bridgette nodded in nervous agreement, "Yeah, so?"

Audril linked her arm in Bridgette's and started toward the door. "Come on. I think it's time to show the Solom Clan what we can do."

CHAPTER VIII

THE SCHEMER

"Don't tell me how to feel!" Bridgette screamed as she burst into the hall in such a rush that it startled the four Solom who were diligently standing guard.

"I wasn't trying to tell you how to feel!" Audril snapped back, standing just inside the door. "You never listen!"

"Now, now girls, what is this all about?" one of the female Solom guards questioned.

Bridgette ignored her and bellowed, "*I* never listen, HA! Miss 'daddy, daddy, why can't I go to Earth?' What a laugh!"

"How dare you?" Audril seethed. "I am the atoh! You will not speak to me like this!"

"Oh, that is it!" Bridgette retorted angrily, and stormed off in the direction opposite the foyer. Once she was a few yards away, though, she stopped, reached into the pocket of her jeans and pulled out a small hot pink device. She spun around and, sneering, pointed it at Audril. "Choke on this, Atoh!"

In an instant, all four of the Solom were on top of her, tackling her to the ground. This was Audril's chance.

She bolted from the room and ran toward the entrance hall. By the time the Solom realized what was happening, she had already accelerated to an acceptable speed. Two of them started after her, but before they were able to reach her, she looked up and yelled, "The Anaria!"

With a bright flash and a pop, Audril disappeared and reappeared inside the massive tree cave.

Almost immediately, an orange glow started to permeate the sap-covered walls which were rippling and darkening to black. Audril sprinted into the dark tunnels, running almost blind. "Delovic Transendar!" she shouted, and was instantly transported to the top of a sprawling staircase outside of a large shimmering building. She raced down the steps and out into the straight stone road that ran in front of it. This time, she was able to get up to a full run before any indications of the Solom manifested. With a devious smile, she lifted her eyes toward the starry night sky and yelled, "The Caverns!"

In a flash, she appeared next to the entrance of a huge cave, quite out of breath from all the running. Huffing and puffing, she rushed into it, and hid off to one side. There she waited, watching for any sign that she'd been followed — but none came. She was alone, or so she thought.

"Clest Anaria?" The voice came in a whisper and was accompanied by a soft white glow which seemed to be brightening by the second. "I was beginning to think you wouldn't make it."

"H . . . hello?" Audril replied, her voice shaking with trepidation.

"Approach the platform, my dear."

As Audril followed the path upward toward the large rock that jutted out over an endless pit in the center of the chamber, she realized that both the voice and the light were coming from deep within the chasm. "Uh . . . are . . . are you the s . . . soul of Lor Mandela?" she stuttered.

"I am," the voice responded, stronger than before, but calming. The voice was somehow male and female, yet neither. It was unlike anything Audril had ever heard before. "I am glad to see you, Atoh. How did you know to seek me?"

"A note . . . in my chambers . . . from out of a shadowy corner."

Eight

Audril cautiously made her way out onto the rock. For the first time, she got a good look at the caverns. They were stunning with long, crystal-covered rocks hanging in jagged cones from the ceiling, and glistening in lights that seemed to be coming from out of nowhere.

"A Shadow Dweller?" the voice chuckled. "I think you and I both know who that would have been."

"Lortu?" she tried.

"A being of great worth and importance . . . but can he be entirely trusted?"

Audril smiled and rolled her eyes, "I've been asking myself that since I met him."

"Hmmm," the voice responded, "and yet we are going to have to trust him implicitly . . . trust him to be more admirable than any Dweller has ever been, and to forget his instinctive desires for gain."

"I don't understand."

"What was the message he delivered to you? Do you remember?"

Audril pulled the note from her pants pocket. "I brought it with me, just in case," she answered. "It says 'Who did tell of the Advantiere? To make it so in merely one year."

"Ahhh, which is why you came to find me," the soul observed.

"Yes," Audril answered before continuing to read. "Then it says, 'Share with the Schemer; the Channeler stays, to keep what was lost for four hundred days."

"And have you discovered the meaning of the rest?"

Audril sat on the rock platform. She was now completely at ease with the situation, and felt that the spirit with which she was conversing had prompted her telepathically to sit. "I think that the last part may have something to do with the line in the Advantiere about balance being maintained for the exact time balance was missing," she tried.

"I believe you are correct," the voice affirmed. "As it happens, from the time you were taken from us, until the time you restored my spirit . . . exactly four hundred days."

"But what about the other part, 'Share with the schemer; the Channeler stays'?" she asked.

"We've already discussed the biggest schemer either of us knows," the soul responded with a chuckle, but then its tone changed, "and it is what you must share with him that concerns me the most."

"Wh . . . what do you mean?" The nervousness in Audril's voice was back. "What *exactly* do I have to share with him?"

Lor Mandela's spirit was slow to answer, and did so with a most peculiar question. "Where is Dallin Doone, Atoh?"

"I . . . I don't know. My dad is sending him to Earth . . . um, I mean Drolana in the morning."

"And you will be accompanying him?"

"Uh, no," she scoffed. "I think my dad is trying to keep us as far apart as possible."

"Yes . . . well he loves you so much that he doesn't want any harm to come to you. This is understandable."

A twinge of guilt twisted through Audril. She had been pretty horrible to her dad the last day or so, and he hadn't deserved it.

"Don't worry; he will forgive you, my dear."

"Can you read my thoughts?" Audril asked quietly.

"Your feelings," the soul answered, "and they are most true to you. You want to go to Drolana, and that is a destiny you cannot avoid. You want to be with Dallin, and he will not live unless you accompany him . . . Yes, you must go to Drolana at daybreak. Your father will understand in time." There was a moment of hesitation and then the spirit added, "Which brings us back to what must be shared."

"And what is that?"

Eight

Again the voice answered with a question. "Do you know the real meaning of 'Clest Anaria'?"

Audril was quick to reply. "Child of Balance."

The spirit was quick to correct. "That was the translation of the Council, yes? But they are mistaken. The meaning of the ancient Derite term 'Clest Anaria' means *eternal ruler of balance*. If the Clest Anaria leaves Lor Mandela before the four hundred days is over, Lor Mandela may meet the same fate it would have met had you never saved us in the first place."

Audril jumped to her feet. "Wait! What? You just said that I *have* to leave! Are you saying that I have to choose between Dallin and the whole world? That's not fair!"

"That is not what I said," the spirit answered with authority.

The frustration which had washed over her so quickly was all at once replaced by a soothing calm and she lowered back to sitting.

"There are three things that make you the Clest Anaria, the *eternal* ruler of balance," the soul explained. "One is your appointment as such. Another comes from your parents . . . a Trysta and a Borloc . . . but if your parents were, say, a Trysta and a Lortus Dweller, it would have still been the same. The Lortus Clan of Dwellers is descended from a Noble family that was nearly destroyed a millennia ago by its love of profit."

"And the third?"

"The third, which is no longer a necessary attribute, is that you were unborn at the time that my soul needed to be restored. Only a pure and perfect child, one untainted by life's temptations would be able to receive the power to create and unite worlds."

Audril listened attentively as the spirit continued, "Lortu could have also been the Clest Anaria. His mother was Dweller, and his father was a Trysta. He didn't meet the third requirement, however; he was already born when my soul became corrupted. But as that is no longer a requirement . . . what you must decide is whether you can trust him to care for your powers in your absence."

"Care for my powers?" Audril's eyes widened.

"Yes. You have it within your abilities to transfer your powers to Lortu, but there is substantial risk. You will not be immortal while he is the Clest Anaria; he will be . . . and if he chooses not to transfer the powers back to you within the four hundred days . . . twenty-two of which have already passed . . . he will become the Clest Anaria permanently." The spirit paused as though thinking. "I wish there was someone else . . . another way . . . but Lortu is the only one who meets the requirements."

"He's bailed me out before," she tried.

"Yes . . . he has. Surely you realize, Atoh, that your powers will be more appealing to him than any other prize he could hope to acquire. It will be nearly impossible for him to return them."

"Oh," Audril sighed, "yeah . . . I didn't think about that . . . but I don't really have much of a choice, do I?"

"There is always a choice, dear Atoh, but I know your spirit; you've already decided."

Audril smiled and nodded. "If Lortu doesn't give my powers back, at least you and Dallin still have a chance. If I don't give him my powers, one of you will have to die, right? That's a risk I'm not willing to take." She looked down at the crumpled sheet of paper she was still clutching, and started to shove it back in her pocket when she remembered that there was still a line that had not been addressed. "Wait, what about the Channeler?" she asked. "I don't know what that part means, 'the Channeler stays'. Who or what is the Channeler?"

The soul of the planet didn't answer for a few seconds. "I'm afraid even I don't know the answer to that question, Audril. It is a legend among the Trystas that in every generation there is one being who can channel any Trysta power. That being . . . the Channeler, as she is called . . . when in the presence of another Trysta, will possess all of the powers of that Trysta; the Channeler can even channel the vritesse powers in the presence of the vritesse. But there has never been any evidence of a Channeler existing, and all the better.

Vritesses can be very proud, as you are aware, and the idea of anyone being as powerful . . . if not more powerful . . . than the vritesse . . . well, this has been a worry of the Trysta High Court for centuries."

"But if the Channeler is a myth . . . ."

"Why is it mentioned in your riddle?" the spirit guessed.

"Exactly," Audril replied.

"I am uncertain, but perhaps our friend Lortu will know the answer . . . assuming that he *was* the one who delivered the message to you."

"I see." Audril stood and brushed some dust from the legs of her pants. "Well, then I'd better get going; I think it's time for me to find Lortu. Thank you for your help."

"Yes," the soul answered, "but be on your guard, Atoh. Choose your words to Lortu wisely. If, in the end, he succumbs to temptation and refuses to restore your powers to you, his greed will eventually consume him. And then I fear that all you have done to save this world . . . will only have prolonged its death."

CHAPTER IX

THE NEW CLEST ANARIA

With no idea how to find Lortu, and even less than no idea how she was going to transfer her powers to him, Audril left the Caverns and transported to the north side of the Sybran Forest, near the Bogs — the favorite hunting ground of Lortu's clan. She figured that she would have as good a chance of finding him there as anywhere.

After scoping out a place to sit near a tall outcropping of rocks, she made herself comfortable on the soft, dewy grass and waited.

The weeping branches of the massive Greelan trees at the edge of the forest swayed from side to side, and despite the overwhelming nature of every single thing that had gone on in the last twenty-four hours, Audril couldn't fight their hypnotic power for long. After a few seconds, her heavy eyelids slid shut and she fell fast asleep.

She had just started to dream about drifting down a winding stream on a pink-sprinkled donut, when a familiar and alarming sound startled her back to reality — the whooping and wailing of Lortu's clan of Shadow Dwellers.

Audril sprang to her feet. Her heart beat through her chest as the mischievous — and rarely lawful — clan circled her, slipping in and out of the shadows.

"Where's Lortu?" she asked.

Nine

A pale, somewhat obese Dweller with coarse, matted hair and what appeared to be dried blood around his lips smiled menacingly. "Where is Lortu?" he repeated in a growl. "What is eet dat you want wit de noble Lortu, Atoha? I tink we can take very good care of you wit out de Lortu." The creepy Dweller zipped up next to her and ran his dirty, rancid smelling hand down the side of her hair, prompting an uproarious burst of laughter and taunting from the throng.

Audril knew enough about the Lortus Clan to know that they enjoyed seeing their victims cower in their presence; she wasn't about to give them the satisfaction. "You will bring Lortu to me this instant," she commanded loudly with a disgusted scowl. "I have no business with you or your . . . friends."

"Dat weel be for me to decide," the Dweller barked as he leaned down and wrapped his filthy, fleshy arm around her knees. With a jerk he hefted her into the air and flipped her onto his back.

Audril rolled to the side and struggled to escape, but the Dweller reached around with his long arms and forced her back. She kicked and punched at him but was in such an awkward position that her efforts were not very productive.

The Dweller snarled and let out an animalistic hiss. Within the blink of an eye, several dark shadows rushed to him, pressing tightly against him on all sides so that it was nearly impossible for Audril to move. She twisted as much as she was able — fighting to break free, and fully aware that if the clan moved into the Bogs she was in big trouble. The Dweller lowered his knuckles to the ground, a sign that he was getting ready to run. In a last desperate attempt, Audril opened her mouth and let out an ear piercing scream.

What happened next was quite unexpected. No sooner had the shriek left her mouth, than she was dropped with a thud to the ground. She watched in surprise as the entire wide-eyed clan bowed with humility, slinked backwards into the tree line and disappeared.

Amazed that a simple squeal had produced such a reaction, she glanced around to make sure that the Dwellers weren't frightened away by something more terrifying than the high-pitched scream.

There, standing just a few feet in front of her, looking both irritated and apologetic, was none other than Lortu. "Wat are you doeeng heah?" he asked in his usual deep, flowing drawl as he helped her up from the ground. "Testeeng yoah eemortality?"

"Looking for you, actually," she replied as she brushed herself off and tried to regain her composure. "But then, I think you know that, don't you?"

"Know dat?" Lortu shrugged, feigning innocence.

"Oh, come on, Lortu. We both know that you delivered that note to my room earlier. Give me *some* credit for having a brain."

Lortu paced slowly back and forth — just one of several of his habits that made Audril uneasy; he always seemed nervous, or like a big cat preparing to pounce on its prey. "I tink you are very eentelligent, Atoha. Dat note could not be deciphered by one witout de brain. But why are you out heah lookeeng for me at dis houah?" he asked.

"Well what did you expect?" she replied, a little annoyed by what seemed an unnecessary guessing game. "Share with the Schemer? Ring a bell?"

Lortu paced for a moment or two more and then stopped cold in his tracks. A look of horror, shockingly uncharacteristic of the overly confident leader of the Shadow Dwellers, washed over his face in a visible wave. "I . . . I am not de Schemer," he gasped.

"Of course you are," Audril insisted. "The Spirit of Lor Mandela told me you are . . . Wait! How can you not know this? You're the one who brought me that stupid riddle in the first place!"

Lortu seemed to be frantically searching his thoughts. His icy blue eyes darted from side to side as he took several shallow breaths and began to pace again. "I cannot . . . dis is a meestake . . . de Spirit knows . . . ." he muttered. He continued rambling in panicked bursts for several seconds, but then stopped, looked Audril squarely in the eye and shouted an emphatic, "No!"

Without hesitation, he hunched over, his knuckles nearly on the ground, and in a hazy, dark blur raced away into the forest.

"Lortu!" Audril shouted after him. "LORTU! Get back here! I need you to take my powers!"

Before she was able to finish her sentence, Lortu was back, standing inches away from her, looking like an excited child on Christmas morning.

Audril jumped and clutched at her chest. "Aaaaaa! What's wrong with you? Are you trying to give me a heart attack?"

"Of course Aye weel take your powahs from you," he panted, his mood very different from what it was just a moment ago. "Anyting to help de beautiful atoha." There was an awkward sense of ecstasy in his tone.

"Um, okay," Audril answered slowly, unnerved by his apparent pleasure in being so close to her. "Lortu, you're kinda weirding me out here."

Lortu chuckled, but then his mood flipped again. His pale eyes squinted into a look of paranoid suspicion. "And what is eet dat you are trying to do?" he snarled. "Why do you try to trick de noble Lortu? Is dis how you repay a haumble servant for all de help he has geeven?"

Audril pulled back in disbelief, her mouth gaping widely. "What in the world are you talking about? And what's with the mood swings?" She let out an exasperated sigh and tried to regain some sort of control over the situation. "Listen, this isn't easy for either one of us, but like it or not, I'm gonna have to let you have my powers while I go to Drolana. You're the only one who can do it, Lortu."

For the first time since they had met, Lortu appeared vulnerable and timid. He stared down at his feet and whispered a weak, "I know, but Aye do not know eef Aye weel be able to geeve dem back." He rocked side to side, still staring at his bare toes and mumbling softly. He seemed so uneasy that Audril found herself feeling sorry for him.

She reached out and gently lifted his chin with her hand. "It'll be all right, Lortu. I'm sure you'll do the right thing."

There was a long, uneasy silence. Lortu just stood there, studying Audril's face. Finally he asked, "You did bring de Verulcae pod, I assume?"

"De hoobidee what?" Audril replied, relieved that he was no longer staring. "What exactly is a Ver-a-kay pod?"

Lortu grimaced at her and shook his head. His hair floated back and forth with a peculiar delay. "De Verulcae pod is how de powah transfer is done," he replied. "Eef you did not bring one, we weel have to be going to de Westrim."

Before Audril could open her mouth to respond, Lortu hoisted her on to his back and sped into the forest. The big trees lifted their branches like heavy stage curtains as she and Lortu raced under them. She squinted to focus on the forest ahead, but Lortu was moving with such speed that it was nearly impossible for her to make out more than blurred shapes and colors. Within two or three seconds they crossed into the stifling blackness of the Bogs.

Audril closed her eyes, as there was no sense in keeping them open. She listened in horror to the distant growling, screeching and howling coming from the Shadow Dwellers and the animals they hunted. As they sped through the darkness an earsplitting crack, followed by a nauseating squishing sound and a horrified shriek pierced the air not far from them. Audril turned her head away from the sounds, praying with all her might that nothing disgusting or dangerous would fall on her or crash into them in the darkness. This was the first time she had been taken into the Bogs and not fainted, yet now, as the disturbing sounds and the overwhelming black encircled her, she found herself longing for the ignorant sanctuary of unconsciousness. Much to her relief, it didn't take long for them to cross the Bogs and emerge onto the hills south of Westrim.

"Eet was quiet in de Bogs dis night," Lortu teased upon lowering her from his back and observing the look of sheer terror on her face.

Audril nervously dismissed his comment and ran her shaking hand through her hair in an attempt to straighten her curls after the wild ride.

Over the east hills the first rays of morning light were slicing through the hazy dusk. "We'd better hurry. The sun's coming up," she instructed. "Where do we get one of those Ver-a-kay things?"

"Verulcae," Lortu corrected, but his thick accent made it sound like he was still saying Ver-a-kay. "Dis way." He motioned toward what looked like a fruit orchard in the distance. "Watch out dat you do not wake de slarps, though. Dey weel not harm you, but dey can be noisy. We do not want de ownair of de grove to tink we are slarps eating his trees. He weel shoot us wit de spike darts eef he does."

"Oh, terrific," Audril breathed.

They approached the orchard where the sleeping forms of two or three dozen gigantic, furry, worm-like creatures heaved up and down in a bizarre unison at the edge of the field. The nauseating stench of their breath, like a mixture of rotten garbage and sour rags, wafted through the air each time the slarps exhaled.

'Ulllllggh," Audril gagged, trying to keep her retching as hushed as possible. She slapped her hand over her nose and mouth and moved quickly past the revolting creatures.

Most of the slarps' heads were coiled inward so that their squishy, flat faces weren't visible, but the faces that Audril could see were hideously dripping with thick drool. She gagged again and moaned quietly. She raced up behind Lortu, who was now a little ahead of her, and followed him into the orchard.

No sooner had they entered the Verulcae grove, than the foul odor of the slarps was replaced by the most amazing aroma. The Verulcaes' twining evergreen branches were heavy with big, fragrant, white double blossoms and fruit that resembled lemons with chartreuse green patches dotting their yellow skin. The further they moved into the grove, the more heavenly the smell — a combination of citrus and exotic spices — became. Audril couldn't help but inhale deeply through her nose and close her eyes in appreciation of the glorious scent.

Lortu seemed oblivious to the trees' intoxicating perfume. He glanced over his shoulder, making doubly sure that they hadn't disturbed the grove's disgusting guardians, and then twisted his head and upper body side to side, peering from tree to tree in search of the perfect pod. He began weaving his way through the grove in silence, raising onto his toes under each tree and inspecting its fruit. Finally, he located a pod he was satisfied with, and produced what looked like a large animal claw from one side of his knee-length loin cloth. He cut the pod carefully from the branches and held it out to Audril for her to inspect.

"What are we supposed to do with it?" she whispered as Lortu pulled it back and cut a tiny hole in one end. The perfume of the pumpkin-colored juice that flowed out of the hole was divine.

Lortu eyed Audril intently. There was a subtle hint of fear in his icy eyes. "I moust drink de nectar."

"Oh. That's it?" Audril quizzed. "What does the nectar do?"

Lortu drew in a deep breath. "De nectar weel keel me. Eet is poison."

"What?" Audril blurted. "What do you mean, it's poison?"

Two or three of the slarps snorted and wriggled a bit, but then resumed their synchronized snoozing.

"How am I supposed to transfer my powers to you if you're dead?" she whispered.

Lortu placed his hand on her shoulder. "De skin of de pod has de anteedote. Eef you and I bite into eet togeter at de same time, I weel not die."

"Really, we just have to bite into it together? That's it?" Audril sighed in relief. "You had me worried there for a second."

Lortu's eyes still held a look of concern as he explained, "Eet weel not be easy for you though, Atoha. You may deecide dat you don't want to save de Lortu."

"Of course I'll save you. Why wouldn't I?"

"I cannot tell you, but der is a good chance dat you weel not."

Audril half-chuckled. "Lortu, this is silly. I'm not about to just let you die."

He forced a smile as he took Audril by the wrist and placed the pod in her hand. He lifted her hand to his lips and squeezed his hands tightly around it. Rich orange nectar dripped in glistening streams down her palm and into his mouth.

Audril watched him drink the juice as if he hadn't tasted liquid refreshment for days. His long, grey fingers trembled as he squeezed her hands tighter and tighter around the little pod. She strengthened her grip, so she too could help eradicate the sticky nectar. As Lortu drank, she found herself growing increasingly anxious for him to finish so she could get the antidote into him before anything bad had time to happen. After a few more seconds, Lortu pried her fingers from the pod and pulled it away from her. He frantically wrestled the remaining few drops from the collapsing fruit on his own.

As the last bit of nectar slid over his lips, a strange sensation swelled in Audril's stomach. The feeling grew and expanded, filling her to her soul. It was the most amazing, empowering, invincible mood she had ever experienced. For the first time, she felt her immortality. She felt how important and exciting she was. There was nothing she couldn't do — nothing she couldn't be. She knew — not just believed — that anything she wanted would be hers, and not a single creature in this world, or any other for that matter, would be able to stop her.

As the potent thrill enveloped her, the exact opposite washed over Lortu. He dropped to the ground groaning in agony and despair.

The slarps at the edge of the orchard awoke with a start. They grunted and growled as they slithered into the trees to see what had awakened them.

Lortu writhed on the ground, groping for Audril's feet, a look of pleading in his pale, watery eyes. "Please," he begged, "Atoha, please."

"Oh, don't worry, Lortu," Audril quipped, "I'll take care of them." She waved her hand at the approaching creatures, which instantly froze in place. "See, Lortu. I can't be stopped. I'm invincible, you know?" She reached down and patted him condescendingly on the head. "Well, I'm tired. I think I'll go back to the Palace and get some sleep." She turned on her heels and started out of the grove, mumbling about how much trouble she was going to be in with her dad, but how she would handle him like she always did — after all, she was invincible.

"Wait!" Lortu wailed, "Don't leave me heah! You have to save de Lortu, please!"

Audril strolled back to where the poor Dweller squirmed on the dirt and sat down next to him. "Of course, Lortu, I can do anything. What do you need?"

"You have to geeve me yoah powahs," Lortu shrieked, "NAOW!"

"Give you my powers?" she chortled. "That's crazy. I can't give you my powers. Do you have any idea what I am capable of? Why would I do anything that stupid?"

"But I am goeeng to die," Lortu gasped, straining for breath. "Atoha! Time is running out. Geeve me yoah powahs, please."

Audril rose to her feet. She couldn't understand why Lortu was being so selfish. "I am not giving you my powers, Lortu," she snipped. "I'm sorry!" She turned and indignantly marched toward the Sybran. "You just aren't my best offer," she shouted back over her shoulder.

Lortu tried to crawl after her, but did not have the strength to lift himself. "Den Dallin Doone weel die, too," he breathed, so faintly that it took a few seconds for the words to reach Audril's ears. She stopped in her tracks and spun around just as Lortu closed his eyes, let out a short sputtering gasp and went limp.

"Dallin?" she muttered under her breath. All at once, she realized what was happening; Lortu was dying and she was letting him! She raced to his side and frantically searched for the Verulcae pod. She pried his hands open; they were cold to her touch. "Oh, no! Lortu, NO! Come on! Where is it?" she begged. "Where's the pod?" She looked under his arms and legs, and rummaged through his hair trying to find the little yellow fruit. She struggled to roll him over, thinking that perhaps he was on top of it. As she strained to lift his lifeless body, she noticed the shriveled pod lying at the base of a nearby tree.

She slid her hands under Lortu's shoulders. With all of the strength she could muster, she dragged him to the tree and propped him against its trunk. She picked up the pod, knelt at Lortu's side and held it to his mouth. With a deep breath, she leaned forward and placed her lips against the fruit. Her mouth and Lortu's brushed softly against each other and Lortu's eyes blinked open.

"Bite down," she whispered, her mouth moving against his as she spoke.

Lortu raised his hand and placed it on the back of her head. "Ready?" he breathed weakly, "Naow."

Together they bit into the pod. The flavor was rich and sweet. Audril sunk her teeth deeper into the fruit and felt the powerful, greedy feelings flow out of her. A warm light, like the soothing rays of the sun on a spring day flooded over the two of them. Audril could feel a pulsating warmth rising in her, flowing up her body and into Lortu's. The sensation was exquisite and slightly arousing. Lortu was so close; his lips were touching hers. She closed her eyes and waited, suddenly hoping that he would wrap his muscular arms around her and pull her closer. As she sat in silent anticipation, waiting for a kiss that before this moment she had never desired, the last fragments of soothing light slid up her throat, danced across her tongue and slipped out of her mouth. Slowly, Lortu pulled away. He reached out and brushed her cheek with the back of his hand. "Eet is done . . . tank you, maye beautiful Audril."

Audril nodded breathlessly. "I'm so sorry, Lortu. I didn't know," she whimpered. "I didn't want . . . ."

Lortu shushed her, shook his head and rose to his feet. "Do not worry yoahself, Atoha. Dis is what is expected wit de transfair of powahs." He reached out his hand to help her up from the ground.

All of a sudden, a low roar sounded in the air behind where Lortu stood. He yanked Audril up and spun around to see the slarps, who were recovered from their stupor, inching their way toward them.

"That's it!" A voice rang out from somewhere beyond the grove. "Get out of my orchard, you foul slugs!" A thin silver quill zipped through the trees, racing past Audril's curls and lodging in the side of one of the slarps. "Go on! Get out," the voice bellowed.

Lortu grabbed Audril and flipped her onto his back. He raced into the trees so fast that Audril had to cough and sputter in order to catch her breath. Another glistening spike whisked by them, this time narrowly missing Lortu's arm. He ran in an evasive zigzag as Audril bounced like a rag doll on his back. She watched in awe as parts of Lortu disappeared and reappeared in the tree's tangled shadows. They approached the edge of the orchard and Lortu slowed a little; a mischievous smile grew across his face. He lifted his head skyward and shouted, "De farm of Dallin Doone!" With a bright blue flash both he and Audril vanished, and in the blink of an eye, materialized just outside of Dallin Doone's front door.

CHAPTER X

DE NOBLE LORTUS BEST OFFER

"**W**ell, I guess that worked," Audril observed with a look of pure shock on her face.

Lortu gently lowered her to the ground. "Follow," he instructed pointing to one side of Dallin's house and checking the area like a covert agent delivering a top secret message.

He led Audril around to the back, where a large barn-like structure stood, and slid back the wooden door that spanned nearly half the width of the building. He turned toward Audril, and motioned for her to enter.

"What are we doing?" she whispered as she rushed by him, feeling as though it was somehow necessary for her to keep her voice low.

"Der are tings you should know before you embark on yoah journey," Lortu breathed. "Many eemportant tings. But der is not much time so you moust leesten closely."

Audril nodded, and took a quick glance around the inside of the barn while Lortu pulled the door shut. There was not much to see besides heavily worn tools hanging on the walls, and a few scattered here and there across the dirt floor, but as her eyes wandered, they fell upon one remarkable object.

In a corner a few feet behind Lortu stood a flowing sculpture made up of groups of concentric circles, and spanning from the floor nearly to the ceiling. The circles, which were constructed of pounded silver metal, twinkled in the thin beams of early morning sunlight filtering through the high windows overhead. Delicate tubes of blown glass in varying shades of blue, green, yellow and white twisted in and out of the circles, arcing and twining through the entire length of the sculpture. The glass looked fragile, so fragile in fact, that it seemed it would disintegrate at the slightest touch.

The piece was so artistic and beautiful, and not at all something Audril would have expected to find in Dallin's back yard. "Did Dallin do this?" she asked, pointing in amazement at the stunning work of art.

"No . . . hees mutter," Lortu answered, before promptly changing the subject to address the issues at hand. "Atoha, you moust pay attention, naow. We weel run out of de time," he insisted.

Audril bit her lip and apologized for allowing herself to become so easily distracted.

Lortu grimaced and shook his head in disapproval. "Naow, while you are away, Aye shall need to find de Channeler," he explained. "Dis weel be most eemportant. De Channeler moust stay on de Lor Mandela. Eef de Channeler is leaving de Lor Mandela, she weel take wit hair de powahs of de Clest Anaria. Dis weel be a most horrible ting for de soul of ouah world."

"But how will you find her?" Audril quizzed as she permitted herself another quick glimpse of the intriguing art standing in the corner. "No one knows who she is, or if she even exists."

"Aye moust find de Trysta dat can channel maye powahs. Aye weel have to search most diligently. Aye also moust persuade yoah fahter not to allow any utter Trystas to go to de Drolana until de true Channeler is found. Eet has been detairmined dat Mikil is not de one, but no more Trystas moust be allowed to go to de Drolana unteel we deescovair who de Channeler is."

"Sounds good to me," Audril agreed, as if she could do much else.

"Der are some very eemportant tings dat you moust do also, Atoha. Dees tings weel be most diffeecult, Aye tink."

"Oh . . . well, I'm getting used to that, Lortu," she chuckled. "What will I have to do?"

Lortu began his trademark pacing. "Dallin Doone has told you dat de Dwellers know tings. Dis is correct?"

"Yes," she responded.

"And do you know how we know dees tings?" he asked.

"No, not really."

Lortu explained. "De Dwellers see results of ceartain actions. We know tings are going to happen because of what utter creatures do or say."

"Oh . . . kinda like a psychic?" Audril guessed.

"Yes, but moah like . . . eef dis pairson does dis, dis will happen, and eef day do dis, dis utter ting will happen. Do you see?"

Audril nodded even though she didn't entirely grasp the concept. "So what is it that you know, Lortu?" she tried.

"Aye know dat you are de only one who can bring Ryannon of Brashnell back to de Lor Mandela for good. You moust do dis. De consequences eef he remains on de Drolana weel be deesastrous for both of ouah worlds."

Somehow this news didn't surprise her, except for the part about her being the one who could bring Ryannon back; it was as if Lortu knew that Mikil and the Solom would fail.

Lortu put his hand on her arm and looked into her eyes. "Also, Aye know dat eef you allow yoah relationship wit Dallin Doone to go any furter on de Drolana, Ryannon of Brashnell weel find out, and Dallin Doone weel not live to see dis Lor Mandela again. You moust keep yoah feelings hidden deep witin you. Do not let dem surface."

"My feelings?" she retorted defensively, "Lortu, I . . . I mean I like Dallin . . . but just as a friend. I've only known him for a few weeks. Believe me, there is *no* relationship there."

The corners of Lortu's lips raised into a knowing smile. "Dis explains why you neahly kissed him de night of de Celebration in de Anaria, Aye suppose."

Audril blushed violently. In one sentence, Lortu made it abundantly clear that he really *did* know things.

He looked her in the eyes again, but this time seemed to be peering through to her soul. "Keep yoah feelings hidden, Atoha," he cautioned again. "Naow, Aye moust go to de Palace and lead Mikil and de Solom Clan to de portal in de Bogs. Dis is de only way to get to de Drolana at dis moment. Ryannon of Brashnell has made eet eempossible for travelers to penetrate de surface, and yoah fahter has had all of de Squanki portals closed. You moust wait heah until Aye return. Den Aye weel ezcort you and yoah . . . *friend* Dallin. . . to de portal." He bowed and backed toward the corner with the sculpture in it. As he neared the piece, he turned sharply, almost as if he were trying to avoid looking at it. He twisted his body, let out a disgusted growl, and vanished into the shadowy corner.

Audril watched him as he faded away. She sighed, shrugged her shoulders and started toward the sculpture. The way the circles and the ribbons of glass entwined and balanced against one another intrigued her greatly. Near the base of the sculpture a small black plate, engraved with elegant silver letters, bore the words, *"Eternal Companion" by Analie Doone.*

"Eternal Companion . . . ." Audril read aloud, "cool." She began to study an area at the center of the sculpture, where three circles formed a glittering funnel. Suddenly at the back of the funnel, she noticed something moving. An image without shape or form rippled deep inside, and then trickled onto the surface, gathering into a discernible pattern which was familiar.

Audril stared at the image, and the image stared back. She was looking at a reflection of her own face. "A mirror?" she breathed. "Oh, I get it . . . my eternal companion." She couldn't help but smile at the cleverness of the work. As she turned her head to investigate more of the fascinating sculpture, she quickly realized that the vision in the funnel was not the only surprise.

All at once, in every circle and on every twisting straw of glass, small likenesses of her appeared, smiling, frowning, laughing, scowling and gaping at her. The images were all her, some from when she was a child, still others depicting her at an age older than what she currently was. Some were just her face, and others her full body. Some were blinking and looking at her, while others were images of her walking, running, dancing, sitting, reading and doing a myriad of other things.

The plethora of Audrils moving across the bending surfaces of the sculpture seemed to be trying to communicate something through their actions — without any verbal clues — but all at once, that changed.

One of the images began to speak. It was an older version of Audril whose jet hair had streaks of silvery white entwined throughout it. "Why didn't you listen to Lortu?" it asked with sadness in its eyes. "You should have listened."

Another image inquired, "Did you pick up the supplies for the party?"

Still another scolded, "I told you not to go down there! These are things you don't understand."

Suddenly, every Audril in the sculpture was verbalizing — asking questions, making statements, shouting for joy, laughing with delight, and screaming in agony. The voices became so loud and created such an overwhelming sense of chaos that Audril felt physically ill. She slapped a hand over her mouth and tried to look away, but no matter how hard she tried, she couldn't turn her eyes from the sculpture.

"Shut up!" she shouted through her fingers as the voices piled one on top of another, "Just stop!" Her stomach twisted and flipped inside of her and a nauseating lump swelled at the back of her throat. She felt like she was about to lose what little she had eaten, but couldn't stop looking at the hundreds of Audrils, who now all seemed to be rebuking her for something, and were growing bigger and bigger on the odd surfaces of glass and metal. An icy cold fear washed over her as they seemed to take on three dimensional forms and push their way toward her. In a desperate effort, she struggled to lift her foot from the ground and managed to take a small step backwards. She hoped with everything in her that the images would go away, and much to her relief, they did.

Audril stood alone in the barn, but now something inside her — prompted by the images she had seen in the sculpture — brought a flood of emotions screaming to the surface and the full weight of her current situation hit her like a speeding freight train. She was no longer immortal, yet had to go to Earth to try to capture the most dangerous person she had ever encountered. A wonderful and exciting relationship was developing in her life, but now seemed doomed before it could get started. She had willfully disobeyed her dad, and was about to do it again. The tiny town she grew up in had been annihilated and most of her old friends and acquaintances had likely perished in the explosion, and perhaps the most troubling thought of all — the soul of Lor Mandela made it perfectly clear that if Lortu didn't return her powers before four hundred days passed, the entire world which she had just discovered to be her real home would be in mortal peril. Having experienced a portion of how difficult it would be for Lortu to restore her powers, she knew that the odds of him actually going through with the transfer when the time came were slim, and none.

As the swarm of thoughts raced through her mind, tears welled in her eyes and her breath caught in her throat. She folded over, and placed her hands on her knees, sucking in short, shallow gulps of air and trying to calm herself, but to no avail. Within a few seconds she was crumpled in a ball on the ground, weeping uncontrollably.

"What am I gonna do . . . oo . . . ooo?" she blubbered. "What if I fail?"

"Mees . . . mees is sure you will be okays," another sobbing voice replied. "The nices atoh lady will not fai . . . ai . . . il."

Audril sat up with a start. "Who said that?" she gasped.

On the barn door, two large, grey, weeping eyes appeared followed by the tiny pudgy figure of Guddlebee. The areas around his eye sockets were a stinging bright red like he had been crying for quite some time.

"Guddlebee, what's the matter?" Audril sniffled, momentarily forgetting her own distress. "Why are *you* crying?"

Guddlebee staggered over and plopped down onto the ground next to her. His tummy sloshed from side to side for a moment after he landed. "Phaeter," he replied, bursting into mournful sobs.

"Uh . . . I'm sorry . . . um . . . what is a Phaeter?" Audril asked.

"My bestess friend . . . the westerns star," Guddlebee wept. "He, he tolds me . . . he tolds me . . . oooooh! He tolds me some very bads things in the nights. Very bads! Ooooooo!" he dropped his small head onto Audril's leg and wailed.

Audril tried to shush him but the distraught little Squanki would not be comforted. She gingerly stroked his wild white hair in a somewhat feeble attempt to soothe him and asked, "Is there anything I can do?"

"Forgives me, pleases. I should not be drippings despicable tears all over the nices atoh."

"Oh . . . don't worry about me, Guddlebee," she responded, "I won't melt." She wiped at her own teary eyes with the back of her hand and asked, "What did your star friend tell you?"

Guddlebee gulped hard and looked up at her. His chin quivered as he explained, "My dearest Entrusteds . . . she didn't come homes from the Celebration ats the noble palace. She is takens and is hurts!"

"Are you sure, Guddlebee? I mean . . . are you sure that your star buddy knows what he's talking about?"

Guddlebee jumped to his feet and glared angrily at her. "The stars knows! They tells me all things they sees! Phaeter knows that my Entrusteds is in dangers!" he barked.

"Oh, all right . . . I'm sorry, Guddlebee. I didn't mean . . . I was just . . . ." Audril didn't quite know what to say to pacify the ranting little fellow. She had heard rumors that Guddlebee was a bit on the crazy side. His claims that he regularly conversed with stars were infamous on Lor Mandela, and even though he had never done anything dangerous, Audril was afraid that if she said the wrong thing — given his current agitated state — she might drive him to his first harmful incident. "What can I do to help you?" she asked, trying to express the utmost concern.

Guddlebee buried his head in his hands and cried some more. Through his tears he muttered something, but the words were muffled and unintelligible.

"What?" Audril questioned softly.

The weeping Squanki lifted his head and blinked at her with his bloodshot bulging eyes. "Mees wants my Tabbits back," he whimpered.

"What? Wait . . . Tabbit's your Entrusted?" Audril gasped. "Oh no."

"Oh no, whats?" Guddlebee shrieked. "Whats oh no? Why the atoh says 'oh no'? Where is my Tabbits?"

Audril never wished she could retract her words more than she did at this moment. More than anything, she did not want to have to tell Guddlebee that she heard Tabbit screaming in the Anaria, right next to the portal through which Ryannon of Brashnell had gone. Hearing that Tabbit had not returned to her home after the Celebration only confirmed Audril's fears that her poor little friend had been abducted by Ryannon and was being held captive on Earth. She looked down into Guddlebee's anxious face and stuttered, "What I meant to say, is um . . . well, it's um . . . ."

"What she means to zay is dat Ryannon of Brashnell has yoah Entrusted on de Drolana and you moust accompany de atoha there to bring hair back." Lortu appeared out of a dark corner so suddenly that both Guddlebee and Audril jumped at the sound of his voice.

"Whaaaaat? Ryannons of Brashnell?" Guddlebee whispered, trembling in fear. "Why does *he* haves my Tabbit?"

Audril forced a fake grin and motioned toward the far side of the room. "Um, Lortu? Can I have a word?" she asked.

After assuring Guddlebee that she and Lortu would be right back, she grabbed Lortu by the arm and pulled him along behind her. "Are you nuts?" she hissed once they were out of earshot. "He can't come to Earth with us! It's going to be dangerous enough without some psycho little Squanki tagging along!"

A strange, wild look graced Lortu's face, as if he couldn't decide whether to laugh or yell. "Aye have seen what weel happen if dis Squanki does not accompany you. Eet weel be better for you to have heem. He weel not bring you danger, Aye promeese dis."

"This had better not be one of your schemes," Audril cautioned. "If you're trying to get rid of me just so you can keep my powers . . . ."

Lortu's eyes narrowed into an annoyed glare. "You do not understand all tings, Atoha," he seethed. "Aye require you to troust de Lortu." His tone and expression were so deathly serious that Audril dared not retort, and when he pointed toward Guddlebee, Audril simply bowed her head and obediently pattered back across the room.

"Time is getting short. We moust meet wit de Dallin Doone and eenform heem of ouah plans." Lortu walked past Audril and Guddlebee and pulled the big wooden door open. Audril glanced behind her at the "Eternal Companion" sculpture. An uneasy pang twisted in her stomach. She turned and quickly shuffled out of the barn with Guddlebee in tow.

As if it were choreographed, they rounded the side of Dallin's house just as he came through his front door carrying a large, camel-colored knapsack. His brown wavy hair was wet and slightly curlier than usual and his red t-shirt and baggy jeans made him look very convincing as "just any old guy from planet Earth." He walked with some speed, yet hummed a slow, sad, mournful song, keeping his head bowed and his eyes locked on the little bursts of dust that kicked up under his feet. He strode across the yard, not aware that three oddly contrasting characters were rushing up behind him.

Lortu was the first to catch up and fell into pace alongside him on the right. Dallin jumped when he saw him, but barely broke his stride. "I was wonderin' where you were," he started, "I wasn't lookin' forward to searchin' through the Bogs for that portal by myself."

Just then, Audril appeared at his left with Guddlebee next to her. Dallin gasped and stared at her in shock. He turned back to Lortu and asked, "What's goin' on here? What's she doin' here?"

"Oh . . . it's delightful to see you, too," Audril snipped.

Dallin ignored her and asked again, "Lortu, what's goin' on?"

"Guddlebee and I are coming with you," Audril answered, smiling smugly.

"WHAT? Oh no, no, no, no, NO!" Dallin barked, freezing in his tracks. Once again, he addressed only Lortu. "Are you crazy? Her father will have me executed!"

"Eet is deeficult to execute a man you cannot find, Dallin Doone," Lortu offered.

The less than profound reply did little to calm Dallin. He looked at Audril and snapped, "Don't you understand? I would like to be able to come back here someday, you know . . . and not have to worry about bein' murdered by a livid atoc! He's forbidden you to go!" He sighed deeply and frowned. "Is there any point in me askin' why you're doin' this to me?"

Audril placed her hand on his forearm, a gesture that had a far more pleasing effect than Dallin cared to admit at the moment. "We have to go with you," she explained, an excited spark dancing in her azure eyes. "I went to the Caverns, Dallin. I spoke to the soul of Lor Mandela. The soul told me that I *have* to go to Drolana. It also said that you need to protect me while I'm there," she lied, "and Guddlebee . . . he is going to rescue Tabbit. Did you know that she's his Entrusted? Anyway, Lortu believes that she's been captured by Ryannon and that Guddlebee is the best one to save her. Besides it'll be nice to have some Squanki magic with us, don't you think?"

"But your dad . . . ." Dallin whined, gazing at her beautiful face and trying to stay strong, but it was no use. Regardless of how angry Jonathan was likely to be, Dallin wanted to spend time with Audril and here was an opportunity to spend a lot of time with her. He glanced at Guddlebee who was staring up at him with bulging, weepy eyes and then at Lortu who seemed to be growing more and more impatient by the moment. "Fine," he muttered with a huff, "but it doesn't mean I'm happy about it."

Lortu hardly waited for Dallin's complaint to register before he began digging in a small pouch that hung at his side. "Very well den. You weel be needing dis." From the pouch he pulled out a huge roll of cash.

"Good grief," Audril exclaimed, "where did you get that?"

"Dis is not eemportant," Lortu answered with a dismissive wave. "Use eet to find a place to stay and to purchase de tings dat you need. Aye tink der should be enov." He handed the wad of bills to Audril who started counting, but by the time she reached forty-five hundred dollars, her hands were trembling so bad that she just stopped and shoved the money nervously into her pocket.

"Yeah, this should be enov," she gasped, "but Lortu, this is a ton of money. Are you sure you want us to take *all* of it?"

Lortu scowled and replied, "What need have Aye for Drolana currency? Dis is wortless to de Lortu. Naow, what is de town nearest to de Glenhill, Ay-ee-wa?"

"Um . . ." she stared blankly at Lortu and struggled to process what Ay-ee-wa was. "Oh wait! You mean Iowa? Oh, uh, Palmerton, I guess," she answered.

"Squanki," Lortu crouched down to Guddlebee's eye level and instructed, "der is no need for you to be going into de Bogs." He pointed to a nearby rock outcropping and continued, "dis weel be de good place for you to make de portal. Go to dis Palmerton of Ay-ee-wa. When you get der, take care dat you close de portal up again. But make certain dat you remembah de place where you eemerge, and re-open de portal in dis exact spot when you return. Aye weel know when you are coming and weel be prepared. You moust hurry, naow. At dis moment, de atoc and dose membahs of de Solom Clan dat stayed behind are on der way to Westrim to look for de atoha at de home of Dallin Doone. Dey will be passing by us shortly."

"Sooo not good!" Dallin gasped, grabbing Audril by the arm and pulling her to the rock outcropping with urgency. Guddlebee darted along behind them and wasted no time rolling his small brown hand into a fist. As he curled and uncurled his fingers, a thin, yet intensely bright sliver of blue light appeared on the jagged face of the rock.

Beyond the foothills, the not too distant sound of agitated voices filled the air. "I don't care if he'll protect . . . . She knew . . . ." "Don't worry, Atoc. We will find . . . visit the Lortus . . . ."

"But I can't believe she would . . . ."

Audril felt a sense of panic at the unmistakable anger in her dad's voice.

"We've gotta go," she whispered, tugging on the sleeve of Dallin's shirt. "Hurry!"

Dallin was the first to lift his foot to the portal. With a strange sucking pop, the light expanded and swallowed him in less than a second.

"Guddlebee, go!" Audril mouthed. The Squanki nodded and obediently did as he was told.

Audril glanced over her shoulder at Lortu. Her dad's voice and the voices of the Solom were getting closer and closer but there was something that she just had to do. She ran back to where Lortu stood, threw her arms around his neck, embraced him and kissed him on the cheek. "Keep Lor Mandela safe, my friend," she whispered in his ear, "and thank you. Thank you for everything." Without looking back, she raced to the portal and dove into it head first.

Lortu watched in awe as Audril disappeared but then heard the atoc's approaching voice and snapped back into the moment. He moved with great stealth to the rock outcropping, and positioned himself in front of the glowing blue slit just as Jonathan and his entourage of black warriors emerged from behind some trees. "Good morning, Atoc," he greeted, casually studying the back of his hand.

Jonathan's care worn countenance spoke volumes of his displeasure. "Lortu," he nodded. "We are looking for Audril. Have you seen her?"

"Yes, Sire. Aye deed see hair neah Koria joust a few hours ago, but eet was as she was transporting, and Aye was not able to stop hair. Aye deed heah hair yell dat she was transporting to de Anaria, but when Aye checked der, she was no wheah to be found. Aye am very zorry, Atoc. Aye have all of my clan looking for hair naow. Aye am certain we weel find hair befoah long."

"Very well, Lortu," Jonathan replied, "You will let me know the moment she is spotted."

"Of course, Atoc."

Jonathan and his three Solom companions continued toward Dallin's farm. As soon as they were out of sight, Lortu checked the rock behind him; the portal was gone. He smiled deviously, placed his fingertips on the spot that Audril had kissed, and whispered, "No, tank you, maye beautiful Atoha. You have made de Lortu moah powahful den de atoc or de vreetesa combined." With a look of haughty arrogance he surveyed the area around him. "Dis being de Clest Anaria weel be most profitable, Aye tink. So tank *you*, Atoha . . . Tank you foah being de noble Lortu's best offer."

CHAPTER XI

TEEDEE VENILWORTH

Audril stared out over the blackened landscape that was once her home, sickened by the sight of the smoldering desolation. "Why?" she mumbled as a lone crystal tear streamed silently down her cheek.

A few feet away, Guddlebee sat cross-legged on the ground tracing his finger around a smooth rock next to him and dreamily gazing skyward. Periodically, he would stop tracing and whisper something into the air.

Dallin watched both of them, but was far more concerned with Audril's current state of mind than Guddlebee's apparent fascination with the heavens. He walked up behind her and tenderly linked his arm in hers. "C'mon," he whispered, "we've gotta find a place to stay."

Audril gulped back her emotions and nodded with a far from persuasive smile. "We should try the Quik Mart," she muttered. "They've got a couple of bulletin boards in there where people advertise things they have for sale and rooms they're renting out . . . ya know, stuff like that." She reached down and subconsciously patted her pocket to reassure herself that the money was still there.

Dallin slid his hand across her back and up to her shoulder.

"Dallin, don't," she snapped, and then quickly interjected, "I mean . . . I'm fine." She ducked away from him and took off across the small, dusty field in which they stood.

Dallin rushed to catch up, followed by Guddlebee who suddenly snapped back into reality when he realized that his party was on the move. "Hey, you can't leave me like that," Dallin teased. "I might get lost!" Guddlebee grabbed him by the hand and assured, "Nos Master Dallins. Guddlebee will nevers let you gets lost. Athenius is very kinds and tolds me he would bes watching out for all ofs us while were heres on Drolana."

"I was just joking, Guddlebee," Dallin scowled, "and let me guess, Athenius is one of your star buddies?"

Guddlebee nodded enthusiastically, "Yeps . . . just met hims. He says he is lookings for my Tabbits and will twinkle three times whens he finds her."

"Oh, terrific," Dallin snipped.

Audril glanced sideways at the two of them and shook her head; a gesture that did not go unnoticed by Dallin.

"Hey," he tried, "you okay? I didn't mean to upset you back there. I was just tryin' to help."

"Oh, I know. I'm sorry," she apologized. "I'm tired and . . . well . . . she jabbed her index finger over her shoulder, back toward Glenhill.

"Right," Dallin answered.

They neared the edge of the field where a wide gulch was all that stood between them and the small town of Palmerton. At the bottom of the gulch, a shallow, winding stream twisted through the parched soil on either side. The dirty brown water cut through the cracked earth, struggling and straining to quench the thirst of the ground, but failing miserably. Dallin and Guddlebee paused to determine the best spot to cross but Audril didn't hesitate. She headed directly for the place where the stream looked widest, rolled up the bottom of her pant legs, and waded across. Dallin shrugged and followed; Guddlebee zipped after them both.

Once they reached the other side of the gulch and climbed up and out, a large convenience store came into view. The wall that faced them was hand painted with several smiling cartoon pigs in blue overalls, and the words "Palmerton Quik Mart, Home of the Big Pig."

Dallin couldn't help but chuckle. "What exactly is a Big Pig?" he sniggered.

"A heart attack on a bun," Audril answered. "It's a massive chili dog with bacon and tons of cheddar and that gross pumpy cheese stuff, on a pile of greasy French fries . . . nasty!"

Dallin's eyes widened excitedly. "Oh, just wrap one up now," he breathed, smacking his lips. "That sounds like *ecstasy* on a bun if you ask me."

Guddlebee copied Dallin's lip smacking and bobbed his head up and down in agreement; his curly white hair floated side to side instead of up and down.

"Just a question, though," Dallin continued. "What're French fries . . . and chili dogs . . . and all that other stuff you just said? And also . . . what's a bun?"

Audril scoffed and slugged him in the shoulder.

"What?" he laughed, "I'm new to this area of Drolana."

"Tourists," Audril retorted, with a grin. "Listen, Dallin . . . I'll buy you a Big Pig . . . if you want," she shuddered in disgust. "But while we're here, this is called Earth, not Drolana, got it? And you can't be asking me what stuff is in front of people. They'll think you're some sort of freak." Dallin smiled and nodded, relieved that Audril was acting a little more cheerful.

"Guddlebee . . . you'll have to hide. It'll be bad news if anyone here sees you running around. There's nothing on Earth that even comes close to looking like a Squanki. You'll weird 'em out, for sure."

Guddlebee frowned as his shoulders slumped. "Fines," he groaned. Despite his disappointment, he turned and bounded across the gravel parking lot to the big painted wall. After taking a cautious glance around, he leaned against one of the cartoon pigs and faded into the wall right over the top it. His bulbous eyes lined up nearly perfectly with those of the overall-wearing swine. Dallin chuckled and Audril rolled her eyes.

"You probably should go back to calling me Maggie . . . at least while we're in Palmerton," Audril explained. "Ed and Lil Marler run this place and they know me and my dad. Ed'll talk your ear off if you let him, which is funny, 'cause Lil can't hear a thing . . . you'll see." They reached the front of the store, Dallin pulled the heavy glass door open, and they stepped inside.

A startling "bzzzzzzzttt" blasted through the air next to them, causing Dallin to jump behind Audril.

"It's just a door buzzer," she giggled. "Ed had it amplified so Lil can hear it. You get used to it after a while, I guess."

Dallin gulped in a huge breath and punched himself in the chest as if he had to restart his heart.

Inside the Quik Mart rows and rows of shelving stuffed with everything from ice cream to skin cream; from newspaper to toilet paper; and from auto parts to deep fried chicken parts, created a maze of colors and textures that was so chaotic, it was difficult to concentrate on any one area for too long. Dallin gazed around in awe as Audril playfully watched him.

Before long, a stout little bald man with wire-rimmed glasses and squinty eyes came around the corner of one of the aisles and nearly dropped the stack of flat boxes he was carrying. "Maggie Baker?" he blared, "Good heavens! Good heavens! Oh, what a relief!" He quickly placed the boxes on the floor, waddled across the store and threw his chubby little arms around Audril.

"Lil! Get out here!" he bellowed as if he were waking the dead. "Lil! It's Maggie Baker! She's all right!" He held up his index finger, that looked a great deal like a raw pink sausage, and beamed. "Woman's gotta get a hearin' aid! I'm 'fraid she doesn't hear very well. Be back in a second." He smiled again, headed toward the back of the store, and disappeared around the end of an aisle. "Lily Ann! Get out here!" he shouted again.

A moment later, he reappeared accompanied by a frail grey haired lady with a kind face and sparkly eyes. She was wearing a grey polka dotted dress with a white cardigan draped around her shoulders. As soon as she saw Audril she clasped her hands over her mouth and started crying. "My goodness," she half-laughed, half-sobbed, "you're the most beautiful thing I've seen in a long time, young lady!" She shuffled up to Audril and kissed her on the cheek.

"Hello, Mrs. Marler," Audril began, "how ya doing?"

"Oh, never mind 'bout that," Lil scolded. "How are you, dear? Where've you been?" She looked at Audril with moist eyes and apprehensively whispered, "And what about your . . . your dad? Is he all right?"

"He's fine," Audril assured.

Ed and Lil just stared at her like the news that she and her dad were all right was the most shocking revelation in the history of all time.

"But where've you been?" Ed repeated. "We've been worried sick."

"It's a bit of a long story, Mr. Marler," Audril answered.

Ed's eyes shifted from her to Dallin and a look of suspicion spread across the elderly shop keeper's face. Lil was eyeing him a bit tentatively herself.

"Oh, uh . . . this is my . . . um . . . ." Audril stumbled; she glanced at Dallin with a look of desperation.

"Oh, cousin," Dallin offered, thrusting his hand out toward Ed. "I'm her cousin, Dallin Doone, from . . . uh . . . Australia."

Audril dropped her head into her hand and sighed.

Ed cautiously extended his hand. "Ya don't sound much like an Australian," he observed.

"Well, it's just . . . I mean he . . . *he* just moved there . . . from . . . uh, Cleveland," Audril stammered, "about two weeks ago."

Lil locked her arm in Ed's. The friendly twinkle in her eye returned. "Well, welcome back to the states, Mr. Goon."

Ed shook his head, "It's Doone, mother, Doone!" he corrected, emphasizing the D in Dallin's last name.

"Oh! Pardon me, Mr. Doone." Lil bit her lip bashfully. "I think I'm starting to lose my hearing."

Ed chuckled and patted her on the arm. "You've notified the authorities, haven't you, Maggie? To let them know you're all right?"

"Um, of course," Audril fibbed, "yeah . . . they know all about it."

Just then the heart-jolting sound of the door buzzer ripped through the air with all its disquieting fury. Dallin jumped again, and Ed peered past him to see who was there.

"Ah, Teedee," he grinned. "Teedee, look who's come to visit." He scurried over toward the door. "It's Maggie Baker, can you believe it?"

"Maggie, who?" the coarse, raspy voice of an old lady with a slight East Coast accent replied.

Dallin looked over his shoulder and then immediately spun back around, "Slarp drool," he gasped, "*what* is that?"

Audril twisted her head to the side and beheld the strangest, most eccentric woman she had ever seen in her life. She too recoiled instantly.

"I have no idea," she whispered.

Lil was still gazing at her with an odd expression of delight, apparently oblivious to the fact that anyone new was in the store.

"Oh, you know . . . Maggie Baker," Ed tried, "from Glenhill. Surely you've heard . . . ."

Teedee cut him off short. "Ahh, yeah. Maggie Baker of Glenhill! Of course, how silly of me."

Neither Audril nor Dallin dared turn to greet the strange woman, but by the sound of Teedee's reply, Audril knew that she was close behind them. Feeling that it would be rude not to at least say hello, Audril pivoted around and came face to top-of-the-hat with the hunched over little woman, whose appearance was even more shocking at close range. Behind thick lenses — that were framed in shiny black plastic and spanned the entire width of her face — Teedee's hugely magnified, steely blue eyes blinked up at Audril. "How've ya been, Toots?" she grunted, patting Audril on the back of the hand. "Shame that Glenhill was blown to bits, but at least you were outta town, eh?" Audril gaped at Teedee's bluntness and tried to take in all that was before her.

From her head to her toes, every inch of Teedee contained something strange. The straw hat on her head was gigantic, lime green and floppy and concealed any evidence of hair that might have been there. A necklace of fat jade and cobalt blue beetles seemed to be crawling around her neck, making it seem extraordinarily small. Beneath the creepy beetle choker, a bright rain slicker-type smock, with huge flowers printed all over it and easily four sizes too big, gave Teedee's petite body the appearance of a flowery pyramid with neon pink legs. Huge silver and turquoise rings spanned the spaces between her knobby knuckles on every finger; a rainbow of jeweled bangles covered her arms almost to her elbows, and her ankles were dwarfed by the black and white zebra print galoshes she wore on her feet.

The outrageous little lady stood perfectly still, except her twitching, flickering eyes, and allowed Audril a moment or two to process her eccentricity before switching her focus to Dallin, who still had his back to her. She jabbed him forcefully in the shoulder and barked, "Turn around and let me check you out, boy. From the looks of ya, you might be exactly what I need."

Dallin could hardly believe what she had just said, nor imagine what she meant by it, but he had little desire to find out. He stayed put until Teedee gave him another sharp poke in the shoulder blade, and then finally relented and revolved around.

"Ma'am?" he choked.

"*Ma'am?*" Teedee quickly mimicked, squinting at him through her gigantic round spectacles. "Do I look like your mother, boy? My name is Mrs. Teedee Venilworth, but you may call me Teedee . . . not Mrs. Venilworth . . . and certainly not Ma'am." She cringed with contempt. "And my goodness, Ed. Get this young man one of those Pig monstrosities! He's nothin' but skin and bones!"

Ed nodded and scurried off.

Teedee wrapped her arm around Dallin's and smiled up at him. Her hot pink lipstick looked like it had been applied in a moving vehicle by a blind person.

Dallin smiled back, feeling suddenly intrigued by this charming little lady that was insisting that he have food.

112

"Now then, dear," she started, her tone a little less gruff, "you look like you've traveled a long way."

"From Australia," Ed's voice sounded from somewhere behind a set of metal shelves.

"Australia?" Teedee mused. "Well, you just come over here and rest while I do my shopping. If you, or your lovely lady friend, need anything at all, you just let Ed know." She led Dallin to a small grouping of metal tables and chairs and insisted that he sit. Then, setting her sunshine yellow and glittery purple hand bag on the floor next to him, she shuffled back to Audril. "My goodness, aren't you a lovely girl!" she gushed, "You and your boyfriend are quite a handsome couple."

"Oh, uh, he's my cousin," Audril blurted.

Teedee glanced over her shoulder at Dallin who was practically inhaling a mound of chili and French fries; an expression of ecstatic delirium shone in his eyes. "Of course he is, love." She nudged Audril in the side with her elbow and whispered, "It's okay, Toots. I won't say a word . . . although, if my lover looked like that, I'd hardly keep it a secret."

Audril turned as magenta as Teedee's stockings and the bold little lady winked and strolled away. She meandered up and down the aisles, mumbling to herself, and asking questions into the air. At the end of each question, she would stop and stare off into the distance as though she were waiting for an answer.

Audril joined Dallin at the table. "She's nuts," she breathed as she plopped into one of the metal chairs.

"She's wonderful," Dallin retorted, blissfully shoving the last bit of hot dog into his mouth. "Ed, can I get another one?" he shouted.

"Sure thing!" Ed answered, again from a concealed location.

Audril grimaced at Dallin and scolded, "Are you forgetting something? We're supposed to be finding a place to stay."

The words barely left her lips when Teedee appeared from out of nowhere. Audril gasped and Dallin sprang to his feet. "Hodgson and I would be honored if you would stay with us at the Manor," Teedee said as if she was giving an order rather than an invitation.

"Oh . . . oh no, th . . . that's all right," Audril spluttered. "We wouldn't want to inconvenience you. Thanks for the invite, but I'm sure we can find a couple of nice hotel rooms in town."

"Nonsense!" Teedee snapped, dropping a bag of groceries onto Dallin, who fumbled and caught the handles just before the contents were able to spill out. "Bring my handbag, please," she insisted as she scampered toward the door. "Hodgson?" she barked back toward the store. "Hodgson! Oh, where is that man? He always disappears when I need him." She glanced back at Audril and Dallin. "Well? Come along," she demanded. "Don't forget my purse and your other pig."

Dallin snatched Teedee's bag from the floor and grabbed his Big Pig from Ed, who had just come around the shelves carrying it in a foam container. He shoved the container into the grocery sack and started after Teedee.

"What are you doing?" Audril hissed. "We're not staying with her! She's insane!"

Dallin looked down at the bags in his hands and shrugged. "It'll be fine; come on." He crossed the store and pushed the door open for Teedee. "Bye Ed!" he called back, "BYE LIL!" he added, much louder and with emphasized articulation.

"Come see us again," a small squeak replied from somewhere toward the back of the store.

"Come on, Au . . . I mean, Maggie!" Dallin called over his shoulder as he and Teedee crossed the threshold. "Make sure you let *you-know-who* know that we're leaving."

"Oh, good grief," Audril sneered. "What do I owe you, Mr. Marler?"

"Oh, nothin'," Ed answered, "Teedee is a part owner now . . . bailed us out of quite a predicament, she did. She won't take anything for it, so I'll never charge her." He pointed toward the door through which Dallin and Teedee had just vanished and added, "Ya'd better hurry. Doesn't look like they're gonna wait for ya."

"Oh, goo-hood grief!" Audril repeated. She thanked Ed with a quick hug, told him to give Lil a kiss from her, and then hurried out the door. "We're leaving, Guddlebee," she shouted, figuring that with everyone else talking to themselves, there was little point in her being discreet.

Teedee and Dallin were quite a ways ahead, arm in arm and guffawing wildly.

Within a few seconds, Guddlebee sauntered up alongside Audril. "Keep out of sight," she cautioned, as they turned onto a street lined with sprawling hedges and tall metal lamps. "We don't have Squanki here on Earth." Guddlebee ducked behind the nearby bushes and carefully kept to the shadows as, together, he and Audril followed behind Dallin and their new landlord, Teedee Venilworth.

CHAPTER XII

MIKIL'S SURRENDER

Although the day was hot and humid in central Iowa, the billowing charcoal clouds that tumbled in from the southwest brought with them a ferocious and chilling wind. Sharp daggers of flashing silver, originating from every corner of the sky, sliced through the swollen canopy, and were followed by rolling booms which boisterously announced the arrival of the massive summer storm. In the distance, the haunting wail of tornado sirens stirred anxiety in the mind of one unfamiliar with the weather and routines of the Midwestern United States. Mikil Tu Shadow crouched among the black skeletons of burnt plants, the tangled piles of splintered homes, and the acres of dusty gray ash in Glenhill, alert...on edge...and waiting.

"Where is he?" she whispered nervously, as a streak of black raced in front of her. "Dis is where we were supposed to come, isn't eet?"

"Patience, my love," Lonoren's disembodied voice replied from a few feet away. "We have only been here a short time. My warriors have the area surrounded and will notify us just as soon as Ryannon shows himself."

"What is dat awful noise?" Mikil asked, referencing the sirens whose surging cries were increasing in volume.

"They are to warn of tornadoes. This area has them frequently." Lonoren ran his invisible hand through Mikil's black curls. "It is strange to see you like this," he breathed. "I wonder why it is so different here on Drolana."

"Well at least you *can* see me," Mikil replied. "I deedn't know dat you would all be heeden on dis world. I haven't seen you for tree days. Eet makes me uneasy."

"Do not worry, dearest. We will be back on Lor Mandela shortly. My clan will capture Ryannon when he arrives, and then we shall return home and shall see each other as ourselves again."

"I hope so," she sighed.

Just then, another shadowy black mass sped by followed by a provocative female voice oozing out of the shadows. "Lonoren, someone approaches. It is not Ryannon, but the fallen Trysta general, Grayden."

"What?" Lonoren responded. "What is he doing here?"

"He must be in league with Ryannon," Mikil observed, rising from her crouched position to scan the area for Grayden. "We cannot leave here witout Ryannon. Stay close, but remain silent. I weel detairmine what is going on."

"Be careful, my love," Lonoren advised as he kissed her on the cheek and retreated behind a heap of rubble.

Across the smoldering black terrain, the outline of Grayden appeared in a flash of lightning. In the same flash, Grayden noticed Mikil and was now marching toward her with determination. As another jagged bolt lit up the night sky, Mikil observed the thin silver vystoran sleeve in his hand, which he raised and aimed at her as he neared.

"Good evening, Atoh," he greeted over the top of the rumbling thunder. "I must admit that I'm a little surprised to see you."

Mikil cleared her throat. "I wasn't expecting you either, Grayden. Is your boss too much of a weenie to come out in the storm?" Her portrayal of Audril was deadly accurate.

Grayden chuckled. "He's preparing a place for you to stay while you're with us. He wants you to be . . . cozy."

As he stepped over the remains of what was once a picket fence and was nearly to where Mikil stood, he lowered the sleeve and sneered, "So, your daddy actually let you come alone?"

"I'm a big girl," she retorted. "I don't need my dad's permission to do something that I know is right."

"Hmmm, interesting. I thought for sure that he'd have you under twenty-four hour surveillance," he replied. "Now if you'd be so kind as to put your hands behind your back . . . ."

Mikil glared at him with disdain. "Really, you think this is necessary? I'm here, aren't I? It's not like I'm gonna run away." Despite her verbal objections, she clasped her hands behind her back.

Grayden produced a rope from a bag that hung at his side and tied it around her wrists. "If I believed that you came here without so much as a plan to cause trouble, I'd be a pretty big fool," he responded.

"You said it . . . not me."

"Ah, hah, hah, hah. You're such a comic genius," he barked, shoving her forward. "Now let's go. We have a ways to travel."

The force of Grayden's push caused Mikil to stumble over the pile of broken wood in front of her, but she was able to regain her footing just prior to falling.

"Oh, watch your step, Atoh," he snickered as he stepped up behind her and thrust his vystoran sleeve into the small of her back. "We don't want you getting hurt. But wait. I forgot. You're the invincible Clest Anaria, so you can't get hurt, now can you?" he scowled and shook his head. "What a bloomin' freak . . . ."

Mikil was preparing her retaliation when a particularly bright burst of lightning lit up the area, momentarily revealing several rushing figures of shadowy black, circling and dodging all around them. She stopped walking and held her breath, hoping that Grayden wouldn't notice the strange masses. Much to her relief, it didn't seem he did. He jabbed the sleeve tightly against her back and commanded her to keep moving.

They crossed over several acres of the devastated terrain, weaving around and through the silent ruins. As they neared the southern border of Glenhill, Mikil finally asked, "Where exactly are you taking me?"

"Don't worry about it. You'll know soon enough." Grayden answered, reaching into his bag with his free hand and digging around for a few seconds before producing a small set of keys. He pulled the vystoran sleeve out of Mikil's back long enough to point it over her shoulder to a small clearing ahead. In what was likely a parking lot before the explosion, a lone vehicle sat — a large, champagne-colored pickup truck. "Over there . . . my car . . . ."

"Where'd you steal that from?" Mikil sneered. "You've certainly made yourself right at home here, haven't you?"

"I like to adapt to my surroundings," Grayden answered and pressed a button on his keys; the headlights of the truck blinked twice and the interior lights illuminated.

Concerned, Mikil glanced around, hoping that Lonoren would realize that he would have to come up with a plan to transport the clan, and quickly — since Grayden obviously intended to continue their journey in this vehicle.

Another sharp bolt of lightning lit up the sky, slicing a hole in the heavily laden clouds above. A few gigantic raindrops plopped to the ground, and then the heavens burst, unleashing a torrential deluge.

Grayden started fumbling through his bag once more, this time retrieving a long black strip of cloth.

"What? You've got to be kidding me," Mikil whined as she realized he was holding what he intended to use as a blindfold.

"Now come on, Atoh. It'll be much more fun this way." He opened the door and pointed to the back seat. "Into the truck," he commanded.

As if she had a choice, Mikil allowed Grayden to force her into the truck and tie the blindfold around her eyes.

He pulled a seat belt and shoulder strap across her to buckle her in, but then stopped. "Hmmm," he hissed in her ear, "this gives me an interesting idea or two." He clicked the seat belt into place, and then lowered his muscular body on top of her. "Ya know, Audril, we don't have to be enemies," he purred, "and we don't have to tell Ryannon a thing." He coaxed her sopping curls behind her shoulder and ran his index finger down her bare neck and across her collar bone. "It could be our little secret." He paused for a moment, sucked in a deep breath through his teeth, and then continued tracing his finger down the center of her chest. "Here . . . let me help you out of these wet clothes," he panted.

As the tip of his finger touched the neckline of her shirt, Mikil leaned forward as best she could and whispered, "One more inch, General, and Ryannon will be the *first* to know. I wonder which weapon he'll choose to kill you. Your own vystoran, perhaps? Or maybe he'll use the same method that he used on his father. Do you have eyes in the back of your head, Grayden?"

Grayden snarled and pulled away. "Fine! Your loss, sweetheart," he growled, as he climbed into the driver's seat, crammed the key in the ignition, and yanked the door shut.

As he turned the key, a bolt of lightning blazed across the sky followed by an ear-splitting crack, and the whole truck shook — not because of the thunder — but because Lonoren and the other Solom had taken advantage of the fury of the storm, and sprung into the bed of the truck at the exact moment that the thunder sounded.

"What was that?" Grayden barked, checking his rearview mirror. He swung open the door to investigate.

"Oh . . . did the big bad thunder scare you?" Mikil taunted.

Grayden seemed to forget his intention to disembark the vehicle, and slammed the door hard. "You know, I'm getting a little tired of you and your attitude, Atoh! Just keep your bloody mouth shut and do as you're told!" He flipped the truck into gear, stomped down on the gas pedal and squealed out of the parking lot.

Seconds turned into minutes, and minutes into hours as they traveled in utter silence. In what Mikil estimated to be about three hours later, the truck turned left off of the paved road and bounced down what felt and sounded like a gravel trail. A bit later, the vehicle came to a sliding stop, and Grayden opened his door.

"I'll be back in a minute; don't go anywhere," he instructed as he climbed out of the cab.

Mikil felt a sense of relief as he walked away and she felt the bed of the truck rock slightly. "Lonoren," she whispered, "are you der?" There was no reply, but she figured that with him being outside and her being in, there was little chance of him hearing her anyway.

The deep voice she heard a few seconds later, however, instantly sent chills rippling down the length of her spine, and obliterated any confidence she had in the situation.

"Well, what have we here?" The door of the truck screeched open, and Mikil immediately sensed that she was in the presence of Ryannon of Brashnell. "Hello, my darling," Ryannon sneered as he slid his hand up the length of her thigh. The buckle of the seat belt clicked, and she felt his strong hands slip around her back and untie the cord that held her. After her wrists were freed, Ryannon loosened the blindfold and it floated downward, landing on her lap.

It took a moment for her eyes to focus, but the first thing that came clearly into view were the glistening flecks of red in Ryannon's dark eyes. "Audril, my sweet," he smirked. "I was beginning to think you weren't going to make it."

Without warning, he pushed his lips against hers and kissed her hard. Mikil struggled to get away, but her awkward position in the back seat of the truck, combined with the strength of the embrace Ryannon had on her, made it nearly impossible for her to move. As he pulled back, she turned her head to the side and spat angrily.

"Oh, come now, darling," he scolded. "There was a time, not that long ago, when you enjoyed kissing me. Don't you remember?"

"That was before I found out you were a scuz bag," she snarled.

Ryannon's eyes dimmed and his face twisted into a frown. "Maybe you don't realize that I hold all of the cards, Atoh." He slid backwards out of the truck and practically pulled her through the door. He looked at her as though he was seriously considering back-handing her across the face, but just as quickly as his countenance had dropped, it lifted, returning to a confident, conceited sneer. "Oh, never mind. We'll work through these little obstacles later. Just come inside now; your dinner is getting cold."

He led Mikil toward the side door of a large, broken down, red brick building. It seemed to be the only occupied structure for as far as the eye could see — which wasn't far because the entire area was surrounded by shadowy forest.

While the eerie scenery may have been alarming to some, for Mikil, it was quite a comfort. Lonoren and the others would be able to use the abandoned buildings and forested areas as perfect places to hide themselves and to strategize Ryannon's capture — and she was sure that her Entrusted would see the opportunity and seize it. She glanced over her shoulder as Ryannon held the door open for her, and fought back a smile as she caught sight of two dark masses racing toward a building in the distance.

Thirteen

CHAPTER XIII

THE HOUSE THAT TEEDEE'S IMAGINARY BUTLER FOUND

"Where are we going? There's nothing out here!" Audril asked loudly enough to be heard over the commotion of the wind and the distant sirens.

"Sure there is!" Teedee hollered back, nearly deafening Dallin who was walking between them. She removed her floppy green hat to keep it from taking flight, and asked Dallin to stop for a minute so she could stuff it into her purse. Now, the thin wisps of long, yellowish-silver hair that had escaped her tight bun blew back and forth across her face, sticking to her vivid pink lips. "My house is just over that hill," she explained pointing her knobby, ring-clad index finger.

Audril scowled at Dallin and nodded towards the scenery ahead. There was nothing but rolling hills and dirt trails in front of them for as far as they could see.

"I think you might be confused, Teedee," she called back. "I'm sorry, I don't mean to argue, but my friends and I used to come out here all the time to play in the snow; there's nothing around."

Teedee didn't respond at first and Audril feared that she may have offended the off-center old lady, but something had to be done — they were obviously going the wrong way.

123

When Teedee finally turned toward Audril to answer, she didn't appear offended, but rather insanely jovial. Her eyes squinted behind her goggle-like spectacles, practically disappearing in the deep surrounding wrinkles. Her mouth gaped open wide, and her whole stiff floral center began bobbing up and down in laborious laughter. "Don't you . . . hoo . . . hooo . . . think I know where I live?" she cackled. "Oh, that's positively delightful!" She jabbed Dallin in the side with her elbow. "Isn't she delightful, Dallin? My, you are such an adorable girl!" She linked her arm back in Dallin's and pulled him down the trail, shaking her head and laughing as they went.

When they got to the bottom of the first hill, she signaled for Dallin to lean closer, and whispered something into his ear. A devious little smile twisted across his lips as he listened. He glanced at Audril out of the corner of his eye and nodded, and then he and Teedee started sniggering like silly school girls.

"Yikes," Audril sighed, stomping past them. "Come on, I'll show you." She proceeded quickly up the hill, eager to prove that there was absolutely nothing — particularly an eccentric old woman's house — in this area of town. "This is so ridiculous," she grumbled to herself. "I've lived here most of my life and *they* act like I have no idea what I'm talking about."

She marched up the trail, and as she neared the top, a big rain drop fell from the clouds above, smacking her right in the forehead. She turned to warn Dallin and Teedee — who were meandering along, chatting casually as they strolled — of the impending downpour. "We should get out of here!" she yelled as she continued backwards up the hill. "The rain's coming." A few feet behind Dallin and Teedee, a tall spindly weed — just barely visible in the near darkness of twilight — blinked up at her with big, grey eyes. "We can make it over to the elementary school if we . . . ."

As she spun around to point toward the school, a bolt of lightning flashed, and her eyes caught sight of the hard edges of an ornate roof line beyond the horizon.

"Whaaaat?" she gasped in astonishment. "No way." She rushed to the hill's crest and sure enough, about half way up the next bluff, surrounded by acres of pristine, manicured landscaping, stood a magnificent old mansion. "It can't be," she mumbled, gazing in awe at the intricate iron trim that adorned the estate's flat roof and the contrasting peaks of several steep gables. "I mean, how?"

"A big truck and several tense moments," Teedee quipped, as she and Dallin came up from behind. "Moved her fourteen miles from Wheaton Township end of last summer. They were about to knock her down, can you believe? Hodgson saw her first. Normally I'd be jealous of him looking at other women," she winked, "but I fell in love with her too . . . the second I saw her." Teedee fluttered her eyelashes as she gazed though her rain-spotted lenses at her beloved home. "Now let's hurry," she urged as the rain started to cascade down in stinging sheets. "These clouds are getting angry. Once we get inside and dried off, I'll have Hodgson fix us some hot tea, and we'll be able to watch the storm nicely from the Summer Breakfast Room."

Audril leaned close to Dallin and whispered, "I told you she's nuts. Watch the storm? Summer Breakfast room? And by the way, who is this Hodgson guy she keeps talking about? Is he her husband, or what?"

"I think he's her butler," Dallin answered with a grin. "She told me that he takes care of her . . . and this place." He chuckled and added, "Apparently she's in love with him, but she says she's never actually seen him."

"Never seen him?" Audril gasped. "Dallin . . . nuts!"

"Hurry along, dears!" Teedee called back. For as old and bent as she was, she was suddenly clipping along at quite a good pace.

"We're coming, Teeds," Dallin replied, as he scoured the area for Guddlebee.

"Teeds?" Audril smirked, pointing her thumb at the row of tall, billowing junipers lining the walkway to the house. Near the bottom of the tree nearest them, Guddlebee's bulging eyes peeped out.

"Well, she won't let me call her ma'am," Dallin replied as he grabbed Audril by the arm and pulled her quickly down the trail. Teedee had managed to scuttle her way down the hill and was already moving up the walkway, but it didn't take too long for Dallin and Audril to catch up.

Guddlebee hopped from tree to tree, keeping out of sight, and then dove unnoticed under the wooden front steps for shelter.

By the time they all reached the porch, Audril, Dallin and Teedee were all sufficiently soaked. Teedee unlocked the double front doors and clicked the latch on the iron handle. The heavy oak and stained glass doors screeched open to reveal an elaborate and beautiful foyer.

"Whoa . . . impressive," Dallin breathed as they stepped inside the ivory marble hall. He pointed to the dark stone fountain rising from the floor to the second story landing and whistled. "This is some place you got here, Teeds. Look at these things!" He dashed like an excited child on Christmas morning to the bottom of one of the two spiral staircases flanking the room, and ran up a few of the mahogany steps. "Are those real?" he gasped, leaning over the ornate iron railing and inspecting the lush plants growing in scrollwork pockets up and down the length of the fountain. "This place is amazing!" He raced back to Teedee and wrapped his arms around her like she was a wealthy, long-lost aunt.

"Well, I'm glad you like it," she grinned. "Now, I'm afraid I don't have much for you to change into, my dear. Hodgson and the other male servants don't keep their clothes here, but perhaps we can find something that'll work . . . at least until your things are dry." She turned to Audril and patted her warmly on the back of the hand. "I'm sure we can find something in my closet for you too, Toots. I was close to your size when I was younger . . . before all these bones started to shrivel up."

Oh joy . . . crazy old lady clothes, Audril thought to herself, as Teedee snorted at her own humor and signaled for them to follow her up the stairs.

The rest of "The Manor," as Teedee called it, was every bit as grand as the foyer. Rooms with thick wood moldings, lush deep carpets, colorful glass

126

mosaics, and tasteful, stately furnishings appeared around every corner. As they made their way down the maze of corridors, Audril wondered if she would ever be able to find her way back to the stairs.

"Here we are," Teedee smiled, pulling open a tall white door and motioning for Dallin to enter. "You can stay here if you like, Master Dallin. I think there is a bath robe on a hook near the shower. Just leave your things on the bench next to the bed and I'll have them dried and returned. If you come down the back stairs there," she pointed to the end of the hall, "you'll be in our Summer Breakfast Room." She gave him a forceful little nudge through the doorway and sang back, "See you in a while!"

She turned to Audril and bit her lip. "He's quite a catch, that boy. You know, if you don't change your mind about his being your cousin soon, I might just snatch him away!"

Audril tried to fight a smile, but simply couldn't. The image of little ol' Teedee chasing a wide-eyed, bathrobe-wearing Dallin around a huge dining table entered her mind, making it impossible for her to do anything but grin; it only added to her mirth to discover that Teedee had placed Dallin in the room adjoining her own.

"Now let's see what we can find for you," Teedee offered as she pulled the door to her bedroom open exposing what — when compared to the immaculate condition of the rest of The Manor — was a shocking mess. Clothes, hats and shoes lay strewn across the floor and over the large unmade bed; odd charts, tattered maps and colorful photographs nearly covered the cinnamon plaster walls completely; a wooden cheval mirror stood in the center of the room and was cracked right down the middle and smeared all over with lipstick kiss marks. Across the room, in front of a large window, an old, crooked, bald male mannequin sat in a small parlor chair, draped in scarves and wildly clashing fabrics, grimacing in disapproval at the disheveled nature of the scene before him.

"Oh, dear," Teedee smiled bashfully, "I forgot how I left this room this morning. I guess I'll be cleaning tomorrow." She cleared a small area of the floor with her foot for Audril and told her she would be right back. She tootled off across the room and disappeared into the closet to their left. "Do you like pink?" she yelled from behind the wall. "It would be lovely with your eyes, but I'm afraid some people have a real aversion to pink."

"Pink's fine," Audril mumbled as she scanned the room trying to isolate any one thing that wasn't a glaring violation of taste. It seemed that nearly everything in the untidy room was flamboyant and awful.

A loud rumble of thunder echoed through the house, shaking the walls and causing the lights to flicker. "Oh my!" Teedee cried out from the closet as the room went completely dark, but when the lights came back on a couple of seconds later, Teedee was standing next to Audril with an armful of clothes.

Audril jumped and grabbed at her chest. "Yikes!" she exclaimed, "you scared me."

"Oh sorry, Toots. Here ya go." Teedee suddenly seemed in a huge hurry. She dropped the pile of clothes into Audril's arms and pointed toward the hall. "Turn right and follow the corridor to the last door on the left . . . just before the stairs." She pushed Audril towards the door and added, "I'd come with you, but I am chilled to the bone and I need to change before I catch pneumonia. You can't be too careful . . . or care*less* at my age, now, can you?" She barely waited for Audril to clear the threshold before shoving the door closed as far as she could. A few of the articles of clothing on the floor slid with the door, preventing it from shutting all the way, but Teedee didn't seem to notice.

Audril shook her head and started down the hall, but before she had taken two steps, she heard Teedee's voice coming from around the open door. Quietly, she tiptoed back and listened.

"Lay it on the bed," Teedee demanded in a serious tone. "Oh, yes, Hodgson, that definitely looks like one all right. Is this the only one you've been able to find? I'm sure there are more." The room fell completely silent. Audril mustered up her courage and peered around the edge of the door. In the middle of the room near the cracked mirror, Teedee stood like a statue, staring into space and waiting for an answer from someone who clearly wasn't there. After a lengthy pause, she twisted her head abruptly to the side and asked, "So, he doesn't know about it? But I'm sure he'll catch on. He's far from stupid." There was a brief pause followed by, "No, of course not, my love. But it's likely that he'll kill them all if he finds out. You must go back there, and let me know the instant anything happens." Audril watched through the space at the edge of the door as Teedee turned and pressed her lips to the mirror and began kissing it passionately.

"Ewwwwwww," she whispered, cringing at the sight of the old lady smooching and stroking the glass. She shuddered in disgust and then rushed away down the hall.

Audril's assigned room was large and comfortable — more than could be said for the selection of clothing she had been given. Most of Teedee's outfits, aside from being hideous, were far too small. Had she not been certain that Dallin and Teedee would eventually come looking for her, she would have been perfectly happy to climb under the covers of the fluffy bed, in nothing but her skin, and retire for the evening. It had been more than twenty-four hours since she had last slept, and she was beginning to feel it.

After trying — and failing — to come up with a plan that would allow her the rest she craved, she grudgingly picked the least horrible outfit she could find from the pile and wriggled into it. She stood in front of a long, mirrored wall and moaned at the image looking back.

The dress was something she would be hard-pressed to wear in one of the Glenhill High School Drama Club productions. She tugged at the fabric of the knee-length 1930's flapper dress with large pink and black polka dots on a teal blue background and tried to smile. As she turned to examine the back of the dreadful gown, the four bright tiers of silver fringe at the bottom swished in a glitzy flash. She pushed at the poky neck line, hoping to make it lie flatter, but it was held up stiffly by a row of shiny silver sequins that she figured must have been added as an afterthought in order to tie in the sequined edge of the flouncy, dark pink sleeves.

She took a deep breath and finger-fluffed her wet curls. As she turned toward the door she sighed, "I'm going to a psycho costume party."

She moped down the stairs and turned the corner into the Summer Breakfast Room; Teedee squealed with delight. "Oh, I was hoping you would pick that one! Dallin, doesn't she look lovely?"

Dallin was lounging at a small, round table with his feet propped up on one of the chairs, looking less than thrilled until he caught a sideways glimpse of Audril. He stood and motioned for her to sit down while choking back his laughter with marginal success.

Audril slid around behind him to the other side of the table and whispered, "Nice robe," in his ear as she passed.

Dallin's face instantly dropped. As ridiculous as Audril looked, he alone held the honor of being the silliest-dressed person in the room. His robe was a stunning shade of brilliant orange and barely reached to the top of his knees. The cuffs landed midway down his forearm and, like the silky collar, were lined with delicate chiffon lace. Embroidered on the breast pocket in elegant scrolling letters were the initials "T.U.V."

Audril dropped into one of the chairs and mockingly sang, "T, U, Veeee, W, X, Y and Z." Dallin glared at her and growled. "It's all I could find, okay!"

Oddly enough, at this moment it was Teedee who was the most normally attired person at the table. She wore a simple sage green house coat, and her hair was twisted into a sophisticated braid. She had removed her lipstick — or perhaps kissed it off — and simply looked like a nice elderly woman. "Have some tea, dear," she offered. "It's peppermint. Hodgson made it for us before he left again."

Audril glanced at Dallin again and smiled. "Teedee, who is Hodgson?" she asked.

Teedee seemed slightly ruffled by the question. The hand holding her teacup shook as she replied, "Oh . . . Hodgson is my butler, dear . . . well, actually, he's more than my butler. He and I are engaged. We'll be getting married just as soon as we get past one or two little obstacles."

"Obstacles?" Audril pressed.

Dallin looked up from his tea and observed the conversation with an expression of concern.

"Well, yes," Teedee explained, "I can't really see him. No one can. It's been very difficult for us, as I'm sure you can imagine. There are times I think I can see him . . . standing in the corner . . . watching over me . . . but when I try to focus on his face . . . his eyes . . . he's just not there." She gazed dreamily out the window, still holding her teacup midway between the table and her mouth.

"Teeds? You all right?" Dallin tried.

"Fine," she muttered back. "I'm just . . . ." She rose from her chair but stopped half-way up and peered through an arched doorway that led to the kitchen. "Hodgson!" she called out like she was calling a pig. "Hodgson! Hoddddddggssonnnn! Oh, where is that man?"

Dallin rose to his feet and eyed her questioningly. "I thought you said he left, Teeds."

"Oh, don't worry, dear," she assured, ignoring his comment. "I must go speak with him, but I'll return, um, *shortly*." She glanced at the hem of Dallin's robe and chuckled as she shuffled from the room.

Dallin fidgeted with his uncomfortable orange wrap and plopped down next to Audril. "I know," he groaned, "she's nuts."

Audril choked back a giggle. "Amen to that . . . um . . . sista," she coughed and then exploded into hysterical laughter.

"Oh, you're so funny," Dallin scowled. "I wouldn't be laughing if I were you, Miss Chandelier with legs!" He reached under the table and flicked at the fringe on Audril's dress, and then he too started laughing.

Audril leaned her head onto his shoulder affectionately, but then quickly retracted. "Oh, uh, sorry," she stammered, "I guess we both look pretty ridiculous, huh?"

"Nos, never ridiculous . . . always lovelys," Guddlebee's squeaky voice replied from an area on the other side of the room near a large antique buffet against the wall.

"Guddlebee, what are you doing in here?" Audril breathed as she and Dallin both rushed to the buffet.

Guddlebee's eyes materialized on one of the small side cupboards, followed by his whole head. "Guddlebee was talkings to Athenius," he explained. "Him wants mes to ask the atoh lady a questions."

Audril stared at the bodiless head peering up at her. It was disturbing to watch the wild curls on Guddlebee's head form in wood and then drift out and turn white, only to float back and transform into the wood again. "What is your question, Guddlebee? And hurry!" she insisted.

"Athenius wants mes to ask the name ofs the mighty Trysta alterer whos is pretendings to be the atoh right now."

The scuttle of shuffling feet sounded from across the room. "Teedee's coming," Dallin warned.

Audril anxiously checked over her shoulder and answered, "her name's Mikil Tu Shadow, Guddlebee . . . why?"

Guddlebee's large eyes saddened. "Ohs," he sighed, "Tabbits and I do not knows this Mikil Tus Shadow."

Slowly he dissolved into the buffet, just as Teedee turned the corner into the room.

"Isn't that a lovely piece?" she asked. "I found that sideboard at a garage sale . . . Crazy Yanks, didn't know what they were giving away." In her hands, she carried a tray of beautiful pastries, which she sat down in the middle of the table. "Come have a treat," she grinned. "My Hodgson is quite the chef. Of course, he's had hundreds of years to perfect his recipes." Audril and Dallin looked at each other sideways and without saying a word, returned to the table.

Audril gazed over the delightful spread of pastries and chose a heavenly looking cherry-filled croissant. She bit into it, but then stopped, and stared wide-eyed at Dallin as a look of horror washed over her face.

Thirteen

"What is it?" Dallin whispered. "What's wrong?"

Audril slowly lowered the pastry from her lips. "Mikil doesn't know Tabbit," she muttered, "but *I* know Tabbit."

It was clear by the mystified look on Dallin's face that he was not making the connection.

Teedee grimaced and asked, "What's a Tabbit, dear?"

Audril ignored Teedee entirely as her face went pale. "How could I have forgotten to tell Mikil about Tabbit? I knew Ryannon had her. That explains why Lortu acted the way he did." She turned to Dallin and looked helplessly into his eyes. A sickening lump swelled at the back of her throat. "Oh, Dallin . . . Mikil and the Solom . . . they're going to fail," she panted. "They're gonna fail . . . because of me!"

CHAPTER XIV

A SQUANKI

"You haven't touched your salmon, my love. Aren't you hungry?" In a spacious concrete room, lit only by half a dozen flickering candles, Mikil glared at Ryannon from across an elegantly appointed rectangular banquet table. Near the middle of the table, an unknown figure sat alongside Grayden, hunched over the exquisite white plate in front of it, eagerly devouring its meal. The stranger spoke not a word and was completely veiled by its dark grey hooded cloak and the overall dimness of the room.

"Come now, you must eat," Ryannon tried once more. "I'm sure you'll enjoy this. It's quite delicious."

Mikil glowered at him in disdain. "It's not the food that's the problem. It's hard to eat when you're being forced to look at something so disgusting . . . and don't you dare call me your *love* again."

Grayden and the stranger stopped chewing and awaited Ryannon's reaction to such an insult, but he simply chuckled and returned to his meal.

After a few more bites, he lowered his fork and wiped his mouth with the red linen napkin from his lap before dropping it onto his plate. "You surprise me, Audril," he began. "I didn't expect you to give in so easily."

Mikil scowled at him in silence, and then threw her own napkin angrily onto the table. "What choice did you leave me?" she snarled. "You disintegrated my entire home town! You murdered thousands of innocent people! Why, Ryannon? Is there some sick thrill you get from destroying people? Is killing just a game to you?"

Again the cloaked individual and Grayden stopped what they were doing and turned their attention to Ryannon. It appeared as though they passionately yearned for him to unleash his fury on this outspoken, disrespectful girl, but once more, they were disappointed. "I had to get your attention. I needed you here," he calmly responded, "and it worked, didn't it?"

Mikil turned her head away in abhorrence. "I fail to see what you hope to gain from all of this," she sneered. "I guarantee that you won't get a single thing from me."

"Oh, on the contrary," Ryannon replied, rising from his chair and moving around the table until he stood next to her. "You will give me everything I need . . . and as to what I will gain from it," he leaned down and put his face very close to hers. "I will gain more than you or anyone else could possibly imagine." He circled slowly behind her as if he were examining her every detail.

As he came around the side of her chair, he stopped. "Such beauty," he sneered. "Think, Audril. We will be the most powerful couple in existence. I understand your anger, you know. You weren't exactly brought here under the best of circumstances . . . for which I apologize. . . but before long I'm certain that you'll remember how much you love me."

"Love you?" Mikil gasped, "I can't stand you! You disgust me! You're nothing but a spineless, sniveling worm that deserves to be crushed and burned! Why don't you just slither into a corner, shrivel up and die?"

Ryannon smiled and started back toward his seat, but then suddenly spun around and slammed his boot into the bottom of Mikil's chair with such force that it and she went crashing and tumbling across the hard cement floor.

Grayden and the stranger gasped in delight, taking some twisted form of vicarious pleasure in Ryannon's barbaric actions.

Before Mikil could process what had just happened, Ryannon was leaning over her. He reached down and grabbed a handful of her raven curls,

135

and yanked her to her feet. "You have only two choices," he growled. "You can give me what I want, or you can sit quietly and let me take it."

Grayden was panting like a dog and watching with aroused excitement from the other end of the table. The cloaked figure's shoulders heaved up and down with animalistic delight as Ryannon wrapped his chiseled arms around Mikil and slowly dragged his tongue across the side of her lips.

To this point, the Trysta commander had refrained from utilizing her years of training, but she had taken about all she was going to take. In a move that caught Ryannon completely off guard, she swiped her foot under his boot and knocked him off balance. He teetered awkwardly, struggling to maintain his footing as well as his grip on her. He stumbled backward and Mikil took full advantage of the situation. She rolled her arms in tightly against her body and then slid down and out of his arms. In a motion that seemed more like a choreographed dance than a self-defense tactic, she spun to her feet, thrust her arm upward, and slammed the heel of her palm powerfully against the bridge of his nose.

Ryannon bellowed as his nose made a horrible cracking noise and streams of crimson blood began to pour down his face.

Mikil came at him again without giving him any time to recover. She twisted her upper body to the side, and with all the force she could muster, spun back toward him and rammed her elbow into his rib cage. Again, a sickening crack resonated through the room as Ryannon doubled over in pain. As she moved to strike again, Ryannon took advantage of his hunched posture and grabbed a hold of one of her legs. He yanked it skyward with such force that Mikil's whole body flew off the ground and launched backward through the air.

She tried to break her fall with her arms, but the angle at which she was traveling through the air made it impossible. Her head hit the hard floor first, with a nauseating *thwack*.

Tiny white flashes of light filled her eyes. She strained to lift herself from the ground but her skull pounded so violently that it felt like it was going to explode. As she raised her head off of the cement, the room went blurry and then slowly faded into black.

When she awoke, Grayden and Ryannon had their arms in hers and were dragging her from the room. They moved past the cloaked stranger, who appeared riveted to Ryannon's every action. Ryannon stopped in front of the mysterious figure and signaled for Grayden to do the same. "I think we need to teach this *brat* a lesson, Lique," he instructed. "Go to Lor Mandela. You are familiar with her best friend Bridgette, right?"

Lique nodded with rapt enthusiasm.

"Well, I don't think our little Bridgette is necessary anymore." Through the blood, an evil smirk spread across Ryannon's lips. "Be sure not to kill her quickly, though . . . I want her to suffer for a good, long time."

"NO!" Mikil shrieked, hoping to be as convincing as possible. "You can't! Please! Please Ryannon, don't! I'll behave myself. I promise! Please! Just don't hurt Bridgette!"

Ryannon drew in a deep breath and wiped some of the blood from beneath his nose. "Hmmm, I think we've found a weak spot in the character of our clever little atoh, Lique. Very well," he sighed. "But from this point forward you must do exactly as I say. Do I make myself clear?"

Mikil looked into his flickering eyes. She couldn't tell whether it was the throbbing pain in her head, or her total disgust with the sight of his face, but she felt quite sick.

"I asked you a question," Ryannon smirked condescendingly.

"Yes," Mikil muttered, "you make yourself clear."

"Good," answered Ryannon in his usual deep, suave tone. He and Grayden adjusted their grip under her arms and continued dragging her from the room. "It's a pity, really," he began once they were through the door. "If not for your appalling outburst in there, you would have had the pleasure of staying in my room tonight, but there are far too many weapons you could get your hands on. Besides, you'll need your rest. We have a big day ahead of us tomorrow."

A Squanki

As the perverse men escorted Mikil through a labyrinth of halls and darkened corridors, the sound of their footsteps pulsated and pounded in her aching head. It was the only sound resonating through the abandoned building — at least until they turned into a narrow passageway and the cry of a tiny, squeaky voice penetrated the silence. Mikil strained to listen, trying to decipher the faint message and to determine its origin.

"Squankis don't tells . . . lady comes backs . . . lady comes backs . . . return the powers . . . four hundred days . . . four hundred days." The small voice grew louder as they neared the center of the passage. "Squankis don't tells . . . lady comes backs . . . lady comes backs . . . return the powers . . . four hundred days . . . four hundred days."

As they neared a dark room with a heavy metal door, Mikil dug in her heels and stopped. "What is that?" she asked, pointing to the door which was cracked open slightly.

The flecks in Ryannon's eyes magnified with excitement. "Oh, yes," he grinned, "I nearly forgot to show you." He pushed the thick door open and stepped into the room.

Nothing could be seen; there was no light in the room except for three buttons alongside the door which glowed vivid green.

Again, the timid voice echoed its cryptic refrain from out of a dark corner. "Squankis don't tells . . . lady comes backs . . . lady comes backs . . . return the powers . . . four hundred days . . . four hundred days."

"Who's there?" Mikil asked, looking to both Ryannon and to the voice itself for the answer.

Ryannon smiled and pushed one of the green buttons, and a single fluorescent light blinked on overhead.

Mikil gasped at the sight of Tabbit who was perched on a hard stone bench, squinting her large, blue eyes in an effort to adjust them to the room's sudden illumination. Her skin was dirty, caked with dust and dried blood. Her long, white hair formed scraggly, matted clumps all over her small, bobbling head. Her dress was filthy and torn in several spots and a horrible, deep purple gash covered nearly half of her frail thigh.

"What have you done to her?" Mikil gulped.

"Nothing," Ryannon answered, "she's done all of this to herself. She's gone mad, hasn't she Grayden?"

"Like I said, off her truglunt," the general replied.

Mikil's heart sank as she watched Tabbit rock back and forth mumbling her message once again. "Squankis don't tells . . . lady comes backs . . . lady comes backs . . . return the powers . . . four hundred days . . . four hundred days."

Ryannon observed Mikil's reaction, and took a fiendish delight in her displeasure. "Oh, come now, Atoh. Having a Squanki here to open portals and to handle other little details has already proved itself quite useful."

"You're a monster," Mikil seethed as she ripped her arms free. Grayden moved to restrain her again, but Ryannon held up his hand.

Mikil cautiously approached Tabbit and crouched down beside her. "Hello . . . are you okay? Can . . . can I help you?" she whispered.

"Squankis don't tells . . . lady comes backs . . . lady comes backs . . . return the powers . . . four hundred days . . . four hundred days," mumbled Tabbit without as much as a glance at Mikil.

Mikil turned her head and scowled at Ryannon. "She needs help, you jerk! She's not your puppet! Why are you so heartless?"

"That's enough," Ryannon barked. "Let's go." He nodded to Grayden who walked up behind Mikil and pulled her to her feet. As they moved past him, Ryannon gave her a shove out the door before clicking off the light.

"You deserve to rot in Hell," Mikil hissed.

"Be that as it may, my dear. I know an opportunity when I see one. I was not about to leave Lor Mandela without a sure-fire way to get back."

"But to harm a Squanki," she argued. "This poor, innocent little creature is not a toy! And she's certainly not meant to be your slave." Ryannon stopped in his tracks and stared inquisitively at her and then at Grayden. "You know,

139

perhaps you are right." He seemed lost in his thoughts for a moment but then added, "Audril, I suggest that in the morning you and I deliver this Squanki back to Lor Mandela. We'll have her create the portal herself. After all, I hardly need her anymore . . . now that you are here."

Mikil eyed him suspiciously. She could tell he was up to something, but had no idea what.

At length, they reached the last door in the corridor and Grayden pushed it open. Inside, a tall, heavily cushioned, four-poster bed with luxurious, pale blue linens filled the center of the room. Copious floral arrangements stood in the four corners, camouflaging the plain damp cement construction of the room, and a large, ornately-carved wardrobe with a mirrored front spanned a sizeable portion of the wall opposite the door.

"I wanted to make sure you were quite comfortable," Ryannon explained, clearly proud of himself for the exceptional arrangements he'd been able to put together in a place as ugly as the old saw mill. "I'll be back for you in the morning."

Together he and Grayden backed out of the room. Ryannon pulled a small silver device from his pocket and pointed it at the door. There was a faint click, and the door locked. As they strolled away, Ryannon turned to the general and asked, "Did you notice anything strange about how she acted with our dear friend Tabbit?"

Grayden thought for a moment. "Didn't you expect her to be concerned?" he asked.

"Of course I did," he grimaced and stared at the floor. "It wasn't anything she did or said, General, but rather what she didn't say."

"What do you mean?" Grayden inquired.

Ryannon pulled the silver device from his pocket and handed it to Grayden. "Go back there," he instructed. "Don't let on that we suspect her of anything."

That shouldn't be too hard, since I have no idea what you're getting at, Grayden thought to himself.

"Tell her that I sent you back to find out if she knows where this Squanki lives."

Grayden's eyes suddenly lit up. "She didn't know her, did she?"

"Very good, my friend. She didn't know her. She referred to her as 'a Squanki' . . . certainly not what I would expect her to call one of her closest comrades. I just can't believe I didn't make the connection when she injured her head."

"So what are you thinking? That this isn't really Audril?" Grayden seemed pleased with himself for deducing such a thing, and so did Ryannon.

"That is exactly what I am thinking," he replied, patting Grayden on the back. "See if you can glean any more information as to whom she really is and what she's up to . . . and remember . . . don't let on that we know. I want to keep it a surprise."

Grayden bowed and turned to do as he was instructed.

Almost immediately following Ryannon and Grayden's departure, Mikil crawled up onto the bed to rest. The pressure in her head was excruciating and she needed to lie down. She was close to dozing off, when a deep, soothing voice sounded in her ear. "Do not sleep, my love. You must try to stay awake for a while."

"Lonoren?" she gasped. "What are you doing heah? You must go, dearest. Eef you are found, dey will keel you."

"I have come to care for you, Mikil . . . you are injured."

Grayden approached the door and aimed the small silver box towards the knob. He was just about to push the button that would unlock the door when he heard Lonoren's hushed voice coming from inside the room. He pressed his ear to the cold steel and listened.

"Here . . . take this. It will help your head to feel better."

"What about de rest of de Solom, where are dey?"

"They are safe, Mikil. They are hidden in the village. Do not worry about us, my love."

Grayden pulled back from the door. "Mikil Tu Shadow," he gasped, "of course. That explains those moves."

Without waiting for further details, Grayden strode down the corridor, through the maze of halls and back to the make-shift dining room. "She's Mikil Tu Shadow of the Trysta Command," he blurted as he burst into the room, "and apparently, the Solom Clan are here as well . . . hiding in the town."

Ryannon, who was sitting at the table, conversing with the hooded creature and sipping on a glass of red wine, slowly rose to his feet and began pacing around the table. The cloaked person jumped up and rushed to Grayden's side.

"How foolish of the atoc," Ryannon sneered. "Clearly he has underestimated me once again." He stopped pacing and slammed his fist against the wooden table; glasses, plates and silver clanged together loudly. "Go to Tabbit's room and force her to open a portal," he insisted.

"Are you really sending her back to Lor Mandela?" Grayden inquired, confused as to how this would fit into their plans.

"No, General . . . I am not. Have her open one of her *special* portals at Síoraí Castle located in County Antrim, Northern Ireland. Make sure that the passages are not visible to one another. Both of you go there tonight and place this at the first coordinate on the screen." He reached inside his jacket and pulled out a small, glowing, purple crystal that resembled hands with interlocking fingers. After fiddling with it for a few seconds, he held it out to Grayden. "Hold down this button when you are in the specified location, and it will dissolve into the air."

"A Catorian," Grayden beamed as he studied the small device in his hand. "I've never actually seen one before."

"Yes, General," Ryannon replied, "a Catorian." He placed his hand on Grayden's back and coerced him toward the door. "Lique," he barked, turning to the person in the cloak, "Take a vystoran sleeve and make sure that the general is not disturbed." The hood of the cloak bobbed up and down, but still no words came from it. "Now go," he commanded, "and report back to me the moment you've returned."

CHAPTER XV

THROUGH THE PORTAL

In bold contrast to the thick, smothering curtain of greenish-black that covered central Iowa the night before, the morning brought with it soft, dewy beams of sunlight floating to Earth from behind lazily drifting puffy white clouds. The sun's shimmering rays danced through the air and blanketed everything in sight, including the thin, dust-covered pane of a narrow window, which sat so high on the wall of Mikil's room that she hadn't even noticed it was there.

The warm sunlight slipped in and danced across the room creeping over the bed, inching its way from the silver crushed velvet throw draped along the foot of the bed, up the cocoon of soft blue sheets and blankets wrapped around Mikil's legs. As the sun continued its ascent, the beam progressed steadily upward until, at last, it came to rest on her sleeping eyelids.

"Ughhhhh," she groaned, fumbling to find anything she could use to block out the offending light. Her hand landed on a pillow which she promptly pulled over her head, but as it dropped onto the sizeable goose egg near her left ear, she instantly regretted it. "Curse dis world," she grumbled, drowsily pulling herself upright and flopping her legs over the side of the bed.

"Good morning, my love." The soothing sound of Lonoren's voice came from somewhere near the wardrobe.

"Oh, good morning," Mikil answered with a smile. "Have you been here all night?"

"Off and on," Lonoren replied, "when I was not meeting with the others to coordinate our strategies."

"You have made plans den?"

"Yes. We have assessed Ryannon's weapons. He and his two assistants are heavily armed. He is also carrying several Catorian explosives. We shall have to be very careful or the results could be disastrous for us all. What we plan to do is . . . ."

Lonoren's briefing was interrupted by a loud pounding followed by Grayden's gruff shout. "We're returning the Squanki shortly," he bellowed through the heavy steel door. "Ryannon will be here for you as soon as the portal is ready."

Mikil gasped and spun back to where she thought Lonoren was. "He is up to someting," she blurted, "he has a Squanki locked in one of dees rooms and says dat he is going to send her back to Lor Mandela, but I could tell dat dis is not his plan. Gatter the rest of the clan. Pairhaps we can seize him at the portal."

"Yes," Lonoren breathed, "this may work to our advantage, my love." Mikil caught a quick glimpse of black out of the corner of her eye, and then felt cold pressure against her lips. "I will return with the Solom shortly. Do not go through that portal until we are back."

"But how will I know when you've returned?" Mikil asked, "I cannot see you, remember?"

"I will kiss you as I just did when we are ready."

Mikil nodded and touched her fingers to her lips. She was about to make a snippy playful comment, when a sudden sense of aloneness washed over her. She didn't see the shadow of Lonoren depart, but somehow she knew that he had left.

Not a second later, there was a faint clicking noise from the hall and the door swung open. Ryannon appeared in the doorway, clothed in his usual all-black attire and sporting his signature diabolical smirk. "Hello, my dearest Audril," he began as he looked her up and down. "Oh, come on. Did you really sleep in your clothes all night? Your pajamas are in the wardrobe!"

"Nothing in that wardrobe belongs to me," she sneered. "I was perfectly fine wearing my own stuff."

Ryannon chuckled and strolled across the room to the large armoire. "Everything in this wardrobe belongs to you, darling. I purchased it all specifically for you." He pulled out a pair of strappy silver sandals and a hanger on which a flowing lavender sundress hung, and held it out to her. "You should wear this today. I've been anxious to see you in this one ever since I bought it," he insisted.

"No thanks," Mikil retorted with an annoyed scowl.

"That wasn't a request," Ryannon snipped. He moved very close behind her and breathed heavily down her neck. "I'll wait in the hall while you change," he panted as he flipped the dress over her shoulder and tried to sneak a peek down the front of her shirt.

"Why don't you do me a favor and just get away from me, you disgusting slime bag?" Mikil hissed.

Ryannon grinned and pressed his lips against her neck. "I seem to remember someone promising that she would do as she was told. We don't want anything unfortunate happening to your sweet little friend now, do we?" He crossed the room and stepped out into the hall. "I'll be back in a couple of minutes," he barked as the door slammed shut behind him with a loud bang.

Mikil was left alone with her thoughts. She couldn't wait for this assignment to be over and to be away from Ryannon and his revolting crew of miscreants. She couldn't wait to be back on Lor Mandela, sleeping in her own bed, training in her own yard, and seeing and holding her beloved Lonoren again.

As she wondered what he was trying to tell her about the Solom's plans to snare Ryannon and deliver him to Atoc Jonathan, she reluctantly changed into the pale purple dress. Only one thought in her mind kept her from ripping the flouncy chiffon gown to shreds—the image of the shocked expression that was sure to be on Ryannon's face upon realizing that his villainous scheme had been thwarted. She finished dressing and stood in front of the mirrored doors of the armoire gazing at the stranger looking back. "Well, at least she's not ugly," she sighed as she ran her fingers through her jet curls. "But how does she deal wit dis mess of hair."

The lock on the door clicked twice and Ryannon pushed it open. "Shall we," he asked, motioning toward the hall with a gloved hand. "Mmm, very nice," he smirked, scanning Mikil's body with a lustful gaze. "Just the way I visualized it looking on you."

Mikil stomped toward the door and marched out into the hall. "Can we just get this over with?" she snarled. "Where's the Squanki anyway?"

"Oh, Grayden has already taken her through. They're waiting for us near the Sybran."

They started down the corridor and had only gone a short way before Mikil decided it was high time for Ryannon to cough up some answers. "Okay, so what exactly are you up to, Ryannon?" she tried. "Do you really expect me to believe that you had a sudden outburst of charity towards that poor little creature? And what do you need me for? I doubt you've brought me here just so you have someone from home to keep you company."

Ryannon's eyes glistened red in the rays of sun filtering through the occasional broken window overhead. "Hmm, I guess there's no harm in divulging my plans to you now," he answered. "After all, we've gotten all of the unpleasantries out of the way, haven't we?"

"I'm not going to clobber you again, if that's what you're asking."

"Precisely," he smirked. "I'll tell you a bit of a secret. I couldn't care less about that Squanki. She is nothing more than an added burden, now that I have the most powerful being alive here with me." His eyes narrowed into glinting slits as he spoke. "You are aware that my late father dabbled in some of the ancient Derite arts, aren't you?"

146

Fifteen

Mikil nodded and played along. She knew little of Ryannon's father, Darian, except that he was just as depraved as his son.

"Well," Ryannon continued, "I've done some studying myself. He left behind quite an extensive library of . . . I guess you would call them reference books. I've learned quite a bit."

"Yeah, so?" Mikil pried.

"So, there's a wonderful ritual that allows the Clest Anaria to transfer her powers to another. Did you know that?"

Mikil shook her head.

"Exactly," Ryannon simpered. "I was rather surprised myself. Furthermore, it's delightfully simple. The only thing we need is a Verulcae pod. Isn't that interesting?"

Mikil acted unmoved. "So that's what we're doing then? We're going to Lor Mandela to pick up a Verulcae pod so that I can transfer my powers to . . . um, let me guess . . . you?"

"Oh no, my love," Ryannon replied, shaking his head and smiling. "I already have a pod. I haven't been without one since I first found out about the process. I like to be prepared, you see. At any rate, we'll take care of that later. Right now, we have other more pressing problems to attend to."

"Problems?" Mikil questioned as they reached the end of a hallway and Ryannon pushed open a creaky maroon door to the outside.

"Yes . . . well, it's nothing that you need to concern yourself with at the moment, my dear. I have everything under control."

"I'm sure you do," she breathed to herself.

They walked along a gravel path without saying anything more. The crunching of the rocks beneath their feet combined with the chirps of nearby birds offered ample noise to fill the tense air. In the distance, Mikil noticed the same hooded figure that was at dinner the night before standing next to a thin slit of blue light. The creature seemed to perk up as they approached.

"Good Morning, Lique," Ryannon greeted. "I trust all is prepared, and that Grayden has done as he was instructed."

Lique nodded energetically.

"Excellent. After we have gone safely through the portal, you may go, if you like. Grayden mentioned that you had things to attend to in Palmerton this afternoon. Is it what we were discussing last night?"

Again Lique's hood moved up and down.

"Doesn't say much, does he?" Mikil interjected, watching Lique with a suspicious eye.

Ryannon paid no attention to Mikil's observation. "That's good. I'll look forward to your return." He patted Lique warmly on the arm, and Mikil thought she saw Lique shudder like an excited puppy.

"After you," he insisted, smugly grinning at Mikil as he pointed toward the portal.

"Me?" Mikil questioned. "Don't you wanna make sure that the coast is clear before we go through?"

Ryannon wrapped his muscular arm around her shoulder and pulled her tightly against him. "Don't worry, my dear. I'm sure Grayden has checked . . . um, the coast."

As he relinquished his hold and motioned toward the blue light again, Mikil glanced around anxiously. Lonoren had told her not to go through the portal until he signaled the arrival of the clan. "Um . . . hang on a second," she blurted, "I . . . uh, I . . . I have to adjust my shoe." She reached down and removed one of her sandals and clumsily fidgeted with the buckle. "Uh, sorry . . . I have one foot that's bigger than the other. This always happens; my shoes never fit right." As she fiddled with the strap, the icy cold brush of Lonoren's mouth moved over her lips.

"Are you quite finished?" Ryannon barked impatiently. "We're on a tight schedule, dear, and Grayden is waiting for us."

"Oh, of course. I forgot that Grayden was waiting," she sighed with relief, but then, with a distinct note of sarcasm in her tone, added, "How could I possibly be so inconsiderate?" She slipped the sandal back onto her foot and lifted it to the sliver of light. With a pop and a blast of blue, the light stretched open and she disappeared into the portal. Ryannon took a few minutes to consult with Lique, and then followed.

Lique turned back toward the mill and started away, when all of the sudden, the portal began expanding and contracting wildly. The frightened hooded being ducked behind a nearby tree, cringing in fear as the sliver of light flashed open and an ear-splitting buzz permeated the air. Violent burst after violent burst ricocheted from the portal and off the surrounding forest, flashing like unnatural lightning across the nearly cloudless sun-drenched sky. Finally, after several seconds of the ferocious onslaught, the portal stilled and returned to its normal, thin, docile appearance. Lique inched out from behind the tree and scurried away quickly, apparently unaware that the tempestuous light show had been caused by the Solom Clan successfully following Ryannon and Mikil through the portal.

CHAPTER XVI

SÍORAÍ CASTLE

Mikil exited the portal ahead of Ryannon, and stepped out into the middle of a windy green field. In front of her an ominous cave, carved into the base of a moss-covered foothill, gave the scene a certain sense of foreboding. Jagged basalt rocks surrounded the chasm and created the appearance of fang-laden jaws waiting to snatch up anything unfortunate enough as to wander too close.

Mikil took no time concluding that something was wrong. Having an extensive knowledge of her home world, she knew that she was most certainly not on Lor Mandela. The landscape in front of her was unfamiliar and unlike any place she had seen.

Cautiously, she inched closer and studied the cave, fully expecting something horrible to burst out at any moment. She bent down, picked up a small rock and tossed it into the darkness, poised to react should something threatening appear. To her relief, there was no movement or sound, other than the rock bouncing across the cave floor and fading into an echo.

With a deep breath, she turned her attention from the cave to the surrounding area. To her right, an endless sea of emerald meadows rolled toward the horizon for as far as she could see. To the left, a crooked staircase made of long, flat rocks snaked up a gentle incline, ending abruptly underneath several flagstone arches, which formed the base of a seemingly endless grey stone bridge. Through the arches, curving away from the bridge, harsh brown cliffs reached into the sky like arms stretched out in a desperate attempt to be saved from the pounding ocean waves below.

Mikil glanced into the cave once again; still, nothing stirred. Slowly, she made her way up the side of the small foothill behind her to better take in the view. As she neared the top, a spectacular sight literally took her breath away.

Consuming the entire top of the hill with the cave at its base, as well as the hills on either side, the crumbled ruins of what must have once been a truly grandiose stone castle stood perched against a backdrop of bloated charcoal clouds. The structure's stacked rock walls and angular roof peaks were majestic and beautiful, even though large chunks of them were now missing.

She gaped in awe at the lofty building, assuming that in its day, this was likely the most elegant edifice in...well, wherever she was. She closed her eyes and fantasized about the grand feasts, lively parties and courageous battles that must have surely been a part of this place's history. She imagined flickering torches lining the walls; myriads of important political figures coming and going; and ill-intentioned criminals attempting to scale the fortress in the dead of night, knowing that their plans would likely fail, but trying regardless, in the hopes that their success would bring them wealth untold. It was disheartening when she opened her eyes again and saw the castle as it now stood: untended, alone, and left to rot and decay.

Mikil's thoughts were suddenly interrupted by a burst of light followed by Ryannon's low voice which shook her back to the bleak situation at hand. "It is lovely, isn't it?"

"Uh . . . whatever," she replied casually, refusing to show Ryannon any hint of the fascination she felt. "Where exactly are we, Ryannon? You said we were going to Lor Mandela, not some random place I've never been before. What are you trying to pull?"

"Nothing, my love. Don't worry. We'll be on Lor Mandela soon enough. I just wanted to show you this very special place before we go."

"Yeah? And what makes it so special?" Mikil snipped.

"At the moment, this is one of the most intriguing places on Drolana," Ryannon answered. "Síoraí Castle, a glistening jewel of Northern Ireland." He nodded toward a cylindrical tower with a large crack down its center. "You see, my dear, I was here just the other day, and thought to myself 'I should bring Atoh Audril to see this place. She would simply love it'." He strutted up beside her and wrapped his arm around her shoulders. "I can tell by that look that you're trying *so hard* to hide that I was right."

"I thought you said we had to hurry," she barked in reply. "We don't want to keep your precious baby Grayden waiting."

An unpleasant scowl moved across Ryannon's brow and down to his lips, but was quickly replaced by his conceited grin. "All in good time, my dear," he replied, "all in good time. First, a history lesson."

"Is this really necessary?" she asked, glancing sideways at the portal and wondering why there had been no sign of the Solom Clan coming through it yet.

"Oh, yes, my love. It is very necessary. I want you to be informed of everything I'm doing. It will make things so much more interesting."

Mikil scoffed and turned away. Her black curls slapped across her face in the whipping wind.

"Now . . . Síoraí Castle," Ryannon continued, "built in the late thirteenth century by an Earl, or a Lord or something . . . they are equivalent to Council Advisors if I understand it correctly. Anyway, at some point, part of the castle dropped off into the sea, which apparently made the owners a bit uneasy . . . can you imagine?" he chuckled. "Now, rumor has it that a clan of Shadow Dwellers, often referred to on Drolana as Shadow People, phantoms or even demons, moved in shortly after the humans moved out." He paused to check Mikil's reaction, and snickered as he caught her eyeing the portal again. "Are you listening, darling?"

"Yeah, sure . . . Shadow People . . . demons," she mumbled, but then her eyes suddenly grew wide. "Wait! Did you say that Dwellers live here?"

Sixteen

"No," Ryannon responded, "I said that this is the rumor. I've made a thorough tour of the grounds and feel confident that there are no Dwellers living amongst these ruins."

Mikil happened to glance up toward the castle as a streak of black moved in front of an arched, glassless window. "What makes you so sure?" she sniggered.

"I'm surprised you would ask, Audril. What with all of your delightful Clest Anaria powers . . . . Do you even know what Trysta powers you possess?"

"What do you mean?" she replied, trying to devise a way to signal the Irish Shadow Dwellers and solicit their help.

"Come along," Ryannon answered as he grabbed her by the arm and pulled her away. "I'll show you."

They moved swiftly over a roughly paved path, up a slope, and then across a meadow that led to the footbridge. Mikil squinted across the lengthy expanse. A salty mist, rolling up out of the turbulent ocean, floated through the balusters and made it difficult to see, but even through the murky veil, she was able to catch periodic glimpses of a shadow darting here and there inside the ruins.

"For you to best understand, we must continue our little lesson," insisted Ryannon.

Mikil looked up at him with disdain. "Yeah . . . fine, it's not like I have a choice."

Ryannon snickered and shook his head. "Trust me; this bit of history will grab your undivided attention." He squeezed her hand and explained. "Since you were raised on this world, you may not fully understand how Lor Mandelan birth lines play out. For example, my father was a pure Brashnellan. My mother, as you know, was a pure Trysta . . . and the former vritesse."

Mikil's stomach lurched as she thought of Ryannon being the son of Ultara, truly one of the greatest vritesses ever to rule. It flopped once more

153

when she remembered that — due in no small measure to Ryannon's actions — Ultara was now dead.

"Trysta descendants can be born with amazing powers," he continued. "Your own mother was able to torture with her eyes, seal rooms to hide them from view, create gaping chasms in the ground that would swallow up anything too close, and probably half a dozen other things that I am not fully aware of. My mother, as the vritesse, had command of every Trysta power in existence."

Mikil's focus was centered on the movement inside the vast ruins. With each break in Ryannon's recitation, she turned to him and nodded as though she were hanging on his every word, but the moment he began to speak again, she would shift her eyes forward, watching and waiting with an intrigued fascination for these strange Shadow People to make a move. Ryannon seemed oblivious as he prattled on. "Did you know that my mother was supposed to put me to death when I was born?" he asked.

Again Mikil acted like she was paying attention and responded by bobbing her head up and down.

"As far as I know, other than me, no first-born male heir has ever been spared, so I have little to use as a point of reference." He stepped in front of Mikil, blocking the footbridge from her sight. "Evidently the eldest male in the vritesse line inherits just as many gifts as would a first-born female."

"Great . . . so you have a billion powers. So what? Why do I need to know all of this?" Mikil snarled.

"I'm getting to that, my dear," he replied with the arrogant smirk that Mikil was beginning to grow used to. "That little Squanki that I was . . . um, *caring* for . . . ."

Mikil couldn't hold back a disgusted scoff.

Ryannon raised his eyebrows and proceeded, "That little Squanki . . . Tabbit is her name . . . has helped me out more than you can possibly imagine. You see, she created the portals that brought both of us to Drolana; she also created the portal that transported us here today, and yesterday, she helped me realize just how handy one of my own powers can be." He stepped back to Mikil's side and this time slid his muscular arm around her waist.

"And what power is that?" Mikil queried, wriggling uncomfortably.

"First, let me ask you a question," Ryannon replied. "It has to do with what I told you earlier about searching this place for Dwellers."

"Yeah? What?"

"As a Trysta heiress, can you sense Dwellers?"

"Yeah, I guess," she replied.

"Well . . . so can I," Ryannon retorted. "What exactly has captivated you over in the castle, my dear? You've been quite intrigued by something. Could it be the Dwellers that are there at this very moment?"

Mikil's heart sank — so much for getting assistance from these Drolana Dwellers. "No," she lied, "I thought I saw something out of the corner of my eye, but when I tried to look at it straight on . . . there was nothing there."

Ryannon appeared thoroughly amused by her comment. "I wonder . . . do you know that Tabbit has the ability to create a single portal that leads to two separate places?"

"And?" Mikil snapped impatiently.

"And . . . realizing this has made her most valuable to me . . . Were it not for my marvelous power of sensing Dwellers, having Tabbit create a portal to both the north and southeast sides of this peninsula would have been pointless, but as it turns out, it's worked beautifully. You see, my dear *Commander* . . ."

Mikil's heart rose into her throat.

"Not only can I sense Dwellers, I can see them . . . even when they are invisible. I'm sure it will come as no surprise when I tell you that the Dwellers here today are tall, have orange eyes, are black from head to foot, and have spiraled horns on either side of their heads." He looked deeply into Mikil's terrified eyes. "Solom, I believe . . . the Solom who came with you to find me and bring me back to Lor Mandela, no doubt . . . the Solom who have been following us around this whole time. Isn't your Entrusted a member of the Clan?"

155

Suddenly, a deafening hiss blasted out above the thunder of the waves.

"Ah, perfect timing," Ryannon sneered.

"What is that?" Mikil cried. "Is that a Catori . . . ?" The word caught in her throat as panic flooded over her in a sickening wave. "LONOREN!" she shrieked, lunging forward toward the bridge.

Ryannon caught her around her middle and lifted her into the air.

"MIKIL!" Lonoren's deep voice boomed back. "Ryannon! Get your hands off of her!"

"LONOREN, GEET OUT OF DER! IT'S A CATORIAN! RUNNNNN!" Mikil kicked and thrashed, trying to get away.

The sound of dozens of footsteps started to pound across the opposite side of the bridge.

Mikil thrust her foot backwards and felt the thin heel of her sandal imbed in the upper part of Ryannon's leg.

"Aaaaarrrhh!" Ryannon growled and doubled over, dropping Mikil hard to the ground.

"LONOREN! HURRY!" she pleaded, scrambling toward the bridge on all fours.

Ryannon yanked the shoe from his leg and raced after Mikil. Crimson blood soaked through his black pants and flowed down his thigh. "That's going to cost you, Commander," he growled.

It didn't take long for him to reach Mikil who he quickly grabbed around the midsection. He hoisted her over his shoulder and turned and started walking away. Mikil hammered her fists against his back. She could see the bridge behind them, but her Entrusted and the rest of the Solom remained invisible to her. The sound of their pounding feet, the horrible hissing of the Catorian explosive, and the unrelenting gnashing of the waves against the rocky shoreline created a chaotic frenzied roar.

"LEAVE HER ALONE!" Lonoren bellowed, his voice still coming from across the bridge.

Sixteen

Again Mikil fought to free herself. She struggled with such fervor that — although Ryannon outweighed her by easily sixty pounds — she was able to force him off balance, and they both tumbled to the ground. She jumped to her feet and took off in a frantic run. "LONOREN! PLEASE! HURRY!" she screeched, as the sound of the Catorian explosive grew louder and louder. Ryannon chased after her, tackling her to the ground just before she reached the edge of the bridge. She thrashed and squirmed, and extended her hand out in desperation, longing to feel the cold touch of her Entrusted. The thundering footsteps drew closer and closer.

"MIKIL!" Lonoren called out again. His voice was close this time, just a few yards away.

Mikil stretched her arm out further and caught a glimpse of a wisp of black flying through the air, followed by the unmistakable thwack of a body landing against the stony bridge. An icy sensation grazed the tips of her fingers. "Lonoren! Oh, dearest," she sighed as his hand wrapped around hers and an overwhelming sense of relief washed over her.

No sooner had their hands entwined, than a colossal explosion blasted through the air ripping the bridge from its supports, and sending it, and a portion of the land on either side of it, plummeting into the valley below. The horrified cries of the Solom shot through the air, and then fell silent as everything between where Lonoren lay and the shore disintegrated into dust.

There was a brief delay, and then Lonoren's body dropped suddenly, practically yanking Mikil's arm from the socket. Ryannon looked up and could clearly see what was happening. He stood and brushed himself off, and then gave Mikil a little push with his side of his boot. He watched with twisted delight as this deceitful woman — who he knew would never let go of her Entrusted — began to slide, inch by inch, closer to the edge of the cliff.

Mikil clawed at the ground with her free hand, trying to anchor herself on something — anything — but the dewy moss was slippery, and there was nothing at all for her to grab a hold of. She kicked and tried to dig her feet into the ground, but with one bare foot, and one dainty tread-less sandal, it wasn't working. Her shoulder burned in agony as Lonoren's body became heavier and heavier. She fought to hang on, but she was moving ever nearer to the edge. Just as the arm holding Lonoren started out over the cliff, a faint whisper rose up from below. Lonoren's voice was weak and labored; it was clear that he was hurt. "Courage . . . my love . . . courage," he spluttered. Mikil felt his hand move, and the coldness she was fighting so hard to cling to slipped away.

"LONOREN!" she shrieked.

There was no reply.

"LONOREN! PLEASE! NO!"

Ryannon smiled in triumph.

Mikil grasped desperately at the air over the crater in front of her. "Lonoren! Please! Lonoren, answer me! Please!" Tears spilled down her dusty cheeks. She collapsed onto her face and sobbed, "My love . . . my . . . my love."

Ryannon stood over her and allowed her to mourn for a second or two, but then yanked her up from the ground and glowered at her in disgust. "Nice try, Mikil," he hissed.

Without blinking, Mikil rolled her hand into a fist and bashed Ryannon across the chin with such force that his head jerked to the side and the bones in his neck cracked loudly. "HOW COULD YOU!" she shrieked. "YOU KILLED DEM . . . YOU KILLED DEM ALL!" Her eyes started to glow a vibrant blue, but her powers seemed to have little to no effect here.

In a fluid motion, Ryannon grabbed the arm that was dislocated, and wrenched it up behind her back. He jammed one of his knees into the back of hers and pushed her face-first to the ground.

Mikil cried out in pain as Ryannon dropped down on top of her with the full weight of his nearly six-and-a-half foot tall body, and slammed his elbow into the back of her injured shoulder.

"I warned the atoc!" he snarled. "I warned him not to toy with me." He looked skyward and shouted, "You've brought this war upon yourself, Jonathan! The blood of billions of people will be on your hands now . . . not mine." He reached into his pocket with his available hand and angrily jerked out a clear, round device with flashing green symbols scrolling across it. He dropped it to the ground and, with a primal yell, smashed it hard with his fist.

A few moments later, in Rosamond and Fairclough — each bustling suburbs of Liverpool, England — a strange hissing began to slice through the pale blue skies above. Residents flooded out of their homes, their schools and their businesses, attempting to locate the source of the irritating noise. The volume of the sound grew, escalating quickly into an ear-splitting screech.

As the confused throngs collectively pressed their hands to their ears, a brilliant flash and an earth-shattering bang erupted through the air; Rosamond and Fairclough, along with their combined population of nearly forty-eight thousand souls, exploded into millions of pieces right up to — but not past — their borders.

CHAPTER XVII

HODGSON CAN HELP

Dallin stumbled groggily down the back stairs and into the breakfast room to find Teedee scurrying about the kitchen. Her ensemble — which made the one she had worn the day before seem quite normal — knocked the drowsiness right out of him. Wrapped from neck to ankles in greenish-yellow glittering fabric, she looked like some sort of fluorescent glow-in-the-dark mummy. "Good morning, handsome," she sang, "tea?"

"Uh, no thanks," he muttered, squinting to focus on the strings of tinkling metallic blue jingle bells dangling from the big puffs of curls protruding from either side of Teedee's head.

She skittered around the room in tiny shuffling steps, grabbing bone china cups from a shelf, digging through the refrigerator for fresh lemons, and filling a black lacquered tea kettle with water from the sink. With every step and movement her strings of bells would tinkle softly.

"How do you walk in that thing, Teeds?" Dallin blurted. He immediately regretted his words, but Teedee didn't seem to mind in the slightest.

"Years of practice," she smiled as she dug around in a silverware-filled drawer for spoons. Suddenly, she stopped digging and froze in place like a statue. "What?" she gasped, staring into the distance. "Oh no. Not again." Without any explanation, she clutched Dallin by the arm and pulled him out of the room.

Seventeen

"Come on, we'd best get into the news room immediately."

"News room?" Dallin queried as Teedee guided him through the summer breakfast room, down a wide hall and into a spacious lounge. She shuffled toward one of the four mauve velvet couches which were set in a square at the center of the floor, and picked up a small remote. "Why would you call this the news room?" Dallin asked as he scanned the elegant room. Teedee just smiled and pressed one of the remote's buttons.

In a fluid synchronization, the doors of the dozen gilded armoires surrounding the room swung slowly open, revealing big-screen televisions, which clicked on and started loudly spouting special reports from twelve different news stations.

"The news room . . . ." Teedee quipped, holding her arms out as if she were welcoming him to observe the wonder before him. She let out a tiny snigger, and then plopped onto the couch nearest her; her legs shot straight out, as her outfit was not conducive to bent knees. She picked up a cup of steaming hot tea from a small glass table next to her and took a sip.

Dallin grimaced at the suspiciously-present tea cup, but before he could think too much of it, the overwhelming commotion on the television screens stole his attention. Reporters broadcasted excitedly in several languages, their words heaping one on top of the other. Dallin glanced at Teedee who was glued to one screen in particular, holding her tea in front of her lips but no longer drinking. He tried to concentrate on the screen but, with all of the other voices echoing through the room, it was nearly impossible.

"What's going on?" he yelled over the din. "Can we turn a few of these off?"

"Oh no, dear," Teedee replied loudly but without breaking her stare. "We might miss something, ya know? Some little clue or . . . ." her voice trailed off as she leaned over and picked up the remote from the table. "Here . . . I'll turn this one up for you."

What Dallin heard next made him wish she hadn't. The conversation between two female reporters — one in a studio and one obviously on location somewhere — stabbed like a dagger in his chest.

". . . . *What they were hoping Natalie, but it appears that this is indeed the work of the Glenhill bombers. Currently, I'm standing just outside of what used to be the town of Fairclough, in the United Kingdom. As you can see by the 'Welcome to Fairclough' sign here behind me, the blast didn't extend even an inch beyond the town's borders. Furthermore, the other explosions . . . in the neighboring borough of Rosamond and at Síorai Castle in Ireland . . . were absolutely identical in their precision.*"

The other news woman, Natalie Wilson of the United States News Network, quickly replied. "*Now Robyn, you say that this is the work of the Glenhill bombers . . . not bomber. Initially, authorities believed that evidence from the Glenhill bombing pointed to a single perpetrator. Have they changed their views in light of yesterday's events?*"

There was a short pause while Robyn waited for the message to reach her. "*That's correct Natalie, but it appears that at this point they are looking into every possibility. Of course, it's too early to know for sure, but the explosion in Northern Ireland . . . at more than two hundred fifty miles away . . . occurred within minutes of these other two blasts, so investigators are no longer ruling out that this could be the coordinated effort of a terrorist group. Several . . . um . . . of the smaller terrorist organizations have tried to take credit, but none of these groups have access to the type of advanced technology necessary to carry out this kind of attack.*"

Dallin stood wide-eyed staring at the screen. The rest of the news reports on the other televisions were just a buzzing in the background. "Maggie!" he shrieked in horror, "you'd better get down here! NOW!"

Teedee smirked at him incredulously. "Maggie?" she sighed under her breath.

Audril, who had already come downstairs and was enjoying a quiet moment alone in the kitchen, jumped out of her chair and raced toward the sound of Dallin's terrified cry.

She ran into the room, and slapped her hands over her ears to drown out the noise. "Aaaa!" she yelped. "What's going on?"

Dazed, Dallin pointed at the armoire. The same report was still on and at the moment Natalie was speaking.

"... Those numbers stand right now?"

"Sadly, Natalie, our latest figures show seven thousand twenty-six confirmed dead, but those numbers are, of course, growing rapidly. We've been told that an accurate count may not be available for several weeks. Fairclough and Rosamond were both considered small towns, however, Fairclough's population alone was nearly twenty-five thousand, and Rosamond's was only about two thousand less than that. Also, many individuals from surrounding cities worked and visited this area regularly. Local authorities fear that the final death toll will be in the tens of thousands."

Audril glanced from television to television without saying a word; the look on her face spoke volumes. After several stunned seconds, she looked at Dallin, and in a much more sober tone than before asked, "What's going on?" She knew what the answer was. She could see by the pictures flashing across the screens that Mikil had failed, and that Ryannon was carrying out his terrible threats.

Much to both her and Dallin's surprise, it was Teedee who replied. "I think it's that Ryannon fellow." She leaned forward on her chair and drew a long, slurping sip of tea.

"What?" Dallin gasped, "I . . . I mean, who?"

"Have you forgotten him already?" Teedee quizzed. "You two were just talking about him last evening. You remember, don't you, Toots? You said that he had that Tabbit thing and that Mikil and the Solom were going to fail because of you. You mustn't blame yourself, though. Why, there was this one time when I bought an old painting worth millions, and wouldn't you know?

163

That very day, the truck delivering it broke down in a snow storm. They about had it fixed . . . I think it was something with the transmission . . . when another truck, hauling live chickens, slid on the ice and smashed into it. Bye, bye painting, not to mention the poor little chickens! The painting even had little chickens painted on it. Oh, they were blue and yellow, and the loveliest shade of mauve . . . ironic . . . but still . . . not my fault. No more than this whole thing is yours. Nope . . . it's gotta be that Ryannon character. He sounds like an absolute cad!"

Dallin stood gaping before her.

Audril shook her head and moaned, "Um, okay . . . reality check, please! Dallin, we have to do something. We've got to stop him before he does this again."

"Yeah, I know," Dallin replied, "but how? We don't even know where he is!"

Teedee set her cup on the table and twisted her legs to the side so she could stand. "You kids worry too much," she scolded as Dallin rushed to help her up. She patted him warmly on the cheek and added, "Hodgson can help. I've already sent him to find out what he can about Ryannon. He has friends that will help us, too." She looked Audril squarely in the eyes and reiterated, "Don't you worry, Toots. Hodgson can help."

At that moment, something in Audril's mind simply snapped. She had lived in Teedee Venilworth's Fa-la-la House of Fantasy for long enough. "Will you *please* stop?" she bellowed. "There is no Hodgson! He isn't real! YOU'VE NEVER SEEN HIM BECAUSE HE ISN'T REAL! This is a serious life or death situation, and we don't need you or your *imaginary* friend getting in our way!"

"MAGGIE!" Dallin yelped, in shock that she was insulting the woman who had shown them such hospitality.

"No, no dear," Teedee assured, patting him on the arm. "It's quite all right. Many people feel that I'm not firing on all cylinders . . . if ya know what I mean." She smiled and wrapped her frail arm around Audril's. "Come along,

Toots. I want to show you something." She started to lead Audril toward the door. Audril glanced over her shoulder at Dallin with a look of, "why aren't you stopping her?" blaring in her eyes.

Dallin just shook his head in scolding disappointment.

Teedee escorted Audril back through the kitchen and to a door that looked as though it might lead outside. "Are you kicking me out?" Audril asked quietly, now feeling a tiny twinge of remorse for the way she had ripped into Teedee.

"Of course not, Toots, but there's someone I want you to meet, if that's all right with you."

"Um . . . sure, I guess."

When Teedee pulled the door open, it was clear that it did not lead outdoors, but instead to a long, dark staircase and down into the cellar below the house. This did nothing to ease Audril's growing nervousness.

"What's down here?" she squeaked, hoping to get some sort of reassurance that this crazy little lady wasn't about to murder her in the basement.

"Just a moment . . . you'll see." Teedee's answer was not the comforting one she hoped for.

"Ya know, Teedee? I'd really feel more comfortable if Dallin came down here with us. I'm . . . uh . . . I'm afraid of . . . um . . . no . . . actually mortified of spiders."

"You really *do* worry too much, honey. You'll get grey hairs early if you keep this up. Why, I didn't get a single silver strand until I was nearly seventy, but of course, looking at me now, who'd believe it. Auburn . . . that's what it used to be . . . not as curly as yours though."

At the bottom of the stairs was another door, this one big, wooden, and heavily carved. There was an electronic key pad on the wall next to it, and Teedee raised a bony index finger and began punching away. She entered six numbers, which Audril tried to memorize over her shoulder, but Teedee turned slightly as she pressed in the last two buttons, blocking the keypad with her upper body. A click followed by a loud clunk echoed through the stairwell, and the door swung slowly open.

Teedee gave Audril a little nudge into the room which was nothing more than a large cement and wooden framework storage area. "See those boxes over there?" Teedee asked, pointing to a wonky pile of cardboard a few feet away. "Go grab the top one and bring it over, please. Oh, it's not heavy," she added as she noticed the concern on Audril's face. Audril was hardly worried about the weight of the box.

Apprehensively, Audril moved toward the boxes. Teedee flipped on a light switch near the door that did very little to light the space, but did help a bit.

As Audril raised her arms to grab the box, she heard the door slam behind her and whirled around to find that Teedee was nowhere to be seen. "She's locking me in?" she gasped. "You've gotta be kidding me!" She ran to the door and started pounding. "Teedee! You let me out of here THIS MINUTE! This is kidnapping! It's against the law! You'll go to jail! You can't do this! Do you think Dallin won't notice that I'm gone! TEEDEE! Get back here! RIGHT NOW!" She stopped beating the door and listened. She could hear the tinkling of Teedee's bells moving further and further away. "TEEDEE! GET BACK DOWN HERE NOW!" she demanded, resuming her assault of the heavy door. "YOU CAN'T KEEP ME HERE!"

Suddenly, a strange, electrically charged iciness crept across her right shoulder, followed by a wave of chills surging throughout her entire body. Instinctively, she spun around, but nothing was there. She peered into the darkness at the other side of the room. A slight shuffling sound, followed by what sounded like a box sliding across the floor, emanated out of a shadowy corner. "Huh . . . hello?" she breathed, in not much more than a whisper. "Is somebody there?"

Much to her horror, the next thing she heard and felt was a freezing breath of air across her nose and cheeks.

Her heart leapt into her throat as she nervously stuttered, "Huh . . . huh . . . hello? Who's there?"

A low, drawling, scratchy, unworldly voice answered back as if laboring to enunciate every syllable. "Hellllooooo, Misssss. I ammmm Hodgggggg-sonnnn." Terror washed over her.

She stared straight ahead for a second or two, and then let out a blood curdling scream. Shrieking wildly, she began prancing frantically in place. "Hod . . . Hod . . . Hodgson!" she yelped. "Hod . . . Hod . . . !" She ran to the door and started yanking hysterically on the knob. "Dallin!" she screamed, "Dallin! Help me! Hod . . . Hod . . . . Anyone! Helllllllp! Daaaaaaddy?"

Hodgson chuckled maniacally behind her. The sound of his eerie cackle caused her legs to feel like gelatin. She whirled back around but something about there still being no one visible pushed her over the top. "Hod . . . Hod . . . Hod . . ." she repeated in a whimper. Her eyes rolled back in her head and she collapsed with a thud onto the cement floor.

Chapter XVIII

ACCUSATIONS AND REVELATIONS

The air in Audril's chambers was thick with tension. Jonathan paced . . . Kahlie paced . . . Bridgette paced . . . Glaron paced, none of them knowing what to say, and each of them anxiously awaiting any news from the Palace Guard regarding the whereabouts of Audril.

"Are you sure that's all you know, Bridge?" Jonathan finally asked, breaking the tense silence.

"I swear! She told me she was going to those cavern things and that she wouldn't be gone very long." Bridgette's wide brown eyes glistened with tears of concern.

"Why would she want to go to the Caverns?" Kahlie breathed, more to herself than to anyone else.

"She was going to try to talk to the soul," Bridgette sniffled. "I tried to tell her that it was crazy, but she thinks that because she's the Crest Anaria . . . ."

"Clest," the other three corrected in unison.

"Whatever!" Bridgette snapped, sounding more like Audril than her usually amiable self.

"I should go to the Caverns and summon the spirit," Kahlie offered. "Maybe it will know where she's gone."

"We all know where she's gone," Glaron retorted with a look of disgust on his face. "You all may be in denial, but the reality is that no one I've ever met is more stubborn, bull-headed, and 'let's not think before we risk our necks' than Maggie Baker."

Jonathan stopped pacing. "She wouldn't dare! I specifically told her . . . ."

"When's that ever stopped her, Jonathan?" Glaron interrupted. "She's always done stuff like this . . . running away from home when she was seven because you wouldn't let her have a puppy . . . and remember when she was ten? She set off for the North Pole in the middle of the night, during one of the coldest winters in Iowa's history, just to prove to Michael Tucker that Santa Claus was real; she nearly died of hypothermia! She's driven both of us crazy with this kind of crap for years! So what makes you think that because she's the atoh of Lor Mandela she's just gonna stop all of a sudden?"

Kahlie could see the anger building in Jonathan's eyes, and quickly interjected, "Listen, we're all on the same side here, and none of us will be able to think clearly unless we calm down a bit." She laid her hand gently on Jonathan's forearm. "I'll go to Koria right now and summon the spirit. Why don't you and Glaron check in with General Statlen and see how the search is progressing . . . and Bridgette . . . please try to think if Audril said or did anything else that you might have forgotten. Let's meet back in the Galia Chamber in an hour and compare notes." She kissed Jonathan on the cheek and, without waiting for a retort from any of the others, slipped out of the room and closed the door.

"Darn that stupid note!" Bridgette blurted, dropping down on the edge of the bed.

Both Jonathan and Glaron turned their heads and eyed her suspiciously.

"Note?" Jonathan quizzed, "What note, Bridgette?" His tone was a little on the scary side.

"I told you," she began with a flustered look on her face. "Remember? The stupid riddle that came out of the wall? That was like the first thing I told you."

"You said something about the Advantiere," Jonathan corrected.

"No, no . . . she *did* say that this all started when that stupid riddle came out of the wall!" Glaron chimed in. "I assumed you were talking about the Advantiere, too, sweetie. You weren't?"

"Aye yi yi!" Bridgette sighed, dropping her head into her hands and shaking it back and forth. "I wasn't talking about the Advantiere! Man, this place is confusing! I was talking about the note that came out of the wall right after you left. That's why we moved all of this stuff into the middle of the room!" She motioned toward the huge mound still heaped in the center of their makeshift race track. "The riddle said something like 'who told you the Advantiere' or 'go see the teller of the Advantiere'. Audril thought it was her grandma at first, but then she clicked that it was the soul of Lor Mandela, 'cause . . . well . . . you know . . . her grandma's . . . um . . . dead. Anyway, that's why she wanted to get to the caverns so bad." She stood and walked over to Glaron and playfully slugged him in the shoulder. "I know what the Advantiere is, duh! I can't believe you thought that's what I was talking about!"

Even though it didn't hurt, Glaron rubbed his shoulder as Jonathan scolded, "That's what we all thought, Miss Clark!"

Bridgette twisted her mouth to the side and breathed, "Well, I guess maybe I coulda explained it a little better, huh?"

"You think?" Glaron quipped.

Bridgette lifted her fist again and Glaron flinched in an exaggerated manner.

"What else did the note say, Bridge?" Jonathan asked.

"Lemme think for a sec," she said and plopped down on the bed again.

Jonathan and Glaron both stared at her intently as she tried to remember the lines of the odd message.

After a few seconds, Glaron glanced sideways at Jonathan just to make sure his patience was holding out. At that moment, the atoc's facial expression changed from one of intense concentration, to one of someone who had just been electrically shocked.

"What is it?" Glaron pried.

Jonathan directed his answer to Bridgette. "Bridge, did you say the note came out of the wall?"

"Uh . . . yeah."

"Where, exactly?"

Bridgette pointed to the shadowy corner from which the note had appeared.

"And you didn't see who brought it?" Jonathan quizzed. His face was growing increasingly rigid by the second.

"No, Audril turned on the lamp and there was no one there." Bridgette answered.

"Lortu," Jonathan hissed. "How else would she have gotten to Earth?"

"But why in the *world* would Lortu do that?" Glaron asked. "He knew as well as the rest of us that you were adamantly against her going!"

"But if Ryannon made him a better . . . ." Jonathan stopped short and barked, "General, follow me! Bridgette Marie Clark . . . you stay put."

"Yeah . . . okay," she moaned as the atoc and her boyfriend strode from the room. She waited until she thought they would be safely out of range and shouted, "but I didn't do anything wrong!"

"Just stay put!" Jonathan's voice called back from somewhere down the hall.

Glaron chuckled. "I bet she thought we wouldn't hear that . . . she's never quite understood why we're all constantly shushing her. It's pretty funny."

Jonathan didn't so much as crack a smile; he seemed intently focused on his current mission — whatever it happened to be. Glaron didn't push the issue. He just marched along obediently alongside the atoc.

As they approached the entrance hall, a sophisticated-looking Squanki appeared in the corridor across from them. This Squanki was not like Tabbit and Guddlebee. Although she was small in stature and had the typical white hair and large round eyes, her skin was a lovely, deep rich brown and her appearance was far more refined; there was something mysterious and immensely alluring about her.

"Good evening, Your Highness . . . Your Excellency," she waved. "I am pleased to have found you." She glided confidently across the foyer and lowered into a graceful curtsy.

"Hello, Sauvina," Jonathan replied. "If you'll excuse us, we're quite busy right now."

"Forgive me for interrupting, sire, but I've just received an urgent message sent for General Glaron from Commander Branlor of the Trystas."

"What is it?" Glaron asked.

Sauvina kept her eyes on Jonathan until he nodded for her to proceed.

"Your Excellency . . . Commander Branlor is traveling, at this moment, towards Mandela City, in the hopes that he might meet with you and the atoc." She straightened her already perfect long, wavy hair with her small hand and continued. "He humbly requests that you meet him at the edge of the Sybran near Westrim so that he might discuss the purpose of his visit with you in advance. The commander states that his mission is of great importance, and that if you leave within the hour, you should both reach Westrim at approximately the same time."

"I'm sorry, Sauvina, but I have urgent business here to . . . ."

"No, Glaron. I think you'd better go," Jonathan interrupted. He leaned toward the general and whispered, "He may have news about Mikil. I can handle things here."

"Right," Glaron nodded, "then I'll just be going."

Sauvina, who respectfully turned her back to them as the atoc whispered, swirled back around and curtsied again. "Thank you, sir. Is there anything else, Your Highness?" she questioned, while straightening the already perfectly straight hem of her tailored powder blue jacket.

Glaron cleared his throat and bowed to excuse himself as Jonathan answered, "Just one thing."

Sauvina waited with rapt attention.

"I've told you that it is not necessary for you to be so formal with me. Please call me Atoc . . . or even Jonathan would be fine."

The elegant little Squanki looked up at him, with her stunning smoky brown eyes nearing tears, and breathed, "With all respect, Highness, I would feel awkward and highly out of line. I know my place and am quite grateful, and extraordinarily honored, to be of service to the vritesse and yourself, but it would not be right for the ator's companion, or *any* servant for that matter, to be so familiar."

"All right," Jonathan conceded, shaking his head, "I wouldn't want you to feel awkward or highly out of line."

Sauvina let out a relieved sigh and bowed as she backed away.

"Oh, just a moment, Sauvina," Jonathan blurted, "have you seen General Statlen?"

"Why, yes, Highness," she beamed, showing a mouth full of pristine white teeth. "He just came in. He is in the lounge adjacent the Galia Chamber briefing a few of his officers."

"Excellent . . . thank you." Jonathan turned on his heels and strode quickly away in the direction from which he had come. He marched past Audril's room and passed the two Solom clansmen who continued to stand guard like large, black statues on either side of the door. Normally, he would have stopped to dismiss them, but there wasn't time for that right now. He had an assignment for Statlen — an assignment that had been delayed for too long already.

He reached the lounge and burst through the door without knocking; three men and three women immediately jumped to their feet. The atoc didn't wait for formalities. "Statlen," he boomed, "I need to speak to you . . . alone."

Without hesitation, the other officers scurried from the room.

"Is there a problem, sir?" Statlen asked, worried that perhaps he had done something wrong.

"Yes, but not with you," Jonathan replied, sensing the general's concern. "I need you and your men to find Lortu as soon as possible. Tell him to report to the palace immediately."

"Of course, sire . . . we will do our best, but you know as well as I that Lortu can be quite elusive."

"If you are not up to the task, General, I'm sure I can find someone who is," Jonathan sneered, leaving Statlen with no question as to his sincerity.

Statlen cleared his throat and pulled back his shoulders. "No, sir . . . we'll find him."

Jonathan's stern expression seemed to soften slightly. "Statlen, I think Lortu knows how to get Audril back. I *need* you to find him."

The hardened, battle-worn general placed his hand on Jonathan's shoulder and assured, "We've been friends for a long time, Jonathan. I will do everything I possibly can . . . you know that."

Jonathan nodded and forced a smile, a gesture that Statlen mimicked; he turned from the room and set off to inform his troops of their difficult mission — one that suddenly became unnecessary.

Within seconds of Statlen's departure, the wall directly in front of Jonathan began to ripple and none other than Lortu materialized in front of it. "You wished to zee me, Atoc?"

Jonathan struggled to hide his surprise and replied, "Yes, but I did not expect to see you so soon."

"Well, eef you would like me to leave and return later, I can do zo." There was a more than usually arrogant smirk on his face.

"No . . . no," Jonathan quickly replied, "I think you and I both know what this is about."

Lortu didn't answer at first. He seemed lost in thought as he paced back and forth in his hunched, eerie manner. After a few moments, he locked his crystalline eyes on Jonathan's, and snarled, "Aye tink dat you are accusing de Lortu of aiding de Ryannon of Brashnell . . . a stupid ting to do zince we are alone in dis room."

Eighteen

Jonathan crossed the room quickly and grabbed Lortu by one arm. "Don't you dare threaten me, Lortu," he hissed.

Lortu yanked his arm away and growled.

"Need I remind you that you are a general of Lor Mandela?" Jonathan barked. "I've trusted you more than I should have, haven't I?"

"Aye weel not stand in dis place and be accused of tings dat are untrue by anyone, not even de *noble* atoc. If you trusted de Lortu, den why have aye been summoned 'ere at all?"

"I want Audril back on Lor Mandela immediately."

Lortu chuckled and shook his head from side to side, his white hair floating along behind it. "De only one who can bring de atoha back is de atoha herzelf. She has a mission on de Drolana. No *changeling* Trysta can do eet for 'er. But do not worry, Atoc. She is protected."

"Protected?" Jonathan bellowed. "You know as well as anyone what Ryannon is capable of! There's no way that Dallin can protect her by himself! You helped her get there, so now you can go and get her back!"

Lortu pulled himself to his full height and casually flicked some dirt out from under one of his fingernails. "Eef I go to Drolana, she weel never be getting back."

A look of horror washed over Jonathan's face at the mention of the possibility of never seeing his daughter again. "What do you mean?"

"I mean dat maye mission right naow is here on de Lor Mandela. I moust find de Trysta Channeler. Witout her powers, de fair atoha weel be in great danger. Zend no more Trystas to de Drolana, Atoc. Dis will be how you can protect yoah daughter. Leave it to maye brothers to protect 'er der."

"Your brothers?" Jonathan replied. "You've already sent Dwellers to Drolana?"

"Der was no need. Dey 'ave been der for centuries." Lortu's answer came as a shock.

"Dwellers? On Drolana?"

175

"Yes," Lortu responded, maintaining his nonchalant demeanor. "Maye cousin de Hodgson of de Brustabala tribe is wit 'er now, keeping 'er safe. His tribe has been de ruling tribe of Dwellers on de Drolana for more den fouh hundred years."

"Lortu, I lived on Drolana for thirteen years. How is it that I never saw a Dweller there?"

"You would never zee me eef I did not weesh it," Lortu laughed.

Just then, a rumbling, ground-jolting blast echoed through the corridors of the palace. "What the . . . ?" Jonathan yelled over the roar. As soon as he was able to gain his footing, both he and Lortu sprinted out of the lounge and toward the palace foyer to see what was going on.

Chapter XIX

RYANNON RETURNS

"**G**ood Lord! What was that?" Branlor exclaimed. He and Glaron were nearing the East Mystad Field at the edge of the Sybran Forest when they too heard the thundering explosion. Glaron didn't waste time answering; he broke into a full run toward the palace. Branlor didn't stand around waiting for an invitation either. Within seconds, he and Glaron were racing side by side through the last row of weeping Greelan trees. As the branches of the graceful trees lifted, the palace and field became visible, revealing the awful result of the explosion.

It seemed as though the whole northern half of the field was engulfed in huge orange flames. At the edge of the inferno, the dark silhouette of a man, with someone flung lifelessly over his shoulder, blocked out the light of the fire behind him. Despite the distance, there was no question as to the man's identity.

"Ryannon!" Glaron shouted.

A sickening, icy wave washed over Branlor. "Oh no," he breathed as he and Glaron both turned their attention to the limp, seemingly dead figure that Ryannon carried. At that moment, neither could tell if it was Branlor's niece or the atoh, but either would be equally as devastating.

They rushed out onto the field. Just as they passed the twisted roots of the Ator's Anaria, the unexpected happened. Mikil gained consciousness and

177

— in a manner true to her training as a Trysta warrior — flipped herself over Ryannon's shoulder and landed gracefully on the ground behind him.

"Mikie!" Branlor shouted excitedly. Within a fraction of a second, Mikil faded into the angular shadows being cast by the blaze. She weaved silently in and out of the flames like a tigress stalking her prey. Ryannon cautiously backed away from the fire, watching intently for any sign of her. For a brief moment, the outline of one of her legs rippled along the edge of the fire and then vanished. As Ryannon turned toward where he'd just seen her, she pounced on him from behind, catching him completely off guard. She grabbed his hand and wrenched his arm up behind him, taking a hold of his spike dart glove and ripping it in two. As it fell to the ground, Ryannon threw his elbow backward, hitting her in the cheekbone. Intense pain and the nauseating sound of cracking bones twisted in her head as she fell to the ground.

As they drew nearer, Glaron bellowed over the boisterous crackling of the fire, "You get to Mikil! I'll check on the others and get more help!"

Branlor nodded and rushed to his niece's aid.

Ryannon smiled and lifted his boot above her head, preparing to crush any bones in her skull that weren't already fractured.

Mikil, taking full advantage of his only having one leg on the ground, slammed the heel of her foot hard against his ankle. Now it was the sound of his bones shattering that filled the air. His leg buckled and he landed hard on the ground beside Mikil.

"That's m' girl!" Branlor shouted from a few feet away.

In the blink of an eye, Ryannon rolled to the side, snatched up one of the halves of his glove and launched a dart directly into Branlor's chest.

The commander stopped cold; his eyes widened and he gulped hard. His gaze locked on Mikil for a second before he shrugged apologetically and then crumpled into a heap on the lawn.

Mikil shrieked. She sprung up from the ground, kicked Ryannon forcefully in his injured leg again, and then faded into the fiery shadows.

Nineteen

Ryannon bellowed in agony; he was not about to let Mikil have any advantage over him though. He clenched his teeth and moved his hand over his leg. His eyes began to glow an intense red. The bones in his leg twisted and strained against his skin like a white hot fire singing his flesh. He moaned as the bone fragments fused themselves together with a raw, pounding pain that finally subsided to a dull ache. Within seconds, his leg was healed and he jumped to his feet to wait for Mikil to emerge.

At that moment, Jonathan and Lortu burst through the palace doors, meeting Glaron at the top of the palace steps. "What's going on?" Jonathan yelled.

"Ryannon!" Glaron huffed, struggling to catch his breath. Before Jonathan or Lortu had a chance to respond, a flash of blue light shot through the air, and two figures emerged from a rapidly dissolving portal onto the palace's front landing. Glaron immediately recognized one of the two as the exiled Trysta spy, Grayden.

At the sight of him, Lortu faded backwards into a dark corner.

"I hear you're the vritesse's puppet boy once again . . . congratulations," Grayden sneered as he easily pinned the still out-of-breath Glaron face first against the palace wall.

"Why, hello, your Highness," a female voice drifted out from underneath the grey hood of Grayden's cloaked companion. "I've never met a real king before." She had exited the portal right behind Jonathan, and subdued him quickly by holding the long, curved blade of a dagger against his neck.

"He's not a real king, Lique," Grayden corrected. "He's just pretending to be one until his accounting job pays off."

Both Lique and Grayden exploded into laughter. "Well, be he king or accountant," Lique sniggered after regaining her composure, "may he rest in peace." She slid the dagger slowly across Jonathan's neck. Small, round beads of blood popped up on his skin following the trail of the sharp blade.

"Stop! NOW!" Glaron commanded. Grayden shoved him harder against the wall.

179

"Oh no, my dear," Lique hissed, "Ryannon will be so proud of me when I deliver him this accountant's noble head. Oh, and then, when I bring him his precious little girl . . . mmmmm . . . we will rule all of Earth and Lor Mandela side by side." She seemed to shiver with anticipation as she carved a little deeper into Jonathan's flesh. "I want to see how long we can make this last." Jonathan's blood was now flowing down the front of him in trickling streams. Lique drew in a deep breath through her nose as if the smell of it was somehow intoxicating.

"Knock it off, Lique," Grayden barked. "Just get it over with so we can get out of here."

Jonathan struggled to pull himself away from the sharp blade, but Lique had a surprisingly strong hold on him.

Suddenly a flash of bright light emanated through the palace doors from inside, and Kahlie appeared in the foyer. She locked eyes with Glaron and immediately, Grayden flew backwards through the air and landed flat on his back with a thud on the bottom few steps. Lique gasped and dropped the dagger as a searing hot pain ripped through her body. Jonathan coughed and staggered, but then turned and lunged toward Lique. As he did, however, she lost her balance and rolled down the marble staircase, landing just a few feet away from Grayden. Grayden struggled his way back to his feet and yanked her up by her cloak.

"Let's go!" he boomed, pulling her behind him as they started in a sprint across the field.

"Come on!" Jonathan bellowed.

He and Glaron raced down the steps, followed closely by Kahlie. They were almost to the bottom stair when Lortu suddenly materialized out of a large, potted topiary right in front of them, pacing quickly back and forth and stopping them in their tracks.

"Lortu . . . MOVE!" Jonathan demanded.

Nineteen

Lortu looked first at Glaron, with both shock and elation glowing in his pale eyes; then he shifted his gaze to Jonathan's throat. He briefly studied the cut across it, shook his head side to side, and then burst into wild laughter.

"Get out of the way!" Jonathan shouted again.

The Shadow Dweller continued laughing as he turned with amazing stealth and dashed across the field — knuckles on the ground like front paws — after Lique and Grayden.

"Ryannon! We've got company!" Grayden bellowed from half way across the meadow.

Ryannon, eyes were fixed on the towering flames as he waited for Mikil to show herself, momentarily glanced over his shoulder and was met with an opportunity he could scarcely resist. Jonathan was racing across the field after Lortu. He was completely unguarded and out in the open — and Ryannon had a clear shot. He raised the piece of glove he was still holding and took aim. As Jonathan moved into the most opportune spot, he inched his finger toward the button. "Now," he breathed as he depressed the trigger. The small mechanism inside the glove clicked; the dart zipped from the chamber with a *shink*.

No sooner had the end of the long needle slid from the glove, than Mikil appeared from out of nowhere and threw herself in front of it. The spike dart pierced into her chest at amazing speed, sending her flying backwards before lodging itself in the bone of her shoulder blade and coming to an abrupt stop. Seemingly unfazed, she rushed at Ryannon, swung her hand upward and smashed him in the bottom of his nose. Again the sound of bones crushing mingled with the snapping of the flames as ruby red blood spilled down over Ryannon's mouth and chin.

He raised his ripped glove again, but much to his disappointment, there were no darts left. Without the slightest hesitation, he sped toward the other half of his favorite weapon which still lay on the smoldering lawn near the edge of the fire.

Mikil lunged through the air — a spike dart still protruding from her chest — and landed face-first. The long dart shifted to one side and scraped

181

against her scapula, sending an almost unbearable pain exploding through her body, but she knew that she had to beat Ryannon to the partial glove, or the atoc would be dead. With all the strength she could muster, she sprung upward, hurling her body toward it and literally snatched it from Ryannon's fingertips. Before Ryannon could react, she rolled onto her back and flung the glove over her head and deep into the engulfing flames.

"NO!" Ryannon roared. With no thought to reinjuring his recently healed ankle, he kicked Mikil hard in the head. The brutal force of his kick flipped her from her back to her stomach, knocking her completely unconscious.

Glaron and Jonathan both saw Ryannon's brutal blow, and stopped their pursuit of the others. As they sped toward Ryannon he realized that he had to leave — now. He quickly assessed Mikil to make sure she was no longer a threat, glanced back at Jonathan and Glaron, then sprinted toward the trees separating the East Mystad from the Delovic Region and vanished into them.

Within seconds, the raging fire seemed to disintegrate into thin air, leaving behind a heavy smell of burnt brush and a blackened landscape.

Glaron ran to Branlor and Jonathan raced to Mikil who was still breathing, but barely. Jonathan turned her over and lifted her upper body into his arms. It was shocking and terrifying for him to see someone who looked exactly like his daughter badly injured and fighting for her life. Her eyes fluttered open and she cringed in pain. "I . . . I . . . am . . . zorry, Atoc."

"Just relax, Mikil," Jonathan said. "We'll get you help." He hoisted her up from the grass and started toward the castle; her eyes rolled back and her body went completely limp.

Glaron looked up from Branlor and shook his head. "He's gone," he whispered.

"We'll send someone back for him," Jonathan instructed. "Get back to the palace and get her a doctor."

Glaron took another glance at Branlor and rose from the ground. He had barely taken a step when he noticed a dark mass on the lawn near the edge of the field. "Vritesse," he bellowed. "Kahlie!"

He took off like a flash, racing past Jonathan in a blur.

It only took Jonathan a second to see what was wrong, and even with the added weight of Mikil, he too started running across the lawn.

Glaron raced up to Kahlie and dropped to his knees at her side. "Vritesse? Come on! Wake up," he pleaded, patting her cheeks.

Kahlie suddenly gasped hard, and bolted upright. "What's going on?" she blurted loudly.

"Are you all right? What happened?" Glaron shrieked, stunned by her abrupt recovery.

"Kahlie, what is it?" Jonathan huffed.

Kahlie didn't answer. She looked at the lifeless form of Mikil and slapped her hands over her mouth in horror. "Audril?" she muttered through her fingers.

"No," Glaron replied, "Mikil."

"She needs a doctor, now," Jonathan added. "Are you all right, love? Can you transport to Koria and bring back Salera?"

"I can try, but you should try to find Michelan. He's staying here in the infirmary for the week instead of being on-call at home."

"I'm on it," Glaron responded as he dashed up the palace steps, skipping two or three stairs with each stride.

Jonathan followed and shouted back to Kahlie, "Are you sure you're okay? I don't think Michelan can handle this one. We need Salera."

"I'm fine . . . Just get her inside! I'll do everything I can." Kahlie stood and dusted herself off and started in a run across the field. When she'd picked up sufficient speed, she looked up and yelled skyward, "Trysta Palace!"

Nothing happened.

She kept running, pushing herself to go faster, and faster. Again she shouted, "Trysta Palace!" — still nothing.

She tried a third time...and a fourth. Finally, she could run no further and had to stop to catch her breath. "What's going on?" she panted aloud. "Why is this happening?" Worried, and resigned to the fact that she was not going to be able to reach Koria in nearly enough time, she sucked in a deep breath and raced back toward the palace.

By the time she reached the infirmary, Dr. Michelan was busily hooking Mikil up to several devices and gadgets; the long, glinting dart was still lodged in her chest. Jonathan and Glaron were leaning against a wall, watching anxiously.

At the sight of Kahlie, without Dr. Salera accompanying her, Jonathan grimaced and shrugged his shoulders. The vritesse chose to ignore him at the moment and focused her attention on Mikil.

"What can I do, doctor?" she asked, moving closer to Mikil's operating table.

"Try your healing powers, Vritesse," Michelan replied. "I'm not sure there's time for me to save her."

Kahlie approached the table and lifted her hand above Mikil's badly battered face. Suddenly, Mikil's appearance began to change. Her raven curls lightened into long waves of white; her face transformed from that of a slightly freckled seventeen-year-old to a tanned, exotic warrior in her mid-twenties.

"Vritesse, hurry!" Dr. Michelan pleaded, "We're losing her!"

Kahlie closed her eyes and fought to conjure her powers. It should have been easy, yet it was taking everything in her, and still nothing was happening. "Please," she begged out loud. "COME ON!" She clenched her jaw, squeezed her eyes even more tightly shut and thrust her hand over Mikil.

"Kahlie, now!" Jonathan shouted. "Now!"

Mikil's face was now her own, and only the very tips of her hair were still black. Dr. Michelan rushed around the table and draped a dark green cloth over her torso. He flipped a switch on a machine with orange and yellow blinking buttons that sat near the table; Mikil's whole body jolted violently. The doctor watched for a moment, and then hit the switch again. This time, nothing happened.

As the last strand of black slipped from the tips of her hair, Mikil Tu Shadow took her final breath, and fell silent.

Nineteen

Jonathan stared at Kahlie in disbelief. She stared back at him like a frightened child and ran from the room out onto an adjoining balcony.

The atoc moved across the room to Mikil. He lifted her thin hand in his and bowed his head. "What have I done?" he sighed quietly. Glaron slid sideways along the wall and slipped out onto the balcony with Kahlie. She was standing near the exquisitely carved marble railing, sobbing. "Why couldn't I do it? Why couldn't I save her?" She looked at Glaron as though desperate for him to answer.

"I don't know," he muttered as he walked up behind her and placed his arm around her shoulder. She turned her face into his chest and wept.

"Sweetheart . . ?" the tranquil tone of Jonathan's voice from the doorway gave her a small dose of relief; she had convinced herself that he would be angry with her. She took a deep breath and pulled away from Glaron to face him. "Oh, love . . . please . . . don't cry," Jonathan soothed. "You tried. You did everything you could."

He crossed the balcony and took her hands. "As soon as Michelan finishes up inside, he'd like to take a look at you."

Kahlie nodded as tears continued to pour from her eyes. Jonathan embraced her and held her tightly to him.

A few moments later, Dr. Michelan came through the glass doors from the infirmary. "Vritesse? Let's take a look and see if we can figure this out for you." He spoke gently. "I've already sent a messenger to Koria to request that Dr. Salera join us."

Kahlie lifted her head and wiped her eyes. She drew in a deep breath and followed Dr. Michelan back into the room.

"I'll be there in just a moment, my love," Jonathan called after her. He waited for her to be out of earshot before losing the serenity in his tone and replacing it with a harsh intensity. "What happened out there, Glaron? How did he get back here?"

"I don't know," Glaron replied, his fingers pushing against his temples. "He's got to have a portal somewhere."

"There's only one portal left," Jonathan replied.

"Surely, you're not accusing Lortu of . . . ."

Jonathan's usually handsome face bore an unbecoming scowl. "Who else, Glaron? Why do you think Lortu disappeared as soon as Grayden showed up, and then conveniently stopped us at the stairs? To slow us down, perhaps? He laughed at us, Glaron! He didn't seem to be chasing after them; he was running with them. It would be nothing for Lortu to convince a Squanki to open a portal on the palace steps; Squanki are terrified of Dwellers. Besides, what part of the Sybran did they seem to be heading for?"

"The Bogs," Glaron conceded, "but Lortu has always made it pretty clear that he despises Ryannon. Why would he *ever* help him?"

"Ryannon's no boy scout," Jonathan retorted, "he knows what entices a Dweller . . . especially Lortu. He's offered him some sort of power or dominion over something that he knew Lortu couldn't resist." Jonathan paused for a moment and then added in a low voice, "Lortu is now our enemy, Glaron; I want him found. Statlen is already looking. Find him and tell him to double . . . no, triple his efforts. Don't stop looking until that Dweller is found."

"Yes, sir," Glaron sighed, far from convinced that Lortu would have turned so quickly against them.

"You oversee things. I'm not sure if Statlen fully understands how important it is to find him. I need to go check in on Kahlie and then I'll come find you." Jonathan started toward the doors, but then stopped and turned back toward Glaron. "I've never seen a vritesse become completely powerless before, have you?" he muttered. "It's strange. Her powers worked just fine when she sent Grayden flying and used her eyes against that Lique woman. What changed in those few minutes?"

"Uh, Jonathan?" Glaron fumbled, "I . . . I don't think it was Kahlie; I think that was me."

"What? What're you talking about? It happened right when she showed up."

"I know. But she looked at me . . . I could hear her voice in my head telling me what to do. I felt strange all of a sudden and extremely powerful. There was this weird burning sensation in my eyes . . . I just concentrated and visualized it. That's when it happened. That's when Grayden went flying and Lique . . . well . . . you know."

Jonathan contemplated Glaron's words for a moment. "Vritesses have been known to transfer powers briefly to another Trysta, but it's rare. Maybe she was able to do that with you. I wonder if that's what's going on with her now. I'll go discuss it with her and Michel . . . ."

Jonathan suddenly stopped dead in his tracks. From where he stood he had a clear view of the portion of the field that had been on fire.

"What is it?" Glaron asked, following his gaze.

"What the devil . . ? Jonathan breathed and walked over to the edge of the balcony. "What's he playing at?"

Below them, the blackened field still smoked and appeared to be smoldering in spots. Only now, upon closer observation, Glaron and Jonathan could see that the places that were still crackling with orange cinders were spelling out a message. The atoc took a step backward so he could view the entire area again. "Nice try, Atoc," he read aloud. "It's your daughter this time, by herself, or the blood of billions — including hers — will be on your hands."

Glaron could see panic building in Jonathan's eyes. "Come on, Jonathan. He knows Audril is immortal. He's just trying to scare you into doing something stupid. He knows he can't hurt her . . . he's already tried, remember?"

"Ryannon's no fool, Glaron. He obviously knows something we don't," Jonathan seethed. His terrified eyes seemed to stare right through to Glaron's soul. He turned and marched back toward the infirmary and barked, "Find Lortu, General . . . NOW!

Chapter XX

GUARDS OF THE DEAD

"Maggie? Hey, come on . . . ." Dallin chuckled as he gently shook Maggie's unconscious form which was sprawled across one of the big sofas in the News Room.

"I didn't thiiink I would scare herrrrr so baddddly," Hodgson's eerie voice moaned from somewhere behind him.

"Oh, she'll be all right," Dallin assured. "She hasn't slept much the last few days . . . it's made her jumpy, that's all. I'm bettin' she's enjoyin' the rest."

Just then, Audril, whose arm and a leg were flopped off the side of the couch, began to stir, which caused her to lose her balance, and sent her to the floor with a thud. "HEY!" she shrieked, supposing that she had been shoved, and not that gravity was her true enemy.

At that moment, Teedee, who had left the room a few moments earlier to go get "something", scuttled into the room with a deep purple towel draped over her shoulder and carrying a different, larger cup than the one she'd had earlier. She shuffled across the room in a direct beeline to Audril and promptly flung the contents of the cup — freezing cold ice water — into Audril's face.

The strangest high-pitched screech, somewhere between tires squealing in the distance and a wrenching hiccup blasted from Audril's gaping lips. Her wide-open eyes adequately expressed both her outrage, and her lack of breath caused by the face full of frigid water. "Wh . . . what was that about?" she squealed, jumping to her feet and violently flipping the water from her hair. "First you lock me in the basement and then you try to drown me? What is wrong with you, lady?"

Teedee ignored the tirade and maneuvered around Audril to the sofa, where, with the purple towel from her shoulder, she started dabbing at the few spots of water that had splashed onto the upholstery. After she finished, she casually held the towel out to Audril.

"No, thank you!" Audril snipped.

"Suit yourself. If you want to stand there all soaking wet, what's it to me, Toots?"

Audril opened her mouth to retaliate, but in her state of shock, she couldn't even squeak anything out.

Dallin, who watched the whole scene unfold while fighting back the laughter threatening to explode out of him, sniggered a bit under his breath and then took Audril's arm and guided her to another of the couches.

"Did you . . . ? She just . . .? What the . . . ? Aren't you . . . ?" she rambled, periodically glancing back at Teedee and pointing with her free arm.

"Shhh, it's okay," Dallin soothed. He leaned closer to her dripping curls and whispered, "I'm sure she was tryin' to help. She's just got her own way of doin' things."

Audril's initial urge was to fling a bitter insult loudly across the room, but the sudden twinge of near-gratitude that she was no longer trapped in the cellar with the freaky phantom-butler-slash-fiancé surfaced, keeping her from abandoning all tact for the moment. "Her own way of doing things, Dallin? She's insane," she breathed in response.

"Yeah, well you gotta admit, some of the best people we know aren't exactly what you'd call normal," he teased. "Besides, I think Hodgson can really help us out. Did you know that he's related to Lortu?"

"H . . . Hodgson?" Audril slapped her hands over her eyes at the mention of his name. "No . . . I didn't know that. We, uh . . . we really didn't have time for much of a conversation." A faint hint of an embarrassed smile played across her mouth as she peered at Dallin through her fingers. "Man, I feel like such an idiot," she chuckled.

Dallin took this as a sign to unleash what he'd been holding back. "Yeah, I know," he snickered. "I can't believe that a Shadow Dweller, or um, a Dark Watcher . . . that's what they call 'em here . . . made you pass out! We have 'em all over the place back home, but one talks to you here and you're out like a Smytle bug!" The laughter he had been fighting so hard to contain was now rolling out of him in uncontrollable waves.

"Okay, first," Audril snapped, "I've lived *here* most of my life and I'd never even heard of a Dweller until, like, a month ago! Second, I was locked in a creepy, dark basement, and third," she paused long enough to slap him across the shoulder, "I have no idea what a Smytle bug is!"

Her scolding did nothing to subdue Dallin. In fact, now Teedee was giggling and snorting right along with him. Within a few seconds, their laughs escalated to a point of infectiousness that Audril could no longer resist. She shook her head and surrendered into a carefree chortle of her own — carefree, until a low, grumbling "Huuuuhhhh, huuuuuhhhh, huuuuuhhhh," scratched through the air right next to her.

"WAIT!" she yelped loudly, causing an immediate hush to fall over the room.

Dallin and Teedee stared at her like concerned parents. "What are you fussin' about now?" Teedee sighed. "Grey hairs, Toots . . . I'm tellin' ya . . . grey hairs."

"How am I supposed to talk to this Hodgson guy, or, I dunno, realize he's standing right next to me, if I can't see him?" Audril asked in exasperation.

"Wouuuuld you liiiiike meeee tooo tapppp you onnn the shouldddderrr next tiiiiime?" Hodgson growled with a hint of joviality.

"Uh . . . no thanks," Audril whimpered in the general direction from which the voice had come.

"Verrrrrryyyy welllll," Hodgson replied. For a split second, Audril thought she caught a glimpse of him — or at least his inky black shadow — out of the corner of her eye. "We mussssst hurrrrrry then. Ryannnnonnn willll be returniiiing to Earth veryyyy sooooon. We must gatherrrrr the othersss to helllp."

"The others?" Audril breathed to herself; she had to know, but was afraid to ask. The small, twisting ache in the center of her soul echoed the answer over and over again, but she had to hear it out loud from someone else. "Hodgson?" she began with trepidation, "are these others . . . by any chance . . . members of the Solom Clan, or Mikil Tu Shadow?"

There was a long silence that felt like an eternity to Audril. Finally, Hodgson's low, droning voice answered, "They diiiied with honor, Misssss."

Audril's face paled instantly and she fell backwards onto the sofa and dropped her face to her knees. Dallin sat down at her side and draped his arm over her back. "It's all my fault," she muttered through sobs.

"No, Maggs," he corrected, "None of this is your fault. This is *all* Ryannon's fault. He killed Mikil and the Solom; he destroyed those towns . . . your town; he abducted Tabbit; declared war against Mandela City; killed your mom; killed his own father, and his own mother!" Teedee gasped as Dallin recounted Ryannon's terrors. "He's murdered thousands of innocent people and now it's up to us to stop him. You've gotta be brave . . . you've got to be strong."

"Heee is right, Missss. If you give up nowwwww, Ryannnnonnn winsss. If you fiiiight with ussss, all of those losssst willll not have givennn their livesssss in vainnnnn."

Audril gulped hard and sat up, focusing on where she assumed Hodgson was. She wiped her eyes with the back of one hand and asked, "How? I mean, how can we stop him? Even if we find him, no one knows where he's planning on striking next!"

"And thaaaat is why we neeeeed helllp," Hodgson droned from pretty close to where Audril was gazing.

"Whatta we need to do?" Dallin asked. "Just tell us."

Hodgson sped to the door and leaned out into the hall — or at least that was what it looked like. This time, both Dallin and Audril caught a quick glimpse of a black mass moving with incredible speed across the room and into the doorway. "One of my fellow Darrrk Watcherrrrs, Trebor, willlll be here shortly. He and I willl briiiing you to the others. We will travel to The Rock aaaand convince them to helllp us."

"The Rock?" Audril inquired. "What's that?"

"Reallllly, Atoh?" Hodgson replied, startling both her and Dallin with his formal — and accurate — address.

"Eh hem?" Teedee cleared her throat. "Maggie, Audrey, A toe? Why, this young lady has more nicknames than a coffeepot has handles!"

Dallin grimaced and looked at her with his head cocked to one side, wondering if anyone else found her statement odd, but then he shook it off when he realized who he was looking at, and that nothing Teedee Venilworth said should ever come as a surprise.

Another almost undetectable blur of black raced back toward them as Hodgson returned and explained, "I'mmmm surprised you would asssssskkk, Missss. You should know of the Rock. You did your finalllll sixxxth grade project onnnn it."

"What?" Audril gasped, unsure what was more alarming: the proposition of visiting the Rock, or the fact that Hodgson knew the subject of her sixth grade project. "Wait a minute! You're not saying that we . . . but it's clear across the country! We don't have time!"

"With Trebor's hellllp we cannn get there quickly, and that is where my brotherrrrs live," Hodgson answered. "They keeeep the badddd ones . . . the criminalllls who used to resiiiide there . . . from escaaaaping. They are the Guardddds of the Dead."

"What is he talking about?" Dallin asked nervously. This rock place was sounding less and less appealing by the second.

Audril paced from one side of the room to the other. "Guards of the Dead? Great! He's talking about Alcatraz," she groaned. "Alcatraz Penitentiary . . . apparently we're taking a vacation to an old . . . reportedly haunted . . . inescapable prison in San Francisco."

Dallin stared at her.

Another wisp of black shot from the armoire nearest the door before vanishing into thin air. "Ahhhh," Hodgson snarled, "Herrrrrre's Trebor nowwww."

Chapter XXI

THE GHOSTS AT THE ROCK

Trebor's voice came as a nice surprise to Audril; it wasn't low and scratchy, excessively drawn out, or thick with any sort of strange accent like the voices of the other Dwellers she'd met. It sounded like a normal American man's voice. "Hello, young lady," he greeted warmly, "I hope I haven't startled you."

"Oh . . . no," she responded with a giggle, "I'm starting to get used to not seeing who I'm talking to."

Trebor chuckled as Teedee shook her jingling head side to side. "Okay, Mr. Trebor," she scolded, "enough chitty-chatty. These young folks have to get themselves moving."

"Why, of course, Ms. Venilworth, please forgive me," he replied without the slightest hint of resentment. Audril found his voice soothing; something about the manner in which he spoke reminded her of the romantic heroes in the old black and white movies she and Bridgette would sit around watching on Sunday afternoons.

"Hodgson," Trebor began, "would you prefer me to escort Miss Baker or Mr. Doone?"

"I thinkkk your size is bettterrr suited to carrrrying Dallinnnn, wouldn't you agggreee, my frienddd?"

Twenty-One

Audril heard what sounded like a vigorous pat on a shoulder. She looked sideways at Dallin who smiled and gave her a playful wink.

"Excuuuuuse me, Atoh." Audril felt long arms wrap around her legs just above her knees and the all too familiar sensation of being hoisted onto a Shadow Dweller's back; only this time there was one distinct difference — the smell of a clean, masculine soap or cologne rather than dirt and sweat. It reminded her of how her dad smelled in the mornings after showering. The smell eased her nerves somewhat, although she was still freaked out by Hodgson. Again, she looked to Dallin for consolation. She let out a nervous giggle upon seeing him floating in what looked like mid-air.

Dallin smiled again, but his smile was different this time. There was intensity in his eyes, an intensity that made Audril feel all at once weak. "Don't worry," he assured without breaking his captivating stare, "I won't let anything happen to you."

"Norrrrr willll I."

"Nor I." Trebor must have straightened up as he spoke; Dallin shifted and suddenly appeared to be standing upright a couple of feet off the ground. "Now, on the count of three, you will both need to hold your breath for a moment. The initial take off can be a bit overwhelming for humans, but I assure you that once we reach traveling speed, you should find the remainder of the journey most agreeable." Trebor paused to wish Teedee a pleasant afternoon and then began to count. "One . . . two . . . three!"

Audril and Dallin sucked in huge gulps of air. All at once Teedee's News Room vanished with a pop. Wind raced through their hair as they moved with amazing speed down a long, greenish corridor. The corridor began to twist and spin into a dizzying, spiraling ripple before transforming itself into a magnificent arched tunnel of thick-trunked trees, each covered with plentiful white blossoms.

"Youuuu cannnn breathe now," Hodgson instructed, his voice unwavering as if he were standing completely still.

195

"C . . . can I?" Audril gasped, finding it difficult to let air flow freely in and out of her lungs due to the beauty and magical quality of her surroundings. "This has been here . . . on Earth? For how long?" Her voice, too, was remarkably steady and clear.

"Hundreds of years," Trebor replied. "Our people discovered the vast dimensions of this planet nearly a thousand years ago. You see, *some* of the Dark Watchers need not travel in shadow as our brothers on Lor Mandela do. It is in this way that Watchers like Hodgson and I stay hidden nearly all of the time."

"So we're moving in another dimension?" Dallin asked.

"It's somewhat complicated to explain," Trebor replied. "We are not really moving at all, rather the dimension is moving through us. The tunnel is under the control of our thoughts, yet it is as real as you and me. Hodgson and I are collectively commanding the dimension to move through the four of us, refracting the angle of the dimension, and bending it toward our destination. Now, when Alcatraz comes near — in about four minutes — we simply need hold our breaths again, and this dimension will freeze in time, and be waiting for us when we are ready to go back."

"Four minutes?" Dallin gaped.

"Yessss, this is the fastest mode of transsssportation known to Dwellllers."

"Man, I guess," Dallin agreed.

"You said that only *some* of your people can do this?" Audril quizzed. "What about the rest of them?"

"There are other dimensions in which they can travel, but none as secretive . . . or as rapid. I, myself, used to move in those other dimensions . . . we call them the Secondaries, and this one is called Light. A few years ago, I became so weary of being spotted by tour groups and the others who toured Alcatraz that I forced myself to learn how to access the Light Dimension."

"Somethinggggggg no other Dwelllller has beeeeen able to dooooo beforrrre or sinnnnnce," Hodgson interjected.

Trebor chuckled and the ensuing thud told Audril, that again, one of the two of them had been thumped on the shoulder by the other. "You misrepresent me, my friend," Trebor modestly replied. "It was you who explained the process in terms which I could understand. Once I fully grasped the physics and the logistics, entering the dimension itself became the easy part."

"Anddd stillll, there has beennnn none otherrr . . . not gifteddd with the skillll at birth . . . able to figurrrre it outtt . . . with or withouttt my instructionnns. Trebor, my friends, is ourrrr mosssst intelligent ally."

"Would you like to see what it is like for yourself, Master Doone?" Trebor asked, seeming ill at ease with Hodgson's compliments.

"See what?"

"How it feels to travel as a Dark Watcher on Earth. I can show you, but you must remain in contact with me at all times or we may accidentally leave you behind."

"I want to try too," Audril whined.

"But of course, Your Majesty," Trebor obliged. "First, you both must reach your right arms straight out in front of yourselves. You'll have to grip tighter with your left arm and legs to avoid slipping off. When you feel Hodgson and I grip your wrists, just relax everything. You'll seem to be flying wildly through the air like a sparrow for a moment, but then we will lower you safely to the ground."

"How will we know when you've gripped our wrists?" Dallin asked tentatively.

"You willllll knooooow," Hodgson sniggered. "Ready? NOW!"

Audril thrust her arm forward and tightened the muscles in her legs. Within a split second, an uncomfortable coldness constricted painfully around her wrist — as though a tight cuff of rock hard ice had frozen and contracted around it. She shut her eyes and made a concerted effort to relax, but it was becoming increasingly difficult with Hodgson bearing down his icy hand. She forced a deep breath, and as she did, she was jerked violently into the air, whirling around like an out of control kite.

The trees raced by faster and faster, turning in on themselves, forming a ferocious vortex all around her. Occasionally, she would catch a blurred glimpse of Dallin whizzing by in the twisting trees. He seemed oddly contorted and disfigured; a twinge of self-consciousness flooded through her, knowing that she likely looked the same to him. The wind intensified, pushing and pulling her in every direction, forcing a silent scream from her lips as her arms and legs simultaneously felt like they were about to be ripped from the trunk of her body. Intense pressure pushed down on both the inside and the outside of her skull; it felt like it was mere seconds away from exploding.

All of a sudden, she dropped fast, like she was falling into a deep hole — a still, silent, amazingly peaceful and bright hole. Hodgson's grip became warm and gentle as she drifted slowly to the ground, landing effortlessly on her feet. Dallin stood inches in front of her, looking into her eyes, and even with the disoriented expression on his face, he was suddenly the most stunning man she'd ever set eyes on. Behind him, the brown, white and green blur of trees glowed, adding a mystical romance to the moment.

"Wh . . . where are we?" she mumbled as she grew more lost in Dallin's rich brown eyes.

"You are in the epicenter of the dimension," Trebor replied. "Have you noticed that we are not moving . . . that it is our surroundings?"

"Uh-huh," Audril nodded distractedly.

"Now, listen," Trebor advised, "There is only one rule in here. Do not touch the trees, or you'll be pulled into the funnel and likely be killed. Don't worry, though; as long as Hodgson and I keep a hold of you, you will be perfectly safe."

Neither Dallin nor Audril seemed at all worried about being sucked into the tornado swirling around them — or even aware that either of these Dark Watchers still had a hold of them. They were completely mesmerized by each other.

Twenty-One

"Loooook upppp," Hodgson offered.

It took a moment or two, but eventually they did as instructed, and turned their eyes skyward. It took Dallin a little longer, though; he didn't want to look away from Audril, not even for a second. At the top of the cyclone, tiny glittering specks in every color imaginable drifted in and out of sunlight. Small birds twittered and danced on the flecks of light. It was spectacular, more glorious than Audril could've possibly imagined.

"Is this what it's like to be in the eye of a tornado?" she asked breathlessly.

Neither Hodgson nor Trebor answered.

Dallin lowered his gaze and looked back into her stunning cobalt eyes. "No, it's like being in paradise," he whispered. "Audril . . . it was you . . . how could I have missed it?" He ran the back of his free hand gently down her cheek. "I've had guilt about feelin' like this since the first time I saw you! But I . . . I misunderstood. It was *actually* you the whole time!"

"Wh . . . what are you talking about?" she muttered as Dallin moved closer and placed his forehead against hers. His warm breath caressed her suddenly flushing cheek.

"It was you the whole time," he repeated. "Oh, my angelic Audril! I thought I loved . . . I mean . . . ." His breath caught in his chest as he whispered. "It was you . . . I love *you*." He smiled and slid a few strands of hair back from her face. "That explains these gorgeous curls."

Slowly, he tilted his head and touched his lips to hers sending an irrepressible shudder quaking through her body.

She retracted a bit at first, shocked, and not knowing how to react, but then, longing — a fiery and inescapable longing — flooded over her. She looked into his eyes, lifted her chin upward, and pressed her slightly open mouth to his.

As their lips met, a wave of scintillating heat surged to her core. She whimpered as Dallin's free hand traced down her arm and around her waist to the small of her back. With a sudden heave, he pulled her more tightly against him, meshing their bodies perfectly and harmoniously together.

Audril melted into ecstasy, and the world faded, and would have stayed far, far from them, had Lortu's warning not begun to replay inside her head

"Eef you allow yoah relationship wit Dallin Doone to go any furter on de Drolana, Ryannon of Brashnell weel find out, and Dallin Doone weel not live to see dis Lor Mandela again."

She wanted to pull back — she had to pull back — but she couldn't. Wave after warm wave of passionate emotion washed over her, breaking any will she had to resist. She loved Dallin Doone; she loved him with every fiber of her being and never wanted to be without him, from this moment and into the eternities.

As she pressed her lips tighter to his, Lortu and his ridiculous warning slid out of her consciousness. Ryannon couldn't possibly find out — they were so well hidden — and in an entirely different dimension. There would be no chance of him knowing — no chance at all..

"Pardon me, Atoh," Trebor's voice quietly interrupted after several blissful seconds. "We've arrived at our destination."

Dallin groaned and slowly backed away but he and Audril continued to look into each other's eyes for as long as they could.

"Deep breath," Trebor reminded as the tornado of trees vanished with a jolt.

Audril became a little disoriented with the abrupt change and tripped over her own feet, but Dallin was there to catch her. He flashed another smile, which instantly turned her legs to rubber, almost causing her to stumble again.

"Mmmm hmmm," she mumbled, pulling away and straightening her hair. Even her imagination couldn't chase away the fact that she and Dallin would be vulnerable to Ryannon now. "I'm sorry, Dallin" she blurted looking down at her feet. "I don't know what came over me in there. We should be focused on finding help right now. This is not appropriate behavior for the atoh, especially considering our mission."

It nearly broke her heart to watch Dallin's expression plummet.

"But . . . but, I just . . . ." he stammered

"Trebor . . . Hodgson?" she interrupted with a discernable blush gracing her cheeks. "Where are these other Dark Watchers?"

As her gaze shifted outward, she observed the stark contrast from the heaven in which they had just been, to where they now stood. Darkness; old dirty paint flaking from the horribly colored mint green and ivory walls; a thick acrid odor; and metal bars running the length of the seemingly unending corridors — it was everything she imagined Alcatraz to be except for one thing — the wave of emotions. Overwhelming feelings of anger and sadness, of fear and bitterness, all mixed with her own anxiety of having to keep Dallin at arm's length. The sensations permeated the air as though they were trying to blanket the oxygen. These feelings had weight to them — a density. It was something Audril had never experienced before, and she was quite anxious to stop experiencing it as soon as possible. If the Light Dimension was — as Dallin put it — like being in paradise, the interior of Alcatraz was its purgatorial opposite.

"Thissss way," Hodgson hissed as he pressed his hand firmly against Audril's back. "Trebor . . . you and Dalllllin come behind ussss. Make surrrre we arrrrre not follllowed by any of the ghosssstsssss."

"Oh, awesome," Audril gasped under her breath. Hodgson's cold hand moved from her back, down her arm, and to her wrist, where again, he took hold with amazing strength. "Let'sssss go!" he growled, and with a jolt they started to run — almost faster than Audril was able.

"Relaxxx," he demanded, "and stopppp trying to runnn!"

"But I can't run like. . . ."

"Jusssst stopppp moving yourrrrr feeeeeet!"

She squeezed her eyes shut and braced for the crash that was sure to follow if she stopped at this pace, but no crash came. Instead, her legs flew up backwards from underneath her, pulling her body parallel to the floor.

When she opened her eyes, she was flying along rapidly, about a foot and a half off the ground. She looked down and noticed that the tips of her hair were dragging along the dingy floor.

"Ugghh!" she groaned and tried to lift her curls with her free arm, but Hodgson scolded her sharply, saying that she was going to throw him off balance.

As they raced past cell after cell, more black forms darted out of the shadows toward them with amazing speed. Audril flinched more than once as a shadow bulleted straight at her.

"Don'tttt worrrry," Hodgson assured. "They won'ttt hittt you." His tone was a bit softer than before, but still gave the distinct impression that he was ordering her to stop fidgeting.

Behind them, Trebor occasionally shouted out something that sounded like "Harkara!" and there would be a thud or a crash, followed by the echoing slam of a cell door. Audril assumed that he was using some kind of spell to command the "ghosts" back into their cells — an assumption which was not at all settling.

"We'll meet in D thirrrrteeeen," Hodgson bellowed. "Tell the others, Marlas . . . and hurry!"

Audril craned her head over her shoulder to see who Marlas was. Behind them, a huge mass of black, an ominous and terrifying presence rolled in waves. The cells were blocked from view; the hall was blocked from view. There was no sign of Dallin or of anyone else — nothing but a dense fog of darkness consuming every inch of the hall — and it seemed to be gaining on them. Audril gasped and quickly turned back around.

One quick corner followed by another, and she and Hodgson stopped suddenly inside a closet-sized room. Her feet hit the floor with a thud and she tumbled onto her backside. "Ouch!" she groaned as Hodgson's icy hands grabbed her upper arms and hoisted her from the ground. Before she could regain her full footing, the room became black — darker than the blackness of a starless, moonless night; darker, it seemed, than the black mass she'd seen following them. She could hear rustling all around her and feel small, unsettling blasts of breath moving through her hair and down her neck, but she could see nothing.

"Mr. Doone, Atoh," Trebor's voice cut through the thickness. "Are you both all right?"

"I am," Dallin answered, "Audril?"

"Yeah . . . I guess so," she mumbled.

"This is crazy isn't it?" Dallin laughed.

Audril didn't answer.

"Excellent, now that we've determined that everyone is as right as rain, can we hurry this up?" A female voice snipped. "There's an investigation team over in Broadway, and who knows when they'll be here to set up their equipment. Especially with all the racket you caused coming in!"

"Thank you, Marlas," Trebor replied. "To the issue at hand then. Does anyone have any new information regarding Ryannon of Brashnell?"

One of the Watchers, with a voice similar to Glaron's, responded. "He's back from Lor Mandela, and still holds the small Squanki as his hostage. He is forcing her to open portals, and we can only assume that he plans to use her as some sort of bargaining tool for the atoh."

"Is she all right?" Audril blurted. "If that monster's hurt her, so help me, I'll . . . ."

"Her physical condition is stable now, but she has fallen into some sort of disoriented stupor. She keeps repeating the same thing over and over again."

"What is it? What is she mumbling?" Trebor asked.

"She says, 'Squankis don't tells, lady comes backs, return the powers and four hundred days.' Does this mean anything to either of you Lor Mandelans?"

"A Trinkle Trance!" Dallin exclaimed, sounding and looking like a kid on Christmas morning, which seemed all too befitting of a name like Trinkle Trance. "She's trying to tell us somethin'!"

"Tell usssss somethingggg?" Hodgson questioned.

"Yeah," Dallin answered. "Squanki are famous for giving hints like that. She's fine! Don't you see? We've gotta get to her as soon as possible! She knows something important! They only do it when something critical is about to happen! It's probably somethin' that'll help us bring Ryannon down! Where is she? I'm tellin' ya! Tabbit knows how to put an end to all of this!"

"They are hiding in an abandoned saw mill in Northeast Iowa. You'd be best to return to Ms. Venilworth's and coordinate your efforts from there. We will provide you with the exact location."

"Verrrry welllll," Hodgson agreed. "Marlas, can you spare approximatelyyyy one hunnnndredddd Watchers?"

For the first time Marlas didn't sound bitter when she spoke. "Of course, sir. This is our slow time of year, and it will give us a little more room to move around here. Take the Infirmary team. There are one hundred and three of them."

All of a sudden, the air in the room started swirling and became bitterly cold. Several of the Dark Watchers cried out, "Harkara!" and the twisting chill shot from the room in an instant, and three of the big iron doors somewhere down the hall crashed shut.

"Ohhhh . . . that was a mistake," Marlas sighed under her breath, her cynical attitude appearing to have returned.

"Did you SEE that?" A woman's voice cried from outside of the room.

"All three of those doors slammed at once!" another woman exclaimed.

Marlas, who must have moved very near Audril, whispered, "Ghost hunters! Stay perfectly still! They won't be able to see you through us."

As the women ran by, they yelled into walkie-talkies, overlapping each other's sentences. "No! We're in D Block!"

"Right! Sherry said she saw a shadow and . . . !"

"Three cell doors . . . all at once!"

"I think we should get a thermal and a camera over here? Quickly! I'm heading down . . . ."

When the last of the investigator's voices trailed off into the distance, Hodgson whispered, "Infirrrmary team, come withhhh meeee. Trebor, pleassse make sure that ourr guestssss remain surrrrounded."

"Have a safe journey," Marlas breathed quietly.

Twenty-One

"Thank you for your help, dear Marlas," Trebor replied as Audril and Dallin suddenly became visible to each other in the center of a ring of black.

Once again, an icy grip enveloped their wrists. "All right ,Atoh. Mr. Doone, just relax like you did before," Trebor instructed. You may feel others of us on your ankles or shoulders, but be assured it is only to keep you hidden from the paranormal investigation team. We'll be back to the Light Dimension shortly."

As the group moved silently down the hall there was no sign of any of the investigators anywhere. Audril and Dallin floated along side by side, surrounded by blackness. Dallin smiled, enjoying both the company and the adventure.

All at once, the collective of the Guards of the Dead came to an unexpected halt and Audril and Dallin's feet thudded with some force against the cement floor.

"Whoa! What was that?" a startled male voice exclaimed from what seemed just inches away.

"What? Did you see something?" another answered with the same excited tone.

"Yeah, on the thermal . . . look, it's still there, only it is more vertical now."

"What the . . . ?" The second person's voice fell off; Audril watched as the group of Dwellers inched in more tightly around her and Dallin.

"Don'ttttt mooooove," Hodgson whispered, but luckily the ghost hunters didn't seem to hear him.

Audril and Dallin stood like statues, unable to see why they should, but somewhat understanding the importance of doing so.

"Crap! It's gone . . . it just vanished . . . did you see that?" one of the investigators shouted.

"Is anyone here with us?" the other asked.

"Central command, this is Sean and Pete. We just had some interesting hits on the thermal." The static of two-way radios filled a momentary silence.

"Awesome," a female voice responded. "Hey Pete, from over here it looks like there's something blocking the light from the camera to your left. Can you see anything?"

"Negative . . . wait!"

Inside the circle of black shadow people, the ends of human fingertips pushed through the black and swooshed by in front of Audril.

"I'm getting a definite cold spot right in front of me!" Audril assumed this voice to belong to Sean. "Hey, Sherry . . . we're going to try to do some EVP work."

"Roger that," Sherry replied. "Mike wants you to try the K2 also."

"Will do."

A moment later, a strange little device poked through the circle of Watchers, and pointed at a very awkward area of Dallin's anatomy. Audril slapped her hand over her mouth to stifle a giggle. Dallin sucked in his mid-section and tried to back away, but the group of Watchers were so tight against him that there was nowhere for him to go.

"Hello . . . my name is Sean and this is my friend Peter."

"Hello," Peter echoed. "We're not here to harm you or try to make you leave or anything; we just want to communicate with you or possibly help if we can."

"This device is something we have used in the past to communicate with people like you. Can you light up the lights on it for us? Just move in front of it."

A snigger escaped through Audril's fingers — not only at the hilarity of Sean's request, but also at the look of sheer terror on Dallin's face as the device moved further into the circle, threatening to become his intimate, personal friend. Dallin was growing increasingly agitated at the little gadget violating his personal space and didn't think it at all nice of Audril to be laughing. "This is ridiculous," he hissed, grabbing the K2 meter and jerking it forcefully out of the investigator's hand.

”MY K2!” Sean shrieked. “DID YOU SEE THAT? DUDE! SOMETHING JUST TOOK MY K2!

“SERIOUSLY?” Pete gasped. “DUDE, WHERE’D IT GO?”

“Pete! Sean! Over here!” Audril recognized the voice as one of the women from before; she was shouting from a fair distance away. “Things are going nuts in the Citadel! Mike wants us all down there now! Hurry!”

“Things are going nuts up here, too!” Pete replied. “Something just took Sean’s K2 . . . it just disappeared.”

“Well, c’mon then!” the woman insisted. “We need to tell the others about this.”

Her proclamation was followed by the sound of footsteps running away. Hodgson groaned, “We can’ttttt afffffforddd any morrrrre mistaaaakes like thatttt one Mrrrrr. Dooooone!”

Dallin’s face was nearly purple with embarrassment, and Audril was biting her lower lip, still struggling to hold in her laughter.

“Light Travelllerrrrs, follow meeee. Secondarieeeees, you’re with Trebor. “GO!”

Audril held out her arm and waited for a frigid grip on her wrist, but as the black fog around her dissipated, none came. Quite suddenly, she found herself standing alone in a long corridor with neither Dallin nor any of the Guards of the Dead anywhere in sight; the supposed missing K2 meter was lying at her feet.

One of the investigators running toward the opposite end of the hall just happened to glance over his shoulder and froze dead in his tracks. “Oh my heav . . . STOP!” He flailed his arms wildly capturing the attention of others with him. All of them, four in all, paused and slowly turned around. Their eyes grew wide as they stared at Audril like deer caught in oncoming headlights. She, herself, stood paralyzed, gazing at them with a similarly stunned expression. She didn’t know what to do or where to run.

One of the men, obviously part of the team's filming crew, raised a large camera to his shoulder. At that instant, a dark shadow lunged between his clear shot and Audril.

"Bumbling brood of misfits . . . every last one of them!" Trebor's voice came as a relief. "Are you all right, Atoh? I apologize for the ineptitude of my colleagues."

"I'm sure glad to *not* see you!" Audril shakily quipped.

From the crew at the end of the hall, shouts could be heard of "Full-body apparition," and "she just vanished," and "not sure if the camera caught it."

"Back slowly around this corner," Trebor instructed. "I'll keep myself in front of you so they won't see you again. Just move very slowly."

Audril inched one foot backward, paused, and then moved the other. "Is this okay?" she whispered.

"Perfect," Trebor breathed in response. "Now . . . as soon as we're out of their line of sight, be ready for me to take your wrist. We won't be able to return to the Light Dimension just yet. We must wait until they move their investigations to cell block A, but I know a place where we should be protected, at least for the time being."

Once Trebor and Audril were safely around the corner, the welcome, yet unpleasantly chilling bite of Trebor's freezing hand grasped Audril's wrist and they took flight through the halls of Alcatraz.

They stopped in the last place Audril would have expected. It was a place familiar to her from her sixth grade studies. "We're in the Birdman's cell," she muttered, "I studied him for my report."

"Yes, he's such a brilliant and misunderstood soul," Trebor responded. "He was labeled a disruptive prisoner . . . that's why they supposedly brought him here. But many things happened in his life . . . many unfair things . . . that is what caused him to have the bouts of anger that would surface from time to time. He's actually been a perfect gentleman the whole time I've known him."

"You know him?" Audril gasped. "Is he still here?"

"Yes, he is," Trebor replied.

"Wow," Audril breathed, "why do these people hang around here after they're dead? I would think they would finally want to be out of prison."

"They do, but they aren't given that choice. Well, I mean they're given ways to do it, but it's pretty close to impossible to get out once you've been sentenced. Take Mr. Stroud here, all he wants is to be with his birds. He was the happiest of his life at Leavenworth when he was studying and breeding those birds." Trebor's voice noticeably saddened. "Here . . . it wasn't allowed."

"You know, at first, I thought he was just a victim of his circumstances," Audril interjected. "The entire cosmos seemed to be against the poor guy. But then I wondered, why did he stab that other guy, or kill that guard?" She walked over to the outer cell door and ran her hand down the cold iron. "And why did they have to strengthen these doors to his cell? I read that he would try to grab at people through the bars . . . creepy."

There was a long silence. "Have you ever wondered what it must have been like for him, Atoh? Being beaten by his father . . . forced to leave home at just thirteen . . . coming home from work one morning at only eighteen years of age to find his only friend beaten, raped and robbed? He had to kill that Charlie, ya know. It was the only way to get back what was stolen. When he turned himself and the gun into the police they didn't understand though . . . nobody did. They made up this ridiculous story that he knocked Charlie unconscious and then killed him in cold blood.

"While he was at Leavenworth, he made such breakthroughs with his birds; he was trying to straighten out his life, but the warden was down on him and took everything away, at least everything he could under the corrupt umbrella of the laws of the time. Eventually, everyone . . . even his own mother turned on him. He spent most of his life in prisons that were unfair and brutal, despite what the newspapers reported. It must have been hell. I'm sure he reached through those bars longing for contact, any contact . . . even negative . . . from another human being."

Audril stood listening, looking in the general direction of his voice. When he finished his account, she glanced over at the picture of "The Birdman of Alcatraz" perched on an easel in the middle of the cell. She looked at his eyes. They seemed lost and confused; she imagined what his voice would've sounded like — being from the nineteen-thirties and all. Suddenly, her heart began to race and her pulse quickened as the pieces of the puzzle all clicked together.

"Trebor," she began slowly, "that's . . . that's Robert spelled backwards." The color drained from her face. "Muh . . . Mister Stroud?" she whimpered.

"At your service, mademoiselle. See! I told Hodgson you were a smart one."

"Does . . . does he know?"

"Of course not . . . he thinks I'm one of them. I've learned how to appear like one of them, of course, by studying them like my birds." He paused momentarily. "Mmmm, my birds. The closest I've been able to come is the sparrows in the Light Dimension . . . I summoned them there myself . . . but they never come down where I can hold them. They always stay way up in that blasted light."

Audril began backing away slowly, "Wh . . . what do you want from me?" she stammered.

"Oh, don't worry, Atoh. Hodgson and the others will be here soon enough to find you."

His answer supplied a bit of relief, however, the sheer terror of being with an infamous murderer was still the dominant emotion grinding in the pit of her stomach.

"You know," Robert began, "I met a very interesting person the other day . . . probably one of the few intellectual equals I've had the pleasure of coming across. He has actually provided me a way to resume my research, even from beyond the grave. I can be with my birds again and continue my studies. Isn't that lovely?"

Audril's courage seemed to be rising by the second. "Let me guess," she tried, "this person's name wouldn't happen to be Ryannon, would it?"

"Oh, you *are* an intelligent girl," he said. "The only thing Ryannon requested of me was . . . ."

"Let me guess . . . . me?"

Robert's cold grip squeezed around her wrist again and he pulled her to the back of the cell.

She struggled, but he was brutally strong. "After you," he insisted, shoving her face-first against the back wall.

A small blue light appeared between her eyes. It expanded and made a loud popping sound as a portal opened . . . and Robert Stroud, The Birdman of Alcatraz, pushed her forcefully through it.

Chapter XXII

DALLIN'S TURN

After pushing Audril through the portal, Robert wasted no time. He rushed down the prison's corridors toward the Light Dimension, dodging undetected through the now active paranormal investigation team. He reached the entrance, took a deep breath and popped into the rapidly moving dimension. Within minutes, he arrived at Teedee's house and burst into the room where Hodgson and the other Dark Watchers were gathered.

"Do you have her?" he gasped, panting as though he'd been running for miles. "Please tell me you have her!"

"What do you mean?" Dallin blasted. "You went back to get her! Where is she? Where would she have gone? We can't leave her there! Take me back! Take me back there NOW! I'll find her myself!"

"You know . . . that may not be such a bad idea," Robert replied, playing the part of concerned comrade very well. "Dallin and I can go back to Alcatraz just to double check. My hunch, however, is that she ended up with the Watchers in the secondaries. Hodgson, perhaps you and a few others should search there. Don't worry, Dallin. I'm sure that's where we'll find her."

Dallin's feeble nod expressed both his concern and his doubt. "Fine, let's get goin' then!"

Just then, Teedee poked her head into the doorway. "Oh, hello Dallin . . . Hodgson, dear, have you seen my purple running suit?" She barely waited for an answer before adding, "Where's my little girl of many names?"

"Sheee is missing, darrrrrling," Hodgson growled. "We are on ourrrr way to findddd her now."

"Oh dear," Teedee gasped, "missing? Well then I guess I'll have to wait 'til you get back for my jog. I'll keep an eye out here, in case she shows up unexpectedly." She shuffled over to a small antique chest of drawers and picked up a pair of large, teal, pointy-rimmed glasses and slipped them on; her eyes magnified to easily three times their normal size through the thick lenses. She looked directly at Dallin with those buggy peepers and said, "Okay, you'd best be off now."

In a flash, Dallin was hoisted onto Robert's back and several wisps of black shadow moved silently, yet with amazing stealth, across the walls.

"Take a deep breath, Mr. Doone," Robert reminded as they popped into the Light Dimension. No words, and four minutes later they were back at Alcatraz.

"We'll meet in the hospital wing," Robert instructed in a hushed tone. "See that opening to the right? It's just around that corner. I heard the investigators say that they were going to the Citadel and then they were going to send a team to the infirmary. I'm assuming they'll be there soon, if they aren't already. Try to stay out of their view . . . I'll cover you best I can. If Audril is still here anywhere I'm sure they will have spotted her by now. Instead of running aimlessly through the prison, this will likely be our best way to glean the information we need."

"Shouldn't we try to find Madras and the others?" Dallin tried. "They would know if she was here, wouldn't they?"

"Don't worry, they'll find us," Robert answered. "Just head for the hospital wing and look for Robert Stroud's cell. I'll meet you there . . . and remember, keep out of sight!"

Unbeknownst to Dallin, Robert stayed very near him as he slid along walls, ducked in and out of open cells, and used the cover of the dark prison to stay hidden in the hallways. This area of the prison was oddly quiet. There was no sign of the ghost hunting team, or any other of the Dark Watchers here, although voices could be heard echoing from other sectors. It didn't take long for Dallin to find Robert Stroud's cell as it was clearly marked with a red plaque and a large photo of the infamous prisoner.

"Trebor?" Dallin whispered, "Trebor are you in here?"

Robert's reply floated out of the shadows like a deadly poison, eerily fluid and strange. "Have you ever killed a man, Dallin Doone?"

"Excuse me?"

"You haven't . . . have you?"

"What does this have to do with findin' Audril?" Dallin barked.

"It has much to do with you finding her," Robert replied in the most chilling of tones. "You see, Dallin . . . once you've killed one man, it becomes easy . . . even intoxicating to do it again . . . once a murderer, always a murderer."

A wave of terror ripped through Dallin as he assumed that — Audril's immortality notwithstanding — Trebor was admitting to killing her. He stared at the corner, wide-eyed, waiting for the confession that would destroy him.

"You cannot find Audril, because you do not think like a murderer," Robert continued. "I, on the other hand do think like one, because I *am* one."

"You son of a . . . !"

"Calm down, Mr. Doone. Your sweetie pie isn't dead," Robert interrupted.

Dallin had to fight back tears as he choked in relief.

"Do you know what I get for being brilliant and trying to make my life better, Dallin? Fifty-four years of imprisonment and no one who would listen. I lost everything and everyone I ever cared about . . . finally even my own mother turned on me. However, being a murderer still has its benefits. Other criminals respect you . . . even seek you out . . . make offers you can't refuse."

Twenty-Two

"Where is she?" Dallin seethed. "Just shut up and tell me where she is."

"Oh, I can do one better than that, my friend. I can show you."

The black figure of Robert's ghost rippled up from the ground, materializing into a black blob. He stood there for a second or two but then, with amazing speed, he blasted toward Dallin. Dallin tried to jump to the side, but wasn't fast enough; Robert crashed into, and then right through him, knocking him to the ground.

An overwhelming fear bled through every fiber of Dallin's soul as images and feelings of every tragic and horrific thing that had ever happened — or that he ever imagined might happen — flooded through him. He was completely paralyzed and freezing, helpless as Robert grabbed his feet and dragged him to the other side of the room.

Once they reached the corner where the portal was hidden, the inky shadow lifted his foot to the wall and a sliver of blue light appeared near it.

Dallin fought to push the morbid images from his mind so he could regain some control, to no avail. Robert was strong and seemed to have a link to his thoughts. If Dallin was able to muster the strength to shield one horrible image, Robert would somehow throw ten new horrific scenes into his head. Dallin laid limp and shuddering on the ground, unable to do anything, as he was dragged into the portal by the black figure of Robert. With a faint crackling, the portal flashed and expanded.

"Time to go visit your lady love, Mr. Doone, although I'm relatively sure Ryannon won't let you live long enough to spend much time with her . . . once a murderer, always a murderer." Robert gave Dallin's legs one more big tug and pulled him into the portal, which promptly collapsed and disappeared just before two of the investigators and a camera man from the paranormal team walked into the cell.

Chapter XXIII

BARGAIN FULFILLED

Traveling via Squanki portal was a surreal experience under normal circumstances. It often happened so quickly that one barely had time to realize they've moved — yet they may have been transported millions of miles between the flash and pop at the entrance and the hazy darkness shrouding the exit. This time, however, Audril was not going to go quickly and quietly if there was anything she could do to prevent it.

She knew from past experience that being inside the portal had caused her to feel claustrophobic, and hoped that there was something nearby — walls of some sort, other exits, rough spots — anything she could grab a hold of that would slow, or altogether stop her from reaching the Birdman's intended destination. She lifted her arms just a little and discovered that, in fact, there were walls within mere inches of her.

The portal grew darker and darker; she would have to hurry. She pushed hard against the walls with her elbows and felt a thick liquid material form around them.

The force of her elbows had slowed her momentum considerably. *It's working!* the voice in her head practically screamed. She dropped to the ground and quickly thrust her hands and feet into the walls with as much strength as she could muster, and with an abrupt bump, came to a full stop.

The inside of the portal was a long, lumpy tube of the most sickly shade of grayish-pink, coated in what looked like thick green mucus. "Awwrrgggh! No wonder you move through these things so fast," she gagged as she looked around. Both her hands and feet appeared to be gone — enveloped completely in the slimy goo. Fortunately, there was no foul stench, as she was sure that would likely make her vomit.

"Okay, so now what? How do I get outta here?" Slowly, she pulled her left foot out of the green gunk and immediately started moving forward again. "No!" she gasped, thrusting her foot back in. "All right . . . so not like that," she panted.

She thought for a moment, and then dug her heel in and slid her foot back towards her body. It was hard to move through the slimy stuff which had very little elasticity to it, and seemed to be resisting, as though this backwardness was simply not allowed. The slime made a vile, wet, squishing pop as her foot slid through it, causing her stomach to turn.

When her foot was back as far as she could get it — nearly against her behind — she did the same with the other foot; then she slid her right arm back and then her left. She looked a little ridiculous all scrunched up like that — kind of like a four-legged spider — but it was working so she didn't care. She pushed down as hard as she could with the balls of her feet and slid her body backwards until her arms and legs were extended again. She could feel the slurping mucus straining and struggling against her backside. "Well, this is the grossest workout I've ever done . . . vile," she cringed in disgust.

She dug in again, and was just beginning to slide her heel back, when something bizarre happened. The walls of the portal became almost transparent, and a man who was obviously a Shadow Dweller zoomed past her — or rather *through* her — passing without resistance through her right arm and leg, as though they didn't exist. Instantly, the ugly, bumpy, muck-covered walls reappeared and all was as it had been before. "Okaaayyy," she breathed, "that was weird."

Once again, she dragged her feet and arms back and then extended them as she slid backwards through the gunk. Her progress was slow, but it was progress nonetheless. After about ten of these intense back slides, the muscles in her limbs started to become less and less cooperative. They burned and, while she was pushing back, shook and quivered uncontrollably. She needed to stop and recuperate for a moment, just a little time to rest.

As she sat in the murky portal, sore and out of breath, the walls began to evaporate again. This time a fat, little Squanki swished right through her midsection. It was strange to watch it happen, and yet not feel a thing.

In less time than it took for her to blink, the Squanki stopped in his tracks, hopped in two large bounds back to her, and shoved one of his pudgy little fists into the wall of the portal — which had rematerialized. He stood there for several seconds, just staring.

"Hello?" Audril tried.

"Whats is ladys doing?" the stout miniature creature squeaked. "This is nots how you do its."

"Well, I know that! Do you suppose I'm sitting inside here for the scenery?" she scolded. "Exactly how do I get out of here?"

The Squanki widened his pinkish-green eyes and looked at her like she was completely mad. "Lets gos," he grimaced almost as if he were reprimanding her.

"I don't want to *lets gos*!" she barked. "I was pushed into this portal and there's a man waiting to kill me on the other side. I want to go back to where I came from." She could barely believe she was telling this rotund Squanki that she wanted to get back to the cheerful loveliness of Alcatraz, but it certainly beat the alternative.

The Squanki's eyes saddened. "You can'ts go backs . . . only forwards."

Spooked a bit by his comment, but convinced that she had been moving backwards already, she replied, "Thanks . . . I'll just keep doing what I've been doing then."

"You wants to keeps getting eated?" he replied with a look of horror in his eyes.

"WHAT?" Audril shrieked. "What do you mean 'eated'?"

"Portals is alive and they eats whats gets stuck in thems." He pointed to the ceiling above with his free hand and added, "See? Alive."

Audril looked up and noticed for the first time that the top of the portal was moving up and down — it was breathing! "Oh, you've got to be kidding me," she yelped. "I've gotta get out of here!"

"Only way outs is to lets gos!" With that, the Squanki pulled his fist out of the wall and zipped down toward the dark end of the portal. "Better chances of livings if you fight that mans, Atoh," he yelled back, "and don't tells the atoc abouts this portal!"

"Great," Audril snipped as she began scooting backwards more quickly than before. "He's more concerned about getting busted by Dad than saving me from this thing!" Her muscles screamed at her, but she refused to be eaten by a portal! Likewise, she refused to just let go and see what fun was awaiting her with Ryannon.

She had moved four or five times more, when a strange tingling sensation started in her toes. It was a little ticklish at first, but then began to sting — and then flat out hurt. Frantically, she tried to move faster, but the sensation was biting at her fingers now as well.

"Aaaagghhh!" she groaned as the pain traveled up her toes, into her feet and throughout her hands. She glanced back over her shoulder at the portal that stretched as far as her eyes could see. "Stop it!" she yelled. "STOP IT!" She stomped down with one foot which only resulted in a stinging twinge shooting up her leg.

Finally, she couldn't hold on any longer. She fully expected that her toes and fingers were already half gone; the pain was unbearable. Screaming in agony, she yanked her hands and feet out of the mucus and rocketed toward the end of the portal. *I have to fight . . . I have to fight!*

She blasted from the portal, and before her eyes could adjust to the light, ran full-speed ahead swinging her fists wildly. As her eyes cleared, she saw Grayden standing a few feet in front of her, watching her with amusement.

"Not recommended," he chuckled.

Audril didn't stop. She was resolved to fight! She ran at him until she was inches away, then she spun around and thrust her elbow up and backwards, nailing him right between the eyes. As he lifted his hand to his head she struck again, planting a knee firmly in his groin. He doubled over in pain, giving her the opportunity to pick up what looked like some sort of short, wooden paddle. Before he could stop groaning and straighten up, she swung the paddle down as hard as she could and shattered it against the back of his head.

Grayden, the massive warrior, collapsed to the ground.

"Yes!" she hissed, amazed that she had taken down a man who outweighed her easily by eighty pounds. Holding tightly to the piece of paddle that remained in her hand, she checked her feet and fingers. Her shoes were pretty chewed up, and there was no sign of socks, but her toes — though swollen, purple and a little bloody — seemed to be intact; her hands were just slightly puffy and red.

Aside from avoiding Ryannon at all costs, her number one goal at this point was to find Tabbit. Not only was she deeply concerned about her little friend, but Tabbit could get them back to Lor Mandela. Once there, she was certain that she and Lortu could figure out how to bring Dallin and Guddlebee home.

She kicked off her mangled shoes, removed the remains of her socks and began carefully maneuvering through the saw mill. Apart from the room in which she'd waylaid Grayden, the whole mill seemed to be lit only by tiny lights placed at equal intervals along the top of the walls. Over half of them were burned out, so it was fairly easy for Audril to keep to the shadows.

She inched down a darkened hallway and around a corner; there was no one to be seen or heard. As there were no doors along this new corridor, she decided to traverse it quickly. She ran full speed and was just rounding the next corner, when a blue light flashed towards the middle of the passageway in front of her. With a startled gasp, she ducked back into the door-less hall and cautiously poked her head out to see what was going on.

Dallin lay twitching and softly groaning on the ground. "Oh no," she breathed. She started toward him but then noticed that his legs were being held awkwardly in the air. Fighting another gasp, she pulled back, hoping that Robert hadn't detected her.

The next thing she heard was the sound of heavy boots walking down the hall, followed by Robert's now appalling voice. "And here is the other one, Ryannon, my friend. That should fulfill my end of the bargain."

"The other one?" Ryannon's voice held a hint of surprise. "I haven't seen Audril yet. Where is she?"

"What?" Robert replied, echoing Ryannon's confusion. "I sent her through the portal several minutes before we came."

"LIQUE!" Ryannon bellowed so loudly that it made Audril jump. She heard the sound of soft footsteps shuffling hastily down the hall.

"What is it, m'lord?" There was something familiar about the voice. Audril couldn't put her finger on who it was, but she would have sworn she'd heard that voice before.

"Go get Grayden immediately."

"Of course," Lique whimpered.

Audril pushed herself tightly against the cold cement wall as a cloaked woman rounded the corner and rushed past her.

Great, she thought to herself, *now I'm in the middle!* She scoured the hall for the darkest spot she could find. Just across from her was a section where three lights in a row were out. It was her best chance of not being spotted. She took a deep, yet silent breath, glanced side to side, and dashed across to the other wall. From her new position, she could see the ends of Dallin's feet which were still being held in the air.

"I thought you were intelligent," Ryannon chided in his usual cool manner.

Robert's reply was quite the opposite, charged with anger. "Don't pin this on me, Ryannon! She went through that portal! If your stooges can't take care of a little girl, then you're the one who should be questioning *his* intelligence!"

"Watch your tone, Robert, or I'll squash every last one of your little friends with my boot!"

Just then, Lique came barreling down the hall, once again missing Audril standing against the wall. "Grayden's been knocked out! He's unconscious in your lab!"

"WHAT?" Ryannon bellowed. "She's here in the mill! Both of you . . . split up and find her! NOW!"

"What about our deal?" Robert asked smoothly.

"Our deal isn't a deal until I have Audril!" Ryannon barked.

"Well then, sir, allow me to do you one more little favor. I feel sorry for you . . . as you seem to be surrounded by incompetents."

Audril watched Dallin's feet fall to the ground. Before she could respond, Robert's voice chilled her ear. "Hello, Atoh." She felt a blast of cold air all around her followed by Robert's frigid hands on her back. "Here's your missing princess, Ryannon!" With a forceful shove, Robert pushed her out into the middle of the corridor. "Bargain fulfilled."

Chapter XXIV

TABBIT'S TRINKLE TRANCE

At the sight of Audril, Lique immediately scurried back down the hall. Audril thought she could hear the sound of sobs floating out from underneath Lique's cloak.

Looking over the shoulder that stung under Robert's bitter cold grip, Audril seethed, "If you weren't already dead, Mr. Stroud, I'd kill you myself!"

Her feistiness gave Ryannon a good chuckle. "Isn't that a bit harsh for you? Although, I must say, this new attitude certainly suits you, my dear."

"Don't you dare call me that, you pig! Everything about you repulses me!" She glanced over at Dallin who was still twitching on the hard floor. "What have you done to him? Tell me!"

Ryannon moved up to her and stood with his face inches from hers. "I'll call you whatever I want, *my dear.* You are in no position to be making demands, especially if you want your phony lover boy here to survive. That's right . . . I know all about that kiss. He's lucky I haven't killed him already . . . I must be feeling merciful today." He ran his hand through her jet curls, grabbing a fistful and taking in a deep whiff. "Speaking of which, I should probably kill you, too . . . after the whole Mikil and Solom fiasco . . . but you can't be killed, can you?" He looked into her eyes as if he were searching for a hint of fear. "No, I think 'my dear' suits you perfectly, and I've picked out a name you can call me, as well."

Audril turned her head in disgust. It was the first time that someone with clean, minty breath had sickened her.

"Oh come on," Ryannon continued. "Don't you want to hear it? I think you should call me . . ." He tightened his grip on her hair and yanked, pulling her face back towards him. ". . . Entrusted." Smiling deviously, he pushed her forward and kissed her hard on the lips.

"Not if you were the last man alive," she sneered, spitting in disdain.

"Oh, really? Well, I think you might want to consider your answer more carefully, my dear. You see, the lives of farm boy Doone here, and your cute little Squanki, depend on it." Ryannon loosened his grasp and added, "Now why don't you kiss me like you mean it." He slid a vystoran sleeve from his jacket pocket and aimed it at Dallin's trembling body. "Convince me this time."

Audril glanced sideways at Dallin's convulsing form. Her heart ached as she viewed the horrified look in his eyes. She thought of poor little Tabbit and what she must be going through — wherever she was. As much as it sickened her, she would have to do whatever Ryannon asked.

She closed her eyes and locked the image of Dallin, just before they had kissed in the Light Dimension, firmly into her mind. With a deep breath, she leaned forward and touched her lips to Ryannon's, kissing him with the passion she felt for the person whose face she held inside her head.

A second or two into the kiss, Ryannon snapped his fingers, a code for Robert to let go of his torturous hold on Dallin's subconscious. Dallin sprang to his feet, but then dropped to his knees upon seeing Audril in Ryannon's arms, her mouth moving fervently with his. Ryannon slowly pulled away and ordered Robert to take Dallin to the room they'd prepared for him.

"That was better, wasn't it?" Ryannon smiled, caressing Audril's back.

She turned away and shuddered in disdain, only to see Dallin struggling to escape Robert's grasp, all the while watching her over his shoulder. His energy was depleted; he could barely walk. As Robert yanked him around the corner, Dallin reached his hand out to Audril and muttered, "Why?"

Audril's heart lurched. "Please, Ryannon. Let them go," she begged. "It's me you want; you don't need them anymore! You have me, so please, let them go home."

"Answer me one little question," he replied. "Why did you kiss him?"

Audril's stomach jumped as Lortu's warning replayed in her mind. "I . . . I was just caught up in the moment. It shouldn't have happened. I told Dallin that." Just saying the words hurt. "Come on . . . I mean, I'm the atoh; he's a farmer from Westrim. I swear . . . he'll never be more than just a friend."

"But he seems to think he is in love with you, and to be quite honest, he's a nuisance to my plans. Give me one good reason that I shouldn't have him killed right now."

Audril's mind raced. What possible reason could she give without revealing her true feelings for Dallin? After several seconds she blurted, "Well, if he really is in love with me, wouldn't it be torture for you to send him back to Lor Mandela without me?"

Ryannon nodded. "Perhaps . . . perhaps, I suppose I can spare him a little longer . . . but I'm not sending him back . . . not just yet. I think I'll use him for a little experiment. At any rate, I commend you on your diplomacy, my dear. Every great leader should be quick to think of answers so eloquently expressed."

Her fear for Dallin's safety gnawed even harder on her insides. Ryannon wouldn't care about keeping him alive after his experiment — whatever it was. In all actuality, she doubted that Ryannon would allow Dallin to survive the depravity he had planned for him. But at least she had bought some time — time for him to live, and time for her to think.

"Now then, Audril, let me show you to your room. I have a couple of tiny things to take care of, but when I return we will begin the ceremony." He took a hold of her arm and escorted her toward the lab.

Her preferred reaction at this moment would have been to give Ryannon the same treatment she'd given Grayden, but she couldn't risk it. She fought every urge within herself to slam an elbow into his face and instead feigned a calm, unaffected demeanor.

"Ceremony?" she tried innocently. "You were just kidding about us becoming Entrusted, right? I mean . . . come on Ryannon . . . we hardly know each other, and I'm only seventeen."

"Yes, but have you looked in a mirror, my dear? Of course I was serious. Besides, you have something that I want, don't you?"

As they passed the lab and turned into another dark corridor, she could hear Lique asking Grayden what had happened. Audril concentrated on that voice, trying to figure out why it was so familiar.

"Something you want?" she muttered in response to Ryannon.

"Well, actually two things. First, the Clest Anaria powers, and second . . . your father." He stopped at a big, red, steel door and pushed it open.

Audril's voice quivered slightly. "What are you talking about? What does my father have to do with any of this? This is between you and me now. He's got nothing to do with the Clest Anaria powers."

"Oh, this is not only about the powers . . . I've known for weeks how to get those. This is about vengeance; this is about your daddy attempting to trick me. You see, I know what he is most protective of." He stopped and stared her down before continuing. "Any guesses, my dear? It's not Lor Mandela and her people. It's not the new vritesse. It's you . . . and you know it. When he learns that you and I are Entrusted . . . when he sees me with black hair and blue eyes . . . it will tear him apart. You giving me the Clest Anaria powers will be, as they say here on Earth, the icing on the cake."

Audril sighed and closed her eyes, knowing that what he was saying was true. "Why do you have to do this, Ryannon?" she said. "Why do you insist on torturing and killing good, innocent people? What makes you so cold-hearted and monstrous?"

Ryannon smiled as though he'd been complimented. "Your feelings will change in time, my dear. Now, let's not linger here in this dreary hall any longer." He motioned toward the room behind the red door, and guided her in with his hand on the small of her back. "See the wardrobe along the back wall? Inside is the closest thing I could find to a Noble Exalting Ritual Dress. There is also a copy of the exalting vow on the shelf for you to memorize. I have to go, but I'll be back at around ten o'clock this evening, and then we'll begin. Grayden will bring your dinner in at seven. If you need anything in the meantime, press the green button near the door and he will attend to you."

Audril nodded and stared into the distance. Inside her mind she prayed for any brilliant idea to get everyone out of this mess. At that moment, she remembered what Dallin had said about Tabbit's Trinkle Trance; maybe the answers would lie there.

"Ryannon, wait," she called as he started toward the door. "Can you at least let me see Tabbit?"

Ryannon threw back his head and laughed wildly at her request. "And have her wiggle her fist and open a portal for you? I think not."

"No! I swear! I won't try to get away. You can have your guard people . . . you know, Grayden and Robert . . . or that Lique lady . . . you can have them watch me. I just want to make sure she's okay."

Ryannon strode back to face her and looked deeply into her eyes. The crimson flecks in his dark irises flickered brightly in the sunlight coming from the window high on the bedroom's wall. "Fine . . . I will have her brought here for ten minutes . . . but mark my words, Atoh, if you try anything, everyone you care about will be dead before the week is out."

Audril nodded. "Thank you," she said, forcing a small smile of appreciation.

"See now," he schmoozed, "things can be worked out between us. I told you your feelings for me will change." He kissed her on the forehead before adding, "Make sure you're ready by ten, my dear." With that, he backed out of the room, shut and locked the door, and strutted away.

Audril walked to the stately bed in the center of the room and plopped down on the edge of it. She looked up at the single-paned window and judged from the sun pouring in that it was mid-afternoon. "This is a disaster," she muttered to herself as she dropped her head in her hands.

Questions suddenly began racing through her mind. *What if Tabbit doesn't have the answers? How am I going to get her, Dallin and myself all out of here? What's happening on Lor Mandela right now? What if Dad doesn't forgive me? What if Dallin doesn't forgive me? What if Lortu won't give the powers back? What if we all . . . .*

A knock on the door interrupted the panic building inside of her. "Die!" she blurted aloud. "Uh . . . um . . . I mean . . . yes?"

Grayden's voice replied, "Your Majesty, may I come in? I've brought your Squanki friend to see you." There was something odd about his tone of voice. It was almost as if he was frightened.

"Yeah, but I can't open the door, doofus . . . it's locked."

"Oh, of course, Atoh . . . I have the key," he replied shakily.

His keys jingled and then scratched against the lock. With a click, the door unlatched and he pushed it open.

Tabbit was in his arms, silent, and looking directly at him with her bulgy eyes. He quickly brought her over, dropped her on the top of a big wooden dresser and backed away . . . bowing to Audril!

"What's the matter with you?" she asked, not really waiting for an answer before rushing to Tabbit's side. "Hey Tabbit," she smiled, "Tabbit? Can you hear me?"

The little Squanki turned her face toward Audril; her scraggly, white locks floated all around her head and shoulders. "Can you hear me?" she mimicked slowly, sounding almost like Audril. "Squankis don't tells," she mumbled weakly.

"What is it?" Audril tried, "Are you hurt?" Then she turned to Glaron and asked, "Is she hurt?"

Glaron cleared his throat nervously and replied, "She, uh, she hurt her leg a few days ago, but Lique's been taking care of her, Majesty."

228

Audril grimaced at his strange show of humility and turned back to Tabbit. "Tell what, Tabbit? What is it?"

"What is it?" Tabbit repeated. "Lady comes backs? . . . lady comes backs?" She looked pleadingly into Audril's eyes.

"Do you mean me? Do I have to go back to Lor Mandela?"

Tabbit's mannerism changed in an instant. "Do I have to go back to Lor Mandela?" she barked angrily. "Return the powers!"

Audril's mind was reeling. "I don't understand." She glanced over her shoulder at Grayden who was standing obediently, albeit wide-eyed against the wall. "Lortu?" she whispered.

Tabbit jumped up on the dresser, standing on her own two legs for the first time in days. Her eyes filled with rage and her petite body shook all over as she lunged toward Audril and wrapped her arms around the atoh's neck, and her legs around her midsection. Audril nearly toppled over backwards as the crazed Squanki yelled, "LORTU!"

Grayden rushed to Audril's aid.

Tabbit climbed Audril's chest, perched herself on her head and screamed at Grayden, "FOUR HUNDRED DAYS! FOUR HUNDRED DAYS!"

"Tabbit! What are you doing?" Audril shrieked from behind a scrawny brown leg. "Are you all right?"

"ALL RIGHT? FOUR HUNDRED DAYS! FOUR HUNDRED DAYS!" She slid back down, and started shaking Audril by the shoulders. "FOUR HUNDRED DAYS! FOUR HUNDRED DAYS!" she squealed again.

Grayden spun past Audril's side and wrapped his massive arm around Tabbit's waist. "Let go, you little demon!" he commanded, yanking her backwards. "You're hurting the atoh!"

Tabbit's grip was so strong that the muscular general was having a hard time besting her. He had to use his free hand to pry her fingers from Audril. "FOUR HUNDRED DAYS!" she cried out again.

"She's not hurting me, Grayden!" Audril bellowed. "Besides, since when do you care?"

All of a sudden, Tabbit let go, sending the three of them toppling backwards to the floor. Tabbit scrambled across Grayden and bounded quickly to the door. She jumped up and took hold of the handle, planting her feet against the cold metal. She tugged and wiggled and pulled, trying to get the door to open, screaming, "FOUR HUNDRED DAYS! FOUR HUNDRED DAYS!" over and over again.

Grayden sprang to his feet and in three giant steps reached her. "You're off your Truglunt, you little monster," he barked, as he picked up a green rock-like object that was decorating the marble top of a side table nearby, and clobbered Tabbit in the back of the neck with it. Tabbit's body went limp. Her head flopped to the side as she hung by her intertwined fingers from the doorknob.

"What did you do?" Audril gasped.

"I knocked her out," Grayden replied, out of breath. He bent over and dropped his hands onto his knees. "It's my job to protect you, Atoh."

"Protect me?" she screeched, "From what? One of my best friends? If it's your job to protect me, then send me back to Lor Mandela! Ryannon is the murderer here, not Tabbit!" Her face was nearly purple with rage. She stomped over to Grayden and shoved him hard in the shoulder.

He pulled to his full height. "She attacked you! Ryannon is the one who told me to keep you safe! I'm just following orders!" He turned and lifted Tabbit from the door. "Visit's over," he snipped. "If you don't mind, Atoh, could you take a few steps back?"

Audril crossed her arms and looked away. "Or what?" she responded. "You'll whack me with a rock, too?"

"Don't tempt me," Grayden sighed and flipped Tabbit over one shoulder. Then he stepped up to Audril and lifted her from the ground and dropped her over the other shoulder. She squirmed and punched but didn't want to hurt Tabbit by accident, so her assault was far from effective. Grayden walked her back to the bed and dropped her onto it. "Forgive me, Majesty." He bowed and strode back to the door.

"I don't think so," she sneered.

As he opened the door, Tabbit's eyes blinked open, and she mumbled, "Return the powers . . . four-hundred . . . ." Her voice trailed off as her eyelids slid shut along with the door.

Chapter XXV

A PERFECTLY ORCHESTRATED PLAN

It was another, separate tragedy that brought together a country still reeling from the destruction of Glenhill, Iowa. This time, in the rural agricultural communities of Central California, a lone gunman, a young student consumed by paranoia that his town was next on the list to be blown up, decided that he was preordained of God to end the lives of as many as he could before the impending apocalypse. When the bullets stopped flying, sixteen were wounded, and the gunman, along with four of his fellow students, three professors, and a federal judge visiting Rosmore University to speak to the law classes, were dead.

Ryannon entered Spencer Auditorium at the university with a group of nearly ten thousand at 4:35 p.m., three days after the shooting. He cleared security without incident, as he'd brought nothing with him, and made his way to his seat, an excellent one, three rows from the stage, which Lique had procured through a prominent contact she knew at the school. This was the perfect opportunity for him to implement his plan. Ten thousand sold out seats, at least that many people outside the building — he would have a large and captive audience.

The president of the United States was introduced at 5:30 exactly. The crowd applauded for nearly five minutes before the tall, sophisticated, forty-two-year-old Commander In Chief began her tribute.

Twenty-Five

President Langley's mood was solemn in comparison to her usual gregarious demeanor, and tears threatened to spill from her generally sparkling green eyes more than once during her opening comments. Ryannon was almost impressed by her sensitivity and ability to boost the crowd's morale during this time of sorrow. "What an inspiration," he whispered under his breath as he observed the overall adoration of the assembly.

The minutes ticked by. It was now 5:42. Having lost all interest in the president's diplomatic prowess, Ryannon diligently scanned the room. Although he could see no Secret Service or Law Enforcement agents, he knew that they were there, but that did not concern him as they would be no match for the highly skilled Brashnellan Minister of Defense. As long as he made it to the stage by 5:45, everything would go according to plan.

At 5:44 precisely, the attention of the gathered throng turned suddenly from the president's stirring eulogy to the disruptive sound filling the auditorium — a high-pitched, screeching hiss. Panic ensued as those assembled realized the significance of the eerie wailing sound. Their screams of horror and pounding footsteps added to the intensity of the air-shattering noise and literally shook the arena.

In the frenzy, no one noticed Ryannon maneuvering through the stampeding crowd towards the third of fourteen shallow alcoves lining the west wall of the auditorium. He peered around with a smile and pressed his foot into the back of the niche, disappearing in a blue flash. Within seconds, he rematerialized in the lab at the saw mill, where he slid a crystal detonator and a large stack of papers from a metal supply shelf into his pocket before jumping back into the portal.

He arrived back on the stage with over fifteen seconds to spare. Just as he anticipated, a full contingent of armed officers was rushing the president off the stage toward the nearest exit at the opposite side of the arena. "Wait!" he yelled. "You're going the wrong way! You're going to get her killed!"

Two of the officers spun around to see Ryannon running towards them at top speed. One of the men drew his weapon, but not fast enough. Ryannon launched himself through the air and kicked the gun from the guard's hand as his elbow planted squarely in the solar plexus of the other, who fell to the floor in a heap. One by one he quickly disarmed and took down the agents, the entire time bellowing, "You're going the wrong way! You're going to get her killed! You've got to trust me! You're going the wrong way!" He grabbed a hold of President Langley's wrist. "Hurry, this way," he insisted as he pulled her back to the other side of the stage.

"Let go of me! What are you doing?" she cried, struggling to get away.

"I'm saving your life," he yelled back. "You've got to trust me!"

As soon as they were a few feet away from the last crumpled form of her protectors, Ryannon pushed the president to the ground and dove on top of her while simultaneously pressing the button on the detonator. A deafening explosion ripped through the air sending the auditorium lurching violently and knocking all of those remaining to the floor. A cloud of debris blasted from the front to the back of the room, enveloping it in a thick, choking mist.

As the dust settled, Ryannon rolled off of President Langley and helped her to her feet. "My apologies, ma'am," he coughed as the president stood in a stunned silence, staring with awe at the scene just inches in front of her. The whole east side of the stage, where she had been moments before, and part of the front of the auditorium were gone, replaced by a gaping crater. There was not a trace of her secret service agents, or the big floral arrangements that were set for the occasion, or the large American flag that adorned the curtain at the back of the stage, nothing but a big hole.

Behind the descending grey fog, hundreds of people raced towards them from a parking lot adjacent to the building, among them, dozens of wide-eyed police officers with guns drawn. They zigzagged their way through the bodies sprawled across the ground, intent on getting to the president as quickly as possible.

"President Langley," Ryannon began, startling her out of her state of shock. "I know who's responsible for this."

"Who's responsible? And just who are you?" she replied shakily, noticing for the first time the fiery flecks in Ryannon's eyes.

"My name is Ryannon, ma'am. I am here to help you."

President Langley looked from Ryannon to the approaching officers, with their guns trained on the man next to her, and signaled for them to lower their weapons.

"I'm fine," she assured. "This man just saved my life. He's all right." She motioned toward the people lying on the floor of the auditorium and commanded, "Leave him alone and see to the injured." Her "grace under fire" poise — arguably one of the deciding factors in her election to office — was more evident by the second. "Okay, Mr. Ryannon . . . you have my attention."

"Forgive me, Mrs. President, but I am sure that you won't be left here alone with me for long, and this is not a matter that can be discussed in thirty seconds or less. But you, and you alone, are the only one I can trust with this information."

She glanced in the direction of Ryannon's gaze to see two Secret Service Agents moving towards them, and then paused for a moment to think. "Very well, I am staying at the Airport Winston in Fresno. I will see you this evening when I get back there. Unfortunately, Mr. Ryannon, in light of these events, I have no idea when that will be."

"I'll only be available until nine o'clock," Ryannon replied coolly. "After that, you're on your own."

"I could easily have you detained for questioning," she retorted.

"Not likely," he chuckled. "Listen. I'm not trying to be demanding, ma'am, but we do this my way or we don't do it at all. Trust me. Once I reveal what this is all about, you'll understand my position fully."

"I certainly hope so, Ryannon." President Langley stared at his strange eyes. "I'll be back at the hotel at 8:30. Right now I think these people could use our help."

"Understood, ma'am."

Ryannon acted the part of concerned citizen well. He administered first aid with proficiency to many of the people he himself had injured.

At 7:40, the president was escorted from the building, skillfully avoiding questions from the hordes of waiting press. Her motorcade cleared the campus at 7:55 and headed north towards Fresno.

Ryannon stayed at the school helping until 8:28 when he excused himself to go to the restroom, but instead walked into the portal in the alcove. A few bystanders observed the flash, but passed it off as an arc from the damaged electrical system.

Ryannon transported to the lab, and without hesitation proceeded to Tabbit's room. She sat, curled on her cement bench, chanting and rocking.

"You . . . portal to Airport Winston in Fresno, California."

Tabbit obediently raised her hand in the air and rolled it into a tight fist. "Portal to Airport Winston in Fresno, California," she repeated, convincingly mimicking Ryannon, and then went back to reciting the lines of her Trinkle Trance.

"Very good," he chuckled, patting her on the head as he stepped into the new portal.

He emerged in a moving elevator which hummed downward, stopping after a few seconds in the hotel lobby. Ryannon stepped out into chaos, as several reporters scurried around on cell phones with their camera crews in tow, while others interviewed hotel staff about a situation of which they knew nothing. A moment or two later, he was approached by a man in a black suit who solemnly asked, "Are you Ryannon?"

"I am . . . such wonderful service," Ryannon mused. "Secret Service," he blurted as he gave the agent a good thump on the back.

The stoic agent was not amused. He pushed a button on the coiled wire running from under his shirt to his ear and said, "I've got him," before escorting Ryannon through a door marked, "Employees Only," and down a long service corridor.

At the end of the corridor another agent waited with a metal-detection wand. "Sorry sir, standard procedure," he explained as they approached and he began waving the wand over Ryannon. This man seemed far more relaxed than the first one. "I'm surprised they don't have us scanning each other after what happened."

"Keep your jokes to a minimum," the staunch guard barked before heading back to his post.

"Aye aye, sir," Ryannon mocked with an exaggerated salute. "Is this guy for real?"

The genial agent shook his head and answered, "Who? Bill? Yeah, he's all right. Maybe he takes his job too seriously, but he's an excellent agent." He set the wand down on a small, glass-topped table and pointed to a freight elevator off to the left. "This way, Mr. Ryannon."

"Thank you, Agent . . . ?"

"Dawes, sir."

"Thank you, Agent Dawes."

"No problemo."

After the elevator ride up several floors, Agent Dawes opened the inner and outer doors and pointed down the hall. "See those two ladies down there? They're standing at President Langley's suite. They'll let you in. It's been a pleasure meeting you, Mr. Ryannon."

"You as well, Agent Dawes," Ryannon bowed and smiled. "Stay safe out there."

The agent nodded and pulled the elevator doors closed and Ryannon strode off in the direction of the president's room.

When he reached the door, the taller of the two brunette guards announced his arrival into her wire, as the other slid a card key through a reader on the wall and typed a nine digit code into the keypad next to it.

"Here you are, sir," the tall agent pushed the door open to reveal a spacious, elegant hotel suite.

President Langley paced back and forth in the middle of the room, less formally attired than the staunch grey suit she wore earlier that evening. She looked ready for a trip to the gym in her conservative black exercise pants and white t-shirt.

"Ah, Mr. Ryannon," she smiled as she shook his hand. "Forgive me. I don't believe I thanked you for saving me earlier."

"No problemo," he joked. "That was the reason I came to the service today."

"The reason you came? From where, exactly? Judging from those eyes, I'd say you're either wildly eccentric or from somewhere far, far away."

"So you've guessed it, have you?" Ryannon smiled. "You are clearly a very intelligent woman."

"Get to the point, sir. I hardly have time for petty flattery."

Ryannon genuinely liked this woman. She was charming yet direct. "Very well," he began. "I am from a place called Lor Mandela in the Lorma System, a galaxy outside of your universe." He paused to gauge the president's response.

She seemed unmoved. "I assume you understand that your claim is rather . . . shall we say . . . unbelievable?"

"Yet you have already entertained the idea, haven't you?"

The president began pacing again. "I've entertained several ideas, Mr. Ryannon. Outside of you being a sorcerer, wizard or vampire, this was the most far-fetched, of course, but frankly, I don't care if you're Santa Claus, as long as you tell me who's responsible for these explosions."

Ryannon moved in front of her and explained, "Just as you don't have time for flattery, ma'am, I don't have time for skepticism. The fate of your world depends on your believing me. If that doesn't snap your mind open, then you cannot be helped."

President Langley squinted and studied Ryannon's face intently, but didn't respond.

Twenty-Five

"Here's how it is, Mrs. President. The monarch of my world . . . a very dangerous man named Atoc Jonathan . . . has placed these explosive devices in nearly seven hundred locations on your planet. His plan is to detonate them one at a time until there are not enough people left to fight. He is a tyrannical conqueror and has singled out Earth as his current prize. Once he's wiped out a significant portion of the population, he will bring his troops in and take over. Anyone left alive will be forced into slavery."

"So, you're telling me that some power-hungry alien guy is blowing up the Earth, bit by bit, just so he can take over? Why would he want a destroyed planet? And if he's okay with a destroyed planet, why doesn't he just get it over with in one shot?"

"Don't you see? By the time he's set off seven hundred of these explosions, the living that remain will have been instilled with such panic and fear that he will be able to get them to do whatever he wants." Ryannon's faux concern was quite moving. ". . . and to answer your other question . . . The atoc knows that intelligent life forms learn from past experiences. As time goes on, the restoration of sites becomes more and more efficient. He waits to invade until most of the populated areas he's destroyed are well on their way to restoration."

"You sound as though he's done this before. Are you telling me that Earth isn't his first conquest?" A sudden change in the president's tone persuaded Ryannon that he had almost convinced her.

"Exactly," he replied, "but this is the closest I've come to stopping him."

President Langley dropped into a comfortable-looking barrel chair and tucked a stray piece of her perfectly styled, sandy blonde hair behind her ear. "Are you for real?" she asked, looking up at him. "I hear what you are saying, Mr. Ryannon, but it is so extraordinary that I can't seem to quite wrap my mind around it. Is there any way for me to know that what you are saying is true, besides taking your word for it? You understand that as President of the United States, I can hardly ask Congress to declare war on another country, let alone another planet without some solid proof of a threat."

"What more solid proof do you need, ma'am? He's already destroyed one town in your country, and tried to assassinate you. This is only the beginning. Where will it be next? Los Angeles? San Francisco? New York? How many more lives will be lost if I'm telling you the truth and you choose to do nothing? I'll give you a rough estimate. It'll be in the billions worldwide. Are you willing to risk that?" He studied her concerned expression and added, "Together you and I have the ability to save worlds. I can't do it without you, and you can't do it without me; it's that simple."

President Langley sat in contemplative silence for several seconds, and Ryannon patiently waited, even though he knew he had her sufficiently fooled. Finally she gulped in a deep breath and sighed, "Fine, what do you need me to do?"

Ryannon reached into his jacket and pulled out the stack of papers he had brought from the saw mill. "I need soldiers . . . and a lot of them," he answered. "These are directions to where we will meet, as well as detailed instructions for the troops. I realize that this will test your skills as an organizer and negotiator, but I need them by 2:00 tomorrow afternoon, assembled and ready for battle."

"Tomorrow afternoon? Impossible!"

"Imperative," he snapped. "There is a very small window of opportunity here, ma'am. I can take five-hundred thousand or more through a portal tomorrow afternoon, but if we miss that window, the number of soldiers I can take dwindles to nearly none. I realize this is a difficulty, but we don't have much of a choice."

"Even if I could get that many troops together, it has to be passed through Congress! Do you have any idea the amount of political red tape I would have to go through to make this happen?"

"Then avoid the red tape, ma'am. You have the authority to mobilize troops, correct? You can deal with Congress after I have the regiment through the portal."

"You're asking me to deploy five hundred thousand, Ryannon. I couldn't possibly . . . ."

Ryannon didn't let her finish, "You couldn't possibly what? Stand by and watch billions of people die, or risk your cushy position? I thought you had more integrity than that!"

"Don't you dare question my integrity!" she retaliated. "What you're asking is ludicrous! It has nothing to do with me risking my position! You want me to send half a million troops to follow you to some unknown planet and then go to Congress and the people of this country and justify it with nothing more than the word of a stranger with red glitter in his eyes? That's what you're asking me to do! You're asking me to risk five hundred thousand lives!"

"Five hundred thousand or six billion . . . yes, I understand your concern," he retorted cynically. "Your options are before you, Evelyn Langley, and I don't have time to wait. Think about it for around five more minutes, then figure out how to make it happen. I'll be waiting here . . ." he slammed his index finger against the papers on the table, "at two o'clock tomorrow."

Ryannon turned and walked out of the room — at 9:00 p.m. exactly.

Chapter XXVI

LOVE INDUCED SUICIDE

Shortly after seven o'clock, Grayden brought in dinner — an exquisite meal of blueberry glazed pork, asparagus, and garlic mashed potatoes. "Where would you like me to set this, Your Majesty?" he asked humbly.

"What's with the whole servant gig, Grayden? Did I hit your head that hard?" Audril snipped.

"I don't know what you're talking about," he retorted, placing the dinner plate on a table near the bed on which she sat.

"That's what I'm talking about! You've been disgusting and vile to me before, and probably woulda killed me if you didn't think Ryannon would kill you for doing it. . . but now you're all like, 'yes, Your Majesty' and stuff. It's fake, and it's annoying!"

"There's no point in me being disgusting and vile right now," he grinned as he walked toward the door, "and yes . . . I would've killed you, but watching you become Ryannon's Entrusted will be far more rewarding. Now, if you'll excuse me, I have an entrusting ceremony room to prepare." His eyes sparkled with delight as he turned and bowed before exiting the room, a trail of devious laughter following him as he went.

Audril was hungry, as she hadn't eaten all day, but her nerves wouldn't allow her to stomach much. After two or three bites, she plopped back down onto the bed and racked her brain for ideas. *What if I . . . no. Or, how about if we . . . ugh! That won't work . . . .*

On the top of a gilded bureau and visible through the thick bed posts, an antique table clock too rapidly ticked away the time. Seven raced to seven thirty. In what felt like five minutes, it was eight thirty and then nine. None of her plans were offering a guarantee of safety for anyone, especially not for Dallin and Tabbit, and their lives were something she was not willing to risk. Finally at nine thirty-five, Audril realized she would have to get ready, no matter how it nauseated her.

Up to this point, the safest plan she could concoct was to just go along with Ryannon's scheme and hope that an opportune moment would present itself.

She walked to the big, ornately-carved armoire and turned the crystal handle. Inside, the most beautiful sapphire blue gown hung by itself, a floor length mermaid style dress, with a full black lace under-skirt, and embroidered in an intricate flower motif which sparkled with tiny black and silver crystals. She lifted it out and held it up in front of her, gazing at her reflection in the mirror that was hanging on the inside of the armoire door.

"How am I going to get myself outta this one?" she muttered. She slipped the hanger back over the closet rod and picked up a folded piece of parchment from one of the shelves. *"A se nalt o talis betrindi,"* she read aloud. *"Kace enalt o madus betrindi. Wes solis e trysta conaye."*

For a moment she let her mind wander. She tried to imagine Dallin with black hair and blue eyes. It was a little hard at first, but then it became so clear in her mind that even when she stopped daydreaming, the image wouldn't leave. "I'm in love with him . . ." she sighed as she silently read over the vow again. "Terrific."

Three years of drama class seemed to pay off as she committed the exalting vow to memory in about a minute — although she was certain that her pronunciation of the strange foreign words was far from accurate. But maybe, if she botched it enough, the spell wouldn't take.

243

With memorizing the vow out of the way, she changed into the gown and tried to do something with her messy hair. "What am I doing?" she snapped at her image in the mirror. "This isn't prom!" She shut the door of the armoire in disgust and dropped into a red velvet chair to wait and hope for a better last minute plan.

The clock sounded off the seconds in irritating ticks that seemed to be screaming for her to do something. In a conscious effort to ignore the annoying clock, her thoughts turned to her poor dad, how he must be so angry with her for leaving, and how, if she was forced to become Ryannon's Entrusted, it would crush him. "I can't let this happen," she breathed. "I can not let this happen!"

The sound of Ryannon's boots approaching the door startled her back to the moment. *Just keep your eyes open, Smaggs,* the voice in her head encouraged. *He's bound to make at least one mistake. Keep up appearances and wait for the right moment.*

Ryannon burst through the door without knocking. He was dressed in an impeccable black tuxedo, and despite his depravity, even Audril could not deny that, at six foot four with chiseled features, dazzlingly shimmering eyes and shoulder-length dark brown hair, he was amazingly good looking. He carried with him a thick, leather-bound book that appeared to be quite old.

"Well hello, my dear," he smiled, eyeing Audril like she was a decadent dessert. "I knew you'd look delicious in that dress."

Any admiration Audril had for his appearance instantly vanished the moment he opened his mouth. "Thanks," she tried, "you look okay too, I guess."

"Don't hurt yourself, love," he chuckled, lowering into another red chair a few feet away. "Why don't you stand up and let me see you better."

Audril's stomach lurched at the thought of him checking her out like a piece of meat. "I'd rather stay sitting, if you don't mind."

"Oh, but I do," he replied, making a twirling motion toward her with his index finger. "Come on," he insisted, "let's have a look."

She took a deep breath and pulled herself to her feet. "There . . . satisfied?"

Ryannon gestured with his finger again. "Around you go."

Audril spun around quickly and then dropped back into her chair.

Ryannon stood and moved to where she sat. He placed the book down on a low curio cabinet near her and held his hands out to her. "Don't be nervous, angel. I won't bite."

"Don't you dare call me angel," she hissed; her conscience practically screamed, *keep up appearances and wait for the right moment! Keep up appearances and wait for the right moment!* Unfortunately, his calling her angel was too much.

"Hmmm," Ryannon smirked, "I think I've discovered Daddy's pet name for his little atoh . . . how precious."

Audril slapped his hands out of the way and stood on her own. "Listen, Ryannon. I will go along with this plan of yours, and I'll even become your Entrusted, but you can't expect me to be all happy about it! I'm only going through with this to save my friends and the people of Earth and of Lor Mandela. You win, okay! You get what you want! Just torture me, and leave everyone else out of it!"

Ryannon studied her eyes for a moment before motioning for her to sit back down.

"I have something I want to show you," he began as he scooted his chair next to hers and picked the book up from the curio. He sat down and flipped open the heavy book, balancing it on the now touching arms of the chairs.

"My father was a superstitious fool . . . a wanna-be sorcerer with very limited power and even less skill, but this book . . ." He stroked the pages and inhaled deeply. "This book may have been the reason he got as far as he did."

He turned a few of the yellowed pages and pointed to a drawing of two black, jagged hands at the top of one of them. "The grasping curse," he said, pausing for a moment to read Audril's reaction, but she showed no emotion. "No doubt you've heard of it."

He rifled through a few more pages until he came to a picture of a crystalline object that looked like entwined hands. "Formula for building Catorian explosives . . . probably good that my father didn't spend too much time on this one. Can you imagine?"

Again, he turned a few pages and pointed at a black sketch. "This one is called 'Time Align.' It will come in useful tomorrow afternoon when we go to see your daddy. You see, I've just returned from a meeting with someone you might have heard of . . . a Mrs. Evelyn Langley."

"President Langley," Audril scoffed. "Yeah, right."

"No, really, dear. She was quite grateful that I saved her when part of the stage she was standing on blew up. She's agreed to help me put an end to these horrible explosions."

"Wait . . . you're serious?" A look of horror washed over Audril's face. "What have you done?"

"Only convinced her that the monstrous tyrant Atoc Jonathan needs to be stopped. She's agreed to . . . shall we say . . . lend me half a million of her best soldiers to put an end to his reign of terror. But, you should be excited to be going back home . . . if only to watch your father's empire crumble."

"That's impossible! She'd never believe you! You're bluffing!"

"Think what you want, angel," he smirked. "It doesn't matter to me."

Again, he turned his attention back to the book. He picked up what looked to be hundreds of pages and turned to one that was dog-eared towards the back of the book. "This is one of my favorites . . . it is my experiment for your good friend, Dallin Doone."

The drawing was one of two people, an old man and a little girl, embracing while tears streamed down the old man's cheeks. The words underneath were in the same strange language as the exalting vow. Audril studied the picture for a moment. Never had she seen — even in photographs — anything that revealed such emotion.

"As I'm sure that you don't understand written Derite, allow me to translate. This is called 'Love Induced Suicide.' Sounds intoxicating, doesn't it?" Ryannon ran his finger down Audril's cheek and tucked her curls behind her ear. "I asked you a question," he whispered as he leaned over and kissed her softly on the neck. "Doesn't 'Love Induced Suicide' sound divine?"

Audril cringed and leaned away. "Not especially," she grimaced. Everything inside her was twisting and lunging. He was planning a full-scale attack on Mandela City in less than twenty-four hours, and now it sounded as if he was going to do something that would drive Dallin to kill himself. The thought was so horrific that the peachy color slid from her face and she had to force herself not to be sick — a nearly impossible task considering that breathing was becoming increasingly difficult by the second. "What are you going to do?" she finally gasped.

"I've already done it," he sneered. "You see, right now Dallin is being paid a very special visit. His lovely dead mother has been momentarily brought back from the grave."

"Wh . . . what?" Audril sputtered. "What are you talking about?"

Ryannon smiled. "It just so happens that, like you, my dear friend Lique is quite the actress. This spell along with her prodigious skill even convinced *me* that I was talking with Analie Doone."

Audril listened in horror as he mapped out the scenario.

"I imagine that right now, Analie is telling her only son that she has been granted temporary life by the soul of Lor Mandela in order to save him from a gruesome end. As he marvels over the similarities of her eyes to his, his dear mother convinces him of the pain he's had to endure . . . how he lost both of his parents, and dear Gracielle. How Atoc Jonathan was happily restored to Lor Mandela, only to turn against him by sending him on a dangerous, life-threatening mission, just to keep him away from his little girl . . . and how he will be forced to watch as the only woman he has ever truly loved becomes the Entrusted of another.

"But our young Mr. Doone is strong and assures his worried mother that he will be okay.

247

"Deeply concerned, Analie hands him a small pinch of silver-colored crystals and tells him that all he has to do is drop a few of them onto his tongue to end it all. He, of course, refuses.

"His mother reiterates that whether he uses the crystals or not, he is headed for a horrific death, and that he has been granted a wonderful gift by Lor Mandela's spirit . . . the gift of meeting death on his terms instead of at the hands of a ruthless murderer.

"He thinks about it for a moment, but convinced that he will be given one more chance to save his lady love, he tries to give the crystals back.

"His mother lovingly urges him to keep them, and to reconsider, but Dallin will not be swayed. Analie tells him that she must go now, but leaves the crystals with him should he change his mind.

"A mist of smoke rises in front of her, and when it fades, she is gone.

"Young Dallin is left alone with his thoughts, but within a few moments he finds himself being escorted to the exalting ceremony, where it all starts to play out exactly as his dear mummy warned.

"He watches his beloved pledge her affection to another, and grief overtakes him and he swallows every last crystal. His body twitches and writhes in pain before slumping into a pathetic heap on the ground."

Ryannon stood and made a motion like he was kicking Dallin's dead body and then spun around and leaned over in front of Audril with his hands on the arms of her chair. The book fell to the floor with a crash. "I've said it before, and I'm saying it again, *angel*," he hissed, "You are in no position to negotiate. We do this exactly as I've planned or, like Dallin, you'll have nothing left to live for. Your father will die. Your little Squanki friend will die. Your friends on Lor Mandela will die, and I will turn this planet to dust. I expect an affectionate and *silent* Entrusted. Do I make myself clear?"

Audril choked back tears and nodded.

"Good." He picked up the book and strode across the room to the door and pushed the green button alongside it.

"Yes?" Grayden's voice crackled.

"We're ready, General," Ryannon answered. "Oh, and please invite Robert and Mr. Doone to join us as witnesses."

He turned back towards Audril and thrust his hand out toward her. "Come along, my dear . . . we don't want to keep our guests waiting."

Chapter XXVII

THE UNINVITED ENTRUSTING GUEST

R yannon escorted Audril through a maze of hallways and into what must have been a storage warehouse for the mill, except at the moment, the only thing about the colossal room that gave away its past function was the presence of floor to ceiling steel bay doors lining the far wall.

If Grayden was responsible for the transformation of the cold cement warehouse, his skills were indeed impressive, although Audril doubted that someone as hyper-masculine would be able to decorate with such finesse. She guessed that it was more likely Lique who had masterminded the beautiful setting.

The room was dimly lit and towards the center of the floor, a small forest glade had been constructed and lined with what seemed to be at least a hundred quaking trees, each with tiny white lights twinkling in it. Strands of mossy vines hung from the exposed metal beam ceiling, and were similarly lit. Delicate garlands of white flowers wrapped the square support beams throughout the room and cascaded onto the floor in soft, flowing puddles. A lilting melody of string music floated softly through the air and seemed to be emanating from the trees.

"Ah, Grayden, well done," Ryannon complimented. "This was precisely what I had in mind." He grabbed Audril by the hand and asked, "Isn't this lovely, sweetheart?" He squeezed hard as if to remind her that he expected her to be submissive.

Audril looked at a practically giddy Grayden and forced a nod.

"Thank you, Atoh," he sniggered. "Oh . . . I nearly forgot. Lique would like to see you, sir. She said it's very important and can't wait."

"What does she want now?" Ryannon asked. "She knows that I'm busy. What could possibly be so important that it can't wait until after I'm finished?"

"She didn't say. She just told me it's urgent that she speak to you before the ceremony."

"Well then, she'll have to come here. It would be insensitive for me to leave right now. Not to mention, I'm quite enjoying the view." He nodded toward Audril and smiled mischievously.

Grayden also made a nodding gesture toward Audril. "But what about . . . ?"

"Don't worry about it, General. Just tell her to hurry."

"Very well," Grayden replied. "I'll let her know on my way to pick up the others. I told them I'd be back in fifteen minutes, which is just about now."

"Excellent, we'll be waiting."

Grayden excused himself, and Ryannon motioned toward three overstuffed beige chairs that looked quite out of place near the forest glade. "Let's have a seat, shall we?"

Audril remained silent as she was led across the warehouse, but in her head she was still trying to come up with a plan to escape. She scoured the room and made note of all the exits, just in case that opportune moment arrived. She was so engrossed in her thoughts that Ryannon's next question took a moment to register.

"Do you know the meaning of Tabbit's chant?"

"What?" she replied distractedly. "Oh, no . . . of course not. It's just a bunch of gibberish as far as I can tell. I don't think there's a meaning to it, do you?"

"She's a Squanki, of course there's a meaning to it. Grayden told me about her visit to your room. He said you acted like you understood at least part of her message."

It amazed Audril that he actually thought she'd be truthful with him. "Well, I have no idea what it means," she answered.

"Hmmm," he responded with a look of skepticism. "I hoped you wouldn't say that. I guess that means I'll just have to kill her tomorrow after she creates the portals to Lor Mandela. Pity though . . . I really thought she was trying to tell us something meaningful."

"Please, stop it!" Audril snapped. "Every time I do or say something that isn't exactly what you want, you threaten to kill someone! I get it, Ryannon. You don't have to keep bringing it up! I mean, what do you want me to do, anyway? I'm going along with your plan! I've kept quiet and agreed with you! I'm standing here in this dress getting ready to do something that I would *never* do! What more can I do to get you to stop?"

Ryannon paused for a moment to think. "You know . . . you are absolutely right, my dear. Forgive me. I know this may be hard for you to believe, but I really don't want to hurt you. Ever since I met you . . . even after the battle, I wanted you to be mine. When I realized that wasn't going to happen, I became angry and lost my temper. It relieved me that you lived." He kissed her on her cheek and added, "You'll never know how much it relieved me."

Just then, Lique burst into the room. As usual, she was shrouded in a grey cloak, her head and face barely visible beneath the large hood.

"Excuse us a moment, won't you?" Ryannon said as he moved to intercept Lique. He pulled her to the back of the glade, where they were far enough away from Audril for privacy, but yet close enough for Ryannon to keep an eye on her.

Audril sat down in one of the chairs and watched the two of them converse. Lique's shoulders heaved up and down and it was clear from her posture that she was sobbing. Ryannon seemed to be doing nothing to comfort her, but rather seemed to be scolding her.

Midway through their conversation, something happened that neither of them noticed. The music stopped playing, and due to the expansive near-emptiness of the room, their echoing voices became audible to Audril.

"See . . . ee . . . ee you again," Lique cried. "I only want to make you ha . . . ap . . .py."

Ryannon rubbed his forehead and responded, "You're getting all upset over nothing, Lique. You know why I'm doing this. Just look at it this way. You have Grayden and I have her. It's quite an arrangement for both of us, isn't it? You and I will still get together from time to time for our special meetings, but I'm not about to pass up gold to settle for sand."

"What a scumbag," Audril whispered.

"Sa . . . and? Is that what I am to you?" Lique wailed. "I've done everything for you . . . hoo!"

"Let's get real, sweetheart. You don't really hold a candle to her, do you? Surely you know that. Now, be a good girl and stop this blubbering. I need you to go back and keep an eye on the Squanki."

"Jerk," Audril mumbled under her breath. She suddenly felt sorry for Lique. It seemed as though she must have had a horrible sense of self-worth to let Ryannon treat her this way.

Just then, a door creaked open and Grayden pulled Dallin into the room. Audril rose to her feet and her eyes met Dallin's for a brief moment before he turned away.

"Hello again, Atoh," Robert's revolting voice purred right behind her.

"Don't you dare speak to me," she snarled through clenched teeth. "I trusted you . . . Hodgson and Teedee trusted you. You're nothing but a cowardly worm!"

"Trusted me? Well, that was your first mistake. Haven't you learned yet that there's no one you can really trust. Even your closest friends and family will turn on you in a heartbeat if the circumstances are right."

Audril watched as the cushion of the chair she'd been sitting on sunk down under Robert's invisible form. She quickly took a few steps away and scowled in his direction.

"Ahhh! Welcome!" Ryannon smirked upon noticing Grayden and Dallin.

Lique rushed away, apparently too upset to be concerned about anyone hearing her sobs. Grayden tried to comfort her with a touch on the shoulder as she dashed by, but she brushed it off and sped out the door.

"Please, let's begin," Ryannon invited, holding his arm out toward the chairs. "I'm so glad you could join us, Dallin. I wouldn't want my lovely Audril's dearest friend to miss her entrusting."

Grayden shoved Dallin toward the chairs, a move that Dallin did very little to resist. He stumbled forward and nearly fell over. Audril hadn't noticed until he came closer that he was pretty beaten up. One of his eyes was nearly swollen shut and was black and blue. Cuts covered his face and arms, and his lip was still bleeding.

"What have you done to him?" she insisted as Ryannon took his place at her side.

"What? Oh, you mean all of that," Ryannon answered. He lowered his voice and explained, "Well, he sort of went ballistic on Grayden when he saw the surveillance footage of you telling me that kissing him in the Light Dimension was a mistake, and how you could never be with a farmer from Westrim. He seems a little sensitive about that. Grayden was only defending himself."

Audril watched as Dallin was forced into one of the chairs; her heart sank when she noticed his tightly clenched fist. She would have to think of something, and she would have to think of it fast. She found herself longing for her powers, when suddenly it occurred to her. She'd given Lortu her Clest Anaria powers, but did that mean she'd forfeited her Trysta abilities as well? *Could it be that simple,* she thought? If she still possessed any of her Trysta powers, they would surely come in handy right now. The only problem was that there hadn't been time for her to fully figure out what powers she had, or how exactly to use them. There was only one she was sure of, and that was transporting.

"Shall we?" Ryannon asked, holding his arm out to her. She wrapped her hand around it and leaned toward him. "I . . . um . . . I think I've forgotten the vow," she whispered, feigning embarrassment.

"Nice try," he smiled, "but I still have the book, remember. I thought the vow might just slip your mind."

It was precisely what she hoped to hear. With any luck, the book would provide a diversion.

Ryannon escorted her to the center of the glade. "Just one moment, everyone . . . apparently my darling actress is having a bit of stage fright." He looked at Dallin who was glaring at him in disdain, and then turned and kissed Audril passionately.

Audril's attention immediately turned to Dallin, who had looked away when Ryannon kissed her. His hand was still rolled into a fist. She was just about to say something like, "What are you holding?" or "Is that for me?" when Ryannon cleared his throat loudly.

"Let's get started," he insisted, turning to the page in the book with the exalting vow and handing it to Audril.

She looked at the page and pretended to be studying the words, but really, she was hoping that the page opposite the vow would give her something she could use. The picture at the top of the page looked like a Squanki — or at least half of one. The wild haired, bug-eyed creature seemed to be peering out from behind something. Quickly, Audril read the words below the picture and committed them to memory. *Duen e cana voren . . . Duen e cana voren.* "I think I'm ready," she sighed, handing the book back to Ryannon.

He held it out and Grayden walked over and took it from him. "Excellent," he said. "Now, Dallin, you'll want to turn around. We need you as a witness, and you can't very well witness anything like that."

Grayden grabbed Dallin by the face and forced his head around. "Get your hands off of me," he snarled. He looked up at Audril with an overwhelming expression of anger and then dropped his gaze into his lap. The fingers of his closed hand uncurled slightly and he eyed the silver crystals in his palm for a moment.

Audril's heart raced. "Can we get this over with?" she blurted.

Ryannon smiled and took her hands. "*En canlis o canaye, se nalt o betrindi,*" he began.

Time seemed to slip into slow motion. Ryannon lifted one of her hands to his lips and looked deeply into her eyes as he nodded for her to proceed. Out of the corner of her eye she watched Dallin lift his arm and open his hand. He licked the index finger of his other hand and stuck his moistened fingertip into the crystals.

Audril could hear the words she was saying, but didn't feel like she was saying them. "*A se nalt o talis betrindi.*"

Dallin studied his crystal-covered finger for a moment before using his thumb to roll the little minerals into a manageable pinch.

"*Kace enalt o madus betrindi,*" Audril recited breathlessly as Dallin moved his hand toward his mouth. Suddenly, time screeched to a halt. "DALLIN, DON'T!" she screamed. "*DUEN E CANA VOREN!*"

Before Ryannon could respond, a snapping light flashed and a portal opened directly behind Dallin's chair. Tabbit emerged from the portal and, with the strength of ten men and the speed of a Shadow Dweller, pushed Dallin into it and he disappeared.

"LIQUE!" Ryannon bellowed as he instinctively moved toward Tabbit.

"Lady . . . RUNS!" Tabbit screeched before Grayden was able to grab her.

Audril did what she was told and took off through the trees, but running was difficult in the mermaid dress, and Ryannon was in pursuit behind her. She weaved through the dozens of trees with increasing agility, and then raced toward the back of the warehouse and the big bay doors.

Twenty-Seven

Tabbit's voice filled the air of the large room as she yelled in a delighted squeal, "SQUANKIS DON'T TELLS . . . LADY COMES BACKS . . . LADY COMES BACKS . . . RETURN THE POWERS . . . FOUR HUNDRED DAYS . . . FOUR HUNDRED DAYS!"

A few feet ahead, Audril caught a glimpse of a black wisp. *Crap! Robert!* she thought. She knew it was only a matter of seconds before she would be caught. She felt Ryannon's hand hit the back of her dress. It was now or never.

"LOR MANDELA!" she screamed skyward with all of her might. The air around her crackled and a powerful blast of blue ripped through the warehouse, stopping Ryannon in his tracks and making Robert momentarily visible. When at last the light subsided, Audril — heiress to the Trysta throne — was gone.

Chapter XXVIII

DALLIN IS OUR FRIEND

Audril blasted out of the light at the Castine Hills on the southern edge of Mandela City in a full run. The sun was high over the Mandela Mountain Range in the distance. "Mandela Palace!" she shouted into the vivid blue sky, hoping that her dad would put aside his justified anger with her long enough for her to solicit his help. Ryannon still had Tabbit so he could open portals, including the one to Lor Mandela. She still wasn't fully convinced that he was telling the truth about his meeting with the president, but it wasn't something she wanted to risk. Furthermore, she doubted he would stop blowing up places on Earth just because she'd escaped — in fact, she was certain that it would move him to do the opposite.

She materialized just inside the main foyer doors, and was met by a host of startled Solom Guards. "Your father is not amused, young lady," a formidable female guard began, locking her arm around Audril's. "His generals are searching everywhere for you."

"Perfect . . . is he here then? Take me to him," she insisted.

"It's a good thing you are a Noble, Atoh. No one fools the Solom and lives to tell the tale," a muscular male interjected.

Audril stepped up to the foreboding warrior and looked him squarely in his fiery eyes. "I trust that's not a threat, Dweller," she seethed, showing no hint of intimidation. "I believe I said I wanted to be taken to my father."

The guard took a small step backward in surprise. "Of course, Majesty," he nodded, "this way."

No further words were exchanged as an entourage of six guards escorted Audril to her father's chambers. When they arrived, Jonathan was sitting at his desk, staring out the window. He immediately jumped to his feet, rushed to Audril and threw his arms around her.

Audril melted into his chest. She knew a punishment was forthcoming, but it didn't matter at the moment. It just felt good to be in the comfort of her father's embrace.

"Where have you been?" he asked in a much calmer tone than she had anticipated. "And what are you wearing?" He eyed her luxurious gown and observed, "You look like you're going to an entrusting or something."

Audril chuckled at his comment and replied, "I was visiting some ghosts at Alcatraz, Dad. Formal wear is all the rage in today's best prisons."

Jonathan grimaced and shook his head. "You had Kahlie, Bridgette, Glaron and I really worried. I should be livid with you right now, but I'm just . . . I'm just happy you're okay."

Audril looked into her dad's eyes which were nearly spilling over with tears. "Daddy, are you all right?" she asked.

Jonathan forced himself to smile. "You were right, Smaggs. It was wrong of me to send Mikil and the Solom. It's just, if that would have been you . . . she looked just like you, up until she . . ." He tightened his arms around her again.

"It's okay, Dad," she soothed. "I shouldn't have disobeyed you either and I didn't do much better at bringing Ryannon back." She hesitated and took a deep breath. "Though I'm pretty sure he'll be coming here soon on his own."

Jonathan pulled himself away from her. "What? What do you know, Smaggs?"

"He said he went to President Langley, Dad . . . and that he's going to bring half a million soldiers here tomorrow," she answered. "I don't know if he's telling the truth or not, but we have to be prepared. He's probably super

259

ticked since I escaped. Even if he's lying about getting soldiers from the president, I'm sure he'll retaliate somehow."

"You escaped? He was holding you prisoner?" Jonathan quizzed with a combined expression of anger and fear in his sapphire eyes.

"Dad, are you listening? Half a million soldiers!"

"Yeah, angel . . . but how's he gonna get 'em here? As far as I know, there's only one portal still open and it's not nearly big enough."

"Tabbit can open as many portals as he needs. He's been forcing her to open portals for him this whole time!"

"Tabbit?" Jonathan frowned. "So it wasn't Lortu?"

"Lortu . . ? No, Dad, Lortu wouldn't possibly! Not after he . . . ."

"After he what?" Jonathan quizzed.

Audril wasn't about to tell her dad that she'd given Lortu her immortality yet. It would most certainly detract from the urgent matters at hand.

"Nothing, Dad. It's just that Lortu's our friend," she tried, and then quickly changed the subject. "Maybe we should get Kahlie and the generals together, don't you think?"

Jonathan stared at his daughter for a few minutes and then muttered, "I think that's a fairly good idea. Kahlie will be happy to see that you're okay. I think she's still with Dr. Michelan." He placed his hand on the small of her back and guided her from the room.

As they approached the infirmary door, Audril stopped short. "What's Kahlie doing here?" she asked.

"Don't worry, Smaggs. She had a little problem with her powers earlier so Dr. Michelan wanted to check her out thoroughly. I'm sure she can just go to the Caverns and get them restored, but you know the doctor. He tends to be overly cautious."

They barely took two steps into the room before Kahlie jumped up from the table on which she sat and sped to Audril. "Oh, thank heavens!" she gushed as she tossed her arms around Audril's shoulders. "I'm so glad to see you!"

"I'm glad to see you too, Kahlie. How are you feeling?"

Kahlie glanced backward at Michelan, and at Sauvina who was standing at his side, and answered, "I'm feeling better. I think I'm just a bit worn down from everything, ya know?" She raised her voice, so that the doctor and her companion servant were sure to hear her clearly, "I'm sure it's nothing to be too concerned about."

"Michelan, I'm sorry, but I'm going to have to steal the vritesse. I'm afraid it's quite urgent." Jonathan jumped right to the point.

"What is it, dear?" Kahlie asked. "Ryannon, I assume?"

"Yes, Ryannon," he answered, placing his hand on her arm. "Sauvina, would you please dispatch messengers to all of the territories. We need all active army members to report to the palace immediately."

"Right away, Highness," Sauvina responded as she snapped into action and hurried toward the door.

"Send word to Generals Glaron and Statlen as well. I need them back here as soon as possible." The graceful Squanki bowed low and then scampered from the room.

"How may I be of service?" Michelan asked.

"Thank you, my friend," Jonathan answered. "I suppose you'd better ready the medical teams."

Michelan nodded and began gathering instruments and placing them in a large black bag. "I still need to run a couple more tests on you, Vritesse, but I suppose it can wait for now." He hoisted the bag onto his shoulder and kissed Kahlie on the cheek as he too rushed away.

Jonathan turned back to Kahlie. "We're going to need the Trystas, love. Ryannon's force is supposedly five hundred thousand strong. The Mandelan Army hasn't fully recovered from the last battle; I'm afraid we'll be grossly outnumbered."

Kahlie nodded, seemingly worried.

"What's wrong," Jonathan asked.

"How are we going to get word to the Trystas? I don't think I can transport."

"I can," Audril quickly offered. "I can get to Koria and back in just a few minutes."

Kahlie took Audril's hands in hers. "Of course . . . that's perfect."

"She's never been to Koria," Jonathan responded. "She'll have to be told how to get in to the palace."

"All you have to do is recite the seven Trysta disciplines," Kahlie explained. "You can just read them off of the pillars. Start with courage; it will be the furthest from you when you're standing at the gate. Once you've recited the disciplines you'll need to state your heritage."

"Audril Borloc, atoh of Lor Mandela . . . daughter of Gracielle Tu Morning," Jonathan instructed.

Kahlie glanced from Jonathan back to Audril. Her expression became solemn. "Find Commander Pauliss. You'll need to inform her that she's in charge of the Trysta army now. She lives in the Dome of Honor in the Hall of Warriors."

"But . . . Branlor?" Audril breathed, with horror in her eyes.

Kahlie placed a tender hand on her shoulder and answered, "Ryannon."

"After you've notified the Trystas, you'll need to go to Westrim and Castine," Jonathan frowned, seeming more than a little concerned. "Tell General Davids to bring the Western units, and go to the territory offices in Castine. Uprul should be there. He can mobilize the Southern troops."

"But you put Dallin in charge of the Western units, Dad. I'm sure he's back at his farm. Ryannon captured him too, but Tabbit pushed him through a portal right before I escaped."

Jonathan seemed to bristle at the mention of Dallin's name. "I've put Davids in charge for now. Dallin has a problem distancing himself from his emotions when it comes to making crucial decisions. I'm sure Davids will notify him. There's no need for you to tell him."

"What?" Audril gaped. "Dad, that's so unfair! You send him to Earth . . . by himself . . . which looks to me and to everyone else like a special assignment . . . and then you demote him while he's away. He's our friend, Dad. How could you?"

"We don't really have time for this right now, Audril," Jonathan scolded. "You need to get to Koria." He looked her over and added, "You'll probably want to change before you go. I think your battle armor would be best."

Audril looked pleadingly at Kahlie who offered only a sheepish smile and a shrug of her shoulders. "Dallin is our friend," she repeated as she turned on her heels and strode angrily from the room.

Chapter XXIX

THE PRESIDENT'S ARMY

In a remote desert area along the California-Nevada border, the first group of soldiers lined up as instructed, one hundred wide by one hundred deep, at nine o'clock in the morning. A few minutes later, Ryannon, Grayden, Lique and Tabbit arrived via portal, much to the surprise of the assembled troops.

An older, mustached man in camouflage fatigues, a black beret, and dark sunglasses quickly approached Ryannon. "I'm General McIntyre, sir. The president has asked me to assist you in this operation."

Ryannon shook the general's hand warmly with his right hand; in his left, he held his father's old spell book. "Thank you, General," he grinned. "I'm very glad that you and President Langley were able to pull this together so quickly. If we can get started right away, we can get all of our soldiers through to Lor Mandela by two o'clock."

"Understood," the general replied. He glanced down at Tabbit who was rocking up and down on her toes, grinning ear to ear and mumbling her Trinkle Trance and asked, "If you don't mind, sir, what exactly is that thing?"

"This, my good General, is a Squanki. Her race of people is one of the oldest on Lor Mandela. They have certain . . . shall we say . . . supernatural abilities. You saw how we arrived. That is how we will transport your men and women to my planet."

264

"Through some magical light beam? What are the risks, Mr. Ryannon?" the general asked.

Ryannon chuckled. "Don't worry, General. Traveling by portal is perfectly safe. I'll take the first group through myself. My friends here will bring up the rear, and if you would be so good as to coordinate things at the portal line, we should be able to move through quickly and without incident. All your troops have to do is walk through the portal and keep walking when they exit so there is room for everyone."

"Yes, that was in your instructions . . . but do you think you're going to be able to get fifty groups this size through in under five hours?" the general asked, not in a derogatory or doubting tone, but rather one that expressed his willingness to do whatever it took for the mission to be successful.

"I believe so," Ryannon answered. "I've calculated it out, sir. There shouldn't be a problem as long as these people have read their instructions."

"Yes, sir . . . they all have," the general confirmed with a scowl that fully expressed his displeasure in Ryannon questioning his efficiency. "In your instructions, you also said you would be supplying weapons to everyone but the first hundred through. The first hundred are armed, but I don't see any other weapons here."

"Don't worry, General," Ryannon smiled. "The weapons are in a storage facility in my home territory of Brashnell. That is where we'll be exiting the portal. Your soldiers will be supplied there. The first one hundred that I take through only need your weapons so we can secure the area; that's why I wanted them to be your most skilled." He paused and, with condescension, put his hand on the general's shoulder. "With due respect, sir, our weapons are quite superior to yours. They are both more reliable and more effective." Ryannon turned his attention to Grayden and Lique. "Go ahead and start the portal, we're wasting valuable time."

Lique lifted Tabbit into her arms and followed Grayden to the front of the massive group of soldiers. Ryannon explained one or two more details to the general, and then they too moved toward the crowd.

At the front of the line, one hundred gun-toting soldiers watched in shock as a small, wild-haired creature skipped and twirled merrily in front of them rolling both of her hands open and closed – the whole time singing, "Squankis don't tells . . . lady comes backs . . . lady comes backs . . . return the powers . . . four hundred days . . . four hundred days."

Grayden leaned over to Lique and whispered, "Wonder why she's so happy." Lique answered with a shrug of her cloaked shoulders as she and Grayden moved to their place at the back of the regiment.

As Tabbit continued dancing, a sliver of bluish light crackled about a foot off the ground, spanning the entire length of the line of soldiers, and drawing an audible *wuhhh* from the group.

As the second battalion of ten thousand soldiers began to arrive, Ryannon scooped up Tabbit, made a nodding motion with his head, stepped into the portal and disappeared.

General McIntyre lifted one arm high above his head, and moved a hand-held radio to his mouth with the other. He waited until the portal expanded and collapsed entirely, and then flung his arm down and shouted, "NOW!" into the radio. With synchronized precision, the first one hundred soldiers lifted their boots to the light. The portal snapped loudly and popped open, swallowing all one hundred in a flash of pale blue. As the portal snapped again and shrunk back to a single thin line, General McIntyre signaled for the second row of soldiers to hold their position, while he kept an eye on his watch.

Ten minutes passed. The second ten thousand were now lined up behind the first and the third were arriving, creating a bit of a space issue. The general reviewed Ryannon's instructions in his mind. *Wait for one of your soldiers to come back through the portal and give the signal. If no word comes, send the second group through at twenty-five minutes.*

Fifteen minutes...no signal. Eighteen minutes...still nothing. At nearly twenty-three and a half minutes, the portal made an odd buzzing noise, and out stepped a single female soldier. "All clear, General," she reported. "We have secured the armory in Brashnell." The lone soldier turned to reenter the portal with the next row of one hundred, when all of a sudden, the portal snapped loudly and shrunk in nearly ten feet on both ends. General McIntyre eyed the thin light over the rim of his sunglasses as once again it made a violent cracking sound and shrunk towards the middle. "Get those two bozos of Ryannon's up here, NOW!" he barked into his radio.

A younger officer toward the back of the group responded. "I've got 'em, sir. I'll send them up pronto." He turned toward Lique who was busily directing soldiers into position and said, "General McIntyre needs you and, uh . . . your friend up to the front right away."

Before Lique could react, Grayden came from out of nowhere and grabbed her by the arm. "The portal's collapsing!" he bellowed. "Come on!" They rushed to the front of the massive group and met up with the general just as the portal made an anticlimactic sizzling noise and disappeared.

"What the Sam Hill is going on here?" the general yelped, thrusting his arm out towards where the portal had been. "What exactly are we supposed to do now?"

"I don't know, sir, but I assure you that Ryannon will figure this out," Grayden tried. "They probably just had a little difficulty on the other side. I bet he'll have this portal re-opened in just a few minutes." His words were confident, yet his eyes showed concern.

General McIntyre rubbed his forehead and looked off to the side where a large cloud of red dust moved toward them. "Ugh, perfect timing . . . the president's motorcade," he groaned. "Hope you two are good at explaining things." He gave both Lique and Grayden a little shove toward the first limousine in the procession and grumbled, "Hold back units five through eight," into his radio.

"What is it, General?" President Langley yelped as she stepped from her vehicle and saw him moving toward her.

"We're not sure, ma'am," he bellowed back. "Seems Mr. Ryannon is having a little problem with his portal. He took the first hundred through, but when we were ready to move the second team in, the portal disappeared. These are his two assistants, maybe they can explain."

President Langley stepped up to Grayden and Lique and studied their faces intently. "You don't have the same eyes as him," she observed.

"No, ma'am," Grayden explained. "We're from Earth. My girlfriend and I have been helping Mr. Ryannon out, that's all. We didn't know we were gonna get roped into such an elaborate operation."

"So you're just innocent bystanders?" the president asked incredulously. "What is your name, sir?"

"Oh . . . excuse me . . . of course," Grayden stammered. "My name is Dr. Gordon Bentley. I'm a physics professor at University of Colorado." He fumbled around in his jacket pocket for a moment before producing a fake faculty identification card. Lique followed suit and offered her driver's license.

The president handed the IDs to one of her handlers. "Check these out, Clint," she instructed. "How exactly did you get roped into this elaborate operation, Dr. Bentley?"

"Well, ma'am, we were on a bit of a romantic road trip for our first anniversary . . . traveling cross country on Interstate Eighty . . . when we came across Mr. Ryannon and his little Squanki in a rest area outside of Cheyenne, Wyoming. At first, he told us that his friends had dumped them there, but after we drove them back into town and bought them dinner, he told us his real story. Of course we didn't believe him, although, admittedly, the Squanki was unlike anything I'd ever seen . . . Just ask the general here." He pointed to General McIntyre who nodded wholeheartedly. "But then he showed us a portal. We went from Cheyenne to New York in seconds!"

Just then the president's guard returned with the IDs. "They check out, ma'am," he offered as he handed the forms back to Lique and Grayden.

"Well, then what do you propose we do, Doctor? We can't very well go through with this operation without the portal."

Grayden looked down at the ground for a minute before sighing. "I honestly don't know. I think we should give Ryannon a chance to reopen it, though."

The president surveyed the huge horde of soldiers and took a deep breath. "All right," she began. "Mr. Ryannon seemed quite adamant that the troops be through by two o'clock. General, have everyone maintain their current position. If nothing happens by two, we have no choice but to scrap the mission. Let's pray your Mr. Ryannon and a hundred of this nation's finest can figure something out quickly, Doctor."

"Yes, ma'am," Grayden replied. "Let's pray."

Chapter XXX

THE CALL OF THE BIG PIG

H odgson chose to be the one to deliver the news to Teedee. "Weeev'e lossst them, my dearrrrr."

"What do you mean, you've lost them?" she barked, sounding suddenly more authoritative than the eccentric old woman she was.

"Weeee think that Treborrrr is a traitorrrr. One of Madras' guardddds saw himmmm take Dallllinnnn through a porrrrtalll."

"A portal? That Ryannon fellow must've gotten a hold of him. Blast!" Teedee looked toward the sound of Hodgson's voice and shook her head. "Well, there's only one thing to do," she sighed, looking down at her restrictive ensemble. "I have to change."

With that, she started across the room. She had just stepped into the hall, when the telephone in the kitchen let out a startlingly loud ring. "Oh, who could that be?" she muttered to herself as she shuffled toward it.

"Hello . . . Oh, hello Ed. What? Who? Yes, of course, calm down, Ed. I'm sure it's nothing. No . . . the police won't be necessary. I'll be there in just a moment." With a sly grin, Teedee hung up the phone. "I can't believe my luck!" she giggled. "What perfect timing . . . HODGSON!" she squealed, "Hodgson, we are off to the Quik Mart. Ed says there's someone there who I think can help us."

Thirty

Teedee scampered to her room and emerged five minutes later dressed in a red and black corseted top dress, with layers of red chiffon forming a tutu-type skirt. Her scrawny legs looked even more frail sticking out from under the fluffy skirt, shrouded in bright red stockings. Clunky, black shin-high boots did little to add to the illusion of girth. With the appearance of an aged can-can dancer gone anorexic, Teedee headed for the door shouting back at Hodgson to follow.

They made their way down the dew-frosted lane quickly. Hodgson more so than his elderly counterpart, but he would stop periodically and wait for her to catch up. In the sunlight, a black blur here and there could be detected, a shadow without a source, moving over plants, rocks and the ground. As they moved up the hill, the pace slowed, but still remained steady, and within twenty minutes, Teedee stepped through the door at the Quik Mart to the melodious sound of the heart-stopping buzzer.

"Ed!" she called out. She scoured the store which seemed to be deserted. "Ed!" she bellowed again.

"In the back," a faint voice echoed back. "Come on back, Teedee."

Teedee shrugged her shoulders and moved to the swinging grey door behind the counter of the café. As soon as she entered the kitchen she was met with a wide-eyed Ed who was staring in awe at the small creature perched on a stack of milk crates and happily scarfing down a chili-drowned Big Pig.

Guddlebee looked up at Teedee with moist eyes of absolute ecstasy.

"He says he's with Maggie and her cousin," Ed mumbled, not breaking his stare.

Without missing a beat, Teedee thrust her hands onto her hips. "Quentin!" she barked. "Haven't your father and I told you a thousand times that you're not to come into town alone?" She snatched up a bar towel that was sitting on the stainless steel countertop and moved towards Guddlebee's face.

"Quentins?" Guddlebee questioned, shoving more of the half-eaten dog into his mouth before Teedee could assault it with the towel.

271

"I'm sorry, Ed. He does tend to get into some mischief from time to time."

"You know him?" Ed questioned. He leaned close to Teedee and whispered. "What is he?"

Teedee wrapped her skinny arm around Ed's and walked him away from Guddlebee. "He's my nephew," she sighed. "My dear sister . . . rest her soul . . . fell in with a bad group when she was younger." She glanced sympathetically over her shoulder at Guddlebee who was still happily munching away. "It was the drugs," she frowned. "The poor little guy will never look normal."

Ed nodded skeptically, "Uh, I'm sorry, Teedee. I didn't know. He just came in here shouting 'Big Pig . . . Big Pig.' I didn't know what to do with him. I didn't want him scaring the other folks, so I brought him back here. Seems happy enough since he got his Big Pig though."

"No worries, Toots," she smiled and slapped him on the back. "I'll just take him up to my place until his dad gets home from work. We'll find something for him to do there that'll keep him out of trouble. Come along, Quentin," she ordered, "Aunt Teedee will take you home. I think you've taken up enough of Mr. Marler's time."

With his pudgy little fingers, Guddlebee quickly shoved the last few bites of chili into his mouth and smiled through a mouthful of food.

"Ugh," Teedee moaned, "Come on." She lifted him from the milk crates and set him on the ground. "Add that one to my account please, Ed."

"Sure thing, Teedee," Ed answered, still gazing in awe at Guddlebee.

"Aunties Dee?" Guddlebee tried, "Aunties Dee?"

"Yes, Quentin," she replied through clenched teeth.

"Another Big Pigs?" he grinned widely, and tilted his curl-covered head to the side.

"Not right now, Quen," she hissed. "Now, thank Mr. Marler."

"Oh, thank yous, Mr. Marler . . . thank yous," he gushed.

"My pleasures . . . um . . . pleasure," Ed replied almost as though he was asking a question. He watched as Teedee shooed the odd little creature out of the kitchen and toward the front doors.

As they were exiting, a young mother and her small son came through the door. The mother twitched unnaturally at the sight of Guddlebee who just smiled and patted her son affectionately on the head. The little boy giggled with delight and bounded into the store, waving enthusiastically at the playful Squanki.

"What are you doing?" Teedee scolded as soon as the glass doors swung shut. "Surely you were told to stay hidden. Do you want to start a riot?"

Guddlebee looked up at her apologetically. "I is sorrys, Auntie Dees. Guddlebee was hungrys. Big Pigs was calling mes!"

"That's no excuse, Guddlebee, and I am not your Aunt," she corrected. "But I would very much like to know how you got here."

"Through the portals with the nices atoh lady," he replied matter-of-factly. "She is lookings for Ryannons of Brashnell. Dallin is lookings for the momma of the atoh's bestess friend, and I is looking for mys Entrusteds, Tabbits. We all comes to Drolana to look togethers. So far, nobodys finds nobodys."

"Oh, someone has found someone," Teedee corrected. "It would seem that Ryannon of Brashnell has found Dallin and the atoh."

"Yikers!" Guddlebee shouted, stopping in place. "Times to ask Athenius for helps!"

"What?" Teedee asked. "Who is Athenius?"

Guddlebee looked skyward and froze like a statue.

"Guddlebee?" Teedee tried. The chubby little Squanki ignored her completely. "Um, excuse me, but what are you . . . ?"

"Shhhhh!" Guddlebee snapped, waving his hand angrily. "Hes is telling me somethings."

"Fantastic," Teedee mumbled under her breath, "they had to bring the insane one along."

273

"Not insanes . . ." Guddlebee hummed, "In tuuuuune."

"Fine, Mr. In tune, can we just move it along?"

Again Guddlebee forcefully shushed her. He stood staring into the sky while Teedee impatiently rapped her fingers against the fabric of her skirt.

After nearly a minute, Guddlebee turned his gaze to Teedee and whispered, "Nothings is right. Athenius is nots happy. He says that he can't sees anyones anymores."

"Fascinating," Teedee snipped. "Now if you're done talking to your make-believe friends, can we get to the business at hand? We need to find Audril and Dallin. I assume you can open portals."

Guddlebee looked up at her with frustration in his bulgy eyes. "Athenius is nots make believes! Hes is real! Nobodys listens to poor Guddlebee . . . Oh, nos . . . they calls him crazies, and broken-headeds, and one Truglunt shorts of a criwa cake! But my stars friends are reals! They talks to mes and tells me things! Just likes your invisible lovey doveys is real! He talks to yous, but you is nots crazies!"

Teedee placed her hand affectionately on the top of Guddlebee's head. "I suppose you're right, dear. I have no right to judge."

Guddlebee drew in a deep breath and blew a stray curl off his forehead out of the side of his mouth. "Yeah, I is nots crazies," he sighed.

"Maybe . . . what if we just all worked together?" Teedee tried. "Us visible ones, and our not so visible friends? Do you think we could do that?"

Guddlebee nodded and his head full of curls flipped and flopped everywhere. "Where do you needs the portal to, Auntie Dees?"

Teedee glanced around to make sure there was no one within earshot. She leaned down close to Guddlebee and whispered, "How about to Mandela City."

Chapter XXXI

A NEW PLAN

O n the southern border of Brashnell, in a spacious clearing surrounded by tall, thick-trunked evergreens, Ryannon, Tabbit, and the first one hundred US soldiers stepped out of the portal, poised for confrontation. Four Brashnellan border guards who were routinely patrolling the area immediately turned and sped toward town to warn the new territory leaders of Ryannon's arrival. Ryannon gave them a generous running start before signaling the troops to gun them down. In a barrage of bullets, the border guards flailed spastically and then dropped dead to the ground.

"Come on," Ryannon directed, leading the team toward the armory that was only a few hundred yards beyond the trees.

"Avoid the fence," he warned as they approached. A tall fence made of a stringy crystalline material and topped with a row of sharp, jagged black stones surrounded the compound. "It's lethal to the touch."

"Well, I'll be a Lodian slarp," a sultry female voice oozed from a small white gatehouse just beyond the fence. "I thought you had left us to rot with these atoc kissers." A stunning dark-skinned woman dressed in a snug uniform that accentuated the curves of her voluptuous body slid out of the house and surveyed the group. A few of the soldiers smirked or gasped at the sight of her.

"Are you going to just stand there making my men drool, Tora, or are you going to let us in?" Ryannon asked.

"Are you going to fix this ridiculous mess?" she retorted as she pointed a metal wand-type instrument toward the row of locks that ran down the length of the gate. One by one, the locks made a grinding noise and turned ninety degrees to the right. As the last one made its rotation, the gate clicked and slid to the side.

"Who else is here today?" Ryannon questioned before leaning down and kissing Tora on the cheek.

"Just me and Doran," she answered with a sly smile. "I think he's still loyal."

"Doran worships the ground you walk on, my dear. I'm sure he's loyal to whoever you are."

"Well, yes . . . that's true," she sniggered.

Ryannon moved his team of soldiers into the armory yard and toward a sprawling warehouse made of a shimmering, almost liquid-like, grey material. As the troops filed into the building, he paused and flipped to the page in the book with the Time Align spell. "*Seeta barus en dali a Drolana*," he read loudly.

With a booming thud like a bomb exploding in the distance, every visible thing distorted and time seemed to screech to a near halt. The soldiers stretched out and moved either in extreme slow motion or stopped altogether. The warehouse building warped into a towering ripple and the ground took on the appearance of a thick, gelatinous mass. Then, just as unexpectedly as time had slowed, it ripped forward. The building shrunk and squished inward. The soldiers flew toward the open doors like a frantic swarm of bees, and the suddenly solid ground bumped violently. As quickly as the strange phenomenon started, it came to an abrupt stop, sending everyone tumbling clumsily across the dirt.

"My apologies," Ryannon coughed as he scooped up Tabbit and tossed her into her usual flopped-over-the-shoulder position. "I wasn't aware that would cause such a commotion . . . but do not be alarmed. Everything is fine."

Thirty-One

The startled soldiers stood and brushed themselves off as they continued into the warehouse. The last one to reach the building was a stocky woman with a stern countenance.

"Colonel, uh, Perry, is it?" Ryannon read her name from the pocket of her uniform. "Believe it or not, we're now secure," he chuckled. "Would you please go back through the portal and inform General McIntyre that we are ready to proceed?"

As the Colonel rushed away, Ryannon turned to Tora and instructed, "Inform as many of our allies as you can that I have returned, and you and Doran meet me at number three in ten minutes. I am going to need your help with something."

Tora glanced at her perfectly manicured nails and casually replied, "I'll see what I can do. I assume that this thing you need help with is destroying the atoc and his pathetic excuse for warriors. Otherwise, I prefer not to waste my time."

"Would I ask if it were anything less?" Ryannon teased. "Now scamper along, my little vixen. You don't want to keep me waiting."

Ryannon took one step into the warehouse, pointed to the dark-haired man nearest him and said, "You . . . you are in charge until I return. If anyone besides me, Colonel Perry or Commander Tora come through this door, you are to shoot them on sight. Do I make myself clear?"

The soldier nodded as Ryannon turned his remarks to the entire group. "The boxes on that shelf over there contain a weapon called a vystoran sleeve." He motioned with his head toward the lone shelf that spanned the back wall of the facility. "You are each to take one. Their operation is quite simple . . . just point the wide end at your intended target and push the button on the shaft. The disks inside them rupture on contact, and are fatal within seconds. I rely on you, as the first team, to brief the others as they arrive on the vystoran sleeve usage. We return to the portal in fifteen minutes, and you will all need to bring as many of those boxes as you can carry." Concluding his short briefing, he slightly adjusted Tabbit's position on his shoulder and exited, strutting confidently towards the opposite end of the building.

Behind the warehouse was a neat row of smaller structures, each labeled with a large, charcoal grey number on the door. Tora and a man with long, grungy hair and a stubbly face waited for him at building number three.

"Well, aren't you a sight?" the man called out as he approached. "Did you bring us dinner?" he snickered, pointing at Tabbit who was still quietly mumbling her trance.

"Doran," Ryannon laughed. "Speaking of a sight, you look like you haven't bathed in weeks."

"Smells like it too," Tora smirked.

"Awww, you love it, precious," Doran quipped, pulling her close to him as she cringed and tried to pull away. "Whatcha need, brother?"

Ryannon lowered Tabbit and held her out to him. "I've got about half a million soldiers from Drolana on their way here now," he bragged with a smug expression of absolute superiority. "We'll take Mandela City easily if you can manage to lead fifty clueless soldiers."

"What do I want with this?" Doran asked with a scowl as he took Tabbit from Ryannon's hands.

"Use her to open portals to the atoc's weapon stores and the palace. There should still be at least that many Catorians inside here." He pointed to the door of building three. "Set all of them to maximum range and send one soldier to each of the small stores, two to the larger ones, and one to the palace through the portals. Give them each a Catorian and set the detonators to all go off at sundown. That should give us plenty of time to get in position."

"That'll be quite a bang," Doran grinned. "Then what?"

Ryannon turned to Tora. "After the portals are open, take her to Manaque. See if that old Squanki fool can figure out what she's rambling on about. I don't want any Shadow Squanki voodoo messing with my plans."

"No, no," Doran chuckled. "I didn't mean what do we do with the Squanki, I meant what do I do with the soldiers? Do you want me to bring them along with our troops to Mandela to fight?"

"The Drolanans won't be needed," Ryannon assured. "When those Catorians explode they'll wipe out most of Jonathan's army and nearly all of his weapons. The army I've amassed will be more than enough to finish off the Mandelans. Tell these so called 'America's Finest' to stay and guard the Catorians. That'll just be fifty less I have to worry about getting back to Drolana when it's all over. Of course, I'll probably keep all of the Drolanans that live through the battle here. I'll need labor to rebuild it all, won't I? Besides, most of them won't have anything to go back to once I detonate the devices I've already placed on their planet." He smiled and drew in a deep, rapturous breath. He then turned to Tora. "I want to have some of our own with me, though. That's why I asked you to notify our allies. I'll need at least a handful of competent warriors."

"I've already sent word to Telnuk. She's been rallying the faithful in your absence. I believe her group is over two hundred strong and growing daily."

"Excellent," Ryannon smirked. "By this time tomorrow, my friends, we'll not only have control of Lor Mandela, but Drolana will be ours as well."

"Delightful," Tora purred. "I've always wanted to go to Drolana. Maybe I can find a man there that doesn't smell like slarp drool."

Doran chuckled. "Maybe I can find a woman who can reach the door handle without a boost."

Ryannon shook his head. "Could you two please hold off on your little love-fest for now? We have work to do. I'll send your fifty over in a few moments. I'm using them to bring weapons to the portal first. Start getting those portals open immediately." He slapped Doran on the arm and marched back to the warehouse.

The dark-haired man he'd left in charge whipped out his vystoran and aimed it at Ryannon's head as he came through the door.

"Well done, Major Porter," Ryannon smirked, pushing the soldier's arm down. "Everyone grab boxes," he commanded. "Let's move!"

Carrying three or four boxes each, the soldiers marched back across the compound and into the trees. They reached the clearing without incident, but when they arrived, there was no trace of the portal anywhere. Ryannon pushed through the group to where it was supposed to be. "Ghandental," he hissed.

"What's going on here, sir?" Major Porter yelled as the team of soldiers watched. "Where's the portal?"

Ryannon gathered his composure and turned to face the demanding officer. "The portal seems to have collapsed, sir. But not to worry, I'll go get Tabbit and have her reopen it."

As if on cue, Doran appeared at the edge of the clearing, carrying Tabbit with him. "Ryannon," he called over the heads of the soldiers, "a word?"

Ryannon moved toward him taking note of the look of concern on Doran's face. "This Squanki is not right," he began in a hushed tone. "Her portals aren't working."

Tabbit gazed up at Ryannon with a psychotic smile on her face. "Portals aren't working," she giggled. "Squanki don't tells . . . Lady comes backs."

Ryannon grimaced at Doran. "What do you mean, they aren't working? She's been opening portals for me for days."

Doran pulled him behind a particularly imposing tree and lowered Tabbit to the ground. "Watch . . . Squanki, I need a portal to the Mertine Weaponry Post," Doran instructed.

She lifted her arm into the air and repeated, "I need a portal to the Mertine Weaponry Post." She curled her small fingers in and out and in and out. Gradually, a tiny, pale blue light appeared in front of her face and stretched to about the length of her hand before making a strange pop, shrinking back in and fizzling away.

"Every time she tries, this happens," Doran explained. "There's obviously something wrong with her."

"Obviously something wrong with her," she laughed. "Lady comes backs." Her long, white hair weaved and bounced in the air, completely independent from the rest of her.

"This is spectacular," Ryannon growled with a demeaning smack to the back of Tabbit's head. "I'm hours away from my greatest victory, and you decide to lose your senses."

Tabbit squealed with delight. "Lose your senses . . . Return the powers."

"Enough!" Ryannon snapped. "Have Tora take her to Manaque now, Doran . . . while you find me another Squanki!" The flecks in his eyes burned bright red. "I can't believe this," he snarled, kicking angrily at the forest floor. "I am in the midst of seizing control of two entire worlds and this little pest decides to break down now! Will you just get her out of my sight before I take her annoying little head off?"

"Her annoying little head off?" Tabbit repeated. She locked Ryannon in an intense stare and sneered, "Four Hundred Days . . . Four Hundred Days."

Sensing that Ryannon was close to making good his beheading threat, Doran scooped Tabbit from the ground and sped away.

As Ryannon slid out from behind the tree, he was confronted by a tense-jawed Major Porter. "Where's he going?" the terse soldier asked. "Don't we need that Tammit, or whatever it is, to reopen the portal? Seems to me that your plan has a few glitches."

Ryannon did his best to force a smile, but it was far from sincere. "As every plan does, my good man . . . I'm sure you've had to improvise a time or two, yourself, haven't you?"

The major acted like he hadn't heard a word. "What are we supposed to do now? I've got a hundred men and women here who want to be able to go home eventually, and if you don't get those others through, will they even have a home to go back to? You may be okay with screwin' around with the fate of my planet, but I am most certainly not okay with you doing it!" His face was practically purple and a vein bulged in his tan neck. "I suggest you come up with something, and I suggest you come up with it quickly."

A New Plan

It took everything in Ryannon not to pull a vystoran sleeve on this annoying man.

"I assure you that everything is under control, Major," he fumed. "Your troops will be just fine. Besides, it does little good for you to panic at the first little snag. Haven't you been trained to remain calm under pressure? My friend Doran will bring us another Squanki and we'll reopen the portal. It's as simple as that. Now, why don't you get over there and persuade everyone else that we're still on track, instead of instigating a blooming riot?"

The major scowled at him and was about to respond when a rustling in the trees caught their attention. Led by a rather masculine woman with deep set eyes, the Brashnellan warriors — two hundred thirty-four in all — pushed their way into the clearing.

"Ahh, Telnuk, welcome," Ryannon oozed. "Major Porter? This is General Telnuk . . . one of my finest officers."

Telnuk didn't break a smile, but instead nodded smugly.

"Excuse me," Major Porter seethed as he turned and crossed the clearing to rejoin his comrades. He approached a soldier who was squatting and writing something on the ground with a stick.

"Anderson . . ." he whispered. "Anderson!"

Sergeant Anderson looked up and raised to full height. "Yes, sir? What is it?"

The major glanced over his shoulder to make sure Ryannon wasn't looking. "We've got a problem."

Anderson leaned toward Major Porter and listened.

"This guy isn't who he seems to be," the major explained. "I overheard him talking to one of his men. I'm pretty sure he's the one responsible for the explosions back home. He's planning on overthrowing this planet and ours."

"What?" the sergeant gasped. "Are you sure?"

"Yeah," Porter sighed.

"So what do we do now?" Sergeant Anderson asked. "He's given us weapons. Shouldn't we take him out?"

"We can't right now. He's got his group of yahoos over there that outnumber us two to one, and we're on their home turf. It would be suicide." The major leaned in a little closer. "No . . . spread the word, Sergeant. As soon as he reopens that portal we need to get word to General McIntyre. Tell everyone to keep their eyes and ears open, and if anyone has any brainy ideas, tell them to report to me."

Sergeant Anderson made a small nodding motion with his head to indicate that Ryannon and his group of Brashnellan warriors were moving toward them. The major pretended to be scratching the side of his leg and observed their position. He turned back toward the Sergeant with an expression of intense concern on his rugged face. "I hope we've brought some strategists with us, Anderson," he breathed. "We're definitely in need of a new plan."

Chapter XXXII

DECLINE OF A VRITESSE

A udril sulked through the halls of the palace until she arrived at the staging room, a three story high chamber that housed all of the suits of armor worn by the Nobles and their respective courts for hundreds of years. In the center of the room was a high shelf loaded with various weapons and big, leather-bound books. It had four sides, each with a rolling ladder attached, necessary because the shelf reached nearly to the top of the middle level of the room. On the first and third floors, wood-paneled alcoves lined the walls, each spanned by a thick, wooden rod. The alcoves held the more streamlined suits which hung by black metal hooks on the rods. The second floor contained rows of gleaming metal armor, more like the bulky medieval suits that Audril was familiar with on Earth.

She maneuvered around the shelf to the wall furthest the door and made her way directly to her mother's suit of armor — one she'd only learned existed three and a half weeks earlier when her dad had given it to her for protection, the last time Ryannon attacked Mandela City. She ran her hand down the sleek charcoal fabric that looked like polished rock, and over the steel scrollwork that formed an elegant protective breastplate of sorts. An icy chill washed over her as her fingertips bumped across a patched area within the scrolls. This was where Ryannon's dagger had plunged into her chest following the last battle — on the day that she learned she was immortal.

284

This time she wouldn't be as lucky. If Ryannon or any of his followers were fortunate enough to find the weaknesses in the suit, she would die just like anyone else. The reality of it made her feel a little sick, but the feeling wasn't based in fear. It stemmed from a different, more complicated emotion.

Her thoughts at the moment centered on one thing and one thing only — Dallin Doone. The mere idea of never being able to tell him how she really felt, of never truly being his was the sole cause of her anxiety.

She contemplated going to his farm first, and getting it all out into the open, but she knew that would be blatantly irresponsible. She had to alert the Trystas and the Mandelans first, but she decided there and then that when she went to Westrim to find General Davids, she would make a stop at Dallin's. If a battle was about to take place where something dreadful might happen, it couldn't wait. She had to tell him. She longed to kiss him again and feel his arms around her.

She slipped out of the dress and into her armor and headed out of the palace.

As soon as she reached the bottom of the steps, she took off in a run across East Mystad Field. "Trysta Palace!" she shouted once she reached an adequate transporting speed.

Beyond the scrolling gate, a group of female warriors practiced sparring exercises, while other Trystas milled around the grounds. None of them seemed to notice her arrival, despite its bright accompanying flash.

"Courage, strength, wisdom, honor, self-control, unity in nature, and dignity in death," she recited loudly, reading from the plaques attached to each pillar. The word death seemed to catch in her throat as she spoke the seventh Trysta discipline. "I am Audril, atoh of Lor Mandela and daughter of Gracielle Tu Morning." As she finished, the large gate creaked open and several of the Trystas turned from what they were doing to see who had arrived.

"Atoh," one of the warriors breathed as she lowered to one knee.

"Clest Anaria," another whispered, humbly bowing as well.

As this Trysta rose, she approached Audril. "You are wearing your mother's battle armor," she observed, pointing to the pair of angels etched into the abdominal shield below the scrollwork. "Should I send for Branlor?"

Audril shook her head sadly. "I'm afraid Commander Branlor was killed," she announced. "He died with honor while engaging Ryannon of Brashnell." The sculpted Trysta let out an animalistic hiss at the mention of Ryannon's name. "I've been sent by the vritesse to notify Commander Pauliss. Do you know where she is?"

"I will locate her immediately, Atoh," the woman offered. It was obvious that the news of Branlor's death at Ryannon's hands deeply bothered her. She gulped hard, pulled her shoulders back and strode off toward the Hall of Warriors.

Audril had nearly reached the doors to the main dome when Commander Pauliss, a stunning red-haired woman in a suit of armor similar to her own, and the Trysta who had gone to retrieve her came through them.

"Atoh," the commander began, "I hear you bring news from the vritesse." She too bowed respectfully to Audril.

"Yes, Commander. First, in case you haven't heard . . ." she glanced at the other Trysta who shook her head somewhat surreptitiously. "Oh," she continued, "I guess you haven't." She drew in a deep breath. "Commander Branlor has been killed by Ryannon of Brashnell, Pauliss."

Commander Pauliss' green eyes widened in shock. "What does the vritesse require of me?" she asked, dropping her gaze to the ground.

"You're in charge of the Trysta Army now," Audril explained, "and we need your help. Ryannon may be bringing a very large army from Drolana to attack Mandela City. Vritesse Kahlie and the atoc request your immediate assistance."

The commander made a visible effort to collect herself. "Notify the troop leaders, Kanali," she instructed. The other Trysta nodded and raced away. "We will bring our army as quickly as possible, Atoh, and we will avenge our brother, Branlor."

"Thank you, Commander. I'm sure you will," Audril replied. "When you're ready, bring your army to Mandela Palace. The vritesse will be waiting. Now if you'll excuse me, there's no time for me to hang around. I have to go to Castine and alert the Mandelans." Of course, she was only revealing part of her motivation for leaving so quickly; she was now one step closer to seeing Dallin.

She transported to the Castine Territory offices and quickly found the old Shadow Dweller, Uprul. After she delivered her message, the aged Dweller asked her to wait for a moment. "Der is someting of grave eemportance dat you moust know, Atoha."

"What is it, Uprul?" she asked, not at all expecting what happened next.

"Dis is not someting dat de wise Uprul can tell," a familiar voice replied, as Lortu materialized from the side of a large, wooden desk, and Uprul faded into a corner. "You are not supposed to be heah, Atoha," he growled. "Yoah meesion is on de Drolana."

"I've been to Drolana, Lortu," she snipped. "As you see, I've come back."

"No come back!" he hissed angrily. "Yoah meesion is not complete!"

"My mission, Lortu? Do you even know what it is?"

Lortu paced as he always did, but there was something extra creepy about his posture at the moment. "Eez de Squanki back? Eez de Ryannon captured?" he slinked around behind her and leaned his head over her shoulder to her ear. "Deed you let yoah feelings for de Dallin Doone be seen?" he whispered.

"Dallin?" she gasped. "How do you know about that?"

"Dwellers know tings, remembah?" He came around to face her and added, "Yoah meesion has been destroyed."

"What?" she snapped. "Listen, Lortu, I have no idea what you're talking about, and I really don't have time for your little riddles right now, so if you could just explain to me in simple terms what it is you're talking about, I'd really appreciate it."

287

Lortu pulled his shoulders back and stood at his full height, something Audril had never seen him do before. "You have sent de Dallin Doone to a place dat weel not be found. Der eez no one to protect yoah powers . . . eegnorant girl . . . eempulseeve, stupeed girl!"

"What are you talking about?" Audril bellowed. "Dallin is at his farm! Tabbit pushed him into a portal to keep him from killing himself! Don't call me stupid, Lortu, when you're the one so wrapped up in being mysterious that you can't even see the obvious, simple answers!"

"Obvious and seemple?" Lortu fired back. "Have you seen de Dallin Doone der? And de Squanki Tabbeet . . . weel she even be alive tomorrow because of you?"

Audril fought back tears as she looked into his pale, crackled eyes. The things he was insinuating were horrific. They weren't true. They couldn't be. Without saying another word, she turned and ran from the building. She would show him. She would prove that Dallin was home — right where he should be.

She ran across the courtyard of the territory offices and was about to transport when Lortu appeared at her right, running beside her. "He won't be der . . . you know dis," he said.

"That's enough!" she shrieked. "Just shut up, Lortu! Just keep my stupid powers and my stupid mission and leave me alone!" She sped her pace and looked skyward. "THE FARM OF DALLIN DOONE!" she screamed and disappeared in a flash.

She sprang out of the light at the end of Dallin's front walkway and raced toward the house. "Dallin . . . Dallin?" she called out as she burst through the unlocked door and maneuvered through the dark house. "Dallin, please . . . where are you?" Frantic, she headed for the back door and out into the yard. "DALLIN!" she yelled once more as she ran towards the barn. She pulled the sliding door open and called out again. "Dallin? Are you in here?" There was no reply.

Out of breath and panting, she stepped inside the barn. Lortu's words, *You have sent de Dallin Doone to a place dat weel not be found* burned in her head like a fire. Her heart felt like it was being squeezed in a vice, and it was getting tighter and tighter with every passing second. She glanced around the quiet barn. "Dallin?" she whimpered. "Dallin." Her knees suddenly felt like rubber and went out from under her and she fell to the ground and wept.

After a few torturous moments, she heard a faint rustling coming from behind the Eternal Companion sculpture, but she didn't have the energy to pull herself up.

"Aye am zorry, Atoha," Lortu whispered as he moved from the shadows and approached her.

Audril ran her hands over her eyes and tried to regain her composure. "What have I done, Lortu?" she sobbed, "and how can I fix it?"

Lortu sat down on the ground next to her and lifted her so that she could lean against him. He stroked her hair gently and breathed, "Der iz noting dat can be done for de Dallin naow, Audril. Eet eez in de hands of de Lor Mandela. But you moust go back to de Drolana, or none of dis weel end."

Audril lifted her face and looked up at Lortu through red eyes. "What do you mean? Why do I have to go back if Ryannon is coming here?"

"Dis eez de mystery dat even de Lortu does not understand, Atoha. Aye only know dat eef you remain on de Lor Mandela, de Ryannon of Brashnell weel not be stopped." Lortu slid away from her and pushed himself up from the dirt floor and back to his feet. "Aye weel find de General Davids and tell heem about de Ryannon. You go back to de palace and let yoah fautter and de vritessa know dat de Trystas and de Mandelans are coming. We can feegure out how to get you back to de Drolana after you have had some rest."

Audril reluctantly stood and brushed the dirt from her armor. "Lortu?" she began, "Will you answer me something honestly?" She studied Lortu's eyes for a moment and then asked, "Will I be the Clest Anaria again? Will you give my powers back to me?"

Lortu tilted his head and grimaced. He kept his eyes focused on hers as he moved toward the dark corner behind the sculpture. "You know someting,

Atoha?" he asked. "Yoah mutter's armor eez good on you." With that, he disappeared into the corner and left Audril alone with her questions.

"Terrific," she sighed, sucking in a huge, quivering breath and starting for the barn door, "absolutely terrific."

She wandered across the yard, still fighting back tears. It took a few minutes for her to motivate herself to run, during which time she just sauntered along slowly down the dirt road that led from Dallin's farm to the Sybran Forest.

When she finally transported back to the palace she was met with the sight of several Trystas rising out of Mystad Lake. There was something artistic and lovely about watching them ascend through fountains of crystal water, and she couldn't help but stop and take in the spectacle.

After a few minutes, Commander Pauliss emerged out of a large, sparkling jet towards the center of the lake. Upon seeing Audril she leaned forward and the jet bent and deposited her gracefully alongside the atoh. "We are here to serve," she smiled, bowing.

Audril liked Pauliss and thought she was very beautiful, and even though her coloring was similar to what Kahlie's had been prior to her exalting, her strong features and tall build gave her more of an exotic warrior-type look; her position as the leader of the Trysta army certainly suited her.

"Hello again," Audril greeted, although it was difficult for her to force any expression of happiness, "thanks for pulling your troops together so quickly."

"Of course, Atoh," the commander replied. "We are sworn to protect the vritesse and her interests."

As they started toward the palace, Pauliss commanded seven of her soldiers to accompany them and told the rest to stay near the lake and await orders.

Audril led the Trystas through the palace to a dim, yet luxurious lounge a few doors away from the atoc and atoh's chambers. "I'll go get my dad and the vritesse," she explained. "Make yourselves at home."

Besides Kahlie and Jonathan, Uprul, Glaron, Bridgette, Michelan and Statlen were all in the room.

Bridgette rushed over to her and hugged her. "I am soooo glad you're back," she whispered. "Do you have any news for me?"

"Not yet, Bridge," she answered with a sympathetic smile.

As Bridgette studied her eyes, a frown spread across her face. "What is it?" she tried. "What's happened?"

Audril didn't answer but put her hand on Bridgette's arm to let her know that everything would be all right. "Dad, the Trystas are here," she said. "Commander Pauliss and a few others are waiting in the Atoc's Lounge for you guys."

Without a word, the four Mandelan generals and Jonathan and Kahlie all moved toward the door. As they were about to exit, Jonathan put his hand on Audril's shoulder. "I know you two girls want to talk, but I'm afraid it'll have to wait. You are needed every bit as much as these others."

Audril nodded weakly. It felt like she was in a bad dream, floating along without any control over her movements or the circumstances, and what happened as they reached the lounge only added to that feeling.

All of a sudden, a loud boom shook the palace and everything stretched and distorted as though it had been put in front of a carnival mirror. Audril tried to lift her foot, but it was heavy and felt like the ground was swallowing it.

Bridgette's head was easily three feet long and her saucer-sized eyes bore an expression of pure terror.

Then, with a deafening "whhhhhah" sound, everything shrank and collapsed inward. Audril's body hurled toward the entryway of the lounge as her feet moved back and forth with incredible speed on the marble floor. She was just about to crash into the molding surrounding the door when there was a jolting bump that sent her, and everyone else, sliding across the room.

"What was that?" Jonathan gasped as he staggered to his feet.

He reached his arms out to Pauliss, and to a male Trysta who had landed near him. "Th . . that was a Time Align," Pauliss coughed. "I've been through one before."

"A Time Align," Glaron echoed as he helped Bridgette up.

"What's that?" Bridgette asked.

Commander Pauliss looked at her and replied, "It's an ancient Derite spell used to align the rotation of two planets. Do you suppose that Ryannon . . . ?"

"I'm way ahead of you, Commander," Jonathan interrupted as he pulled up Michelan, Audril and another Trysta. "My guess is that Drolana and Lor Mandela have just been aligned. But why? Why would he want the time on both planets to be the same?"

"Vritesse?" Pauliss' tone was suddenly one of alarm. "Vritesse, are you all right?"

Jonathan spun toward her voice to see Kahlie once again unconscious on the ground. "Doctor!" he shouted.

Michelan was already moving quickly toward her.

As the doctor dropped to his knees beside her and started digging through the satchel he wore over his shoulder, Kahlie bolted upright and shoved him forcefully out of the way. The doctor flew across the floor like he'd just been hit by a car.

With amazing stealth, Kahlie jumped to her feet and ran at Jonathan, tackling him to the ground and grabbing him by the neck.

"Aaagghhh!" Jonathan bellowed as Kahlie forced her hands against the fresh cuts that had been left by Lique's knife earlier. "Kah . . . lie . . .what . . . are . . . you . . . doing?" he choked.

Pauliss immediately rushed to his aid. Without hesitation, Kahlie moved one of her hands from her Entrusted's throat and knocked Pauliss' legs out from under her. The warrior fell to the ground hard on her back, and Kahlie grabbed her ankle and flung her away like a rag doll. One by one, she fought off everyone who approached, all the while pressing down harder on

Jonathan's throat. His face turned purple and blood started to spurt from the fresh wound as he struggled to pry her fingers off.

"Glaron, do something!" Bridgette shrieked just as Kahlie hurled Audril through the air, slamming her hard against one of the stone walls.

"Stop it, Kahlie! What's wrong with you?" he bellowed as he rushed her and tried to get a hold around her waist from behind. "You're killing him! STOP!" She didn't waste her energy lifting Glaron. She just threw her arm backwards and clobbered him in the face, which was enough to send him sliding across the floor.

Kahlie looked like she'd gone mad. "Come on . . . come on!" she snarled as she went back to a two-handed assault on Jonathan. Her eyes were wide with anticipation. "Come on! DIE!" she seethed.

Jonathan's vision blurred and the room started to spin. The harder he tried to loosen Kahlie's grip, the tighter she squeezed. He could feel his throat collapsing and was about to pass out when all of a sudden, Kahlie's eyes rolled backward, and she collapsed on top of him. Behind her, Michelan crouched with a metallic syringe in his hand. He caught his breath and rolled the tranquilized vritesse off of Jonathan who was sputtering and coughing violently.

"Jonathan, are you all right?" he blurted.

Jonathan didn't answer, but bobbed his head up and down. He pointed around the room at the three Trystas and Statlen who all lay sprawled across the floor. Michelan nodded and immediately scooted away to attend to them.

"Daddy!" Audril cried, throwing her arms around Jonathan's shoulders.

"I'm okay, Angel," he sputtered. "I'm okay." With sadness, he looked at the still form of Kahlie.

As he watched her lying there, she started to stir, and then once again shot to sitting with amazing stealth.

"Get away!" Audril shrieked, jumping in front of her dad.

Kahlie looked at her and started laughing maniacally, but the laugh wasn't her own. She sounded like Ryannon! As she sat laughing, Jonathan peered out from behind Audril and gasped as he was met with a disturbing image from his past. Kahlie's eyes had turned from a rich blue to nearly black and a small fire flickered in each one — a fire of orange and blue and white. "My brother's back," she cackled as the flames in her eyes grew larger.

"Darian," Jonathan whispered under his breath.

"What?" Glaron called from across the room, where he was shielding Bridgette, should another attack occur.

Just then, as if Glaron's voice had rejuvenated the sedative Dr. Michelan had administered, and as abruptly as Kahlie had regained consciousness, she slumped to the side and was quiet.

Jonathan looked over at Glaron with a look of terror on his face. "Glaron . . ." he gulped gently, rubbing his throat, "her eyes just changed . . . they turned into . . . into Darian's."

Chapter XXXIII

THE CLEST ANARIA'S BOOK OF REVELATION

"I'll take her back to the infirmary," Michelan offered as he checked Kahlie's vital signs. "I hate to mention it, Jonathan, but we probably should keep guards on her, at least until we're sure she won't attack you again."

Jonathan smoothed his Entrusted's black, wavy hair and sighed, "I suppose. But when she wakes up . . . if she's okay . . . you're to tell her it was for her own safety." He helped the doctor load her onto a stretcher that was wheeled in by Michelan's assistant and added, "This is because Ryannon is her twin, Michelan. I know it is. Please try to find out what's happening to her."

Dr. Michelan nodded reassuringly and he and his assistant moved the stretcher from the room.

Jonathan turned his attention to Pauliss. "Commander, may I speak to you?" he asked.

The still stunned Trysta moved to his side. "I'm afraid it's necessary for us to place some guards on the vritesse . . . as a safety precaution," Jonathan explained.

"Of course, sir," she agreed. "I'll send Canlora, Deinna and Mahor to the infirmary right away." Pauliss took a deep breath and started to turn away, but then stopped, locked her eyes on Jonathan's and asked, "Atoc? Is the atoh prepared . . . I mean, should anything happen to the vritesse, she is the next in line."

Jonathan knew that Audril was the only remaining Trysta heiress, but he'd never given it much thought. She was already the atoh of Lor Mandela and the Clest Anaria. This was just one more pile of responsibility that he didn't want to heap on his seventeen-year-old daughter. "I think that's a bit premature, Pauliss," he scolded. "Let's cross that bridge when the time comes. We all have enough on our plate at the moment."

Pauliss bowed her head and turned away. She discreetly informed Canlora, Dienna and Mahor of their new assignment and then rejoined Atoc Jonathan, Statlen, Glaron, Audril, Bridgette and the other four Trystas that were in the room. Everyone was a little banged up from the incident with Kahlie, but none had been seriously injured.

Jonathan was the first to speak. "In light of Kahlie's revelation that Ryannon is, in fact, here, I think we need to find General Lortu."

"He should be here soon," Audril offered. "I ran into him in Westrim. He went to go get General Davids."

In a perfect reiteration of his impeccable sense of timing, Lortu's voice oozed out of the shadows. "De General Davids weel be heah with his soldiahs soon," he reported. "De Ryannon eez een Brashnell, and has zent de Doran to find a Squanki for heem. Tabbeet's portals have stopped working."

"What?" Pauliss questioned. "What do you mean her portals have stopped working?"

"Why is that significant?" Audril asked, observing the commander's agitated expression. Her words were directed at Pauliss, but as she said them, she glared out of the corner of her eye at Lortu. She was less than happy with his blatant avoidance of the question she'd asked him earlier.

"De commandair knows de signifeecance," Lortu answered. "Squanki portals are foolproof. Eet is a rare ting indeed when dey stop working."

"Has anyone tried to have another Squanki open one?" Pauliss tried. "To make sure that it's not just Tabbit?"

"Not yet," Lortu answered. "Excuse de Lortu for a moment."

He was already half gone before finishing his sentence, and a moment was all it took. Before anyone else could say anything, he stepped back out from a dark corner. "De Squanki Sauvina weel join us shortly," he informed. "We can have hair open de portal for us."

"What does all this mean?" Jonathan asked. "What do Squanki portals have to do with Ryannon . . . or what's going on with Kahlie?"

"They may have a great deal to do with it," Pauliss replied. "If Ryannon is messing with Derite spells, his attack may be the least of our worries, Atoc."

"Explain," Jonathan said with a frown.

"The Derite people were linked to everything," she explained, "nature, creatures, air, water, earth, space, sound . . . and time. Their ancient writings can take a lifetime to comprehend, and misuse of them can lead to any number of calamitous events. As Trystas, we are taught to have a healthy respect for the Derite spells . . . and to leave them alone. Need I remind you of the nearly devastating results of Anika's actions?"

"No," Jonathan sighed as he recalled the spiral of events that had resulted when the Trysta Anika tried to use a Derite spell to steal the vritesse powers from her sister.

Audril started to pace nervously. "I hate to say it, Dad, but if the Time Align spell is Derite, then Ryannon's been doing more than just messing up portals." The looks from Pauliss and the other Trystas made her hesitant to continue. "He has a book; he showed it to me. He said it was Darian's . . . and he's been using it, Dad . . . a lot."

"A book?" Pauliss quizzed. "What kind of book?"

"It's a big, thick book of spells. The grasping curse is in it, how to build the Catorian devices he's been using to blow places up, the exalting vow, one called Love Induced Suicide, and the Time Align. He's used them all . . . or at least tried. He is using it almost like an instruction manual for his life." Audril glanced around at the Trystas and their expressions of absolute panic.

"Atoh," Pauliss panted, "these spells . . . has he been using them in order?"

Audril thought her question odd. "I didn't really pay attention," she answered with a confused scowl.

"Audril," Glaron spoke for the first time in the conversation. "It's pretty important that you try to remember, Boo. We need to know if he was going in order." His eyes held the same terrified look as the rest of the Trystas.

"I really don't know, Glaron. He only showed me . . . no . . . wait." She seemed lost in her memories for a moment before continuing. "The Love Induced Suicide spell was at the back of the book. He skipped a bunch of pages to show me that one."

"Will someone please tell me what's going on?" Jonathan blurted.

Glaron turned to him and explained. "What Ryannon has is not just some random book of spells, Jonathan. It is a book of revelation."

"A book of Revelation? You mean like in the Bible?"

"No," Glaron continued. "Not a book of Revelations. It's not meant for mankind. It's meant for one person, and one person only . . . the Clest Anaria."

"What?" Audril questioned. "If it's meant for me, how did Ryannon . . . or Darian get a hold of it?"

"It was stolen from the Hall of Warriors over thirty years ago. We thought it had been destroyed," Pauliss answered.

"You see, Boo, if the book was destroyed, the Clest Anaria's life would just play out the way it should. Nothing would interfere," Glaron elaborated. "It was almost a relief when we thought it had been destroyed."

Pauliss looked at Audril and added, "Long before you were born, Branlor found burned pages that we assumed were from the book."

"So what does it mean if Ryannon goes out of order?" Bridgette asked.

"It means that the order of the Clest Anaria's life has been tampered with, Bridge, which in turn means that the order of Lor Mandela has been tampered with," Glaron explained. "It will cause all kinds of chaos."

"You've gotta be kidding me," Audril chuckled. "Are you saying that my life and Lor Mandela have been thrown all out of whack because Ryannon read my book backwards? That's ridiculous."

"We'll soon find out," Pauliss answered. She seemed annoyed by Audril's lack of belief. "My hunch is that no Squanki will be able to open a portal." She motioned with her head toward the entrance of the room where Sauvina stood, waiting for the opportune time to announce her arrival.

Jonathan walked over to her and said, "Thank you for coming Sauvina, I need you to open a portal for me."

"Of course, Highness," she replied, "but, if you please, sir, haven't you forbidden the Squanki from opening portals?"

"Yes, Sauvina," he answered, "but this is an emergency."

Sauvina lifted her hand into the air. "I see. Where would you like the portal to, sire?"

"Um . . . let's see . . . how about down by the lake," he suggested.

Sauvina grimaced. "I am capable of opening a portal further away, Highness."

"The lake will be fine," he said.

The elegant little Squanki shrugged her shoulders and began rolling her hand. After three rolls, a tiny sliver of light appeared near her left arm. The light stretched upward and downward from the ends until it was nearly a foot long. All of a sudden, the ends of the portal shrunk inward. Sauvina jumped and started rolling her hand faster and faster. The portal regained a little length, but then shrank in again, this time more quickly than before. The Squanki looked around at everyone watching with a stunned expression on her lovely face. "What is happening?" she gasped as the portal took another leap in on itself. Despite her frantic efforts, the tiny light sizzled and then disappeared with a miniscule pop. Sauvina gazed up desperately at Jonathan. "Forgive me, Atoc. I seem to be out of sorts," she whimpered.

"No, Sauvina," he replied, rubbing his forehead. "It's not you. Something has happened on Lor Mandela that is affecting the portals. We just needed you to confirm that for us. Thank you."

The confused Squanki bowed and backed out of the room.

"See," Pauliss snipped, "we have a problem here."

Glaron eyed Jonathan. "Jonathan, you have to trust us. The consequences of messing with the Clest Anaria's book of Revelation can be catastrophic. The portals are just the beginning."

"So what do we do?" he asked.

"We have to get de book back," Lortu answered. "And we have to be putting de order of tings to de right."

"Fine, Lortu," Jonathan replied, "then go ahead and get it. Surely the Shadow Dwellers . . . ."

Lortu's uproarious laughter interrupted him. "Dis can only be done by de Clest Anaria, sire."

Audril gasped and glared at him. "Lortu . . . I'm sure *you* can go get it," she seethed. "You don't need my help."

"Oh no, Atoha, Aye am not worty to do what you ask. De noble Lortu would surely fail."

"The noble Lortu, my eye!" she snapped.

"Out of the question," Jonathan blurted. "She just got away from Ryannon. It's too dangerous!"

Audril scowled at Lortu. "I'll be fine, Dad. The *noble* Lortu can accompany me," she insisted.

Jonathan tried to come up with a reason not to let her go, but he knew that if Lortu was saying this was the only way, there was no alternative.

"All right, but you had better keep her safe, Lortu."

Lortu grinned smugly and made a dramatic low bow. "I weel protect hair wit maye life, Atoc."

"Yeah, easy for you to say," Audril retorted in a scathing whisper.

Chapter XXXIV

A STRANGE, BUT LUCKY COINCIDENCE

Once they had moved far enough away from the atoc's lounge that she wouldn't be heard, Audril shoved Lortu in the chest and barked, "I can't believe you! I'm not the only one who can get the book. Ryannon's not the Clest Anaria, and he's been toting it around for who knows how long! This is all some big game to you, isn't it?"

Lortu grinned at her assertiveness and replied, "Yes . . . eet eez most certainly a game, Atoha, and de Clest Anaria's book of Revelation eez a wonderful addeetion to dis intrigue."

"What are you talking about?" she huffed. "How can you act this way when everything that's happening is so out of control?"

Lortu slowed his pace as they entered the palace foyer. Several people milled around the elegant room, so he chose, at least for the moment, not to answer.

As they moved through the bright, stained-glass chamber, many stopped what they were doing to bow to Audril.

"Ahhh, dis eez nice," Lortu hummed, "de respect . . . and de feah."

"They don't fear me, Lortu," she corrected with a smirk. "They just do it because they think they have to."

"Because dey feah what weel happen eef dey don't." He glanced at her sideways with a cocky sneer on his face.

Audril was growing tired of Lortu's apparent fascination with challenging her. "Fine, Lortu, they fear me . . . whatever," she sighed.

They stepped out onto the sprawling veranda outside the palace doors and moved towards the stairs. "So what's our plan then?" she asked.

"Seemple . . . we go to de Brashnell. De Lortu gets de book and geeves eet to you. Aye come back and say dat you have gone to de Drolana. De atoc gets angry wit me. Aye go eento hiding. When yoah meesion eez completed, you come back." He looked her deeply in the eyes and added, "and aye return yoah powers . . . seemple."

"Oh, simple," she snipped. "So this was all a plot to get me out of the palace and send me back to Earth. You know, Lortu, I'm not convinced that I have to go back. I mean, what am I supposed to do there? Besides, how are we gonna straighten out this book thing if I'm there and you're here?"

"Dis eez a good point," he muttered as they started across the emerald field.

"Yeah . . . it is. Maybe *you're* the one who is supposed to go to Drolana. Have you ever thought of that?"

"Reedeeculous," he replied, "De powahs moust remain on de Lor Mandela, remembah?"

"Yeah, I remembah."

Lortu looked at her like a concerned parent and shook his head. "Shall we transport?" he asked.

"I suppose it would be silly of us not to," she sassed.

Lortu didn't reply to her snarky comment but instead, within a fraction of a second, hoisted her into the air and dropped her onto his back.

"Never *not* humiliating," she groaned as Lortu started off in a powerful sprint.

Audril wrapped her arms around his shoulders just as he yelled, "Westrim Nort Forest" into the sky.

With a flash, they arrived in a densely wooded area that was nearly dark, despite it being midday. Tall pine trees with unusually large, decaying trunks stretched as high as the eye could see, shielding most of the sunlight. Only tiny streams filtered through, but by the time they reached the ground, they were so far from their source, and so interrupted, that they were nearly nonexistent. The nauseatingly strong scent of evergreen trees mixed with stagnant wet vegetation hit Audril's nostrils the second they arrived.

"Creepy," she gagged as she climbed off of Lortu's back.

"No . . . not creepy . . . conveenient," he whispered, pointing straight ahead with an only partially visible finger. "Look . . . ."

Through the trees, Audril could see movement. She leaned around the peeling grey trunk of the tree directly in front of her to try to get a better view and saw what looked like two soldiers in camouflaged fatigues, conversing.

"Ryannon's camp?" she asked, but there was no reply. "Lortu?" she whispered. "Lortu? Are you here?" Her question was answered with nothing but silence. "Oooh, that man!" she hissed, stomping on the damp ground.

Cautiously, she weaved around a couple of the towering trees, instinctively flinching as she peered out behind one and saw Ryannon moving nearby. He was strolling back and forth, carefully studying the pages of none other than the book.

"Oh, smashing," she sighed.

Suddenly, a commotion broke out in the camp. Audril pulled her head back, but then inched it out around the tree. All she could see were men and women scrambling frantically while they shouted and pointed. She smiled, shook her head, and muttered, "Lortu."

As the chaos continued, she tried to keep Ryannon in sight, but a soldier who was nearly the same size as him jumped out and blocked her view. Curious to determine what exactly was going on, she slinked around another tree. Suddenly, half of Lortu appeared next to her, causing her to jump and let out a startled yelp.

The part-visible Dweller slapped his hand over her mouth and pointed down to where his other hand should have been, but wasn't. There, seemingly floating in air was the Clest Anaria's Book of Revelation.

Audril pried Lortu's fingers away from her mouth. "That was quick," she whispered, glancing over her shoulder to make sure that Ryannon was still otherwise occupied.

"Aye told you . . . seemple," Lortu grinned.

Audril smiled in reply, but their apparent delight in the situation was quickly dashed by the sound of Ryannon bellowing, "WHERE'S MY BOOK?"

"Let's get out of heah," Lortu whispered, grabbing her by the hand and leading her deeper into the trees. Little twigs and half-decomposed pine needles crunched beneath their feet so loudly that Audril was certain Ryannon, or someone from his camp, would hear.

They continued through the darkness; Lortu leading their nearly blind flight, until he was certain no one was following. When he was confident that they were alone, he lifted Audril onto his back again and broke into an amazingly fast gallop.

This quickly became one of the rougher rides on which she'd been. There were several moments as he navigated through the thick forest, dodging around low branching trees and leaping from elephant-sized boulders that she felt as though she had left Lortu's back entirely, and was free flying through the air.

"Hang on," he yelled as they came to what looked like a steep hill.

Audril screeched as Lortu leapt from the edge of the hill and they plummeted downward. She glanced over his side and realized that they had literally just jumped off a cliff, and a huge one at that. She squeezed her eyes shut, waiting for the inevitable crash, when she heard Lortu cry out, "Mandela Ceety!"

A brilliant blast of icy blue light shot through the air and shone through her eyelids as her stomach rose into her throat like she had just mounted a hill on a roller coaster and was rushing down the other side. Perhaps because they had transported from mid-air, it now felt like they were hurtling through space at the speed of sound.

Thirty-Four

Audril slowly opened her eyes, and the image that met her blew her away. They were surrounded by amazing color — pastel lights in every imaginable hue shooting upwards from around their feet. Lortu's normally alabaster tresses shone pink and blue and yellow as the spectacular light show reflected off of them.

"Are you seeing this?" she called out, lifting one of her hands and moving it into the beams of color which separated around her fingertips. "This is amazing!"

"Amazing," Lortu repeated in a shriek, "but when eez eet going to end?"

"Are you scared?" Audril giggled, hearing the horror in his voice. "Just enjoy the ride, Lortu!" She let her mind wander for a moment and imagined the leader of the feared Lortus Clan, wide-eyed and hugging the safety bar on "The Terminal of Terror," an airport-themed thrill ride at "The Peaks" amusement park back in Palmerton.

"Aye am not scared," he insisted in a tone that clearly manifested the opposite. "Aye joust do not weesh to be stuck in dis ting forever."

"Don't worry, Lortu. I'm sure it's just because you transported when you weren't touching the ground." She leaned down and gave him a reassuring squeeze on the shoulders. "Look, I think we're already coming out of it." Sure enough, the lights were starting to fade to grey and were being replaced by obscure shadows darting below their feet. Audril squinted, trying to identify the source of the shadows when she realized that their trajectory would land them in a not so good place.

"Lortu! Watch it!" she shrieked.

The blurred shapes had stopped moving and were solidifying into three human-like forms, and Lortu was on a direct collision course.

"Looks out aboves!" a squeaky voice called out, but there wasn't time, or the means, to change direction. With the bellowing cries of five individuals, Lortu and Audril smacked hard into the others, sending bodies flying in all directions. Audril rolled across the ground and into a sizeable Truglunt bush.

"My word!" a raspy, coarse, and familiar voice sounded from beyond the shrub.

"Teedee?" Audril gasped, popping up out of the top of the bush, with a look on her face like someone who had just seen a dead relative.

A few feet away, and dressed in her ridiculous red and black getup, Teedee Venilworth sat on a cobblestone pathway with one leg twisted awkwardly up underneath her, picking leaves and twigs out of her grayish-yellow hair. "Is that any way to greet friends, Toots?" she scolded. "You try to kill em?"

Lortu, who probably took less than a second to recover from the crash, eyed the strange old lady and slowly backed away.

"Hellos, Miss Atoh ladys," Guddlebee sang out as he rushed to help Teedee to her feet. "Aunties Dees brings us backs to Lor Mandelas." He grabbed a hold of Teedee's hands and yanked with his entire body but she hardly budged. "And I ates a Big Pigs," he added with a touch of ecstasy in his tone.

Audril couldn't speak. What in the world was Teedee Venilworth doing on Lor Mandela? How did she come across Guddlebee? And why was Guddlebee referring to her as his aunt?

"HODGSON," Teedee squealed in her familiar pig-calling voice. "Oh, Hodgson!"

There was a rustling in another bush followed by a moan. Teedee scrambled to her feet faster than Audril thought possible and shuffled to the bush. She parted a few of the branches and then pointed her bony finger at Lortu. "You! Funny looking one with the white hair . . . get over here and help me."

Lortu glanced around indignantly as if he was trying to figure out exactly who she was referring to in such a demanding tone. "Maye name eez Lortu, woman, and aye do not take ordahs from de likes of you."

"Lortu? Lortu of the Shadows?" A smooth male voice rose out of the bush Teedee was busily digging through. All at once the large shrub nearly shook out of the ground, and a dazzlingly handsome man with a strong, chiseled jaw, muscular physique and perfectly groomed short, wavy, dark hair appeared from behind it.

"Oh, Hodgson . . . you're all right," Teedee sighed, smiling up at him.

Audril suddenly found her voice. "Hodgson? You've got to be kidding me! You're Hodgson?"

"Strange, huh?" Hodgson replied with a knee-weakening smile and a voice that was no longer labored or drawn out. "Apparently we're visible on Lor Mandela."

"Maye brudder," Lortu chuckled and approached Hodgson. "Eet has been many yeahs since de noble Lortu has seen you."

"Noble Lortu," Hodgson bowed, "indeed it has. I am here as your servant, great one."

"Who eez yoah friend," Lortu asked, sizing up Teedee with his icy eyes.

"This is my fiancée, Ms. Teedee Venilworth," he replied proudly. "We heard that Ryannon of Brashnell has returned to Lor Mandela and we've come to offer our services. Teedee is very resourceful, your nobleness."

"That's one way to describe her," Audril whispered to herself. She moved out from behind the Truglunt bush and asked, "How did you get here?" but before anyone could respond, she turned a glaring eye on Guddlebee and answered the question herself. "A portal . . . of course. Tell me, *noble Lortu*, is this part of your student exchange program? You invite your brudder, or whatever he is for a visit to Lor Mandela, while you send me back to his place? This all seems a little too coincidental!"

"Ahh, there she goes with the worrying again," Teedee mumbled to Guddlebee, "always worrying, this one."

Audril waved off her comments like an annoying fly and continued to scold Lortu. "First you send me a mystical, magical prophecy delivered via invisible man, and then you talk me into going to Earth so you can hold on to my powers for me. You insist that Guddlebee go with me, and now, he's opened a portal to bring your long lost family through. Not only that, but you have been adamantly stressing that I go back and complete my mission, which I'm guessing will be finished on exactly the four hundredth *and first* day. You set me up!"

"No, no, you silly girl," Teedee cackled. She approached Lortu and wrapped her frail arm around his waist, a gesture that caused him to cringe a bit. "If this is the fabled Lortu, he would never set you up. He would only try to help you." Lortu pulled himself a little taller and grinned smugly.

"Oh great," Audril smirked, "You have a groupie, Clest Anaria!"

"What?" Teedee gasped. "You've given *him* your powers?" She looked into Lortu's eyes for confirmation.

Lortu bowed his head almost as if he were ashamed.

"TIME OUT!" Audril bellowed, "How do you know all of this stuff, Teedee? I want the truth! Who are you?"

"My name is Teedee Venilworth, *Miss Worry Wart*, and I *have* been telling you the truth," she reprimanded. "I know all of this stuff because I'm engaged to a Dark Watcher . . . and a very handsome one at that," she added, winking at Hodgson and blowing a kiss.

"Nauseating," Audril muttered as Hodgson air-kissed Teedee in reply.

"You can tink what you want, Atoha. Dat eez fine, but der eez a great deal at stake eef you do not return to de Drolana zoon," Lortu stated coolly.

"Fine," Audril responded haughtily in Lortu's direction. "Why don't you just show me in my book why I have to go back, then? It's supposed to show revelations about my life, isn't it?"

Audril looked down at Lortu's hands. In all the commotion, she had failed to realize until this very moment that the book was not with him. "Lortu? Where's the book?" she asked as an uncomfortable lump rose in her throat.

Lortu's eyes grew wide and he took a couple of steps backward. Without a word, he turned quickly and raced back to where he had landed when they had crashed into Teedee, Hodgson and Guddlebee. Frantically, he started digging through grasses and bushes muttering under his breath like a mad man.

"Aw, man . . . you lost it?" Audril groaned and moved to help him hunt.

"I wants to play!" Guddlebee exclaimed excitedly. He began ripping grass out of the ground where he stood and then dove head-first into a Truglunt bush.

"What is it?" Teedee giggled nervously. "Surely you're not talking about the Clest Anaria's Book of Revelation."

"Great! She knows about that, too? Is there anything that you don't know about me?"

Teedee sniggered and answered, "Yeah, why you're so uptight all the time." Hodgson snorted as he struggled to hold back his laughter.

"Extremely hilarious," Audril sneered, turning her attention to the next shrub. "I can't believe you lost it, Lortu! So much for seemple!"

"Eet moust not have transported," he guessed, scratching his head above his left ear.

"Yeah, that's convenient," she cried. "Ya can't show me if you don't have the book! This is just great."

Teedee watched with the same patronizing look on her wrinkly face that she always wore when she was accusing Audril of worrying too much. "You're just gonna have to go back to wherever you came from and get it, Toots. The book can't fall into the wrong hands."

"It's already been in the wrong hands," Audril griped. "And how am I going to bring it back if it won't transport. It'll take a whole day to walk back from Brashnell."

"You weel have to go by calandry," Lortu suggested. "Tru de Nort Mountain Pass. De noble Lortu weel find a calandry. In dis way, you weel see dat I am not leading you astray, Atoha."

"Calandry?" Audril quizzed. "What's that?"

Lortu ignored her and instead addressed Teedee and Hodgson. "We moust go to de palace and speak to de atoc. He weel be most eenterested een yoah arrival heah."

"Have you found the Channeler?" Teedee asked anxiously, prompting a scoff and a dramatic eye roll from Audril.

"No," Lortu answered. "We shall speak to de atoc about hair as well." Without further commentary, he hunched over with his knuckles mere inches from the ground and began to whoop like a frantic bird. His cries reverberated off of the nearby trees and echoed through the Sybran Forest. A few seconds later, a cry similar to Lortu's, but far more voluminous, sliced through the air, shaking the needles on the trees.

"Ahhh, heah eez a calandry, now."

With a graceful, undulating motion, the branches of the Greelan trees at the edge of the forest parted and swung upward — a motion that always reminded Audril of the big, plum-colored curtain on the stage at what used to be Glenhill High School. Behind the obliging branches she could make out a large, dark form approaching with incredible speed. As it moved closer and parts of it became discernible, a sense of panic flooded through her. "A rynolt?" she gasped, racing behind a waist-high bush near for protection. "Are you crazy?"

"Dis eez a calandry . . . not a rynolt," Lortu corrected as if she was foolish to think otherwise.

The creature galloped out of the forest and pranced out onto the stone path. As soon as it was clearly in view, Audril recognized it as the same type of creature on which Ryannon had arrived at the last battle, only his had been flying.

The calandry was massive and horse-like, as was a rynolt, but with some distinct differences. Rather than sleek, black scales, it was covered in what looked like pewter, holey gauze. Bits and pieces of it moved in such a way that its skin seemed to be billowing in the breeze. From each coffee can-sized hoof extended three razor sharp, hooked claws, each almost six inches in length. The claws clicked on the rocky path as the creature walked.

Then there was the head. The calandry only had one hooded head as opposed to two on the rynolt; and rather than resembling massive, weaving cobras, the calandry head was more like that of a fairy-tale dragon. The most distinct variation between the calandry and the rynolt however, was that, in addition to traveling along the ground, the calandry was also a flying beast, as evidenced by the black, jagged wings folded against each side of its enormous body.

"I hope you don't expect me to ride that thing," Audril complained.

"You weel be able to get to de Brashnell and back een just a few hoahs, Atoha. Eet eez de only way to bring back de book quickly."

The calandry lowered its head and appeared to be sizing up Audril. Its silver eyes scanned her as its head snaked from side to side. Huge snorts of air blasted out of its nostrils and through her hair.

"Gross," she moaned. "Calandry snot."

"Well, aren't you a spectacular creature," Teedee squeaked in a sad, raspy attempt at a baby voice. "I'm going to have to use you as inspiration for a new outfit."

Audril pictured Teedee wearing ripped up black tulle over the top of a shiny silver body suit, complete with a dragon-shaped hat and a long, uneven black cape. For some reason, the words "Trick or treat?" came to mind.

"You know, Lortu, this isn't exactly inspiring confidence in your concern for my safety."

"De calandry eez pairfectly safe," he explained, "Joust do not anger heem." Lortu slouched over and wrapped his long arm around Audril's legs and tossed her up on to the calandry's back. The gigantic beast spread his sprawling wings, reared upward and roared ferociously.

"Eef he zeems to be getting nairvous, joust hum like dis." Lourtu pursed his lips and emitted a monotone sound, like the idling of an engine. The calandry immediately calmed. "Or feed heem a frolnisk. Der blood eez soothing."

Audril had no idea what a frolnisk was, nor did she have any intention of finding out. Feeding this creature was most certainly not in her plans.

"Do be careful, Atoh," Hodgson said as he stepped forward and placed his hand warmly on her ankle, a gesture that, under the circumstances, should have stirred fury within her — but it didn't. There was something about the way that he looked at her that crushed any anger that might have tried to surface.

"I'm not sure about this," she replied, shaking her head as the calandry shifted from one side to the other and back again setting her slightly off balance. "Shouldn't I know what my own mission is? I still can't believe that running into you all here is some strange sort of coincidence."

Teedee toddled over to where Hodgson stood and grabbed him by the hand. "Have you ever met anyone who was sure of their mission in life, Toots?" she asked with a knowing twinkle in her eyes. "This is not just a strange coincidence. It's a lucky one."

Out of the corner of her mouth, Audril blew a curl off of her own forehead and asked, "What, exactly, is so lucky about it?"

Hodgson flashed another of his perfect smiles. "Once we've met with your father, and you've retrieved the book, Atoh Audril . . . you'll see what was so lucky about it."

Chapter XXXV

HERE WE GO AGAIN

The calandry waited for a slap on the hindquarters from Lortu, and then sped down the stone path and into Mandela City at a full gallop. Several people gaped in awe at the sight of the atoh barreling recklessly through town atop the imposing creature whose skin seemed to move and create an odd, surreal scene of its own.

"How do I steer this thing?" she cried in a panic as they moved faster and faster, heading directly for a short fence that surrounded a perfectly manicured garden at a breakneck speed. Audril quickly tried the only thing that made sense — grabbing a hold of the calandry's hooded neck and pulling it hard to the left.

The calandry seemed to respond, albeit a little tentatively. He made the turn, but not before one of his hind hooves clipped the fence, shattering a few of the boards and sending splinters blasting through the air like fireworks.

"Whoa!" Audril shouted as the calandry compensated too sharply and stumbled off of the path into soft dirt.

She tugged his neck again. This time he reacted with stealth and lined himself back up with the road.

"There ya go, boy," she encouraged, "that's it! We've got it."

By the time they reached the tall, shimmering homes of Anisia Mystad, where the upper-crust of Lor Mandelan society lived, the calandry was sensing

Audril's commands almost before she made them. They soared out onto East Mystad Field, moving as one across the lovely, grassy expanse.

Audril instinctively slid her legs backwards and up so she was lying on the calandry's back.

As if on cue, he unfurled his immense wings which caught a flowery, perfumed current of air, and lifted them smoothly from the ground.

Audril wrapped her arms around the creature and watched the meadow move away.

"We're going to Westrim North Forest," she purred, laying her head against the calandry's broad neck. He seemed to nod and change course a few degrees to the north.

This is it, she thought to herself, *this is what I was born to do.* "I should stay here with you . . . not go back to that stinky Drolana, huh boy?" She sighed aloud and patted the side of the calandry's hood.

The gentle beast hummed in the same soothing tone that Lortu had used before, and then pumped his wings, pushing them higher and higher into the air.

They sliced through wisps of cottony clouds and soft rays of diffused sunlight as the wind rushed playfully through Audril's silky raven curls.

This was heaven, and she didn't want it to end. Up here, there was no Ryannon; no ill or psychotic Kahlie; no Clest Anaria; no stressed out dad; no blown up Glenhill; no missing love; just peace and endless beauty for as far as the eye could see.

The time it took to reach the forest passed far too quickly, and before Audril was anywhere close to ready, they began to descend. As they dropped below the high clouds, the treetops became visible, like a blanket of dark green fur draped across the landscape. Bordering the trees to the north, a large, shining city bustled.

"Brashnell," Audril guessed, watching strange silver vehicles dart around the roadways of a place that reminded her more of the big cities on Earth than anything else she had yet experienced on Lor Mandela.

A crystal blue lake sparkled beyond the trees to her left, and off to the right, the clearing where Ryannon's army was camped came into view.

Audril drew herself up into a ball on the calandry's back to make sure she was well hidden behind his flapping wings. "Over there," she instructed, motioning with her head in the direction opposite Ryannon's camp.

The calandry banked hard to the left and aimed for a clearing much smaller than the one Ryannon occupied, but it looked like one she remembered passing as she and Lortu ran through the forest earlier; at any rate, it looked like the best place to land.

The calandry drifted gracefully into the clearing, touching down into a smooth gallop before slowing to a stop. He lowered his front legs to kneeling so that Audril could slide off more easily.

"Thank you, my friend. That was wonderful," she said, petting the creature's pewter side. "But, I feel like I should call you something, you know? Give you a name?"

The calandry turned his charcoal head to her and nuzzled it affectionately against her cheek.

"All right," she giggled. "Let's see. You're big . . . and mysterious . . . a little frightening at first. Your beauty is, perhaps, misunderstood. You prefer little company . . . I know! I'll call you Phantom. What do you think about that?"

He chuffed loudly and pranced in a circle around her, his raptor-like claws flinging leaves and dirt upward. "Phantom it is," she smiled. "Come on, Phantom . . . we have a book to find."

She moved into the trees with Phantom in tow, uncertain yet hopeful that she was heading in the right direction. The forest seemed even darker and more confusing at this slow pace, and was eerily quiet, except for when Phantom periodically shot a rapid gust of air through his nose. It took three or four times of him doing it before Audril stopped jumping out of her skin.

"Look," she whispered excitedly as the stretched out crest of a hill appeared beyond the trees in the distance. "I think that's it."

315

Her pace quickened as they climbed the gentle incline. The scenery became familiar and Audril realized that they were, in fact, approaching the cliff from which she and Lortu had jumped.

"Yeah, Phantom, this is it! It should be down there at the bottom."

"What should be?" an unfamiliar voice answered back.

Audril spun around to see an unkempt man, smiling wildly, his head tilted to one side awaiting her answer.

"Who are you?" she breathed. She looked around nervously for Phantom, who had apparently been spooked away by this mangy stranger.

"Awww, pardon my manners, Atoh," he bowed, keeping his eyes fixed on her. "My name is Doran. I'm a member of the Brashnellan Security Council."

Audril took a small step backward, but found that she was nearly out of land to stand on. She teetered slightly and barely caught herself before slipping from the edge. "Careful, love . . . that's a long ways down." Doran chuckled, moving closer to her.

"Brashnellan Security Council?" she questioned with a raised eyebrow. "The old one . . . or the new one?"

Doran's chuckle escalated into full laughter. "The new one, of course . . . I never really did agree with that brogger, Darian."

Audril sighed with relief, and stepped more confidently away from the jagged rim of the cliff.

"So whatcha doin' out here by yourself, darlin'?" Doran asked, motioning with his head toward the forest. "There's all kinds of nasties in these woods; you should have a guard. I can't believe that the atoc would approve."

"Oh, I'm pretty sure he doesn't," she smirked. "Believe it or not, Mr. Doran . . . ."

"No, no . . . not Mr. Doran," he corrected with a broad smile, "just Doran."

"Uh, okay, um . . . Doran. My dad and I have reason to believe that Ryannon has returned to Lor Mandela, and is planning an attack on Mandela City again."

Doran did his best to feign astonishment. "Oh, really," he gasped, "Hmmm, Ryannon?" He paced a bit, and then quickly circled around behind Audril. "Now there's someone I *do* agree with." He grabbed her arm and wretched it up behind her back. "And he's gonna be very happy to see you, I think . . . let's go."

She struggled, but Doran was amazingly strong for his ordinary size.

"Let go of me," she protested, digging her feet into the loamy ground; she was not about to go back to Ryannon without a fight.

"Listen, darlin', we can do this the easy way, or we can do it the hard way. Does the mighty Clest Anaria feel pain?" Doran pushed her forward, forcing her arm to extend awkwardly and agonizingly backward. He twisted it higher until her hand was well above her head. Her shoulder cracked and felt like it was about to dislocate from the socket; a searing twinge shot through her entire arm, back, and chest.

"Okay . . . okay!" she grimaced. "Stop!"

Doran slowly lowered her arm until it was bent against the middle of her back again. "I think I said, let's go."

With another shove, Audril started reluctantly forward. Her shoulder ached, and she really wanted to lower her arm and shake it out, but she wasn't about to give Doran the satisfaction of asking. She doubted he would let her anyway.

She thought about calling out for Phantom, but then reconsidered. Without knowing what weapons, if any, Doran was in possession of, it could be risky for her new friend.

"Listen, Doran," she tried. "Why are you doing this? Don't you understand that Ryannon is only in this for himself? He'll use you and get rid of you, just like he's done with everyone else."

"Nice try, Atoh," Doran retorted as they moved into the darkness of the trees. "Ryannon and I have been friends since we were twelve years old. I don't think he's quite ready to ditch me yet. Let's just say my friendship with him has always been quite lucrative. I kinda doubt that's gonna change now."

"He killed his own father. What makes you think you're safe? He'd cut off his own left arm if he thought it would benefit him."

Doran just laughed and pushed her along.

As they moved closer to the camp, the sickening smell that had repulsed Audril earlier grew stronger. "It stinks," she snarled, "we must be getting closer to your boss."

Doran forced her around the imposing trunk of a towering tree and out into the clearing where the last rays of daylight were beginning to fade. "Look who I found wandering around the forest," he called out boisterously.

Ryannon, who was only a few feet away, pointing out the finer features of a vystoran sleeve to one of the US soldiers, turned and nearly dropped the weapon. "Well, if it isn't Atoc Jonathan's lovely daughter!" he grinned. "I thought I'd lost you, my dear. Will surprises never cease today?"

Doran gave Audril another forceful push, this time into Ryannon's waiting arms.

Ryannon held her for a moment and then grabbed her by the face and looked into her sapphire eyes. "My patience with you is just about at its end, Atoh. One more trick like the one you pulled at the saw mill, and . . . ."

Audril didn't let him finish. "I know . . . you'll kill someone I care about," she sneered. "You know something, Ryannon? You really have to try to be a little more creative."

"Why should I when what I do seems to work so well?" He leaned forward and gently kissed her lips. "I think we have some unfinished business to attend to," he breathed as he moved his mouth up the side of her face.

"I am not going to become your Entrusted," she cringed. "I don't care what you say, Ryannon. You don't have anyone that I care about here, and you can't hurt me. You know that."

318

Ryannon moved away from her and started to laugh. "My dear, I don't think you understand the full weight of the situation." He raised his hand in the air and made a small waving motion to a dull looking Brashnellan who was standing at the other side of the clearing. The man looked at him blankly and nodded before disappearing into the trees. "You see, I told you that today has been a day full of surprises."

A few seconds later, and with a little bit of a commotion, the Brashnellan returned; only he wasn't alone now. With him were two bound and blindfolded prisoners — Bridgette and Atoc Jonathan.

Chapter XXXVI

FORCED INTO IT

"You jerk!" Audril bellowed, slamming her fists against Ryannon's chest. "How dare you?!"

"Smaggs?" Jonathan yelped, straining his neck upward in an attempt to see under his blindfold. "So help me, Ryannon . . . if you harm so much as one hair on her head, I'll . . . ."

"You'll what?" Ryannon interrupted with a tone of haughtiness in his voice. "I hardly think you are in a position to negotiate, Jonathan. But don't worry . . . I wouldn't dream of hurting your daughter. I am in love with her."

"Love? Hah!" Audril scoffed. "You don't know the meaning of the word."

Ryannon slid his arm around her waist and whispered, "Play nice, lovey. I don't necessarily need them alive."

Once again, he signaled to the dense looking warrior who removed first Bridgette's blindfold, and then Jonathan's. Even though the sun had gone down and it was almost dark, they both squinted while their eyes adjusted to what little light was left.

Bridgette appeared to be terrified beyond words and was sobbing and shaking. Jonathan, on the other hand, was clearly livid.

"What makes you think this is going to work, Ryannon?" he fumed, scrutinizing what little army was present. "My forces have already begun to assemble and, from the looks of things, we outnumber you ten to one."

Ryannon shoved Audril back into Doran's grasp and strutted to where Jonathan stood. "Well, Atoc," he began, "first of all, I have you . . . and the Clest Anaria. Do you really think your generals will risk losing either of you?"

His answer seemed to do little to impress Jonathan.

"Second, I have a regiment of half a million soldiers on Earth just waiting to come through a portal. Remember the message I sent you on that idiot Glaron's cell phone . . ."

Jonathan recalled all too well how Ryannon had threatened to lie to the world's leaders on Earth about who was really responsible for the explosions.

"Once I informed President Langley that you were trying to take over Drolana with those murderous explosions, she was more than willing to offer up her troops," Ryannon elaborated. "Now let's see . . . if my math is correct, that has us outnumbering you."

"So where are they then?" Jonathan sneered with the faintest hint of a "gotcha" smile moving over his lips. "You've messed up the portals with your little Time Align, Ryannon."

Ryannon fought to remain unruffled, but he knew that Jonathan was right and it showed in his darkening eyes. It was the only logical explanation for Tabbit not being able to open a proper portal.

Jonathan observed the anger and frustration in Ryannon's visage and added, "Yeah! I know all about it! By screwing around with magic you don't understand, you've ruined your own convoluted plans."

Ryannon clenched his teeth and without another word strode back to Doran. "Where's Tora and that Squanki?" he hissed so quietly that only Doran and Audril could hear.

"They should be here soon," Doran answered. "What's going on?"

"As soon as they get back, I want that portal re-opened! Even if she has to try all bloody night," he barked. He snatched Audril by the arm and dragged her back to Jonathan and Bridgette, suddenly appearing on the verge of insanity. "You are both right on time!" he exclaimed with an inflated sense of urgency in his voice. "I think we should finish what we started earlier, don't you, dear?"

"Come on, Ryannon. You've got to be kidding me," Audril groaned.

Ryannon gestured toward a group of three other Brashnellans with vystoran sleeves in hand who immediately moved behind Jonathan and Bridgette. "I have never been more serious in my life," he snarled.

"What's he talking 'bout, Maggie," Jonathan asked.

"Your daughter and I are about to become Entrusted, Atoc," Ryannon blurted. "We would have been already, but we were interrupted."

Jonathan glanced at Audril with horrified shock in his cobalt eyes. "No, angel," he breathed. "Don't let him do this."

"Oh honestly, Jonathan," Ryannon smirked, rolling his eyes in an exaggerated manner. "I can hardly believe that she'd rather watch you and Blondie here die, just to get out of giving herself to me."

Bridgette tried to fight back a mortified whimper, to no avail.

Jonathan lunged forward but was stopped by the two men on either side of him. "I'll kill you! So help me, Ryannon, I will tear . . . ."

"That's enough!" Ryannon howled, turning to Audril. "Either you do this willingly and they live, or you do it unwillingly and they die; it's up to you, my dear!"

The soldiers in the camp, who up to this point had been active with movement and their own conversations, were now quiet and watching with eager interest.

Never one to pass up a chance for attention, Ryannon lifted his arms out to the troops as though welcoming them into his living room and instructed, "Please . . . everyone, try and find a comfortable spot. I want you all to be a part of my entrusting to this beautiful woman."

Bridgette seemed to suddenly find her voice, albeit not entirely. "Audr . . . nuh . . . you can't," she pleaded in a barely audible sob.

Audril looked at her and forced a non-convincing smile. "It'll be okay, Bridge," she tried.

Ryannon nodded to the men who were holding Jonathan and Bridgette. As if rehearsed, the men used the blindfolds to gag them both.

Bridgette was easily stifled by two muscular guards.

Jonathan was more difficult. "Get off me! No! I'll . . . have you . . . rrrrmmmdddrrr," he bellowed as three others fought, and finally succeeded to pull the rag across his mouth.

"Really, Mr. Ryannon . . . is all of this necessary?" Major Porter chimed in. He could no longer stand by and watch the man he knew to be the villain torture these people — especially the dark-haired girl who reminded him a little of his own teenage daughter.

Ryannon approached the major and pointed across the clearing to an unoccupied spot. "May I have a word with you, Major?" he asked.

Porter agreed reluctantly and they moved to the other side of the clearing, away from the crowd.

"I know this may seem drastic, sir," Ryannon explained, "but it is really just for show. Tyranny is the only language this man understands. I am not *really* marrying his daughter." He glanced over his shoulder at Audril. "She's only seventeen, for heaven's sake. But if the people here think that we are Entrusted . . . that's what it's called here on Lor Mandela . . . then I will have some leverage when it comes time for negotiating peace; the Entrusted of the atoc's daughter is a powerful political figure. I'll be in a much better position to secure peace on both of our worlds."

Major Porter squinted at him, far from convinced.

"Don't worry, after everything is under control, I'll let her know that it wasn't real."

The Major glowered at him with his thin brown eyes. "I hope you're not lying to me, sir," he warned.

Ryannon chuckled and shook his head. "Trust me, Porter. I quite like her. I wouldn't dream of harming her. Come on now, let's get back to it," he replied, urging the major along with a hand on the center of his back.

"Shall we begin?" he shouted enthusiastically, more to the crowd than to Audril as he returned to her side. "Do you remember the vow, my dear, or would you like to repeat it after me?"

Jonathan let out another muffled yelp from under his gag. The guards next to him jabbed their vystoran sleeves tightly into his sides.

"No . . . I remember," Audril mumbled.

"Very well," Ryannon replied, flashing a wicked smile at the atoc.

Audril glanced over at her dad and Bridgette. Reality suddenly hit, and it hit hard. She was going to have to go through with it; she was going to have to recite the vow. Their lives depended on it. Ryannon had said that he didn't need either of them alive. She knew this was true. She gulped hard and looked into his red flickering eyes and whispered, "*A se nalt o talis betrindi.*"

A triumphant smile spread across Ryannon's lips. "That's it," he urged, panting like a rabid dog. "Keep going, my dear."

Jonathan's eyes grew wide and a barrage of choked, angry sounds spewed out from around the rag in his mouth.

"*Kace enalt o madus betrindi,*" she forced herself to continue.

Again, Jonathan released an indiscernible flood of bellowing.

Audril turned toward him to comfort him, but all she could see were the silver tubes prodding both him and Bridgette in the sides. With tears forming in her crystalline blue eyes she whispered, "*Wes solis e trysta conaye.*"

Ryannon lifted her hands in his and looked at her with the same evil smirk he had given Jonathan. "*A se nalt o talis betrindi,*" he purred. "*Kace enalt o madus betrindi.*" He paused to kiss the back of her hand and then literally shouted, "*Wes solis e trysta conaye!*"

The dark sky immediately shone glittering gold. Tiny sparks like fireflies spun around the trees and into the camp. Jonathan's protests were all but drowned out by the comments and gasps of those in attendance.

Thirty-Six

The tiny lights collected into glistening ribbons and encircled Ryannon and Audril. Ryannon leaned down and kissed Audril on the cheek. "Finally . . . you're mine," he sneered, words that sent a nauseating lump shooting from Audril's stomach into her throat.

The streams of light danced around them for several seconds before separating from Audril and absorbing into Ryannon's chest. Almost instantly, his hair darkened from deep brown to rich raven black.

It was as if the change in Ryannon's appearance solidified the significance of what just happened in Jonathan's mind. He dropped to his knees in despair.

Audril rushed to her father, but before she could reach him, Ryannon had his arm firmly around her waist and was dragging her backward. She strained and kicked to get away but his grip was too strong.

"Stop it!" she yelled, "I went through with it, Ryannon! Now . . . let . . . them . . . go!"

"In good time," he retorted. "There are one or two little things that we need to attend to, and then, I promise, *angel* . . . I'll send them home to their cozy beds at the palace."

His use of the word *angel* sliced into her core like a red hot knife, and a singeing knot twisted in her chest. She couldn't breathe. Had she really just married Ryannon? Surely it wasn't binding. It couldn't be. She'd find a way . . . a way to get out of it.

"What things?" she questioned in a sullen whisper.

Ryannon turned her to face him and replied, "First . . . this." He pulled her close and — making sure that Jonathan could see clearly — pressed his lips over hers and kissed her with larger-than-life passion. He moved his hands up her back and into her curls and smashed her mouth even tighter to his. After several seconds, he finally moved away and let out a guttural groan. "We'll continue that in a little while," he smirked. "The next order of business is a little ritual involving a verulcae pod. I'm sure you'll find it very pleasurable, dear . . . I know I will."

Oh great, Audril thought to herself, *how is that going to work out?* She tried not to betray with her eyes that she knew anything about the power transfer, but the terrifying thought kept wrenching through her, and she was sure it showed. What would Ryannon do when he found out that she was no longer the Clest Anaria?

"What is it, my love?" he asked as he noticed the look of worry on her face.

"What do you mean, 'what is it?'" she snapped. "You just forced me to become your Entrusted! You're having a field day torturing my dad, and you still won't let him and my best friend go . . . and now you're planning on putting me through yet another one of your weird ritual thingies! What other reasons do I need?"

Ryannon sniggered and pulled her by the hand toward the trees at the opposite side of the clearing. "Maybe the power transfer can wait. I think it's time we had a little . . ." he glanced back at Jonathan and hissed, "privacy."

Both the atoc and Major Porter quickly jumped to their feet. Jonathan bellowed something through the gag, before swinging his arms out from behind him and wrapping the rope that he had managed to loosen from his hands around the neck of one of his captors. Without waiting for orders, the warrior on the other side of him pressed the button on the vystoran sleeve.

Audril screamed at the sound of the metallic click, yanked herself out of Ryannon's grasp and leapt toward her dad.

Jonathan froze in place and looked down at his chest, fully expecting to see green goo running down it, but much to his surprise, it appeared that the vystoran sleeve had misfired — an almost unheard of malfunction.

Audril collapsed to her knees, mouth gaping, with a combination of both overwhelming relief and inexpressible horror in her blue eyes.

"Ryannon, please," she implored in a sob. "Just let me talk to him! I'll convince him not to give you any more trouble! Please!"

In a moment of uncommon compassion, Ryannon agreed. He helped her up from the ground, escorted her back to her dad and yanked the gag out of his mouth.

"Why you . . . you . . . ." Jonathan roared.

"Dad, stop!" Audril insisted. "This won't help any of us! Please . . . please, Daddy. Just do as they say. Please . . . ." Crystal tears jumped from her eyes and streamed down her dusty cheeks; she reached around her dad's shoulders and embraced him and he wrapped his arms around her as well.

"I'll figure this out," she whispered in his ear. "You've just gotta trust me." She pulled back and wiped her face with the back of her hand.

Jonathan nodded and muttered a weak, "Okay, angel."

"There," Ryannon said, sliding his hand around her arm and moving her away. "You've had your moment."

He turned his attention to the guards and barked, "Don't let anything like that happen again. Tie him back up and you . . ." he yelped at the warrior who'd fired the vystoran sleeve, ". . . learn how to use that thing properly!"

He turned to see Major Porter eyeing him suspiciously. As he accompanied Audril past, he patted the skeptical major on the shoulder and assured, "Don't worry, Major. Things are still exactly as we discussed."

He led Audril out of the clearing and into the towering trees. It was now completely dark out and a hazy mist had settled around the tree trunks, taking the visibility down to nothing.

"What are you doing?" Audril tried timorously as they moved into the murky woods. "Why all the secrecy?"

"This won't work with a bunch of witnesses," he replied. "The time has come for me to relieve you of your Clest Anaria powers." The tone of his voice sounded rather like that of a child on Christmas morning. "I should think you'd be happy to be rid of them. They've caused you such trouble."

"It's not my powers that have caused me trouble, Ryannon," she corrected. "I think we both know that."

327

Ryannon ignored her comment and pulled her further into the forest, into pitch blackness. "We're almost there," he breathed excitedly.

A few yards ahead, Audril could see a tiny light flickering between the trees. It almost seemed as though it was groping for breath in the heavy gloom. As they moved closer it became clear that the light was coming from a small fire pit which had been constructed in the center of a treeless patch of moss about the size of a football field.

The light was the result of weak flames that — judging by the charred, white ashy appearance of the wood within — had been burning for quite some time.

A make-shift altar of flat, smooth stones had been erected near the fire, and atop the highest stone sat a small, yellow fruit covered in green spots — a verulcae pod.

Wait a second, she thought in complete shock. *Why didn't I think of this before? I mean, how can he not know this?*

Like a pile of bricks falling onto her head, it occurred to her. The power transfer would require him to drink the verulcae juice — and it was poisonous! If she didn't bite into the skin of the pod along with him, he would die. How could he be so stupid, and what could possibly have led him to believe that she would *actually* save him?

"What's all this about?" she asked innocently, fighting to hide her mirth.

"This," he replied, lifting the pod and holding it out toward her, "this squishy little verulcae pod contains everything we need for you to give me those pesky powers of yours."

"Learn this in your magic book, did you?" she quipped.

"I don't need that book anymore," he answered, waving his arm in the air, unconcerned. "This is the only interesting thing in it that I haven't done yet. Oh, I know . . . I know . . . you thought that if you stole it from me, it would hurt me somehow. Sorry to disappoint you."

"I'm sure I don't know what you're talking about," Audril replied as she anxiously watched him examine the pod.

"You really should have invested a little more in your drama classes," he retorted. "You're a horrible liar." Ryannon reached down behind the altar and pulled out a length of rope.

"What's that for?" Audril asked with just a tiny hint of nervousness in her otherwise excited voice.

"Well, I can't very well have you wiggling around while we do this, and based on your past performances . . . ." He moved toward her with the rope in one hand and the verulcae pod in the other.

Let him tie me up! she thought indignantly. *He's going to die!*

Ryannon's arm slipping around her waist shook her from her thoughts. He pulled her in with his strong arm and sucked in a deep breath through his teeth. "You know something, Audril," he began, "you are a very desirable young woman." He lowered his face into her hair and kissed the top of her head. "I'm looking forward to consummating our union."

"Um . . . ewww! I don't think so," she snarled, struggling to push him away. Her attempt only made him strengthen his grip.

"Don't be nervous, love," he purred hedonistically as he ran his hand over her shoulder and down her arm. "I won't bite . . . much."

Audril shrank back as much as she could. "Can we just get on with whatever you are planning on doing with that magical little fruit thingy?" she sneered. "You don't want to be distracted and accidentally do something wrong."

Ryannon pried himself away and looked at her questioningly. "Why would you say that?"

"No reason," she simpered as a mischievous smile played across her peachy lips. "It's just that without your book, you have nothing to reference. You might screw it up . . . like you did the Time Align."

Anger flickered in Ryannon's blackish-blue eyes where the red flecks had been previously, but then surprisingly, he started to laugh. "I'm going to enjoy watching you suffer," he sneered. "It will be such a turn on." He yanked her roughly to a nearby tree and pushed her against it. Then, with great agility

329

and expertise, he flipped the rope across her and secured her to the coarse trunk. Had it not been for the armor covering the majority of her body, she was sure she would have been severely scraped up.

"I feel it necessary to explain this process to you, my dear," he began, holding the verulcae pod in front of her eyes. "The juice inside of this is lethal. It'll kill a rynolt in just over a minute, so I imagine there won't be much time for us."

Audril watched with rapt anticipation as he drew a knife from his jacket pocket and sliced a hole into the top of the pod. He stowed the knife away again, carefully holding the pod upright to avoid spilling any of the nectar from it.

"Now then," he continued in a reverent whisper. "Every drop must be consumed, and then, we must bite into the skin of the pod together." He paused for a moment, as if trying to increase suspense, before looking earnestly into her eyes. "Understand, Audril. If you do not bite into this pod when I do, you will die."

Ah hah! The voice inside her head screamed. *He doesn't get it! He is doing it wrong!* It was exactly what she hoped for. He had it backwards. He had interpreted the spell incorrectly, and believed that she would be the one to die, when really, it would be him! Either that, or he was bluffing his way into making her bite the fruit. At any rate, she knew what she would do. She would let him go through with it, pretending like she was going to bite down, then, when he was writhing in agony, begging her for relief, she would pull away and watch him fall. Just the thought of it made her feel extreme elation — an intoxicating sense of power and control — an invigorating flood of emotion that, all at once, gratified and startled her.

She had never desired to watch someone die like this, but right now, she wanted nothing more than to see the life go out of Ryannon's eyes — to watch as he gasped for his last agonizing breath. She longed to hear his pleas for help that would go unanswered and, in time, fall silent. She wished him dead; she yearned for it. It was both exhilarating and frightening.

Then it occurred to her. She had seen the embodiment of these emotions in someone's eyes before; she had seen a look that perfectly expressed how she was feeling, but hadn't understood it at the time. It was an expression she had witnessed in Ryannon's mother's eyes — Ultara's — when the vritesse found out that Ryannon had killed his own father.

Ultara, upon learning of Darian's death, had made a comment about Ryannon's priorities being in line. Audril remembered that, when she said it, she had the strangest look in her eyes, like she was ecstatic that her former Entrusted was dead, but all at once miserable that he was.

Could this be some weird Trysta emotion seeping through? Audril thought. She was, after all, half Trysta. She fought to keep her feelings from showing as Ryannon moved nearer to her with the pod.

"Here goes," he breathed as he lifted the small fruit to her lips and began to squeeze.

"WAIT!" Audril shrieked as though trying to wake the dead. "What . . . what are you doing?"

"I think I made that clear," Ryannon grimaced. "You have to drink all of the juice out of this pod. That's how this works!"

"No!" Audril bellowed, "YOU have to drink it! That's how . . . ." All at once she gasped as she realized what she'd just admitted.

"How . . . do . . . *you* . . . know?" Ryannon hissed, studying her expression with the ultimate look of suspicion.

"I . . . I don't," she stammered. "It's just . . . I don't want to drink it! You said it'll kill me!"

Ryannon didn't say a word. He walked over to the altar and gently placed the pod back on top of it. The silence was unnerving to Audril as he returned to the tree and began loosening the knots.

"What are you doing?" she tried, her voice quivering with trepidation.

"Tell me, darling," he began as the rope fell to her feet. "What must I do to make you love me?"

The question was not at all expected. "What?" she breathed.

331

"Maybe you like it ROUGH," he howled as he threw the back of his hand against her face with such force that she flew through the air, twisting and landing on her left arm awkwardly against the rocks of the fire pit. The stomach-churning sound of bones cracking echoed against the large pines.

Audril stifled a whine and lifted her other hand to her lip which felt like it had instantly swollen to the size of a golf ball and was burning and throbbing like it was about to explode. "Oh no," she groaned in a whisper as she noticed crimson blood streaming over her fingers. Quickly she turned her head so that Ryannon wouldn't see.

"What? You didn't like that," he asked. His voice grew nearer as he hissed, "Look at me when I talk to you."

Audril tried to think, but the pain stabbing through her arm was too great.

"I said LOOK AT ME!" Ryannon's gloved hand gripped her jaw and wrenched her neck around. At the sight of the blood, he started to guffaw like a mad man. "You gave them away, didn't you?" he roared. "You gave them away!"

With no thought to the pain she was in, Ryannon ripped her up forcefully from the ground. Audril let out a mournful yelp as the bones in her arm scraped together.

"Who did you give them to, Atoh?" he sneered, no longer laughing. "Your little blonde friend? Or maybe that pathetic loser, Glaron?"

He raised his arm to backhand her again, when a large shadow whizzed past them, and a screeching roar sounded overhead. They looked up to see the blackened form of a calandry soaring just below the tree tops, and it seemed to be descending.

Ryannon's lips spread into a half-smile as he grabbed a handful of Audril's curls and yanked hard. "Tell me who you've given the powers to, or I'll feed you to *him* for supper."

Audril prayed with all her might that the dark creature moving down toward them was Phantom. Her eyes kept darting from Ryannon to the calandry in search of some sign.

Despite desperately wanting to cry because of her pain, she sighed loudly and replied, "I have no idea what you're talking about."

Ryannon uncurled his fingers from her hair and shoved her hard. Again she fell to the ground, but this time could not contain her scream. She cried out in agony as the weight of her upper body smashed against her arm.

The calandry howled again as it swooped within inches of the ground.

"Such a pity," Ryannon said, pulling a vystoran sleeve from his jacket and taking aim at Audril. "But at least our friend here will be well fed."

Just as he started toward the button with his index finger, there was a rushing sound and the weapon blasted out of his hand and landed in the fire. The flames surged just as the calandry retracted one of its crenulated wings, revealing three riders upon its massive back — one was Glaron, one Guddlebee, and the other, Teedee.

Chapter XXXVII

SURPRISE RESCUE

Claron trained a crossbow-type weapon on Ryannon, who looked more than a little shocked that he'd been so skillfully disarmed.

"DORAN! We're under attack!" he yowled as he wasted no time speeding away into the trees, back toward the clearing.

Glaron dismounted the calandry who was, in fact, Phantom, and helped Teedee to the ground before rushing to Audril's aid.

Guddlebee seemed perfectly content to stay perched atop Phantom and keep as much distance between himself and Ryannon as possible.

"Boo! Are you all right?" Glaron gasped as he observed her dangling arm and still bleeding lip. "Where're your dad . . . and Bridge?"

"They're back at the camp," she replied, relieved to see him. "But Ryannon has hundreds of soldiers back there," she added. "We have to get out of here quick!"

Teedee bobbed up and down and rolled her hands into fists. "Let them come!" she squealed, punching at the air in front of her. "I have a few surprises up my sleeves!"

"I'm sure you do," Glaron grimaced as he helped Audril to her feet and moved her toward Phantom, "but you'd better save 'em for later, Teedee. We have to figure out how to get to the others."

"You tells 'em, Auntie Dees," Guddlebee squeaked, sounding rather terrified.

"Why did you bring them?" Audril whispered out of the corner of her mouth. "Of all the sidekicks you could've chosen . . . ." A twinge of pain in her broken arm stopped her mid-sentence and made her whine loudly.

"There now, sweetie, we'll get you taken care of soon," Glaron assured, sounding more like he had in his days as Dr. Brockman. He leaned her gently against Phantom's side and explained, "The calandry wouldn't let anyone but Teedee near it. I couldn't even get close unless she was around, and she insisted that Guddlebee . . . ."

"So what's the plan, Tiger?" Teedee interrupted, smoothing down the front of her frilly red skirt, and motioning with her head toward the forest. "From the looks of it, we'd better come up with something soon."

The trees began to rustle as several dark figures moving through them became visible.

"Get on!" Glaron bellowed, helping Audril grapple her way onto Phantom's lowered neck.

"This isn't a very good plan!" Teedee hollered, pointing back at the trees.

Glaron turned, just as a red disk sped past his face, narrowly missing him.

Phantom reared, sending Audril and Guddlebee lurching backwards. Audril was barely able to hold on with her uninjured arm.

A dozen or so Brashnellan soldiers burst through the trees aiming vystoran sleeves right at them. Ryannon was in the center of the group, looking quite smug for someone who was unarmed.

"Oh, you think this is going to get you somewhere, do you?" Teedee snapped.

Glaron tried to shush her but she was already moving away from him and toward Ryannon.

"I have heard some pretty shocking things about you, Mr. Ryannon, and I must say that I am not a fan of your doings . . . blowing up innocent people . . .

kidnapping . . . tricking perfectly wonderful young men into practically committing suicide, and apparently beating lovely young ladies!" She motioned back at Audril with a bony finger.

Perhaps because they were so stunned by this eccentric old lady, none of the Brashnellans fired. They all stood with mouths open as Teedee continued her diatribe directed toward their leader.

"There's a name for your type, Mister, but it's a name I can't say in polite company!" She reached the fire pit and stood in the glow of the quietly flickering flames. "I should have stepped on the egg when I had the chance!" she barked in her gruff, gravely tone.

"Oh, good grief," Audril sighed aloud, "here she goes again!"

Glaron looked up at her with a strange, terrified look on his face.

Ryannon and several of the Brashnellans broke into thunderous laughter. "Is . . . is this who you have to defend Mandela City? And to think, I was almost worried!" he roared. "Doran! Go get the atoc and what's her name! I'm sure they'll want to know that they're about to be rescued by old Mommy Twiggy Legs here!"

Doran scurried away as Teedee *tsked* at Ryannon's impudence.

"Listen, lady, I don't know if you realize this, but these are *real* weapons. You might want to go back with the other girls over there so you don't get hurt." He smiled at Glaron.

Guddlebee growled his displeasure.

Teedee stood still for a moment, watching Ryannon like a disappointed grandmother, but then bent over and picked up a baseball-sized stone from the edge of the pit and hurled it with all her might at him. The stone fell — several feet shy of him — and again, he and the Brashnellans burst into laughter.

"That's enough!" Teedee scolded. "I'm warning you, Mr. Ryannon. If you don't turn yourself over to the chief advisor right now, you will be sorry!"

"Um, Teedee," Glaron tried, but was instantly hushed by Teedee's patronizing look.

"I will count to three!" she continued. "One . . . ."

"Oh, please," Audril moaned, as Ryannon signaled for his soldiers to turn their weapons exclusively on the off-center old woman.

"Teedee don't!" Glaron shrieked as the Brashnellans took aim.

Teedee ignored him. "Two . . . ." she sneered, an eerie seriousness in her eyes.

"Three!" Ryannon bellowed, but no sooner had he said the word than the entire collection of the vystoran sleeves rocketed from the warriors' hands, and the trees around them lit up in an amazing light show of intense orangey-pink, blue-green and fiery yellow. One by one the shapes of hundreds of Trystas materialized all around them, sending the Brashnellans, including Doran, who'd just returned with Jonathan and Bridgette in tow, collapsing to their knees in pain.

Glaron whooped loudly from his position near Phantom who pranced up and down with delight. "That a girl, Teedee!" he cheered. "How in the world did you know?"

Audril and Guddlebee were hugging and giggling when, all of a sudden, the lights from the Trystas' eyes dimmed.

The Brashnellans stopped writhing, but seemed to be held on the ground by an unseen force.

An icy blast of wind — black and clearly visible — moved through the area, twisting around the Trystas in dark wisps until finally collecting in a loose whirlwind around Teedee.

All at once, the base of every tree for as far as the eye could see began to glow, illuminated seemingly from the inside by a deep blue light.

As the lights spread upward, the shadowy wind rushed around Teedee, blowing wisps of silver hair across her face.

"What's going on?" Bridgette whispered to Jonathan, who indistinctly shook his head and shrugged his shoulders.

Teedee moved toward where Ryannon lay, encircled by rushing ribbons of black, but her posture wasn't hunched over and frail anymore; her gait was smooth and flowing. As she walked, her outlandish ensemble began to change around a body that also seemed to be changing within the cyclone.

The blue light was now slipping into the high drooping branches and long needles of the trees, flooding through the forest like a huge, all-consuming wave.

"Oh . . . my . . . guh . . . ." Audril gasped, unable to finish her words.

Teedee was now wrapped in a deep green velvet gown with scrolling gold trim that hugged her suddenly svelte physique. She continued floating toward Ryannon, taking slow, fluid steps, all the while encircled by the wisps of wind.

A moment later, the blue in the trees began to grow and surge until all at once the forest erupted into a brilliant white glow.

Glaron squinted and shielded his eyes but kept them locked on Teedee from behind.

Her hair started to thicken and change color, transforming slowly into a vivid mane of lava orange. As the wispy wind moved away from her, the light from the trees dissipated and was replaced by a soft gold radiance.

"Great . . . big . . . son of a slarp," Glaron gasped. "Ultara?! It can't be!"

"Hello, Mother," Ryannon hissed from the ground.

Without breaking her calm, methodic stride, she walked to him and lifted her arm upward.

With no effort on his part, Ryannon raised to his feet.

"Like I said..." The harsh, raspy voice of Teedee Venilworth had been replaced by a deep seductive one, as smooth as silk. "I should have stepped on the egg when I had the chance!"

Chapter XXXVIII

KABLAZAM!

The Trystas kept their magical hold on the Brashnellans as they restrained them with silvery ropes, which spun unaided into formidable knots around the warriors' wrists.

Jonathan and Bridgette were freed immediately and reunited with Audril and Glaron.

Glaron held Bridgette tightly to him as she wept quietly.

Jonathan helped Audril off of Phantom's back and assured her that as soon as a Trysta with healing powers was available, they'd get her arm mended.

Still atop Phantom, Guddlebee had risen to his feet; his eyes darted anxiously from side to side as he rolled up and down on his stubby, bare toes.

"Is this what you're looking for, brother Squanki?" A deep, soothing voice lilted out from behind one of the massive trunks.

Audril, Jonathan and Glaron all turned as Hodgson emerged from the shadows.

Next to him, Tora was struggling to free herself from the grip he had on the collar of her uniform. She looked even more petite than usual next to Hodgson who was easily six and a half feet tall.

"Nos," Guddlebee sighed in a disappointed whimper.

"No, my friend . . . not her," Hodgson corrected as a mischievous smile played across his handsome face. He pointed down toward his knee. "Her," he beamed.

All at once, a few floating wisps of white hair appeared from behind Hodgson's leg. The locks drifted dreamily and were followed by a big, blue eyeball on a little, brown, elated face.

"Yippeeeee!" Guddlebee squealed as he sprang off of Phantom's back and bounded over to where they stood.

Tabbit, who looked as good as new, let out a delighted squeak and pounced on him, knocking him to the ground. He threw his arms around her and glanced skyward, grinning from ear to ear. "Thank yous, Phaeter," he sighed, "thank yous."

Audril couldn't help but laugh as Hodgson, along with Glaron and Bridgette, escorted Tora across the clearing to a pleased Commander Pauliss. "Feeling better, Tabbit?" she smiled.

Tabbit pulled herself off of Guddlebee and jumped to her feet. "Oh, yeses, Lady! Yeses!" She pointed at Ultara, looking as though she would burst into joyful tears. "Lady comes backs!"

Audril gasped, staring wide-eyed at Tabbit, and replayed the words of Tabbit's Trinkle Trance over in her mind. *Squanki don't tells . . . lady comes backs . . . lady comes backs . . . return the powers . . . four hundred days . . . four hundred days.* "Oh! So that's what you were rambling on about! How in the world did you know?"

Tabbit locked her tiny arms behind her and rocked up and down sheepishly. "Squanki don't tells," she grinned. "Nopes, they don'ts."

"Guess there's only one thing left to do then," Audril guessed. "I have to get my powers back before four hundred days is up."

Guddlebee suddenly sat up. A wild, startled expression burned across his face. "That's the bestest you can do?" he scolded. "That's the bestest? Come on, ladys . . . thinks!"

Thirty-Eight

"Nos, nos, my friggles," Tabbit squeaked nervously as she held her hands out to him. "It's nots time for thats yet."

"Time for what?" Audril queried. "Time for me to have my powers restored?"

"Oh, nos," Tabbit answered. At this point she was darting back and forth between Audril and Guddlebee like the ball in a ping pong match. "Your powers cans be returned anytimes . . . hes is just being . . . just being . . . sillys."

"I am nots!" Guddlebee retorted indignantly. "Withouts *hims* helping . . . its would be dangerouses . . . she wills never figures its out . . . very, very dangerouses!"

"What are you two talking about?" Audril insisted. "Does this have something to do with . . . with Dallin?" Saying his name was almost more painful than the throbbing ache in her arm.

"I'd like to know that myself," Jonathan interjected. "What *are* you two talking about?"

Tabbit stopped in front of Audril, looked sideways at Guddlebee and rolled her enormous eyes. "He thinks thats the pretty Clest Anarias is needing a protector . . . a Dallins Doones protector . . . but hes is a dorblesnorf!"

Guddlebee huffed loudly and turned away with a stomp of his foot.

Audril had no idea what a dorblesnorf was, nor did she ask. "Lortu *did* say that Dallin needed to protect me." She looked pleadingly at Tabbit and asked, "Do you know where the portal that he went through led?"

Tabbit looked down at her toes and shook her head sadly.

"What is this all about?" Jonathan tried again, becoming more agitated by the second.

"It's nots over yets," Guddlebee breathed with his back still turned. "Tabbits knows this and calls me the dorblesnorfs, she does!"

"What do you mean? What's not over yet?" Audril pressed. "Darlings . . . ." Tabbit snarled through clenched teeth. "Thats is enoughs." Her elfish

341

appearance and the scathing anger building in her bulging eyes created the oddest sort of contradiction.

"I think I'll decide whether it's enough or not, Squanki," Jonathan said. "I insist that you tell me what you know immediately."

Much to Tabbit's relief, they were suddenly joined by Ultara. Jonathan's anger seemed to melt away as he met her with a warm embrace — at least for the moment. "Welcome back, vritesse," he smiled.

"Thank you, Jonathan," she replied. "It's good to be myself again, although I'm seriously considering adapting Teedee's fashion sense." She smiled playfully at Audril and winked. "How are you feeling, Atoh?"

"Well, all things considered . . . ." Audril began, cringing.

"Ultara . . ." Jonathan interrupted and motioned toward Audril with his head. "Would you mind fixing that up?"

"Oh, of course," she replied with a gasp, as she noticed a straining Audril cradling a misshapen forearm with her good hand.

Phantom let out a low, rumbling growl as a soft, golden glow spilled from Ultara's eyes and spread out over Audril's arm.

Tabbit had grabbed Guddlebee by the back of his shirt and was trying to lead him away unnoticed, but Jonathan stopped them by clearing his throat loudly. "I believe you were about to tell me something, Tabbit?"

Tabbit chuckled nervously and let go of her Entrusted's flower print blouse. She took a deep breath and was about to speak when a sudden commotion broke out a few yards away.

Jonathan spun around to see at least half a dozen Trystas sprawled on the ground, and Ryannon moving swiftly toward them.

"Get her out of here!" he shouted to Ultara as he observed that Ryannon's eyes were transfixed on Audril.

His now vivid, cobalt eyes brightened into a concentrated glow and Jonathan crumpled to the ground in agony. Several Trystas and even some of the American soldiers moved to detain him, but he raised his arm in the air and sent them hurtling backwards. "If you want the atoc to live . . ." he snarled as the next wave of would-be attackers advanced on him. Even though he hadn't finished his sentence, his words were enough to stop them in their tracks.

Jonathan wailed miserably and writhed on the ground as a shock of intense electricity jolted through him.

Ultara turned to Phantom and made a strange clicking noise with her tongue. The massive calandry turned his dragon-like head and repeated the odd sound. Ultara waved her arm and he swung his neck downward, hitting Audril behind the knees, sending her teetering backwards. He flipped his long neck up and she tumbled down it and onto his back.

The bones in her not-yet-healed arm snapped in two again with an audible crack, projecting a fiery, painful twinge ripping through her entire upper body, and forcing an agonized shriek from her lips.

"Grab a hold! NOW!" Ultara warned as she smacked the creature on his thigh.

Phantom spread his enormous wings and swooshed them up and down, lifting from the ground.

"No!" Ryannon bellowed as he sent another powerful blast twisting through Jonathan.

Ultara turned to confront him, her eyes now emanating an intense amber glow.

Ryannon winced a little, but did not slow his advance.

Other Trystas' eyes, including Glaron's, began to illuminate, creating a chaotic tapestry of color on the surfaces of the surrounding trees and the mossy clumps of ground, but nothing slowed Ryannon. It appeared as if all of the combined powers in the Trysta Empire would not be enough. In fact, it seemed that the more they tried to stop him, the more powerful he became.

Phantom glided further upward, with Audril nearly passing out from the stabbing pain caused by each stroke of his wings. In between the waves of black twirling through her head, she struggled to urge Phantom back to the clearing — back to her dad.

She could see him twitching on the ground and hear his pleas for help, but rather than getting closer with each swell of Phantom's wings, her father's thrashing form was moving ever further away, shrinking into the distance as they gained altitude.

Ryannon was now standing nearly on top of him, sending deadly bolts of energy through him continuously. Ultara and the other Trystas tried everything they could think of to stop him, but no one could get remotely close. Even the vystoran sleeves weren't working — to the dismay of the U.S. soldiers who tried to use them to subdue him. The vystorans flew at Ryannon, but just before hitting him they rapidly changed course, as if being deflected by an invisible force field.

Ultara stared questioningly at Ryannon for a moment, studying his every move, searching for any sign of weakness.

All of a sudden, a look of astonishment washed over her. She raised her hands in front of her chest, cupping them as if she was holding a ball. Lines of intense concentration formed on her face as a spinning orb of white light expanded between her palms.

With a slight flick of one wrist, the orb raced at Ryannon, hitting him squarely in the chest before exiting through his back. The orb darted around, zigzagging from person to person, emitting a high pitched hiss.

As Ultara watched intently, her eyes widened with shock as the ball stopped less than an inch from Glaron's green eyes, and erupted into a shower of emerald sparks. "Glaron?" she breathed in a stunned whisper, "GLARON! GET OUT OF HERE!" she bellowed across the clearing.

The volume of her command so startled Glaron that he began to run instinctively. "Wait! What?" he asked, catching himself just prior to reaching the tree line. "WHY?" he yelled back.

"You can't be here right now! You're making him too powerful! Go on! GO!"

Glaron could hardly imagine how his presence could make Ryannon more powerful, but he trusted Ultara implicitly. He glanced from her to

Jonathan, who was unconscious, but still jerking spastically with each jolt that Ryannon leveled against him, then shrugged his shoulders and dashed off into the trees.

As soon as he was a fair distance away, Ryannon's assault seemed to drastically diminish.

"EYES!" Ultara howled as a glowing spectrum of color emanated again through the clearing. This time the attack was far more effective. Ryannon collapsed to the ground, bellowing loudly.

"I've had just about all of you I am going to take!" Ultara seethed, standing over the pathetic, writhing form of her son. "Your reign of terror is over."

Her eyes intensified as she prepared to send a final fatal blast through him, but before she could, Ryannon pulled something from his pocket and pointed it directly at her — a shiny silver pistol that he had confiscated from one of the U.S. soldiers. He aimed it upward and moved his finger to the trigger. With a metallic *shink*, a single bullet exploded from the chamber.

Faster than a blink of an eye, Guddlebee raised his pudgy little hand and yelled, "STOP!"

As though it had hit a wall of solid lead, the bullet obediently stalled in its trajectory and dropped into the decaying leaves littering the ground.

Ryannon quickly rolled to the side and this time took aim at Jonathan.

Guddlebee's bulgy eyes seemed to double in diameter. He pulled himself to his full, unremarkable height and held his small hands out in front of him. He whispered something skyward, and as he did, a thin strand of silvery light shot down from a bright star overhead into his palms. He looked directly at Ryannon; a wild maniacal expression twisted across his face. Quickly, as if he'd been stung by a bee, he retracted his hands backwards and yelled, "KABLAZAM!"

A shock wave, like an exploding bomb, rippled through the forest, yet seemed to affect no one but Ryannon. He flew into the air, spiraling backwards like a football, crashing with a loud thud against a tree and then dropping in a lifeless heap to the ground.

Ultara glanced backwards at Guddlebee with an expression of both shock and relief. "How?" she breathed.

"Hes was gettings on my nerves," Guddlebee replied, grimacing.

Everyone stared in disbelief at the diminutive, otherwise non-threatening creature who had just done what an entire army of powerful Trystas couldn't.

The forest was deafeningly silent for a few moments, until, at last, the stillness was broken by the sound of a single voice — Ryannon's. He lay on the forest floor, knees at his chest like a newborn baby, muttering incomprehensibly.

Just then, Jonathan began to sputter and gasp for air. Ultara rushed to his side and helped him to sitting. "Unbelievable," she smiled as she lowered to her knees beside him. "I've never seen anyone take that much and live to tell about it, Jonathan. Here . . . ." The soft amber glow of her healing powers returned to her eyes and washed over Jonathan's entire body. Within a few seconds, his breathing returned to normal and he had the strength to sit without her help. "Take him to Breigarian," he hissed weakly, as soon as he had enough energy to speak.

Ultara nodded and motioned to a few of the Trystas standing near Ryannon, and they hoisted him to his feet. With their arms locked securely around him, they escorted him away. Several unintelligible syllables spilled from his lips as they disappeared into the trees.

"Audril . . ." Jonathan muttered. "Where . . . ?"

"She's safe, Atoc," Ultara replied. "I sent her on the calandry back to the city. I'm sure she's being attended to by Michelan at this very moment."

Jonathan looked up to see Bridgette moving quickly toward him. "Are you all right, sweetie," he asked, his voice a little stronger, but still not entirely normal.

"I'm fine," she answered. "I'm not the one who just got electrocuted," she sighed as a small, silver tear dropped from her lashes and trickled down her cheek.

"I think the atoc could use some water," Ultara offered. "Could you get some from the camp, Bridgette . . . and while you're there, tell your boyfriend that I would very much like to see him now."

Bridgette didn't hesitate. Even though Ultara was kind, she was slightly terrifying to Bridgette, whose exposure to "power" prior to coming to Lor Mandela had consisted of turning on the occasional light switch.

"You'll never believe this, Jonathan," she explained as the light from her eyes continued to cascade over him. "When Glaron gets here, I think you're in for quite a surprise."

Chapter XXXIX

ANY OF THESE ELEMENTS MISSED

A few minutes later, together carrying a dusky blue ceramic bucket, Glaron and Bridgette emerged from the dark forest. Water sloshed back and forth over the sides of the bucket and occasionally plopped out around their feet as they walked.

Ultara stood the moment she saw them and motioned excitedly toward Glaron, who was relieved to see her smiling.

When Bridgette had told him that Ultara wanted to see him, he assumed that he was in trouble for something. Why else would she have sent him away earlier?

"Glaron, hurry," she called out impatiently; seemingly oblivious to the fact that the water bucket was heavy.

He leaned close to Bridgette and whispered, "Coming, your pain-ness."

Bridgette giggled appreciatively. As she made an adoring face at him, she missed a rather large clump of moss directly in front of her. As she stepped onto the slick mound, her foot slipped forward, sending even more water splashing to the ground.

"Will you save some of that for the atoc?" Ultara scolded playfully. She had always enjoyed teasing Glaron. In the days when he was her chief advisor, she would find ways to pester him regularly, just to get one of his usually hysterical reactions.

"Don't worry, ma'am," he chuckled, "I'm not entirely sure we should be giving this to him, anyway. Haven't you heard that you're not supposed to put water on an electrical fire?" He looked at Jonathan and winked.

He and Bridgette carried the bucket to Jonathan and Bridgette pulled a large soup ladle from her back pocket and dipped it into the bucket.

Jonathan, who had regained most of his strength, took the ladle from her and sipped the cool water. "Thanks," he breathed in between drinks. "Now, what is it, Ultara?"

"Glaron," she began. "Have you noticed anything strange about yourself lately? Anything unusual about your abilities?"

Glaron's brow furrowed. "Yeah . . . lots of things, why?"

"When I saw what happened with Ryannon just now . . . how his powers suddenly exploded . . . I knew . . . I knew that there was a channeler in our presence."

"A channeler?" Jonathan gulped, "I thought those stories were just myths. Has there ever been proof of one existing?"

"Not until now," Ultara beamed, her golden eyes flickering in the moonlight and focused on Glaron. "That orb I conjured was no regular spell. It was designed by the Council of Satia to search out a Trysta with enough natural power to become a vritesse, should the bloodline ever fall vacant.

"Naturally, the orb would find the channeler to be the most powerful. I had expected it to indicate Pauliss or Glestran or one of the other females . . . the last Trysta I expected was you, my friend! I should have known though, when I began to alter, I couldn't have done that on my own . . . ."

A dreamy expression fell across her face as she continued, but now she seemed to be addressing herself. "Lortu said the channeler has to . . . but why would he need . . . this is all very unusual."

"Hold on a second," Glaron panted as the color slid from his normally tan face. "Surely you're not suggesting that I'm a ch . . . ch . . . ."

"A channeler, yes," Ultara blurted. "In fact, I think, my dear Glaron, that you are the one and only channeler."

"But I'm a guy!" he whined. "Everyone knows that's impossible!"

"Unlikely, yes . . . but not impossible," Ultara corrected. "Lortu hinted to me earlier . . . said that you did a remarkable thing to save the atoc when he was being attacked. I'm assuming that you did something beyond your normal abilities, and that there just happened to be another Trysta with those extra abilities lingering near by."

"Yeah, Kahlie," Glaron breathed. "But why me? Why now?" he asked, looking not at all thrilled that he was suddenly the stuff of Trysta legend.

"I think you might have just answered your own question," Ultara replied, her face lined with contemplation. "It's because of Kahlie . . . but it can't be though . . . that doesn't make any sense. Oh no, wait . . . they're twins!" she muttered.

"It would be so nice if, for once, you people would stop talking in riddles," Bridgette huffed.

"I quite agree, Bridge," Jonathan sighed. "I'm supposed to be the atoc, but somehow, I'm always the last to find out what's going on."

Jonathan's comment seemed to penetrate through Ultara's deep thoughts, actually making it to her ears. She stopped mumbling and looked at him with her brow furrowed. "I'm sorry, Jonathan. Of course you should know . . . ."

"Know what?" he asked.

"Never in the history of Lor Mandela have so many catastrophic events happened in such a short amount of time," she replied, "and I think it all has to do with that book."

"The book?" both Glaron and Jonathan asked in unison.

"Ah hah!" Guddlebee squeaked from a few yards away. Tabbit rolled her eyes and shushed him.

"Think about it," Ultara continued as wave upon wave of realization seemed to break over her. "Darian started using spells out of the book, who knows how long ago. I seriously doubt he followed any particular order . . . except the one that would benefit him most. My guess is that, between him and

Ryannon, the order of things has become so seriously out of alignment that a channeler and a Clest Anaria would both be necessary."

"Not following," Jonathan grunted.

"Where do I begin?" she sighed.

Just then, Guddlebee bounded over to them and looked up at her. "Whats about withs the twins?" he smiled, prompting a loud chorus of shhhh's from his Entrusted.

"Right," she started, "well, my hunch is that Darian took the book while he was living with me at Trysta palace. The first weird thing that happened was that I gave birth to twins . . . a boy and a girl."

"Yeah . . . but that's not unheard of," Jonathan replied.

"No, but it is very unusual . . . heiresses almost always give birth to a girl first, and I think I'm the only one in history to have given birth to mixed-sex twins . . . others have done it, of course, but as far as I know, no one that's ever been in line to become vritesse."

Jonathan thought for a moment, and then nodded in agreement.

"Not only that," Ultara continued. "You know how uncommon twins are on Lor Mandela, yet mine were only one generation removed from my mother and my aunt . . . that's a little beyond unusual."

"Uh, huh . . . and . . . ." Bridgette urged, not feeling any more enlightened than she had been before Ultara had begun her explanation.

"Well, Bridgette," Ultara snipped, causing her to gasp and her brown eyes to widen in fear. "Let's just list out all of the bizarre, world changing events that have happened since, shall we?"

Sensing Bridgette's discomfort, Glaron placed a soothing hand on her arm. "There's been a lot," he agreed.

"Yes, like the Advantiere; the planet being divided in two; the atoc and the atoh disappearing; the planet being put back together; me *not* dying but instead ending up on Drolana as a little old lady; and the portals collapsing, just to name a few. And now, from what I hear, the atoc's own Entrusted has tried to kill him." Ultara looked to Jonathan for confirmation — confirmation that came instantly in the despondent look in his eyes.

"So what does that have to do with a channeler?" Glaron asked, silently hoping that the answer would not involve anything dangerous or painful for him.

"I believe a channeler is to the vritesse what the Clest Anaria is to the soul of Lor Mandela," Ultara explained, obviously much to Guddlebee's delight.

He skipped around her in a circle, giggling madly. "Finallys they gets it," he sang, looking skyward, "Finallys! Phaeters is telling mes ages ago, but . . ." he looked haughtily at Tabbit, "but Squanki's don't tells!"

"Perhaps Squankis should tell," Jonathan scolded, looking straight at Tabbit, who rolled up and down on her toes and grinned sheepishly.

"I don't understand," Glaron tried. "A channeler channels the powers of other Trystas . . . is that what Audril does with the planet's powers then?"

"I think there's been a misinterpretation somewhere along the line," Ultara explained. "If my hunch is correct, the channeler levels out — or preserves — the vritesse's powers, should they become corrupted, and the Clest Anaria does the same for Lor Mandela's."

"That's right . . . yous is gettings close!" Guddlebee sang as he continued skittering about.

"So, the vritesse powers are corrupted?" Glaron asked.

"I believe so," Ultara answered. "I am the rightful vritesse, but the powers were given to Kahlie . . . problem number one. Problem number two is that Ryannon is her twin. Like I said, a twin male heir is unchartered territory. Who knows how that's going to affect the powers?"

"So what does it all mean?" Jonathan asked, glancing sideways at Hodgson, who had just joined them.

"I'm not interrupting, am I?" the smiling dweller asked, wrapping his arm around Ultara's waist.

Ultara made a playful smirk in his direction before continuing. "There's a line of the Advantiere that says, 'Healing begins following future events,' remember?"

Jonathan nodded as he replayed the lines of the Advantiere in his head. He had spent so much time in the first four years of Audril's life studying and trying to decipher the prophetic riddle, that it was indelibly etched in his memory. "Yeah, so?"

"Well, I don't think Audril has completely saved Lor Mandela yet. I think all that happened at the battle was just the beginning of the healing process. I think the Clest Anaria and the channeler are eventually going to have to restore their powers to their rightful owners."

Her answer sent a golf ball-sized lump lurching from Jonathan's stomach up into his throat. "Excuse me?" he gulped. "Give them back? You mean, she won't be immortal anymore?"

"She's not right now anyway," Ultara reminded him.

"I know," Jonathan replied, "but I thought for sure she'd given the powers to one of you guys, and that she'd be able to just get them back at any time." He looked at Glaron and Bridgette who both shook their heads.

"Wait! That makes sense!" Bridgette boldly interjected. "The note . . . the one that came through Audril's bedroom wall . . . ?" She glanced from Glaron to Jonathan and back. "It said that the answer still lies in the Advantiere!"

"Hold on," Ultara breathed, poking her index finger in the air like she was calculating something. All at once she stopped and walked over to Tabbit who was sitting on the ground, flicking a small Greelan bug with her finger and doing her best to ignore the conversation.

"Tabbit?" she said.

The petite Squanki scooted around so that her back was completely facing Ultara.

Ultara flipped her wild orange locks indignantly and lowered to the ground beside her. "Four hundred days?" she breathed. "Any of these elements missed? You knew this all along, didn't you?"

"What?" Jonathan asked, "What is it?"

Again Ultara was reciting lines of the Advantiere. Jonathan clearly remembered the phrase, *Any of these elements missed, and Lor Mandela will cease.* It was the line that had caused him and Audril's mother the most concern.

Tabbit turned her face toward Ultara; the tears forming in her eyes expressed all too well that she did not share Guddlebee's exuberance. "The atohs lady has to get her powers backs and she has to sets the book rights! She has to return hers powers to the souls . . . and Master Glarons has to return his-es to the rightfuls vritesse . . . both on the four hundredths day, or . . . or . . . or . . . ." She started sobbing wildly and threw her face onto the mossy ground.

Ultara stood and finished her sentence. "Or Lor Mandela will cease . . . not explode, Jonathan, not be destroyed, just . . . cease."

"Wait!" he gasped. "You're telling me that if Audril doesn't get her powers back from whoever she gave them to and return them to the Spirit of Lor Mandela on this day four hundred . . . if she doesn't set whatever has been thrown out of . . . ."

"Balance!" Glaron blustered. "She's the Child of Balance!"

Ultara nodded. "The order of the book must be restored as soon as possible, and the powers of Lor Mandela and of the vritesse have to be given back to their rightful owners on the four hundredth day. On that day, balance will have been maintained for the exact time balance was missing . . . the balance that was missing for four hundred Lor Mandela days when you and Audril were on Drolana." She paused for a moment before muttering, "I guess Ryannon must have made some sort of connection. That's why he preformed the Time Align."

Jonathan struggled to process this information.

"Okay, so the first order of business is helping Audril fix that book."

"That's right," Ultara agreed. "Hodgson and I will gladly help and I'm sure we can count on the Trystas."

"You can count on us too," said Major Porter, who had just walked up and heard the end of their conversation. "I have a feeling we're not going home any time soon."

Jonathan placed his hand on the Major's shoulder. "Thank you for your help, Major, and I'm very sorry about the problem with the portals. We'll try to get them figured out just as soon as we can."

"I know," the Major replied, "but in the meantime, I hope you will allow us to do you some good. I feel bad that we came here to attack you."

"Oh, don't worry about that," Jonathan assured. "I know how Ryannon can be. I'm sure he was very persuasive when he met with President Langley . . . ."

"You know about President Langley?" Porter exclaimed.

"I voted for President Langley," Jonathan smiled. "I lived on Earth for just over thirteen years; course I didn't know I didn't belong there. It's a bit of a long story, but maybe if we get a chance before you go back, I'll fill you in on the details."

Major Porter smiled and nodded. "I think that Private Knox over there may be quite helpful. He's s a bit of a whiz kid . . . joined up to pay for his education." He pointed to a tall, lanky soldier who was assisting the Trystas with the Brashnellans, but rather than searching them for concealed weapons, as the rest of the troops were, he seemed intrigued by the ropes that were being used to bind them.

"He's a cracker jack soldier," Porter continued, as if trying to justify Private Knox's academic behavior. "Sees everything, that one. I dunno . . . he might be able to help figure out those portals of yours."

"That's excellent," Jonathan replied. "The more help, the better. Right now though, I think we should notify the proper Brashnellan authorities that they have a couple hundred prisoners. Glaron, will you and Bridgette join me? And perhaps you'd like to come along as well, Major."

Jonathan turned to Ultara. "I would appreciate it if you and your friend, Hotson, is it?"

"Hodgson," she corrected with a giggle. "Although Hotson is far more accurate."

Jonathan rolled his eyes and shook his head. "Thanks for that, Vritesse," he moaned. "Would you and *Hodgson* get back to the city right away and find Audril? I think logistically, the rest of us are better off camping here for the night and then heading back in the morning."

"Of course, sire," she grinned. "Just let me leave Pauliss with some instructions." She excused herself, and she and Hodgson moved to join the Trystas.

Jonathan turned toward Guddlebee and Tabbit and shot them a disappointed scowl. "And, you two," he grumbled. "Don't you run off. When I get back I think we need to have a little chat about what Squanki shouldn't tell and what they should." Guddlebee struggled to stifle a smug grin without much success, while Tabbit glanced down at her feet in shame.

Forty

Chapter XL

LORTU DECIDES

Phantom swooshed down and landed in the same shrubbery-lined expanse bordering Anisia Mystad where Audril had first seen him. The Greelan trees along the cobblestone path drifted back and forth catching glimpses of flickering moonlight on their long, teardrop-shaped leaves. He pranced up and down, trying to awaken Audril who had fainted mid-flight from the searing pain in her arm.

As Phantom capered around, a low hum, like an idling engine rolled out of the trees. The calandry mimicked the monotone drone and gently lowered to his front knees, folding his legs under himself.

The branches of one of the trees began to ripple unnaturally and Lortu slipped out of the surging shadows. He approached Phantom and stroked his dragon-like neck.

"Well done, maye friend," he whispered and lifted Audril into his arms.

She stirred a little and her eyes blinked open. "Lortu?" she questioned hazily. "Wh . . . what's going on?"

Lortu lowered her onto a small patch of grass, and knelt down beside her. She winced as her arm moved slightly. "Hold steel," he urged and moved a rogue curl from her cheek. "Dis ees going to be ovah befoah you know eet."

Phantom chuffed three times in succession and then dropped his head and drifted to sleep. A few seconds later, he let out a particularly resounding snort, and Audril snapped awake.

"Lortu! You've got to get some of your Dwellers back to the North Forest . . . Ryannon!" she gulped. "He's . . . he's got . . . my dad! Power surges! My dad needs your help!"

"No . . . no," Lortu soothed, "Eet ees ovah, Atoha. De atoc ees fine. De vritessa Ooltara stays wit heem naow."

"Oh . . ." she sighed breathlessly, "Oh, thank you . . . thank you, Lortu." Her head started to spin again and she slumped against his slender yet muscular chest. He placed his arm tenderly around her shoulders, being careful not to disturb her broken arm.

"Atoha?" he tried, fearing that she had passed out again.

"Mmmm?" she whimpered.

"Can you stand on yoah own? I tink dat riding on maye back ees out of de question foah you."

"I . . . I think so," she panted. "Just give me a sec, 'kay?" The pain pulsating in her arm had settled into a deep, pounding throb, which was almost tolerable so long as she didn't move.

Lortu held her as she took several deep breaths in an attempt to steady herself. "All right," she sighed at length, "let's give this a whirl."

Slowly, Lortu slid his arm away and he moved into a squatting position next to her. "I weel help leeft you . . . on tree den?"

Audril nodded.

"One . . . twoa . . . tree."

She leaned forward slightly and Lortu moved his hands onto her waist. With the help of her uninjured arm she was able to shift onto her knees as Lortu slowly guided her upward to standing.

"Der, dat ees bettah," he smiled. "Wait heah a moment," he instructed as he moved towards the bushes alongside the path.

Audril watched as he skirted around one of the taller shrubs and emerged holding something fairly large in his hands.

"I tink dis may help," he offered. As he moved into a wide swath of moonlight Audril immediately recognized that he was carrying the book.

"You found it?" she asked incredulously, not entirely convinced at this point that it had ever been lost.

"Eet was heah in de bushes," he nodded. He grabbed the hand of her good arm and lifted it out in front of her. Then, he placed the Clest Anaria's Book of Revelation on top of it.

"Rest yoah arm," he encouraged, helping her maneuver her injured appendage onto the book. While it did feel better to have her arm against a flat surface, the book was heavy and her other arm shook a little under the strain.

"I don't know, Lortu," she grimaced.

Lortu seemed to ignore her. "Ees eet true dat de Ryannon has taken you as hees Entrusted?"

"So much for making me feel better," Audril snipped as she shifted the quivering book out from under her arm and maneuvered her good arm around it. "Yeah . . . he was going to kill Bridgette and my dad. I didn't have a choice."

"I zee," Lortu acknowledged, stroking his chin contemplatively.

"But, there's gotta be a way to get out of it, isn't there?" she tried.

Lortu began his trademark pacing, not saying a word, but stopping every few seconds and studying Audril's face.

"Yoah meesion ees not complete," he finally replied.

Had Audril's arm not been broken, she probably would have pummeled him.

"Enough about my stupid mission!" she shrieked. "Will you please give it a rest? I don't want to go back to Earth! I want to stay here with my dad, and Bridgette, and Glaron! Don't you get it? Everyone I care about is here!"

Audril expected some sort of profound retort from Lortu, but instead he stopped pacing and looked down at the ground. "Aye am zorry," he sighed, looking rather dejected and forlorn. "Of course, you are een control of yoah own destiny. I weel not mention eet again."

"Thank you," she whispered, feeling a tiny twinge of regret for having gone off on him like she did. After an awkward, momentary silence she asked, "Can we get back to the palace now? I really need to see a doctor."

"Der ees joust one ting more," he muttered, pulling himself upright and approaching Audril with an odd, intense look in his pale eyes. "Aye have to tell you someting." He moved very close to her and locked her in a weighty stare.

"What is it, Lortu?" she asked, suddenly aware of the smoldering heat emanating from his body.

"Shhh," he insisted, dragging his long fingers down the top of her broken arm. "Dis weel make everyting bettah." He stepped forward, his chest and stomach now against hers, except for where the book blocked them. He wrapped his long arm around her and purred, "Der is someting eemportant dat you moust know."

His breathing became deep, nearly panting. "Dis eez someting dat was not to happen, but eet deed." He studied her eyes for a moment and then whispered, "Aye am in love wit you, Atoha."

All Audril could mutter was a shocked, "Huh?"

Lortu tightened his arm, coaxing her even closer.

"Wh . . . what are you doing?" she asked in a squeak as his face moved closer to hers. "Lortu?"

Suddenly she lost all power to resist. She found herself melting into Lortu's mesmerizing eyes. The pain in her arm seemed like an old memory as his warm breath hit her cheek.

"Dis weel make everyting bettah," he repeated in a tone so hushed, it was almost inaudible.

Again, he strengthened his hold on her and their lips touched. An aroused shudder tingled throughout her body. Her legs turned to jelly and her breath caught in her chest. She closed her eyes and let sublime emotion wash over her in warm, energized waves, deeper and more penetrating than anything she had ever felt. Lortu kissed her with such passion as she had never experienced, even when she had been kissing Dallin. She pressed her mouth harder against his, wanting the feeling to continue, longing for it to never end. Lortu coerced her more tightly to him and groaned softly.

All at once, a familiar sensation, and one she had felt quite recently, coursed through her — dizziness — disorienting, almost nauseating dizziness. Small stars ricocheted and swirled behind her closed eyelids.

Lortu's lips were still moving against hers, but she was suddenly aware of how weather-worn and coarse they were. The heat in his touch seemed to be fading and turning uncomfortably icy. A prickly chill burned in her extremities, and then quickly moved through the rest of her until she felt as though she was encased in ice. Still, she did not want Lortu to stop kissing her.

Her head felt strange, like it was separating from her body. She needed air, yet that would require Lortu to pull away.

In her mind, she debated. *You have to breathe or you'll die*, her logical side argued. *I won't die. I'll only faint again and I don't want to stop! I can't! He'll think I don't love him if I . . . ."*

Suddenly, the words stopped and were replaced by heavy black, as Lortu moved away and his mouth separated from hers.

"I am zorry, Atoha," he muttered.

Audril stood with her eyes tightly shut. Try though she might, she was unable to open them.

Lortu leaned over and picked up the book that she had let slip during the kiss, and placed it back in her arm. "Aye can not geeve dem back. You understand . . . ."

Before she could make sense of what was happening, she felt a hard shove against her chest. She stumbled backwards and through her closed eyes saw a brilliant flash of light. With a thud, she abruptly came to rest on her backside in the bottom of a shallow gully surrounded by long, waving grasses. She tried to lift herself, but as she did, an agonizing jolt of pain shot from her arm into her shoulder and a swirling sense of disorientation twisted through her skull. She collapsed backwards and, with a heavy moan, slipped away into a dark oblivion.

Lortu watched the portal expand and then collapse into nothingness; a devious, triumphant smile played across his lips. He turned toward the Greelan trees which graciously lifted their cascading branches upward and to the sides. Uttering a satisfied chuckle, Lortu, the Schemer faded into the undulating shadows.

Chapter XLI

FOUND

Sunshine filtered through the quaking aspens in wide ribbons and floated down over Audril, warming her still unconscious form. Her eyes fluttered open; she squinted, trying to make out the hazy shapes around her but all she could see were blurry, dark spots in the glowing sunlight. Her head ached, and twinges of pain from her broken arm stabbed through her in agonizing waves. As the surrounding area began to ripple into focus, she realized she was still sitting in a waist-high ravine. She vaguely remembered being here the night before, but she couldn't remember why she was here, or how she ended up in this ditch in the first place.

She looked herself over. She was wearing a strange charcoal-colored suit made out of even stranger material that looked like polished granite but was almost flimsy to the touch. Odd extensions hung from both sleeves, and upon closer inspection she realized that they were gloves of some sort.

A big, brown, leather-bound book sat on the ground next to her. She reached over and flipped it open. It appeared to be written in an odd foreign language, yet she had the strangest feeling that it belonged to her.

Her arm did not look good. Under the light fabric, she could see how distorted and swollen it had become. She couldn't remember how she'd broken it, but come to think of it, she couldn't remember much of anything.

Found

Her last memory was of hazy faces, a blonde girl and a dark-haired man. There were balloons, and a large banner draped across a small white farmhouse. There were small flashing lights outside a darkened window and a horrendous noise, but beyond that, there was nothing.

All of a sudden, a familiar sound — the engine of an approaching semi truck — roared somewhere in the not too far off distance. She was near a road...near help.

She struggled to stand, but the combination of the slick, grassy ground in the ravine, combined with the pain shooting through her arm, made it nearly impossible.

After several tentative attempts, she finally managed to get to her feet. The road wasn't visible from her low vantage point, but it sounded, from the periodic whooshing of a car racing by, that it was just beyond a short, steep incline.

"Great," she breathed as she surveyed the dewy vegetation covering the slope. "How am I supposed to get up that thing?"

Taking a deep breath, she tossed the book up out of the ditch and then hurled herself upward. She landed on her behind, alongside the ravine, cringing and whimpering at the pain of impact. She gulped hard and swung her legs around and used the same approach to stand that she'd used in the ditch. It was a little easier this time, and only took three tries for her to get to her feet.

Moving up the slick incline, however, was not that easy. It was every bit as challenging as she had anticipated, especially with a badly damaged arm — and while carrying a large book. She slipped and nearly lost her footing several times, and once, her feet completely went out from under her and she slid down the hill, dragging her mangled arm behind her.

By the time she reached the top and the road, sweat was dripping down her face and she was exhausted and in great pain. She dropped to her knees, lowered the book to the ground, and cradled her throbbing arm. She almost didn't notice when a few minutes later, a silver minivan drove by and pulled to a stop about a quarter of a mile up the road.

The whirring of the van backing up, combined with tiny gravel crackling under the weight of its tires, was a very welcome sound.

"Are you all right?" a kindly female voice called out as the van clunked to an even idle and the driver's door swung open.

Audril didn't answer; she didn't have the energy. It was almost more than she could do to raise her head.

In front of her, and approaching with a concerned grimace on her face, a woman with a perfectly styled blonde bob half-jogged toward her.

"Oh my goodness!" she gasped. "Your arm! What in the world are you doing out here?"

The salty taste of perspiration moved over Audril's tongue as she attempted to speak. "I . . . I don't know."

Suddenly, the woman screeched to a stop and her jaw dropped open. "Maggie? Maggie Baker? Is . . . is that your name?"

Audril glanced up at her and searched her mind. Maggie Baker...the name sounded vaguely familiar, but it wasn't hers; it didn't sound right. "I . . . I don't think so," she muttered.

"Oh," the lady responded with surprise. "I'm sorry, it's just . . . you look just like her."

"Do . . . do I know you?" Audril asked, suddenly feeling a little dizzy and disoriented again.

"No," the lady replied as she moved to Audril's side. "My name's Jessica Philpot . . . but please, just call me Jess." She smiled and knelt down next to her. "Can you get up? I think we'd better get you to a hospital."

Jess picked up the book, and then guided Audril to her feet and over to the van. "Hang on a second," she said as she pulled the sliding door on the passenger's side open.

Inside, a baby boy sat staring at her from his car seat. The binky in his mouth wiggled up and down.

Next to him, a little girl, about six or seven with the same precision haircut as her mom strained to see Audril over her brother.

"Cleo, can you climb in the back, sweetie. I need to move Brayden to where you are so there's room for our friend."

The little girl frowned but obeyed her mom and climbed over the seat to the bench in the back and pulled a seatbelt over her lap.

"Here, lean against this," Jess offered, indicating the side of the seat. She tossed the book over into the front and said, "I'll move the car seat over so you have a little more room."

She scurried back around to the driver's side and opened the sliding door. Within a few seconds, she had repositioned her baby's seat and was back around to Audril.

"Let me help you," she whispered kindly. She placed one hand on the small of Audril's back and put the other under the elbow of her uninjured arm. "Ready?" she asked.

Audril nodded and, with Jess' help, she hoisted herself upward and into the van.

Cleo watched her from behind with a supremely worried look on her face. "Momma, is she a stranger?" she asked quietly.

Jess chuckled and replied, "No, peanut, this is . . ." She gazed questioningly at Audril who shook her head slightly side to side. "Um, this is . . . Kelsey, honey." She just blurted the first name that came to mind. "Kelsey's hurt and we're going to take her to the doctor, okay?"

"Did you call nine-one-one?" Cleo asked with wide, green eyes.

"What a smart idea!" Jess praised. "You are right. We should call 9-1-1. I'll do that right now."

She slid the van door closed and pretended to talk on her cell phone as she moved around to the driver's seat.

"All set," she assured as she climbed in. "9-1-1 just told me to bring her to the hospital. Are you cool enough back there?" she asked, looking at Audril in her rearview mirror.

"Yeah, thanks," Audril answered, even though she was still a little warm. "Thank you, Jess." She leaned back against the seat and closed her eyes.

As Jess maneuvered the van back out onto the highway, the breeze from the air conditioner became cooler and blew more strongly across her face.

"You're pretty, Kelsey," a small voice squeaked from behind her. "My name is Cleo. It's short for Cleopatra . . . Cleopatra Philpot. I'm six. I'm in Mrs. Reynolds' class. She's nice but one day, Kevin Bucher got in trouble for bringing his lizard to school. Then she wasn't very nice. Some of the kids tease Kevin 'cause his last name is Bucher, but I don't tease him . . . just 'cause his name sounds like booger. Momma says that's not kind."

"Cleo, honey," Jess called back, stifling a giggle. "Let's not talk poor Kelsey's ear off. I'm sure she would like a little peace and quiet."

"Oh, I don't mind," Audril corrected, opening her eyes. "She's cute. Besides, it's taking my mind off my arm."

"You're very sweet," Jess grinned through the mirror. "She's inherited my gift of gab, I'm afraid. Mrs. Reynolds isn't too nice when it comes to talking in class, is she, Clee?"

Cleo moved her fist in front of her mouth and giggled sheepishly.

"We should be at the hospital in about five minutes," Jess informed. "We'll take you in and make sure you get all taken care of."

"Are you sure?" Audril asked, now feeling cool and comfortable except for the constant wrenching in her arm. "I don't want to mess up your day."

"Nonsense," Jess scolded. "We were just on our way back from my mom's. I don't have any set plans, other than cleaning and doing laundry, and I'm not about to drop you off at the emergency room and let you fend for yourself so I can go home and clean."

"I made my bed this morning," Cleo chimed in. "Momma didn't even have to tell me to."

"Nice," Audril replied, trying to remember where exactly her own bed was.

"My birthday is October seventh. When's yours?" Cleo asked, but didn't pause for a response. "I'm gonna be seven and I want a princess birthday party at Mower's. Have you ever been to Mower's? It's sooooo cool. They have a

367

princess room and games and pizza. Ellie had her birthday there on Saturday, but she didn't invite Crystal 'cause they got in a fight."

"My stars, little one!" Jess sighed. "Why don't we put on your happy music?"

She popped a CD into the player and the sound of children singing a bubbling song about a rainbow and a teddy bear filled the interior of the van.

Jess mouthed 'sorry' in the mirror and rolled her eyes.

A couple of minutes later they pulled into the parking lot of the hospital. From the large monument sign in front, Audril saw that they were at the Ridgefield View Medical Center of Ridgefield, Iowa.

A nervous knot twisted in her stomach as she thought about telling some doctor that she had no idea who she was, or how she'd gotten dumped alongside a rural highway.

"I wonder if Uncle Tim is here today," Jess asked as they pulled up to the big, automatic doors of the ER. "Dr. Storey is my brother-in-law and a wonderful surgeon."

Just then, a robust, clean-cut man with salt and pepper hair, wearing a long white coat, emerged from the doors waving.

"Ah, there he is," Jess grinned as she shifted the van into park. She climbed out and rushed over to hug him. "Hey, you," she laughed. "Are you working ER today?"

"Yeah, why?" he asked, his happy expression fading to one of concern.

"Oh . . ." Jess blurted. "We're all fine. It's this young gal, here." She slid open the door next to Audril and stepped out of the way. "I'm no doctor, but I'm pretty sure that arm is broken."

"Hi, Uncle Tim," Cleo sang from the back seat.

"Hey, Goober!" he exclaimed. "Now, my dear," he began, sizing up Audril, "what have you got . . . ?" All at once, a look of confusion jumped into his eyes. "Jess! Is this . . . ?"

"I know," Jess answered. "She looks just like Maggie Baker, but she doesn't think that's her name."

The doctor grimaced.

"She's obviously had a bit of a trauma, Tim. She's a little disoriented."

Dr. Storey's grimace rose to a pleasant, albeit not entirely sincere smile. "I see," he replied. "Well, let me get you a chair, young lady."

The doctor wheeled Audril into the hospital while Jess parked the car. After x-rays and a thorough exam, Audril's arm was set and she was moved to a room where she could stay for observation.

"Knock, knock," Jess called out from behind the partially open door.

"Come in," Audril answered, happy to hear the familiar voice. As the door swung open, Cleo bounded into the room followed by Jess who was carrying Brayden in her arms. His binky was not in his mouth anymore, but the red outline of it was visible around his rosy lips.

"Hi, Kelsey," Cleo chirped, climbing up on the bed without as much as a pause.

"Honey, be careful of her arm," Jess scolded.

"She's fine," Audril assured. "Thanks again for sticking around, you guys."

"Oh, you're very welcome, dear. Listen, I was thinking . . . I mean . . . once you're all healed up . . . you're welcome to stay with us if you need to."

Jess' offer probably prompted the opposite effect than she had hoped. It sent an almost paralyzing fear flooding through Audril. She didn't know where she belonged, who her family was, her name, birth date, social security number, or anything. Trying not to come across as ungrateful despite her horrified mood, she muttered a weak, "Uh . . . yeah . . . thanks."

Just then, there was a quiet rapping at the door, and Dr. Storey peeked around it. "Hey, Jess . . . Can I talk to you for a sec?" He smiled at Audril and asked, "How ya doin', Tiger? Ya hangin' in?"

Audril nodded.

"Good," he grinned. "We're just gonna keep you for today and tonight so we can make sure everything's okay, and so you can get some much needed rest. You takin' good care of her, Goober?"

Cleo nodded with a little less energy than she had exhibited thus far, and gave a wide yawn.

"Good," he chuckled. "Will you lovely ladies excuse us for a moment?" Together he and Jess (and Brayden), stepped out into the hall.

"Mmmmm," Cleo huffed, looking up at Audril with her clear green eyes. Audril noticed a pronounced redness around her lids. "I'm really tired," she said and yawned again. She leaned her head against Audril's shoulder and within seconds was out cold.

". . . Think she is," Jess' whisper sounded from the hall. It was faint, but if Audril held her breath, she could hear her and Dr. Storey perfectly.

"That kind of testing won't work," he replied. "I have nothing of Maggie Baker's to compare it to, and there's no way to get anything . . . ya know, with Glenhill . . ."

"So what do we do?" Jess asked. "She seems like such a sweet girl. I'll gladly take her to my place."

"I have Rosa checking . . . she's trying to track down anyone who'd know anything about Maggie Baker . . . a next of kin, or anybody that could give us an ID one way or the other," the doctor explained. "Nobody knows what language that book is, so it's given us zilch-o clues."

"Do you honestly think you can keep the media out of here for long, Tim? If she is Maggie Baker they'll be on her like flies on a carcass!" Jess' voice was no longer a whisper. "My guess is as soon as the first shift goes home, we're toast."

"There are only four of us here who've seen her. I've already talked to the others. They know that this is a sensitive case. They wouldn't dare spill."

Jess scoffed loudly, followed by the doctor shushing her. "Why don't we see how Jane Doe is doing? Don't worry, Jess. We'll get it all worked out."

The door opened and Audril tried to look as though she was engrossed by the satiny floral wallpaper. She acted surprised that they had walked in, and hoping to start a comfortable conversation, motioned with her head to the sleeping girl next to her.

Both Jess and Dr. Storey smiled warmly. "She's not hurting you, is she?" Jess checked.

"Nah, she's fine. Just making me a little sleepy," Audril answered.

"Why don't you go ahead and take a nap," Jess encouraged. "Tim says you're bordering on exhaustion. I brought my needlepoint along . . . that'll keep me busy. I think this little guy is about to go down for his afternoon snooze, too."

"We have a few playpens around, sis," Dr. Storey offered. "I think a nap is an excellent idea." He frowned slightly at Audril and added, "You need your rest, young lady. Just let me know if you can't sleep and I'll get you something in addition to your pain pills to help."

Audril nodded with a smile and Dr. Storey slipped out of the room.

Jess followed him toward the door, and informed Audril that she was going to go grab her needlepoint and Brayden's car seat, and assured her that she would be back shortly.

Audril closed her eyes.

As she lay there, she replayed Dr. Storey's and Jess' conversation in her mind. Apparently, they thought she was this Maggie Baker, and for all she knew, she was. It was weird and disconcerting for her to not know her own identity. She felt like it was in a little box in her mind, just waiting to jump out, but it couldn't for some reason. It seemed so close, yet miles away. *Maggie Baker . . . hmmm . . . it's not a horrible name . . .* It was the last thought she had before drifting off to sleep.

Chapter XLII

A FRIEND TO RELY ON

Audril awakened, four hours later, feeling only slightly rested; she could have easily gone back to sleep, but everyone else in the room was awake, so she would have felt a little awkward.

Cleo was trying her best to piece together a puzzle on the floor and Jess was curled up reading a newspaper on the small, apricot-colored loveseat in the corner.

"Good evening," she smiled over the top of brown, plastic-rimmed reading glasses. "How did you sleep?"

"Like a rock," Audril replied, with a drowsy half-yawn.

Jess took off the glasses and stuck them in her purse. "Good . . . you needed it."

"Hey, Kelsey! Look what I'm making," Cleo cried out.

Audril rolled and leaned over the edge of the bed to get a better look of her new little friend's work.

"Awesome," she beamed, "It's an elephant, isn't it?"

Cleo bobbed her head up and down. "Elephants can come from Asia and from Aprica," she informed.

"Africa," Jess smiled.

Just then, a woman who looked exactly like the older version of Jess, right down to the perfect hair, crept into the room, carrying Brayden. "Ah, you're awake," she smiled.

"This is my sister, Carla Storey . . . Tim's wife."

Considering their similarities, Jess' clarification was hardly necessary.

"She's gonna take the kids home with her tonight. Tim said I could stay here with you. I guess this thing is a pull-out," she added, patting the cushion of the loveseat. "My hubby is out of town on business, so Carla's agreed to sit for me."

"I feel bad that you have to rearrange everything for me," Audril frowned. "I'm fine, really."

"Oh pish," Carla replied. "My kids love having the cousins over. They sort of entertain each other . . . makes my job so much easier." She winked at Audril and smiled widely. "Let's go, Gooberdy Goo." She mussed Cleo's hair and helped her pick up the puzzle.

Jess jumped up from the sofa and strolled over to her sister. "Thanks, missy," she said, as she kissed Carla ferociously on the cheek.

Within a few seconds, Carla had the kids all gathered, and was hurrying them out the door, accompanied by a chorus of *Bye, Kelsey*'s emanating from Cleo.

They had only been gone a few seconds when Dr. Storey came into the room pushing a rolling tray along with him. "Dinner," he sang out as soon as he was sure that Audril was awake.

"Wow, what great service!" Jess laughed. "I bet this is the only hospital this side of the Appalachians where the doctor doubles as a waiter."

"Oh, I have my ulterior motives," he replied, positioning the tray over Audril's bed and raising and lowering his eyebrows in a comical attempt to be mysterious.

"Why does that make me a little nervous?" Audril chuckled. "You're not going to tell me I'm dying or anything, are you?"

"Hadn't planned on it," he grinned. "I just wanted to see how you'd react to . . . duhnt, duhn, duh . . . the dreaded hospital food."

As he lifted the tray cover to reveal a chicken dinner that looked far from dreaded, a thin, elderly woman peered in around the door.

"Hiya, Rosa," Jess sang and waved energetically.

"Oh, hello, Jess," Rosa replied with a strained smile. "Dr. Storey?" she continued, "there's a person here . . . you know . . . um, that thing you asked me to find . . . ."

"Oh, right!" the doctor exclaimed. "Excuse me, girls." Without another word, he set the cover near Audril's feet and followed Rosa out of the room.

"Wonder what's up with her?" Jess grimaced. "She's usually so friendly."

A moment later there was a knock on the door, and Dr. Storey returned. "There's someone here to see you, young lady," he said with the same insincere smile that he'd given Audril at the van.

"Someone to see . . . me?" Audril gasped through a mouthful of chicken.

For some reason, Jess deemed it necessary to rush to Audril's side and take her by the hand.

"Oh . . . okay, I guess," Audril answered with a little trepidation. The thought of this being a person she should know — like a parent, or a sibling, or worse still, a boyfriend— terrified her. What if it was someone close that she should recognize, but didn't? She felt the sudden urge to jump out of the bed and run. Of course, there was nowhere to run to. And what if it *was* a boyfriend and she looked horrifying! At least, she had to check herself in a mirror.

"I . . . I need to visit the restroom first, if that's all right?" she muttered.

"Of course, dear," Jess replied, patting her hand a bit faster and harder than necessary. "You just take your time."

Audril slid the dinner tray away and slipped out of bed. Once in the bathroom, she became extremely grateful that she had asked for a moment to herself.

Forty-Two

Her hair was matted to one side of her head and her face was filthy. It looked like she'd washed it with dark brown dust. She splashed handfuls of water into her face with her one useable hand and watched streams of mud run down the sides of the sink.

"Ughhh!" she groaned as she scooped another handful of warm water and threw it across her cheeks.

She took a little water and ran it through her knotted hair with her fingers, rejuvenating her curls after a considerable effort.

She adjusted her hospital gown, which thankfully was so large that it covered everything, and then some, checked that there was no lingering dinner in her teeth, and flushed the toilet — just so she didn't seem vain to Jess and Dr. Storey — and then returned to the room.

Jess subdued a grin as the refreshed Audril climbed back into bed.

"I'll go show your visitor in," Dr. Storey said.

"Don't worry, honey, I'm right here," Jess soothed, smacking the back of Audril's hand again. "We'll get through this together."

Once more, Jess' over-exuberant caring produced an effect contrary to her intentions. Her fussing was only making Audril more nervous.

A second or two later, the door squeaked open and a woman with long waves of silver hair stood in the doorway next to Dr. Storey.

She was wearing a flowing, flowered skirt in vivid shades of red and orange. A red and gold scarf was folded in a triangle and tied at her thin waist. Tucked into the scarf was an ivory peasant blouse with big orange polka dots, loose billowing sleeves and long ruffled cuffs. Atop that was a short, bolero length vest in the same rich colors as the skirt.

Although the woman's hair was silver, she wasn't old — or at least her face looked decades younger than that of someone whose hair had turned completely grey. Not only did her face seem young, but her hair, despite its color, seemed full and vibrant and showed no signs of thinning.

A charming smile played across her bright red lips as she sighed, "Maggie, dear. I am so happy to see you!" In her voice was the faintest hint of a French accent.

Audril eyed her for a moment and then grinned widely. "Miss . . . Ms. Devereaux?" she gasped, more surprised that she remembered her high school drama teacher, than that she was standing in the door of her hospital room.

"You know her?" Jess quizzed.

"Yeah . . . yeah! I do!" she replied. "This is Ms. Devereaux. She's my favorite teacher. Come in, please . . . don't just stand out there in the hall, come in," she urged.

Ms. Devereaux crossed the threshold and moved to Audril's side. "Oh, how lovely that you are all right, dear. I've been woorried sick for you all these months."

"Months?" Audril asked in shock.

"You deesappeared," Ms. Devereaux explained, "nearly a year ago. You and your father and Brigeet."

"My father?" she asked as a gaping hole seemed to form in the pit of her stomach.

"It's all right, hon," Dr. Storey interjected. "It usually takes a while for all of your memories to come back. We'll just take it nice and slow."

Both Jess and Ms. Devereaux nodded in agreement.

"Wait a second!" Audril snapped. "Are you telling me that I have a dad that I don't remember, but I can remember my drama teacher? That's insane!"

"Well, you haven't *seen* your dad yet," Jess tried. "Maybe you have to actually make visual contact with someone to remember them, isn't that right, Tim?"

"That's one possibility," he concurred.

Audril sighed heavily and groaned. "Well, what if I don't ever remember him?" She dropped her face into her hand and mumbled, "That'd suck!"

Forty-Two

"Hey, I have an idea," Dr. Storey offered. "I'm going to go get Melissa Frake. She's our hospital psychologist. Maybe she'll have some ideas how we can get your memory back."

"Psychologist?" Audril mumbled after he had exited. "Super."

"It'll be okay," Jess assured. "Dr. Frake is awesome."

"I don't need a shrink!" Audril insisted. "Just tell me what's going on, and who I supposedly am!"

Following a lengthy pause, Jess broke down. "We think that you are a girl named Maggie Baker, who disappeared from the small town of Glenhill about a year ago."

She and Ms. Devereaux then proceeded to explain in wave upon wave of information how she and her dad and best friend, Bridgette (whom she couldn't remember, either), had vanished off the face of the planet in late August, and how their disappearances had been highly publicized — both at the time of, and then again a few weeks ago, when Glenhill had been blown to smithereens.

"So, where's my dad?" she asked, looking a bit like a lost puppy.

"We don't know," Dr. Storey answered as he came back into the room. He flashed an irritated look in Jess' direction. Next to him was a short, kind, yet plain woman in her early thirties.

"Maggie," he began, "This is Melissa."

Audril glanced from Jess to Ms. Devereaux and then to Dr. Frake. Suddenly, she didn't want to talk anymore. She just wanted to think.

"Can I have a little time alone?" she muttered quietly.

Jess opened her mouth to respond, but Dr. Frake put a quick hand on her arm and answered in a soothing English accent, "Absolutely, we'll just be outside. Press the nurse button if you need anything."

"Will she be all right?" Ms. Devereaux asked the doctor as they huddled outside the room in the hallway.

"I think so," he responded. "It's hard to tell with amnesia. Sometimes memory comes back fully, and sometimes it doesn't. I'm going to highly recommend that she get some counseling, though, either from Melissa here, or wherever she is most comfortable. It's impossible to say what kind of trauma she's gone through over the last year."

"Doctor," Ms. Devereaux fidgeted with the cloth around her hips as she asked, "may I be allowed to care for her in her father's absence? She has always been a very dear girl to me."

The doctor glanced at Jess, who nodded sadly, and then at Dr. Frake who nodded her approval as well. "Thank you for offering, Ms. Devereaux," he replied. "I'm sure it will be very helpful for her to be near someone she remembers and trusts. As long as she's all right with it . . ."

"And, as long as you'll allow my family to come visit occasionally," Jess threw in. "I've only known her since this morning, but as you say, Ms. Devereaux, she's become a very dear girl to me, also."

Ms. Devereaux's eyes sparkled. "Of course! I would be delighted, and I'm sure that Maggie would be very happy to see you anytime."

Chapter XLIII

FROM ONE NIGHTMARE TO THE NEXT

The next morning, Audril was released from the hospital, into the care of Ms. Devereaux. They left with a bevy of hugs and kisses from Jess, Cleo, Carla and even Brayden, who more or less leaned over and mashed his drooly open mouth against Audril's cheek. As she wiped slobber from her face, she thanked Jess and Dr. Storey again for being so kind and climbed into Ms. Devereaux's powder blue sports car.

She had hardly slept the night before, and as the car purred down the long highway toward Palmerton, where Ms. Devereaux lived, she found it increasingly difficult to hold her eyelids open.

"I'm just gonna snooze for a bit, if that's okay," she slurred. She placed her book up against the car window and leaned her head against it.

Ms. Devereaux responded with a quiet, "Mm hmm."

By the time Audril opened her eyes again they were pulling up in front of a large, stately Victorian encircled by a sprawling veranda.

"Th . . . this is your house?" Audril mumbled as she rubbed the sleep from her eyes.

"It's your house now too, dear," Ms. Devereaux answered.

Audril gazed in awe at the beautiful white mansion with a green roof and rolling acres of pristine lawn. The amount of wood trim on the veranda alone was staggering.

Ms. Devereaux pulled the car into the detached garage at the back of the lot, which looked to be a miniature of the main dwelling. A long breezeway stretched from the garage to a rounded part of the veranda at the back of the home.

"This way," Ms. Devereaux said, pointing down the breezeway toward a leaded glass and cherry wood door.

"After you get settled and rest for a while, we shall go shopping and pick you up some new clothes and things." She eyed Audril's strange suit and offered, "I can lend you some of my clothes for when we go out."

"Yeah," Audril agreed. "I don't really want to be seen in this thing in public. I don't even know where it came from."

As Ms. Devereaux unlocked and opened the back door, a fluffy silver and black Persian cat zipped out past Audril's ankles.

"Oh, Taumina!" Ms. Devereaux exclaimed. "You get back here!" She ran over to where the cat was rolling around ecstatically on the lawn and scooped her up. "Madame Taumina Devereaux, meet Miss Maggie Baker." She walked back, stroking Taumina's thick fur and held her out toward Audril, who ran her casted hand down the back of the softly purring animal.

"How do you do, Madame Taumina?" she smiled.

"Oh, you're going to be such good friends," Ms. Devereaux grinned, tossing the cat gently back into the house. "She's really quite a diva, but aren't all actresses?"

They stepped in through the door — and back in time a hundred years or so — into a room with mauve-striped, fabric-covered walls, a floral tapestry medallion sofa and heavily carved, red velvet chairs, all neatly arranged atop a jewel-toned rose print carpet. Rich mahogany tables, some with marble tops and some with wood, sat next to all of the upholstery pieces. Intricate Tiffany lamps and wall sconces added a warm, colorful glow to the room.

Audril gazed around in awe at the scene. Every inch of the room held something fascinating, and just when she thought she'd seen it all, she would spy another interesting box, bottle or trinket.

"This was supposed to be a breakfast nook," Ms. Devereaux explained, "but I turned it into the parlor."

"Wow," Audril breathed. "It's really beautiful." She walked over to one of the marble-topped tables, set down her book and picked up a cobalt blue etched crystal perfume bottle and studied it.

"This is one room that little Brayden probably won't do too well in," she observed, mesmerized by the way the light played on the little atomizer.

Ms. Devereaux watched her examine the bottle. "Why don't you keep that one up in your room? We'll get you some nice perfume to fill it weeth."

"Uh . . . Oh, no . . . that's okay," Audril sputtered, returning the bottle to the table.

"But it matches your eyes, dear," Ms. Devereaux insisted.

Audril smiled at her and then picked up the bottle again and gazed at it dreamily. She imagined that it was probably the most beautiful thing she had ever seen — of course, she could only assume so.

"Good . . . lovely . . . lovely," Ms. Devereaux tittered. "Now let me show you to your room."

As she guided Audril through the house, it became apparent that Brayden probably wouldn't do well in any of these rooms. They were all just as elaborate, and as exploding with knick-knacks, as the parlor.

By the time they reached the upstairs room where Audril would be staying, she had seen a ceramic elephant holding a large potted fern, a lamp in the shape of a woodland fairy, a monkey holding jewel-encrusted walking sticks, and the most stunning pale green silk ball gown on a wire-frame dress form.

Ms. Devereaux hesitated at the bedroom door for a moment, while Taumina weaved around her ankles, and then swung it open to reveal a large, stunning, pale blue room with heavy white and olive dotted draperies, and burnished gold trim detailing on all of the walls and high ceiling.

"Good grief," Audril gasped. "This is crazy." She gazed at the tall, king-sized four poster bed with hangings on it that matched the drapes; it almost seemed small in the spacious room. Again, a delicate medallion sofa, albeit smaller than the one in the parlor, flanked by two rose-carved, marble-topped tables, created a cozy sitting area in front of a white stone fireplace hearth.

"This is your room now," Ms. Devereaux said. "A room fit for a preencess." She walked across the room and pulled back the curtains to reveal a floor-to-ceiling, multi-paned window. The instant blast of sunlight was all at once startling and breathtaking.

"This is so cool," Audril breathed as she rushed into the luxurious room. She tossed her book onto the bed, and with the perfume bottle still clutched in her hand, ran to Ms. Devereaux and wrapped her un-casted arm around her teacher's thin shoulders. "Thanks so much," she gushed. "I don't even know what to say."

"Then don't say anything, Maggie, dear. Just enjoy yourself."

Ms. Devereaux patted Audril gently on her back and then glanced at her watch. "Oh, dear," she cried. "It's time for you to take your medicine. I'll go make you a sandwich so you're not taking it on an empty stomach, then you'll no doubt want to rest for a while. If you are not up to shopping today, dear, we can go tomorrow. There is no pressure."

All Audril could think to do was thank Ms. Devereaux again and again for taking her in and being a most hospitable hostess.

"Please, Maggie . . . think nothing of it! I am happy to have the company!"

Ms. Devereaux ducked out of the room and returned a few minutes later with a gold-rimmed tray containing the most delicious cold ham sandwich smothered in a delectable honey mustard sauce, a glistening clump of red grapes and a tall glass of fresh orange juice. She was also carrying a stack of neatly folded clothing under the tray.

Audril practically inhaled the sandwich, which was surprising considering that she wasn't even aware she was hungry; but it tasted so good, she couldn't stop once she had started.

382

Her arm was beginning to ache again, indicating that Ms. Devereaux had been correct; it was time for medication, and so she popped one of the large pain pills into her mouth that Dr. Storey had prescribed and washed it down with a big swig of orange juice.

After she had finished eating, Ms. Devereaux gave Audril a more thorough tour of her room, which included a tall, nearly full bookcase tucked into a small corner nook, a bathroom that would probably rival those in many five-star hotels, and a nearly empty closet bigger than the hospital room from which she had just been released.

Ms. Devereaux had placed the pile of clothes in the empty closet while Audril had been scarfing down the sandwich. She surmised that Ms. Devereaux must have inherited a large sum of money from a relative or something; she doubted that this kind of extravagant living would be provided by the salary of a small town high school drama teacher.

Following the tour, Ms. Devereaux told Audril that she was going to run a few errands, and urged her to get some rest.

"If you need anything, this is my cell phone number. Please call if you think of anything you would like me to peek up." She handed Audril a small pink note with her number scrolled across it in an elegant hand, and then headed off on her errands.

Audril went to the closet and changed. She was anxious to shed the bizarre suit she wore in favor of something more normal…and cleaner.

The clothes in the pile were a little flamboyant for her taste, but she finally settled on a pair of heather grey leggings and an oversized red and white striped shirt with tails.

Changing was a bit of a challenge with a broken arm, but following an admirable struggle, she was able to manage the buttons of the shirt and hoist the pants to her waist by pulling up one side, and then the other.

By the time she was through getting dressed, she was thoroughly winded. She crossed the room and lowered herself carefully onto the soft bed.

"Oh, this *so* beats that slab of springs at the hospital," she sighed as she dropped back onto a pile of down pillows.

Out of the corner of her eye, she saw the top of the book peeking out from the puffy blankets that had nearly consumed it. She scooted the mysterious tome toward herself with her good hand and flipped it open.

At the top of the page was a black pencil sketch of two people, a man and a woman. The woman sort of looked like her; she had long curly hair, at least. But it was the male character in the drawing that was mesmerizing, with his strong, chiseled features and dark, penetrating eyes.

As Audril stared at him, she found herself engrossed, wondering who he was, and what he and this woman were supposed to be doing. She studied the look in his captivating eyes, a look that seemed to express passion and desire.

She stopped for a moment to wonder if any man had ever looked at her in that way.

The woman in the drawing, however, seemed indifferent to the feelings of the man. In fact, she was looking away from him with an expression bordering on disgust in her eyes.

Audril studied the drawing — mostly the face of the handsome man — for several minutes before reading aloud the strange, foreign caption below it. "*A se nalt o talis betrindi. Kace enalt o madus betrindi. Wes solis e trysta conaye.*"

Wonder what it means, she thought to herself.

She flipped through a few more of the yellowed pages, but none other captured her attention as this one had. Finally, she turned back to it, and remained staring at the stranger's rugged face until the grog from the medication overwhelmed her, and she slipped away into dark dreams.

It was night time when she awoke with a terrified start. The images dancing through her subconscious had been so real, and so intense, that her mind didn't allow her to continue in them.

Panting heavily and with a pounding heart, she jumped out of bed, raced to the light switch at the door, and flipped it on.

She gazed at the expansive window across the room from her.

A day that had been cheery and bright had given way to a stormy gloom. Grey streaks of rain crackled loudly against the darkened window panes, creating a chaos that only added to Audril's anxiousness.

"It was only a dream," she puffed, "only a dream."

She glanced around the big room and suddenly felt quite uncomfortable with her solitude. She needed company — she needed not to be alone.

Grabbing the doorknob and rushing into the long hallway, she hoped with everything in her that Ms. Devereaux had returned from her errands.

The house was, fortunately, well lit by the multitude of lamps and sconces in every room. This was a relief, as she didn't think she could have handled feeling her way around a strange house in the dark in her present horrified state.

Though she was no longer asleep, she found that she had to fight to suppress the dreadful, lingering images of her dream.

There had been a face — frightening and intoxicating at the same time. It belonged to a strange man who was only ever partially visible. He had tried to kill her, by forcing her to drink something — by poisoning her.

Stop thinking about it! The voice in her head scolded. *It was just a stupid dream!*

When she reached the foyer at the bottom of the stairs, she called out shakily for Ms. Devereaux.

"Yes, sweetie, what is it?" the kindly teacher replied as she appeared in the arch separating the foyer and the living room. "Are you all right?"

At this point, Audril was shaking uncontrollably, and Ms. Devereaux could see the fear shining in her blue eyes.

Audril attempted to restore her composure by sucking in a deep breath, but it didn't seem to help the feeling that she wanted to burst into tears.

"I had a nasty . . . nasty dream," she breathed from behind a quivering lip.

"Oh, my goodness," Ms. Devereaux exclaimed, rushing to her and wrapping a tender arm around her waist. "Here, come into the living room and have a warm cup of cocoa. It will help you feel better."

The kindly teacher escorted her into the living room and to a tall, ornate, white and gold chair. She poured thick, steaming cocoa from a rose-covered coffee pot into a matching cup, and set it on the table at Audril's side. "Would you care to deescuss it?" she asked delicately.

Audril shook her head. She had no desire to relive the thing that, at this moment, was holding her in what seemed an unreasonable state of terror.

She fumbled to pick up the cup of cocoa, nearly shaking it to the point of spilling. "Let's talk about something else," she suggested as she attempted to steady the cup with the fingers protruding from the end of her cast.

"Oh . . . all right," Ms. Devereaux replied. "Well, it's a little late to do our shopping today, so I was thinking we could go into town in the morning, and then maybe take een a movie or something . . . I know how much you enjoy the cinema. We could make a whole day of it, if you like."

"Are there any good movies playing right now?" Audril asked, hoping to continue the small talk for as long as it took to make her dream fade away like the majority of her other memories.

Ms. Devereaux retrieved a newspaper from a nearby magazine basket, and pulled a chair over next to hers.

"Let's see," she hummed as she flipped through it. "Here we are . . . this weekend's film options. We have *Ben of the Burbs*, a cheek fleek about a man from the country who falls een love with his busty, high-powered boss." She glanced over the paper at Audril and chuckled. "I made up the busty part, of course, but she *is* rather well-endowed."

Audril couldn't help but giggle a little. "What else?" she asked, shaking her head.

A mischievous twinkle played in Ms. Devereaux's lavender eyes. "*Spidermole*," she blurted, "What good is having all of those eyes when you can't see a thing?"

Audril sounded like she'd suddenly sprung a leak. "You made that one up too, didn't you?" she sniggered. "*Spidermole . . .* really?"

Ms. Devereaux laughed melodiously. "Wait! Here's one! *Chew Chew Choo Choo*, one man, one train, forty tons of bubble gum!"

"O . . . okay . . . okay," Audril sputtered, now chortling uncontrollably, "How 'bout *Star Warts, Dermatologists in Space*? or . . . or *Master Rapper Emcee Poppins, Nanny from the Hood*."

"Very good . . . very good," Ms. Devereaux rolled. "I . . . I thi . . . ink we are on to something!"

By the time they had invented a dozen or so ridiculous movie titles, they were laughing so hard and having such a good time that Audril's dream was all but extinguished from her mind. Booming thunder was periodically shaking the house, but it didn't faze her at all. In the last half-hour or so, she remembered exactly why she had always liked Ms. Devereux so much.

Their fun evening was suddenly interrupted by the glow of headlights flashing in through the living room window.

Ms. Devereaux gasped and jumped to her feet. "Oh my goodness," she exclaimed, rushing to an intricate mirror that hung on one of the walls, and then messing with her hair. "It's Friday night! I almost forgot! My fiancé is taking me out to dinner . . . to celebrate our one year anniversary together!"

"I didn't know you were engaged," Audril smiled. She stood and moved across the room to the window and looked out at the champagne-colored pickup truck moving slowly up the driveway. "That's awesome! What's he like?"

Ms. Devereaux rushed around as she collected a pair of black high-heels and a bright purple handbag from the next room. "Oh, he is wonderful," she gushed as she paused for half a second and stared out the window with Audril.

"Oh, my . . . seven-fifty," she gasped, glancing at her watch. "You'll have to meet him when we get home."

"No worries," Audril answered. She watched the driver's door of the truck swish open and a tall, muscular man in a long trench coat step out. In the dark and the rain, she could not make out his face, but his presence alone was confident and very attractive.

"He looks handsome," Audril complimented.

"Yes, quite handsome," Miss Devereaux blushed. "I'm sorry, dear. I'm afraid I'm going to have to cut our fun short for tonight. You're okay here now, aren't you?"

"Yeah, I'm fine," Audril answered. "Thanks again, Ms. Devereaux. You've been a real life saver."

Ms. Devereaux hurried over to her and glanced out the window again.

Her fiancé was huddled under a large umbrella and moving toward the door.

"You are very welcome, love," she said as she patted Audril softly on her cast. "But since you are going to be living here now, I seemply can not allow you to continue addressing me so formally."

She moved across the room toward the front door. "My first name is Angelique, dear," she informed. "Please call me that from now on. Or better steel, call me what all of my close friends do . . ."

"What's that?" Audril asked.

Ms. Devereaux grabbed a grey cloak from a nearby hall tree and draped it across her shoulders. She then turned back to Audril before running out the door and hollered over the thunder, "Please . . . call me Lique."

Forty-Three

Meanwhile, on Lor Mandela — in spite of the missing Clest Anaria's Book of Revelation and the Child of Balance — the relentless countdown marched on...the countdown to four hundred days.

www.ingramcontent.com/pod-product-compliance
Lightning Source LLC
Chambersburg PA
CBHW060149260626
47160CB00001B/185